INVADER

SIMON SCARROW

AND T. J. ANDREWS

INVADER

headline

First published in Great Britain in 2016
by HEADLINE PUBLISHING GROUP

1

Cataloguing in Publication Data is available from the British Library

ISBN 978 1 4722 1370 9 (Hardback)
ISBN 978 1 4722 1369 3 (Trade paperback)

Typeset in Bembo by Avon DataSet Ltd, Bidford-on-Avon, Warwickshire

Printed and bound in Great Britain by Clays Ltd, St Ives plc

MIX
Paper from
responsible sources
FSC® C104740

Headline's policy is to use papers that are natural, renewable and recyclable
products and made from wood grown in well-managed forests and other
controlled sources. The logging and manufacturing processes are expected
to conform to the environmental regulations of the country of origin.

HEADLINE PUBLISHING GROUP
An Hachette UK Company
Carmelite House
50 Victoria Embankment
London EC4Y 0DZ

www.headline.co.uk
www.hachette.co.uk

For E. G.

CONTENTS

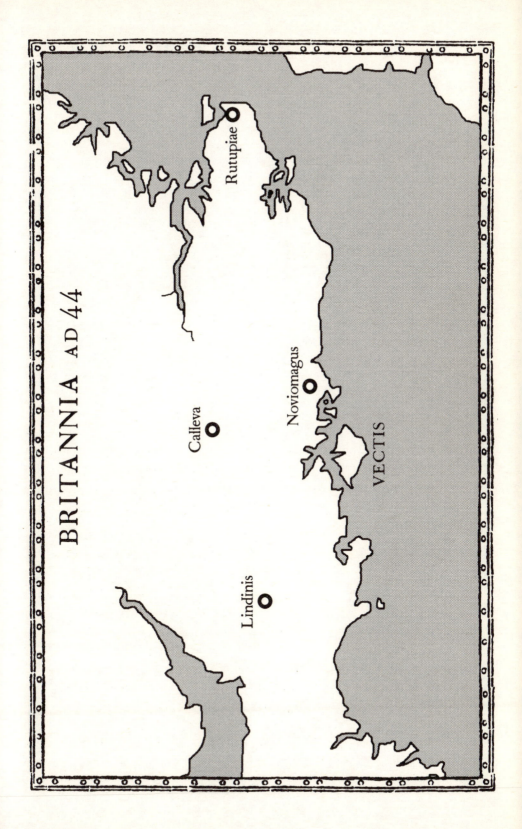

BRITANNIA AD 44

Rutupiae

Calleva

Noviomagus

VECTIS

Lindinis

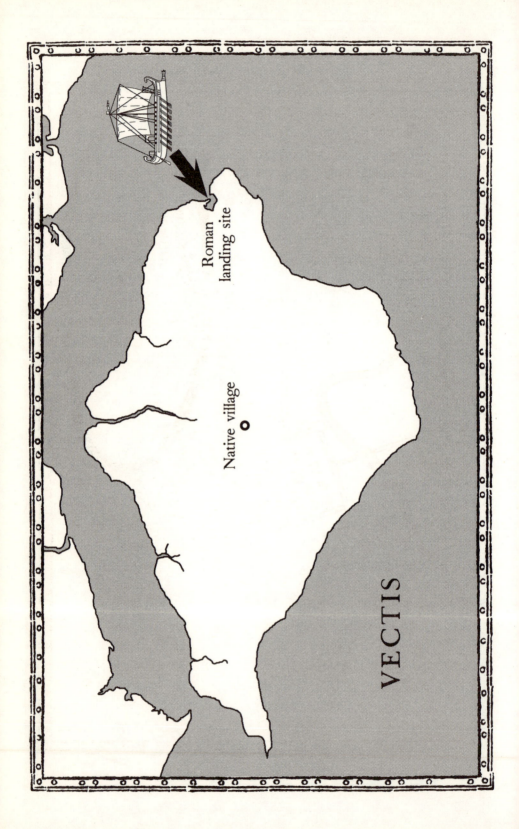

Roman
landing site

Native village

VECTIS

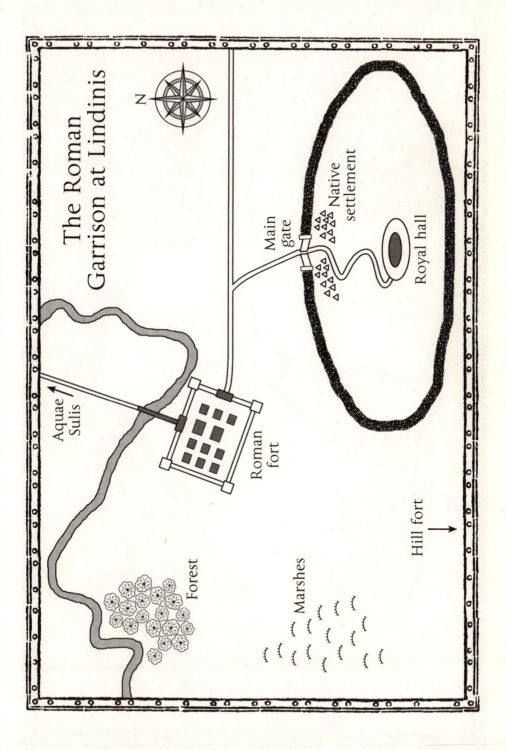

The Roman Garrison at Lindinis

N

Aquae Sulis

Forest

Marshes

Roman fort

Main gate

Native settlement

Royal hall

Hill fort

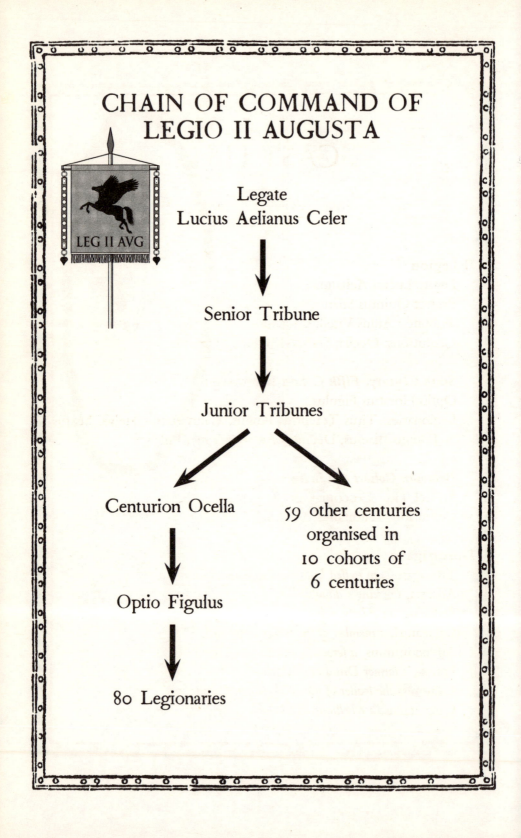

CAST LIST

II Legion
Legate Lucius Aelianus Celer
Prefect Quintus Silanus
Tribunes: Aulus Vitellius, Palinus
Centurions: Ocella, Scrofa, Mergus, Minucius

Sixth Century, Fifth Cohort Detachment
Optio Horatius Figulus
Legionaries: Titus Terentius Rullus, Gaius Arrius Helva, Sextus
  Porcius Blaesus, Decimus Artorius Vatia, Pulcher

Batavian Cohort at Lindinis
Prefect Titus Cosconianus
Centurions: Tuditanus, Vespillo, Ambustus

Durotrigans
Trenagasus, *an exiled king loyal to Rome*
Ancasta, *the king's daughter*
Sediacus, *an elderly noble*
Bellicanus, *a member of the king's inner circle*
Andocommius, *a ferocious warrior*
Petrax, *a former Druid bodyguard*
Calumus, *the leader of the Dark Moon Druids*
Quenatacus, *a rebellious tribal chief*

Others

Numerius Scylla, *an imperial envoy dispatched to Britannia*
Cethegus, *a retired Roman trooper*
Cogidubnus, *king of the Regni tribe*
Magadubnus, *a native scout*
Brigotinus, *a village chief on the Isle of Vectis*

CHAPTER ONE

Calleva, winter AD 44

A chill blast of air swept through the headquarters tent as the new legate of the Second Legion strode briskly through the tent flap.

'On your feet!' the camp prefect boomed to the officers seated inside. 'Legate's arrived.'

The officers fell silent and instantly shot up from their stools, standing to attention as the legate marched past. Lucius Aelianus Celer nodded at the camp prefect, his hands and face tingling from the cold night air. He had only recently arrived from Rome to assume command of the legion and the miserable conditions of the island had come as something of a shock to him. With each passing day he found himself yearning for the blissful warmth of his native Campania. Shaking off the cold, Celer approached a hide map suspended on a wooden frame at the front of the assembled rows of officers. A junior tribune stepped forward from beside the map and handed him a short wooden cane. Celer glanced at the camp prefect and straightened his back.

'Thank you, Quintus Silanus.' The prefect nodded. Turning to the officers, Celer addressed them in his silky aristocratic voice. 'At ease, gentlemen.'

An uneasy silence hung over the gathered men as they sat down. Even in the wan glow of the oil lamps Celer could see the anxiety etched across their faces. Less than a month had passed since the Second Legion, under the leadership of his predecessor, Vespasian, had defeated Caratacus, king of the Catuvellauni and the leader of those native tribes who had chosen to resist the Roman invaders. After a long and bloody campaign, Vespasian had finally routed Caratacus's army in a brutal pitched battle. Victory had come at a heavy price, with the Second Legion suffering grievous losses and

1

Caratacus escaping from his captors. It was the end of the campaigning season, winter was on the way and the soldiers would be spending the next few months bottled up in the legionary fortress until the new campaign in the spring. Celer cleared his throat.

'It's a cold night, gentlemen, so I'll keep this brief,' he declared. 'In the past month, we have received numerous reports of attacks on our positions to the south. Patrols have been ambushed, forts razed to the ground and naval supply depots sacked. We are not talking about the odd opportunistic raid, but a campaign of coordinated attacks. The situation is so grave that I'm told even Greek merchants are now refusing to do business outside of our legionary camps.' That last remark drew a polite chuckle from his audience. Celer paused and half smiled before continuing. 'I know some of us had hoped that defeating Caratacus would bring peace to this benighted land. However, following his escape it appears that our enemies have rediscovered their courage. The Durotriges have taken it upon themselves to redouble their resistance to our inevitable rule. My illustrious predecessor Vespasian may have conquered this territory, but he did not succeed in taming it – a failure I plan to correct.'

Celer turned towards the map depicting that large swathe of southern Britannia which nominally lay under Roman control, extending east from the naval base at Rutupiae all the way along the path of the River Tamesis past Calleva to the edge of the mountainous region to the west. Celer nodded at the map.

'Our intelligence sources indicate that these attacks are the work of Durotrigan warriors operating from the Isle of Vectis.' He pointed with his cane to a wedge-shaped island situated a few miles south of the mainland. 'During Vespasian's lightning campaign across their territory last summer, a significant number of the enemy managed to flee the hill forts. In Vespasian's haste to advance west, however, he neglected to turn back and deal with this rabble, allowing them to successfully withdraw to Vectis.'

Celer turned back to the officers and tightly gripped his cane, his knuckles shading white. He continued.

'From their base on Vectis, the enemy has been able to launch wave after wave of attacks on the mainland, retreating to the isle before our forces can effectively engage them. Gentlemen, it's vital

2

that we subdue Vectis once and for all and stop the Durotriges using it as a base to attack our supply chain along the coast. Accordingly, tomorrow at dawn the Fifth, Sixth, Seventh and Ninth Cohorts will march down to the naval port west of Noviomagus Regnorum. As we speak, a dozen galleys and supply ships from the Britannic fleet are sailing to the port from Rutupiae. Once our men reach the coast, we'll embark the ships, load our supplies and make for Vectis.'

There were low murmurs amongst the officers at the prospect of having to fight again so close to the bitterly cold winter months. Several exchanged wary glances with one another. A few men on the rear rows muttered to themselves. Celer was unmoved. He raised a hand, swiftly silencing the room.

'Thankfully, Fortuna shines on us. Over the past few weeks, our native scouts have been operating in secrecy on Vectis, gathering intelligence on the enemy. They have reported back that the Durotriges have no defensive fortification to speak of.' Celer chuckled to himself. 'As a matter of fact, they're still constructing a hill fort in time for the coming winter. If we act now, we can take the hill fort before the Durotriges have a chance to complete their defences, rout the enemy and be back in the camp before the first storms arrive.' He regarded his men with a smug grin. 'The advantage will be ours. We'll have strength in numbers. The enemy will have nowhere to run. In addition, an advance squadron of ships has moved into position along the coast, cutting off their supplies from sympathisers on the mainland. All things being equal, Vectis should fall easily. Of course there'll be the usual nests of resistance to stamp out. Once that's done we can start dividing up the booty.'

The mood inside the tent quickly lifted at the mention of earning a share from the spoils of war. Each officer, Celer knew, stood to make a tidy sum from the captured natives, who would be shipped to Gaul and sold into slavery, not to mention the treasure troves of ornately decorated weapons and jewellery hoarded by the native aristocracy.

'We'll land here.' He pointed with his cane to a notch of land on the east coast of the isle. 'The enemy won't be expecting an attack from the east. Acting on my orders, our scouts have disseminated false information to the Durotriges. They believe we will approach from the more obvious route to the north.' He drew the cane up the centre of the isle, to an inlet running up towards the northern coast. 'The east of Vectis will be mostly undefended, except for perhaps a token presence.'

Celer sought out a face among the throng and rested his gaze on a man seated on the front row. The man had bright blue eyes and an aquiline nose and he wore a fine cloak. 'Tribune Palinus.'

'Sir?' The man looked up and blinked.

'You'll be in charge of the Fifth Cohort. Your men will land first and secure the beach ahead of the main force. Think you can handle it?'

Palinus puffed out his chest with obvious pride. 'You can count on me, sir. I won't let you down.'

'Good.' Celer flashed him a thin smile before turning his gaze on to the rest of the men. 'Now, then. Any questions?'

A centurion at the back raised a hand. He was a short, pale man with dark curly hair and he lacked the scars of many of his comrades. Celer regarded him coolly.

'Yes, Centurion Ocella?'

'Sir,' Ocella began carefully. 'What kind of force are we up against?'

'According to the spies, several hundred at most,' Celer responded casually; he did not want to dampen the good mood. 'All the more reason to move now, before they have a chance to dig themselves in and reinforce their numbers. Of course, I would prefer for us to attack in greater numbers. But as you all know, the legion is thinly stretched as it is after the recent engagement with Caratacus. Some of your own units are badly depleted. They'll be replenished with the reserves recently arrived from Gesoriacum.' The legate tipped his head in the direction of the prefect. 'Silanus has been overseeing their training and assures me the men are ready for battle. Isn't that right, Silanus?'

'Ready as they'll ever be, sir,' the prefect replied guardedly.

'Quite.' Celer gave a sharp nod of his head. Then he handed the cane back to the orderly and straightened his back. 'Gentlemen, conquering Vectis is vital if we're to continue our advances in the next campaign season. General Plautius has ordered us to seize the territory which lies beyond the Durotriges. Some of the tribes in that distant region have already sent envoys to Calleva suing for peace.' The legate smiled. 'It seems our strategy of total war against the Durotrigans has shaken their neighbours. Which is as well, as the Emperor is very keen for this savage land to be pacified so it can start paying its own way.' His expression abruptly hardened. 'However, we cannot advance west as long as our supply chain to the rear remains exposed to raids. Any more questions?'

He looked round the tent. No one responded and Celer nodded with satisfaction. 'Good.' Then he gestured to an officer seated in the middle of the front row next to Tribune Palinus. All eyes turned to a heavily built man running to fat with a dark complexion that betrayed his southern Italian roots.

'In my absence, Senior Tribune Aulus Vitellius will assume command of the rest of the Second Legion,' Celer said. 'Some of you will already know the tribune from the early days of the invasion. He's recently rejoined the Second after a spell in Rome. Prefect Silanus has been bringing him up to speed.'

Vitellius smiled slowly at the legate. 'And I look forward to fulfilling my duties, sir,' he said in a deep voice before turning to the officers and fixing them with his icy stare. 'Rome has its pleasures, of course. But I must say it is good to be back among true comrades.'

Celer forced a smile to his lips. 'I'm sure Tribune Vitellius will make a fine commander of the legion in the interim.'

Then he nodded curtly at Silanus and headed for the tent flap. The officers rose simultaneously and snapped to attention as the legate strode stiffly out of the tent. Vitellius and the legate's orderlies followed close behind. Once the legate and his entourage had departed from the tent, Silanus stood the officers down with a gruff reminder that they were to collect their written orders from the legate's secretaries before returning to their units to brief their men.

The officers filed out of the tent and emerged into the icy evening. Although it was not yet winter the weather had already taken a turn for the worse, a grim reminder of the long, hard months to come. As the officers dispersed towards their various barracks, Centurion Ocella snorted angrily.

'Wonderful,' he muttered to his optio. 'Just bloody wonderful.'

'What is, sir?'

Ocella stopped in his tracks and glared at his recently assigned subordinate. He was a physically imposing man, broad-shouldered with taut, hardened muscles and a pinkish scar above his right eye. With his wild hair and stubbly cheeks, he had the makings of a competent if unremarkable soldier, Ocella considered. But he made a poor optio. He was hopeless at the day-to-day paperwork and administrative duties required of a junior officer. Whoever had originally promoted him to the post must have been desperate, Ocella decided, or plain mad. Now he was stuck with the burly Gaul. His last optio had died of an infected leg wound sustained in the battle with Caratacus's army, and the legate had taken the unusual step of imposing the optio upon him, denying the centurion the usual custom of promoting his own candidate from the rank and file. A fact which only increased his disdain for the man in front of him.

'What the hell do you think, Figulus?' Ocella snapped haughtily, bracing himself against the brisk wind. 'This mission. What with this foul weather and a sea crossing, it's taking quite a risk. And for what? To deal with a few pathetic stragglers on some remote isle.' He muttered a curse under his breath and looked away. 'Meanwhile the Fourteenth and Ninth Legions get a taste of the real action to the west and north.' He glanced quickly back at his second-in-command. 'More spoils of war to be had there too, I'll wager.'

Horatius Figulus pursed his lips. Despite his commanding officer's strong words, Figulus saw an unmistakable glint of anxiety in the centurion's eyes, and his voice wavered noticeably as he spoke. Figulus had been a soldier of Rome long enough to recognise Ocella as a ceremonial soldier, the type of officer who preferred kit inspections and nights of drinking, gambling and whoring to proper soldiering on the battlefield. As was often the case with such commanders, Figulus sensed that Ocella was driven by a need to prove himself in front of his comrades, whatever the cost.

Figulus shrugged. 'I reckon we've got bigger worries than the size of the booty, sir.'

'Oh?' Ocella cocked an eyebrow. 'What do you mean?'

Figulus scratched his beard. 'The Durotrigans are the hardest warriors in all of Britannia, sir. If there's many of them camped on Vectis, they won't give up without a proper fight. Hill fort or no hill fort.'

'And what makes you an expert on the Durotriges, hmm?' Before Figulus could reply, Ocella stroked his chin and added, 'I suppose being half Gaul, you're practically related to these savages.'

Figulus bristled slightly at the insult but bit back on his anger. Although his father had served in the auxiliary cohort long enough to earn Roman citizenship, Figulus took quiet pride in his Gallic roots. He'd spent his childhood in the town of Lutetia in his native Gaul, the grandson of a Aedui nobleman, before joining the Second Legion at the age of eighteen. If anyone in the legion ever accused him of split loyalties, Figulus was quick to reply that he considered himself more Roman than most Romans. But while his devotion to his comrades was never in question, he knew that the truth was slightly murkier. He felt his Gallic ancestry deep in his blood, and he kept the memory of his roots alive by learning the native tongue, which was similar to Gallic. Over the past few weeks in Calleva, he had become fluent in the local dialect. Some of the rankers joked or gently teased him about his Gallic forebears; Ocella preferred to make thinly veiled digs. Figulus refused to rise to the bait and answered politely.

'Not only that, sir. I fought them. Last summer. Under Vespasian. We drove them from their hill forts, one by one. They put up a fierce struggle, I can tell you. Even the women and children. They'd rather die than surrender.'

'Really? You heard the legate's briefing. The hill fort is incomplete, their supplies have been cut off and they won't be expecting an attack from the east. What could possibly go wrong?'

Without replying, Figulus looked down the sloping ground towards the defensive perimeter of the timber fort. Beyond it lay the town of Calleva, a large sprawl of thatched roofs visible above an earth rampart. The Second Legion had returned to the fort next to Calleva after the recent campaign and yet the town was already beginning to follow Roman custom. New streets had been laid out in a Roman-style grid. Numerous taverns and brothels were open for business. Some of the local aristocrats even dressed like Romans. To Figulus's eyes, the pace of change in this part of the province was remarkable.

Even so, he felt his chest tighten with tension. He glanced back at Ocella. 'I wish I could agree with you, sir. But take it from me. Conquering Vectis is going to be a lot harder than you think . . .'

CHAPTER TWO

Isle of Vectis, Five Days Later

A full-throated scream pierced the damp air as an arrow flashed past Figulus, striking the soldier next to him through the neck. The man jolted and his head snapped back, blood fountaining out of his mouth as he fell into the water with a crash of spray.

'Form up on the beach!' Ocella bellowed to his men as he reached the shoreline ahead of Figulus. 'Form up, for fuck's sake!'

As the soldiers jumped over the sides of the galleys and into the icy waters below, they came under immediate attack from archers perched on the chalk cliffs either side of the narrow beach. Arrows rained down on the legionaries in a constant deadly hiss. Some were struck down as soon as they hit the water, their bodies sinking beneath the surface, arrow shafts jutting out of their necks and torsos. Others clasped wounds as they frantically limped towards the shore along the sandbar, the shallow water running red with blood.

Figulus waded past the dead and the dying, his neck muscles clenching with anger. The landing had been a disaster. At dawn the twelve galleys had launched from the naval base at Noviomagus and made for the east coast of Vectis, their decks heaving with soldiers. The lead four galleys had run aground on a sandbank a short distance from the shoreline, with the men on board forced to leap down from the decks and wade through freezing water almost up to their necks. The rest of the fleet was left floundering further out at sea as the trierarchs gave orders for the ships to navigate around the grounded vessels, delaying their arrival. Figulus glanced back and saw the soldiers huddled on the crowded decks of the galleys, forced to watch their imperilled comrades scramble ashore.

He looked ahead as the survivors of the Sixth Century waded

towards the shore, rallying around Ocella. Driving rain spattered against their helmets in a rhythmic din, the men weighed down by their armour, short swords and shields. Their woollen tunics were soaked through, adding to their weight. As Figulus pushed on through the shallow water he felt something cold brush against his stocky leg. He glanced down and saw the limbs of a pale body beneath the surface. Several arrow shafts protruded from his chest and his dull eyes were wide open, his face locked into an expression of silent agony. Figulus nudged the dead soldier aside with his shield and hurried ashore, dodging arrows, his hobnailed boots squelching on the wet sand.

A scene of grim horror confronted him on the beach. Everywhere he looked soldiers were writhing on the ground, the lapping waves washing faint veins of blood upon the wet sand. Maimed men were struck again by arrows as they clawed their way towards their comrades higher up the beach. Pinned down by the missiles raining down from the cliffs, the survivors of the first wave to land had been unable to form up and provide an effective shield for the freshly landed troops, who were picked off at will by the archers positioned on the cliff tops. A few scattered soldiers had managed to form up on the crescent-shaped beach. As arrows thunked into the sand around him the optio felt a bitter rage fill his heart. Once again, a ragtag army of Britons had succeeded in inflicting terrible casualties on their Roman foe.

'Get over here!' Ocella screamed to Figulus as the century formed up in a rough line, hefting their shields above their heads to protect them from the missiles pouring down on them. 'Today, Optio Figulus!'

As the optio ran on, the air came alive with a furious, wind-like whoosh, and a stream of arrows arced through the gloomy sky, hailing down on the isolated men of the Fifth Cohort to a chorus of pained cries. An arrow punched through the arm of a man in front of Figulus. The legionary released his grip on his shield and pawed at the pointed tip sticking out of his flesh as he sank to his knees. The Gaul hoisted his shield above his head. There was a brittle clang as a missile clattered against his shield boss. Figulus lost his footing as he tripped over a splayed corpse and he crashed to the ground, splashing head first into a puddle of gleaming blood beside the body of a wounded soldier. Blinking salty droplets out of his eyes, Figulus quickly picked himself up and scrambled on. He looked back past his shoulder as a cluster of arrows stabbed the sand a few steps to his rear.

In the next instant Figulus drew up alongside his centurion, catching his breath. Ocella shot him a scolding look.

'What the fuck kept you?' he snapped.

'Sorry, sir,' Figulus grunted. 'Dropped my lucky charm.' Seeing the centurion's quizzical expression, he unclenched his left fist to reveal the silver medallion depicting Fortuna. 'Almost lost it in the surf.'

Ocella was momentarily lost for words. 'You nearly got yourself killed over that?' He shook his head in disgust. 'Bloody Gauls . . . Forget it. Look, there's no time. We're in the shit. Those archers have got us pinned down and the cohort's in complete disarray. Most of our ships are stuck out at sea. Only the Fifth's managed to land, together with one squadron of cavalry, and there'll be no support from the warships until they get round that cursed sandbar.'

Figulus followed his line of sight as Ocella nodded out towards the sea. A bank of dark cloud loomed above the grounded galleys. Beyond them several more warships rocked back and forth on the deep swell of the sea. Among these ships he spotted the vessel carrying the legate, a quinquereme, with a long purple pennant fluttering from its mast. He turned back to the centurion and cleared his throat uneasily. 'The gods only know when Celer and the rest of our lads will get ashore.'

'A token resistance,' Ocella muttered under his breath. 'That's what the legate promised. Look around you. What the hell's token about this?' He pointed out the archers on the cliff.

Figulus tightened his grip on his shield handle as he scanned the beach.

'Where's Tribune Palinus?' Ocella barked. 'He's supposed to be in charge here.'

'There, sir,' a soldier to the right of Figulus shouted. 'Palinus took the cavalry up that way.' He pointed to where the gently sloping beach led up to a bank of shingle, and beyond that stood a low but sheer cliff. A series of small tree-lined gullies were cut into the cliff, providing natural exits from the beach. The beach itself was bounded at either end by rising cliffs.

Ocella snorted through his flared nostrils. 'Typical bloody Palinus, showing off as usual. Idiot thinks he's the new Caesar.'

At that moment the air exploded with a hail of dull thwacks and sharp clatters as javelins replaced the shower of arrows. A shrill cry carried across the damp air as a javelin punched through a legionary's mail armour, goring his flesh. Another soldier on the outer line of the formation howled in agony as a javelin slammed into his boot just beyond his shield. Blood instantly coloured the sand around his foot. The soldier released his grip on his shield and reached down to clasp his wound. A handful of arrows clattered into the shingle and one plunged into his neck; the man collapsed in front of Figulus with a gasping cry.

'Take cover!' Ocella roared at his men. 'I SAID TAKE COVER!'

The men hunkered under their shields as the missiles continued to clatter down on them, crashing off the edges of shields like giant hailstones smashing on a tiled roof. Then Figulus heard a whirring sound as slingers added to the barrage and slingshot struck the Romans' shields with a deafening rattle. The odd cry told of a javelin punching through a shield and impaling its target, or a lead shot shattering a soldier's bones. But for the most part the shields offered the legionaries a solid defence against the frenzied wave of missiles. Figulus felt his shield shudder and heard the sharp crack of splitting wood as a Celtic javelin slammed into it, the tip punching through the wood a mere few inches from his face. He gritted his teeth, his forearm and bicep muscles aching from the strain of keeping his shield raised above his head. He was now drenched in sweat despite the cool weather as the physical and mental stress of battle began to take its toll.

'Hold your ground!' Ocella yelled. 'They can't keep this up forever!'

In the next instant the stream of missiles abruptly ceased, and a still silence fell on the beach. There was only the relentless hiss and suck of the waves on the shore and the groans of wounded men. Figulus peered over the metal brim of his shield at the cliff top to the north, watching intently as the archers retreated from view.

'Maybe Palinus has scared them off,' Ocella mused. 'The glory-hunting fool. He'll take all the credit, as usual.'

Figulus grunted as he wrenched the javelin free from his shield. 'Pity. And there I was looking forward to getting stuck into the lot of 'em.'

'Maybe not,' a legionary next to him muttered darkly.

Figulus glanced at the man who'd spoken. He had a prominent scar running down the side of his face and purpled cheeks from years of hard drinking. He'd been one of the first men to introduce himself to the Gaul after Figulus's transfer to the Sixth Century a few weeks earlier. Titus Terentius Rullus was one of the veterans of the Sixth Century.

'Eh?' Ocella snapped. 'What do you mean?'

Rullus nodded at the widest gully cut into the cliff. At once the centurion and his deputy swung their gazes in the same direction. Figulus spied something moving towards them from the treeline at the crest of the gully. As the object bolted out of the murky gloom and down the face of the cliff, the Gaul realised it was a striking white horse, galloping towards them at a furious pace. Then he noticed something else and felt a cold fear clamp over the nape of his neck.

'Shit,' he growled. 'That's Tribune Palinus's horse, sir.'

The horse drew closer, and reared up as it reached the bottom of the slope. Figulus and the others saw blood streaking the animal's flanks.

'Looks like the bastards have done for Palinus,' Rullus muttered.

A menacing war cry sounded from somewhere beyond the trees at the top of the cliff. Just then a long line of muscular figures lined up on the crest of the main gully, their woad-stained bodies clearly visible. Each warrior brandished a long sword which they thumped repeatedly against their round shields in a gesture of defiance. Some of the Durotrigans intoned strange chants, inciting the native gods to help them crush their sworn enemy. One of the men jabbed his thrusting spear at the sky and Figulus felt his stomach churn as he caught sight of the tribune's severed head mounted on the tip of the spear. Then the native war horns called the warriors to battle. The braying notes sent a cold chill through Figulus and his comrades.

'Durotrigans,' said Rullus. 'Hundreds of 'em by the looks of it. Must have cornered Palinus and his mates when they reached the top of the cliffs. Poor buggers.' He turned to the Gaul. 'Looks like you're going to get your wish after all, sir.'

Figulus tightened his thick fingers round the grip of his short sword and grinned at the Britons lined up on the hilltop as he called out to his men, 'If the bastards want to play rough, then they've come to the right men!'

CHAPTER THREE

The wild war cries of the Durotrigans instantly cut out. There was a moment's pause and then the warriors began storming down the cliff towards the cohort assembled on the beach, swarming through the long grass covering the gully in dense tufts, their lime-washed hair flowing behind their broad shoulders. Swallowing his fear, Ocella swiftly turned to address the century.

'All right, lads! Spread out! Form a line. NOW!'

At once the legionaries broke up from their solid defensive formation and brought their shields down in front of them in a single smooth motion while Ocella moved to take up his position on the front line. Many of the soldiers had abandoned their javelins in the struggle to get ashore, and Figulus herded those who were still equipped with a throwing weapon towards the rearmost rank so that they could launch their missiles over the heads of their comrades. Then Ocella ordered the front rank of men to draw their weapons and the air was filled with the sound of grating metal as swords were unsheathed from scabbards. Similar orders were given by centurions up and down the beach as the men of the Fifth Cohort prepared to face the warriors bearing down on them.

'Javelins . . . ready!' Figulus bellowed.

The men to the rear of the century lifted up their weapons so that they gripped them horizontally across their shoulders.

The dark great mass of Durotrigans had reached the bottom of the cliff and were charging across the shingle beach less than a hundred paces away. Their line stretched in a loose formation across nearly the full length of the beach and at this distance Figulus could see that some wore mail vests over their tunics. Their straggly beards were

14

visible beneath their helmets and swirling patterns were painted on the front of their shields. Most of the enemy were bare-chested, and a handful wore nothing, to express their contempt for their Roman enemy. A few of the warriors were armed with war spears, although most brandished the heavyweight long swords so beloved of the Celts.

The Durotrigans swept across the shingle beach in a mass, some men racing ahead of their comrades. Figulus looked on as the gap between the Romans and the enemy rapidly closed, waiting to give the signal for the men to hurl their javelins at the onrushing Britons. The timing had to be perfect. Throw too early, and the spears would fall short of their intended targets. Too late, and the Durotrigans would be on top of the front rank before the iron heads struck home. Now the warriors were so close that Figulus could see the wild looks in their eyes, their mouths gaping as they shouted their war cries.

'Release javelins!' Ocella thundered.

The men at the rear simultaneously hurled their missiles at the Durotrigans. The javelins arced through the grey sky before plunging moments later amid the warriors a short distance from the century, the long iron shafts punching through the crude round shields. The front rank of Britons toppled as if they had slipped on ice. Some men went down at once. Others stumbled on, clutching shafts protruding from their torsos, before they were thrust aside by the frantic charge of the enraged warriors following them. One naked Briton shrieked as a throwing spear plunged into his groin, blood splashing down his legs and on to his feet.

But even as the wounded Durotrigans fell away, the warriors behind surged past them. Ocella thrust his sword arm in the direction of the enemy horde. 'Forward!' he shouted.

The Sixth Century advanced in line with the rest of the cohort, each centurion sticking rigidly to the tactics that had served Rome so well in countless battles against its barbarian foes. The clash of steel against steel rang out as the opposing forces rippled into each other. The legionaries covered their torsos with their shields and thrust at the throats of the enemy with their short swords in the manner they had practised endlessly in the bloodless battle of training-ground drills. Fighting shoulder to shoulder, their shields forming a solid wall

15

against the enemy, the men thrust at the savage warriors opposite them with precise stabs aimed at the most vulnerable points on the body: the throat and upper chest. For their part, the Durotrigans tried to swing their long swords, forcing them to open up and expose their bodies to the Romans.

Figulus shouted for the men of the second rank to ready their swords as they waited for their chance to take the position of any soldiers cut down ahead of them, swiftly plugging any gaps in the shield wall. Men were dropping at an alarming rate. The surgeon's orderlies scurried up and down the line, removing the severely wounded a safe distance down the beach. Those who could not be saved were dragged aside and left to writhe in agony on the sand as they bled out, clutching at their wounds in vain attempts to stem the flow of blood.

As the legionaries pushed forward, someone shouted a warning and a new wave of missiles hurtled down from the cliff looming over the right flank of the Roman line. There was a cry of agony as one of the men of Figulus's century went down, his thigh pierced by an arrow.

'Rear rank! Raise shields!' Figulus roared, and the men on either side instantly lifted their shields to form a solid screen above them, protecting themselves and, to a lesser degree, the men of the first line. Some of the enemy missiles fell amongst their own warriors, who shrieked at their hideous wounds while their companions hurled themselves against the wall of Roman shields. Peering past the shoulder of the man in front of him, Figulus saw one Durotrigan, sweeping his sword before him, barge through a gap in the line. He was cut down by one of his own javelins before he could get stuck into the legionaries. Ocella, who had retreated from the front line and was frantically shoving men forward into the gaps, turned to Figulus in horror.

'What the hell are they still shooting at us for? Don't they realise they're hitting their own men?'

Figulus hissed in frustration. Despite the peril to their own men the Durotrigans' arrows and javelins were whittling down the Romans. More and more gaps were beginning to open up in the front rank now as the line began to waver. Soon the enemy warriors would be able to push the Romans back by weight of their numbers. He drew Ocella's attention to the tribesmen on the cliff.

'They're killing us, sir. We have to get off the beach.'

Ocella shook his head. Sweat flowed down his reddened face. 'Our orders are clear. We hold the line here until the other cohorts can land and reinforce our position.'

'If we don't do something, there won't be any line left to hold.'

'We make our stand here!' Ocella insisted. 'Here!' He took a step closer to his deputy, lowering his voice. 'Question my authority like that again and I'll have you up on a charge.'

Figulus bristled with rage. The Sixth Century was in grave danger and its commanding officer, gripped by indecision and anxiety in the heat of battle, was more concerned with punishing his subordinate for a perceived slight. Ocella turned away from him with a sneer. As he did, a lead shot from one of the slingers glanced off his helmet. Stumbling backwards, Ocella let out a light groan, his eyes rolling into the back of his head as he collapsed onto the sand. Figulus cast a look at the unconscious officer. Bright red blood trickled down his face. An orderly crouched beside the centurion and examined him quickly before turning to Figulus.

'He's out cold.'

Figulus hesitated a moment and it was Rullus who spoke first. 'Looks like you're in charge, sir.'

'Right, then.' Figulus nodded, tightening his grip on the handle of his shield as he shaped to take up his place on the front rank and take the fight to the Durotrigans.

'We've got to put a stop to those archers somehow.' Rullus nodded at the men injured by arrows lying on the shingle behind them. 'At least then we'd stand a fucking chance.'

Figulus hesitated, blinking blood and sweat out of his eyes. 'How?'

The veteran pointed to a muddy gully cut into the cliff running parallel to the cliffs. 'If we can get a small party to work their way up there, we can teach the bastards a lesson they won't forget in a hurry.'

An appreciative grin crept across the Gaul's grim face. 'Just the job. Take charge here, Rullus.' Then he signalled to the thirty or so men still in the second line and jabbed his sword at the cliff. 'Rear three sections! On me!'

The blood rushing in his ears, Figulus led the legionaries around the century's right flank and charged up the beach towards the cliff. Several Durotrigans caught sight of the Romans manoeuvring past them and broke away from their comrades in an attempt to cut them off, lunging at the soldiers with their long swords. Figulus punched his shield at a charging warrior, the iron boss smashing into the man's face with a dull crunch. As the Romans crossed the shingle beach and scrambled up the gully, the Gaul could feel his calf muscles aching from the exertion, his lungs burning with the effort.

He pushed up the steep incline and at the crest of the cliff he turned towards the huddle of natives lining the cliff edge. The Britons' attention was fixed on the fight taking place along the beach as they rained arrows, javelins, slingshot and even small rocks at the Romans. Figulus felt a hot thrill run through him as he prepared to cut down the unsuspecting barbarians.

'Stay with me!' he ordered his men. 'When we go in, hit 'em hard.'

As the legionaries rushed along the cliff top, one of the Britons glanced round and saw them. His eyes widened with panic and he turned back to his companions to alert them to the onrushing soldiers. At once the Britons turned away from the cliff edge. A few managed to release their javelins at a low angle, but Figulus and his men were already upon them and the soldier to the right of the optio gasped as a shaft smashed into his knee. In the next moment the Romans charged into the native warriors. The Britons snatched at their hand weapons, a motley assortment of axes and knives, quite useless against the broad shields and armour of the legionaries. Step by step Figulus and his men forced the enemy towards the edge of the cliff.

Figulus peered over the top of his shield and saw the glimmer of a javelin shooting towards his neck as a Briton thrust at him. The optio deftly parried the attack with his damaged shield. The warrior snarled as his weapon glanced off the curved edge, angling away from his target and opening up his torso to attack. Figulus took grateful advantage, stabbing the man in the chest. There was a sickening crunch as the blade tip punched through soft flesh, skirting off hard bone. The Briton released his weapon with a shudder as Figulus ripped his sword free and the man fell at the optio's feet.

Those Durotrigans who had survived the initial attack now found themselves trapped between the Romans and the sheer vertical drop of the cliff. Figulus urged the men around him to keep pushing the enemy back. To his left he spotted a naked Briton clamping his hands on the top edge of a legionary's shield in an effort to wrest it from his grip. Figulus spun to face the warrior, stabbing him through the throat before he could claw at the terrified legionary, and there was a soft crunch as Figulus's blade tip scraped against the man's jaw.

With one last effort the small party of Romans pushed forward and the remaining Durotrigans began to plummet to their deaths on the rocks below. Some clawed at their companions, dragging them down as well. One clasped his hands round a legionary's knee as he lost his footing, pulling the despairing Roman to his death with him. Only a handful managed to scrabble free along the cliff edge but they were quickly set upon by the Romans, thirsting to avenge their comrades who had been cut down by the missiles raining down from the cliff. There would be no prisoners taken today.

As the last of the enemy on the cliff top was cut down, Figulus glanced around, his chest heaving as he surveyed the scene. Below he could see dozens of contorted bodies broken on the rocks. Lifting his gaze to the shingle beach, Figulus watched the men of the Fifth Cohort pressing forward and he felt a surge of relief at the sight of the rearmost natives turning to flee from the bloodstained shingle. Within a matter of moments the Durotrigans were beating a pell-mell retreat back up the shingle beach as the last few warriors turned their backs on their slain comrades and ran for their lives.

Out on the waters of the cove one of the warships loaded with catapults had managed to navigate around the grounded galleys. The trireme headed towards the shore, oars rising and cutting the sea in continuous rhythm. Up on the deck the men prepared the catapults to shoot at the retreating enemy. Figulus heard the distant shout of an order and several sharp cracks carried across the water like whiplashes as the catapults unleashed their stone balls, arcing over the heads of the cohort and crashing through the fleeing Durotrigans. The crudely shaped stones shattered skulls and spines like giant fists. More of the enemy were struck down by a final volley of iron-headed bolts shot from ballistas mounted on the deck of the same warship. The surviving

19

warriors, casting terrified backward glances, managed to scramble off the beach and out of sight, leaving behind a scene of slaughter. Some of the legionaries tried to pursue them but laden with heavy armour they quickly gave up and hunched over their shields, gasping for breath.

Figulus led his men back along the cliff edge to head off any enemy fleeing towards them, but there was nothing left for his men to do. The battle was over. As the remainder of the Fifth Cohort emerged from the gullies, the soldiers set upon those natives too injured to escape. They were in no mood to take pity on their vanquished foes and killed the wounded Durotrigans where they lay. Figulus saw several legionaries surround a warrior who was on his knees. The men cheered as they took turns to plunge their swords into his body, one after the other. The warrior remained defiantly upright even as he choked on his own blood. Figulus fought off the urge to intervene and looked away.

Bodies and discarded equipment covered the beach. He was surprised at how painfully thin many of the dead Britons appeared to be. Everywhere he looked he saw protruding ribcages and gaunt faces. Conflicting emotions swirled inside him – as they always did in the grisly moments after a battle. As a soldier in the service of the Emperor, Figulus was acutely aware of the fact that the warriors he slew in battle were Celtic men. Just like his forefathers.

'A bloodbath, sir,' Rullus said as he drew up at his shoulder, his faded grey eyes surveying the beach below. 'Never seen anything like it. They were just throwing themselves at us. Some of them had nothing but their bare fists.'

'It's hard to believe how much they hate Rome,' Figulus responded.

He fell quiet for a moment, then remembered something and directed his gaze towards the cliff.

'Where's the centurion?' he asked, scanning the lines of men.

Rullus tipped his head at the column of wounded men herded on the shingle beach. 'Down with the other casualties, sir. Doesn't look like he'll be waking up for a while yet.' He hesitated to go on, glancing left and right to make sure no one was listening. Then he leaned in close to Figulus and lowered his voice. 'Word to the wise,

20

sir. You'd do well to watch yourself around the centurion. Ocella used to be an officer in the Praetorian Guard, before he transferred to the Second.'

'Why would he give up a cosy position with the Guards to transfer to Britannia?'

Rullus shrugged. 'Maybe it wasn't his choice. Maybe that's why he gives us so much grief.' He sucked his teeth and added, 'The last lad in your boots didn't last long. He was sent back to Gesoriacum to train new recruits. Take it from me, sir. Ocella's not someone you want to cross.'

CHAPTER FOUR

The last galleys were beached as a purple dusk settled over Vectis, the sea glistening like thousands of dazzling sword points in the dying light. The skies had cleared while the deck hands unloaded the supplies that would feed and equip the army. Throughout the afternoon teams of sailors had laboured to clear the triremes run aground on the sandbar. Standing up to their waists in the freezing water, they pulled on ropes tethered to the prow of each ship, dragging the vessels over the bar and refloating them one by one. While the triremes were pulled clear, the rest of the fleet made its way carefully towards the beach in the late afternoon.

Men from each century of the Fifth Cohort were detailed to carry out the grim task of clearing the dead from the shore. A note was made on waxed slates of the name of each dead legionary to present to the centurions to tally up the casualties. The injured were treated where they lay, while a field hospital was set up in the camp being constructed a short distance inland. The dead were gathered up and placed in lines, ready for the pyre that would be constructed to cremate their bodies after firewood had been gathered. Each corpse was relieved of its armour, weapons and boots. These were then sent on to the quartermaster's office to be repaired and placed in stores, ready to be reissued as the need arose.

On the orders of the legate, the Durotrigans were heaped below one of the cliffs and left as a stark reminder of the price paid by those who defied Rome. Their weapons and equipment were removed too, so that they might not fall into the hands of scavengers, who might then sell them on to Rome's enemies.

With his force ashore, the legate dispatched cavalry scouts to search for signs of the enemy further inland while the cohorts at last moved up from the shore, leaving the cliff behind, the memory of the beach-fighting seared into their minds. The fatigued men cleared the scattered thickets on the ground beyond the shore and bent to the arduous task of constructing a marching camp in the face of the enemy. First they dug a twelve-foot-deep outer ditch using their entrenching tools. Then they heaped the spoil from the ditch to form a ten-foot-high inner rampart. This was surmounted by sharpened wooden stakes lashed together with leather ties, designed to act as giant caltrops in the event of an enemy assault.

Once the defensive lines had been completed the men set to work laying out their tent lines. With the legion and its baggage train securely enclosed within the marching camp, the soldiers at last filled their empty bellies with rations of steaming hot salted pork and barley gruel. As night closed in, the men retired to their eight-man goatskin tents. They sat round camp fires warming themselves and their damp clothes, swapping lewd jokes, playing dice, trying to take their minds off the grim memories of battle. Those men on fatigues were assigned the arduous task of cutting logs from the edge of a nearby forest to construct a funeral pyre for their fallen comrades.

Once Figulus had fulfilled his duties for the day he joined Rullus and his section at their camp fire and warmed his hands. He had checked with the Second's surgeon to see if Ocella was recovering but the centurion was rambling incoherently, his head rolling from side to side as he lay on a thin bedroll spread on the ground. Figulus had hoped the man would have recovered his wits enough to resume command of the Sixth Century and let his optio return to his lesser responsibilities. As things stood, it looked as if Figulus was saddled with command for the next few days at least – a situation he resented, for he considered himself a common soldier at heart, and cherished the camaraderie of his fellow rankers. But at least he would be spared the centurion's fussiness in the meantime. Ocella was an efficient officer who prided himself on the presentation and orderliness of his men. Any sign of tardiness was met with a cold glare and a harsh disciplinary charge. Life under Ocella was particularly challenging for Figulus and Ocella ruthlessly seized on every little mistake he made, berating him over a speck of dirt on his polished belt buckle at kit inspection, or the slightest error in his record-keeping. Privately Figulus suspected that Ocella resented him for his much greater combat experience. Perhaps Ocella saw him as a threat to his authority. With a heavy feeling in his heart Figulus realised that unless he could resolve his differences with the centurion, his days with the Sixth Century would be numbered.

Rullus and the other legionaries huddled around the camp fire in silence, their faces illuminated by the glow of the flames. Figulus could see the numbed weariness in their expressions and decided to do something about their mood. 'Now, then,' he said with a forced grin. 'Who wants to see a magic trick?'

Rullus rolled his eyes. 'Gods. Here we go! Another bloody trick.'

Figulus turned to Rullus and winked. 'This one really works. I learned it from a Cilician merchant back at Rutupiae.' He searched the faces of the men around the camp fire. 'All I need is a volunteer.'

'An idiot, more like,' Rullus chuckled.

'I'll do it, sir,' the legionary seated opposite Figulus offered.

Figulus regarded the slender, youthful-looking legionary. Gaius Arrius Helva was one of the new recruits who had been assigned to the Sixth Century the day before they marched from Calleva. He had that mix of naivety and cockiness common to all the new recruits for a short period after they arrived in Britannia – before brutal conflict with the enemy turned them into battle-hardened veterans who couldn't wait to leave these shores. In the short time that Figulus had been with the Sixth Century he'd come to know Helva only slightly; but there was something about the new recruit that he found encouraging. He was eager to prove himself worthy of his comrades and his enthusiasm for army life contrasted starkly with the weary, cynical air of many of the older soldiers.

Figulus took a coin from his purse. 'Right then, lad. Give us your palm.'

Helva dutifully thrust his hand towards the optio with his palm facing up. Placing his hand on top of the legionary's, with his own palm facing down, Figulus then produced the coin, showing it to each man around the camp fire in turn before placing it firmly on top of his hand.

'Now,' he began. 'You can clearly see that this here coin is on top of my hand, yes?' The men nodded. 'Well, what if I said I could make this coin pass through my hand and into your palm?' He was looking at Helva as he spoke. The legionary stared at him with wide-eyed disbelief.

'Through your hand?' he repeated. 'That coin? It can't be done. Only the gods are capable of such things.'

'Gods . . . and rose oil salesmen,' Rullus muttered. 'Four sestertii says it won't work.'

'Deal!' Figulus responded eagerly.

He counted to three. Then, with his free hand raised high above his head, he intoned the words the Cilician had taught him and slapped his hand down on top of the one clasped over Helva's palm. He waited a moment. Helva leaned forward expectantly as Figulus slowly peeled his hand away from Helva's palm. Even Rullus, in spite of his obvious scepticism, craned his head to get a better look.

'Empty!' Rullus declared, slapping his thigh. 'I knew it!' He rubbed his hands gleefully. 'You owe me four sestertii, sir.'

'Bollocks!' Figulus frowned. 'But − I don't understand. I did exactly what the merchant told me to do. I said the right magic words and everything.'

'Pay up, Gaul,' Rullus replied jokingly.

Cursing his luck, Figulus reached into his purse and dug out four coins. He could ill afford the loss, since he had managed to squander the bulk of his modest savings on dice. He found that he had an inexplicable urge to keep playing the game. Each time he lost, he'd walk away in a sour mood, swearing to Jupiter that he'd never gamble at dice again. And yet the following day Figulus invariably found himself back at the gambling table, in the dark corner of some questionable drinking hole, wagering away yet more of his hard-earned pay. Only recently he had lost a full month's salary playing dice in Calleva, losing twenty straight games in a row. A result which led him to strongly suspect that his wily opponent had been cheating.

'Optio Horatius Figulus?' a voice barked.

Figulus spun round as a man stepped forward from beyond the tent lines. From the plume on his helmet, Figulus identified him as one of the legate's personal bodyguards. The man looked directly at Figulus as he spoke. He'd spotted the staff of office, unique to the rank of optio, lying on the ground beside him.

'That's me,' he replied.

The bodyguard nodded. 'The legate wishes to speak with you.'

'Now?' Figulus glimpsed Helva and Rullus exchanging puzzled looks in the dim glow of the camp fire. 'What for?'

The bodyguard's face gave nothing away. 'Right away, if you don't mind, sir. The legate's a busy man.' He gestured to Figulus to follow him and promptly marched down the main alley leading towards the centre of the camp.

What could the legate possibly want with him at this late hour? wondered Figulus as he followed the bodyguard past the barracks and the grain stores. Outside the tents of the field hospital he spied a small line of shrouded bodies. A short distance beyond, they reached the legate's headquarters, a large tent erected at the intersection of the two main routes running through the camp. A pair of guards stood watch outside the tent, with the legion's military standards resting in racks on either side. The soldier escorting Figulus approached the open tent flaps and the two guards nodded at their comrade and stepped aside.

'In you go, sir. Legate's waiting for you,' the bodyguard said tonelessly.

The sweet tang of heated wine filled his nostrils as Figulus entered. It was pleasingly warm in the tent. Braziers in all four corners burned brightly, heating the quarters against the foul British weather. In one corner stood a low table with a platter of cold meats heaped on top, and a brass jug filled to the brim with wine set in a retaining stand over an oil lamp. Thin wisps of steam rose from the jug. A large campaign table occupied the middle of the tent, surrounded by half a dozen padded leather stools.

Legate Celer was sitting behind the table, his brow heavily furrowed in concentration as he read from a waxed slate on the desk in front of him. Figulus stood awkwardly in front of the legate for a moment or two, taking in the luxurious surroundings of the legate's tent. It was a world away from the trappings of a common soldier and inwardly the Gaul felt terribly out of place.

At last Celer glanced up. Figulus gave a stiff salute. The legate regarded him with his cold blue eyes.

'At ease, Optio.'

The legate had an air of self-regarding superiority characteristic of most Roman aristocrats, a confidence verging on arrogance. Figulus had seen men like him occupying the senior tribune ranks: the sons of wealthy aristocrats dispatched to Britannia to fulfil their military service for a couple of years before returning to Rome to pursue a lucrative career in public office. Some such men had little interest in the business of soldiering and displayed an alarming lack of concern for the long-term stability of the province. They cared only about where their next jug of Falernian was coming from and catching up with the latest gossip from the bathhouses and theatres of Rome. Figulus feared that such a man was now in charge of Rome's finest legion.

'Figulus, isn't it?' Celer asked.

'Yes, sir.'

'And you're half Gaul, I understand from your records. My friends in the imperial palace tell me they're letting your people become senators. In Rome. Imagine that! Gauls debating politics. The world's gone mad.'

Figulus kept his lips pressed shut and stood very still as Celer glanced down at the waxed slate on his desk.

'The Sixth Century did the legion proud on the beach today. By all accounts, the Fifth Cohort would've been overrun by those damned Britons had it not been for the Sixth's charge up on to the cliff.'

Figulus shifted his weight, unsure whether the legate expected a reply. After a moment's silence Celer continued.

'I'm told your centurion sustained an injury.'

Figulus nodded. 'Took a blow to the head, sir. He's laid up in the field hospital. Surgeon reckons he'll be back on his feet in a day or two.'

'This legion has lost too many officers lately,' Celer remarked sourly. 'But the plain fact of it is, Ocella isn't here and as his subordinate you are the next in line of command. You showed admirable initiative on the beach, a quality that will be needed again for this next task.'

27

Figulus frowned. 'What task, sir?'

Celer stroked his chin calmly. He had the politician's knack of answering a completely different question to the one being asked. 'Is it true that one of the last acts of my predecessor was to pardon you from a charge of desertion?' Figulus froze in horror but before he could respond, Celer went on. 'Not to mention that the legate also dropped charges of aiding and abetting the escape of condemned soldiers.' He paused, regarding Figulus with his icy blue eyes. 'Those are serious offences. They carry a severe penalty.'

He left the threat hanging in the warm air. Figulus felt his stomach tighten into a painful knot. 'I was only trying to do what was right, sir. An officer I respect and a bunch of other lads were wrongly condemned to death by decimation. I couldn't stand by and see them executed. It wouldn't have been right.'

'Yes, yes,' Celer replied impatiently. 'I'm well aware of the details. It's all here in the report. As is the reason given for the pardon. Apparently you played a vital part in the defeat of Caratacus.'

The optio shrugged. 'I did my duty, sir.'

Celer pushed the waxed slate aside and leaned forward across the desk. 'You might think you can live off past glories in this army, Figulus, but I don't give a damn what you did under Vespasian. This is my legion now. And you're going to have to prove yourself to me. Understood?'

'Yes, sir,' Figulus responded through gritted teeth.

'Glad to hear it.' Celer smiled briefly. 'Now, to the mission. As you know from the earlier briefing, our objective on Vectis is to put an end to the Durotriges' pitiful little resistance. The day after tomorrow we shall resume our march westwards, once the rest of the cavalry have arrived, and attack the hill fort the enemy is in the process of building. I doubt the assault itself will present much difficulty to the men. I find it staggering that these brutes continue to place so much misguided faith in their primitive defence works.'

Figulus bit his tongue. It was a widely held view among those men new to the Second Legion that the hill forts of the Durotrigans had been easily conquered. The Gaul, however, knew differently. The Second Legion had fought hard to take those forts, and but for the leadership of Vespasian and the resolute efforts of the soldiers,

28

they might still be in the hands of the enemy. Only a fool would believe that the Durotrigans had been easy to conquer. He watched Celer carefully as he reached for the silver goblet half filled with wine on the desk and took a swig. The legate set the cup down and delicately wiped his lips on the back of his finger.

'Make no mistake, Optio, I intend to crush every last pocket of resistance on Vectis.'

'Yes, sir.'

'There is, however, a problem.' Celer exhaled deeply. 'We've received intelligence that a number of Roman prisoners are being held on the isle. They were captured on the mainland a few months ago. They're being held not far from here. Our native scout, Magadubnus, learned of their predicament. According to him, the Durotrigan chief holding the prisoners wants to make a deal with us.' A smile tickled at the corner of his lips. 'Their lives in exchange for food.'

'Food, sir?' Figulus wondered. 'Not silver, then?'

The legate nodded. 'I know. Pathetic, isn't it? But understandable. We've cut off their supplies and the islanders cannot feed the refugees from the mainland as well as their own people.' Celer leaned back in his chair and smiled. 'So the Durotrigan chief is offering us a deal. And you, Figulus, along with a small party of your men, are going to make the exchange.'

CHAPTER FIVE

A frigid silence filled the legate's tent as Celer rose from his chair and approached the low table bearing the meat and wine. He lifted the brass jug from the retaining stand and refilled his goblet.

'The prisoners were part of a detachment sent to Vindocladia,' he began. 'Reinforcements for the vexillation fort down there. The men never arrived. A scouting party found the commanding officer and scores of dead soldiers dumped in a nearby stream. Twelve men were unaccounted for. At the time, we assumed they had been sold into slavery, or burned alive in one of those infernal wicker men.' The legate swirled his goblet in his hand, eyeing the contents. 'I should say they're lucky to still be alive.'

'If you say so, sir,' Figulus replied guardedly, his cheeks blazing with rage as he recalled his own period in captivity at the hands of Caratacus: manacled in a filthy animal pen, tormented by his captors. He'd escaped without being subjected to the cruel and unusual tortures for which the Britons were known. Others, he knew, were less fortunate. If the soldiers were indeed alive, the Britons were unlikely to have spared them any suffering.

'How can we be sure that they're really holding the prisoners, sir?' he asked. 'It could be a trick.'

By way of reply, Celer set the goblet down on the low table and picked up a leather pouch next to the oil lamp. He tossed the bag to the optio. Figulus caught it and opened it. Inside was a lead tag, stamped with the seal of the Second Legion. It was of the type worn by Roman soldiers on the march, so that their corpses could be identified if they died. Holding the tag up to the light from the flickering braziers, Figulus could make out the name of a soldier engraved on the reverse, along with his rank and century.

'There are eleven more signaculums just like that one,' Celer said. 'They were handed to Magadubnus by the Durotrigan chief as proof that he's holding the prisoners. We've already checked the names on each signaculum against the records of the missing soldiers. They correspond. So we may be fairly certain that the chief is telling the truth, and has the men in question.'

Figulus looked at the legate. 'Magadubnus has been communicating with this chief, then?'

'He's acting as an intermediary on our behalf. Negotiating between the two parties. The Britons trust him about as much as we do, I suppose. Magadubnus learned about the prisoners shortly after he landed on Vectis several days ago, pretending to be a Durotrigan warrior in order to gather intelligence on the enemy. He heard about the prisoners, and learned that the chief might be willing to cut a deal with us. At which point Magadubnus approached the chief, with my permission, to open negotiations.'

'The local warriors won't be too happy when they find out.'

'Of course.' Celer smiled briefly. 'But with everyone going hungry, I would think that the chief's hand has been forced rather. Perhaps the thought of several Roman cohorts sweeping through his village also had something to do with it. For what it's worth, we've also promised the chief that we'll supply his people with grain and spare his village.'

'And he'll take our word for it?'

'He has no choice. He can negotiate with us or else his people will suffer certain death, either through starvation or at the end of Roman swords.'

'How much grain are we talking about, sir?'

'Four hundred modii. I understand the natives have a crude mill in their village. The grain will provide them with enough bread and porridge to keep them alive through the winter, although quite frankly such a diet sounds miserable. But I think you'll agree such an exchange is infinitely preferable to losing good men in any direct attack on the village. Not to mention the risk of the villagers executing the prisoners before we could rescue them. Besides, these men are highly decorated soldiers of the First Cohort. The cream of the legion's crop. General Plautius was particularly distressed to learn of their abduction.' He smiled to himself before going on. 'Returning them safely to the ranks will please the general. And it'll be a splendid boost to the morale of the legion, don't you think? Quite a coup.'

'Of course, sir,' Figulus responded diplomatically, though something about the legate's demeanour told him that Celer was far more concerned with impressing General Plautius than improving morale among the rankers.

'In time,' Celer continued, 'once we have laid waste to Vectis, the rest of those barbaric Durotrigans will quickly recognise the error of their ways and surrender to us. Eventually every other tribe on this miserable island will follow. Then we shall have peace in Britannia.'

Figulus stayed silent. Celer's aristocratic mind, educated in the certainties of Roman superiority, would not allow for the notion of anything less than absolute victory. Only after a year or more on the ground would he finally grasp the depth of the hatred that the natives felt for Rome. They might defeat the Britons on the battlefield, Figulus thought, but that was as far as any victory would go. He stood without speaking while Celer paced back to the desk and shoved the clutter to one side and rolled out a vellum map of Vectis. Figulus stepped forward and leaned in for a closer look as the legate pointed with a slender finger to a position on the western fringes of the island.

Celer said, 'The village where the soldiers are being held captive is approximately half a day's march from our present location. The terrain is quite navigable, save for a few marshes. Once you reach the village you will oversee the exchange with the chief. If he tries it on, making requests for extra grain or any such nonsense, rough him up a bit. Remind him that he's obliged to abide by the terms of our agreement. Then all you and your men will need to do is unload the grain, account for the prisoners and return them safely to the camp. Should be easy enough.' He pointed a finger at Figulus. 'You're to leave at once.'

Figulus jolted with surprise. 'We're to go tonight, sir?'

'But of course,' Celer replied evenly. 'Moving under cover of darkness will help you avoid any Durotrigan scouts roaming the land. Magadubnus knows the ground well. He'll guide you safely around any nests of Durotrigan warriors. The exchange is set for dawn. If you leave now you should make it in good time.'

Figulus stared at the map. He could already anticipate several problems. Even if he and his men managed to avoid the Durotrigan scouts, any one of the surrounding native settlements carried a threat. It would take only one local to stumble upon their position and soon they would have an army of Durotrigans hunting them. Then there was the physical condition of his men. They had been up since the early hours and in the space of a single day had battled seasickness, fought on the shores of Vectis, cleared away and buried their dead comrades and constructed a marching camp. Many of them were probably already asleep. Figulus could almost picture the looks on their tired faces as he told them they would have to slog through hostile terrain in the middle of a cold, damp night.

'In the temporary absence of Centurion Ocella, you'll assume command of a detachment from your century. Take forty men with you. I've drawn up the necessary requisition for the grain which you can present to the quartermaster.'

'Yes, sir.' Figulus paused before adding, 'We might run into trouble on the return march, sir. Marching in broad daylight with the prisoners, we'll be an easy target for any nearby Britons.'

Celer grimaced. 'Forty soldiers ought to suffice for a rearguard action if you do encounter any resistance. Besides, by then most of the Durotrigans ought to have rallied at the hill fort. I understand that many of them are making their way there now in an attempt to hasten its completion before we attack. The fools.'

Figulus gave a slight nod of the head, unconvinced by the legate's reassurances but unwilling to risk annoying him further by pressing the point. Clearly Celer would not spare him any more soldiers and it would be fruitless to pursue the matter. 'Where will I find Magadubnus, sir?'

'He's in my bodyguard's tent. One of my clerks will send for him. I'll arrange for him to report to you immediately. Now, if that's all . . . ?' Figulus nodded and Celer smiled thinly at him. 'Dismissed.'

Figulus saluted the legate, turned and left the tent, filled with apprehension at his task. So far in his military career, he had managed to avoid responsibility, content with his lot as a second-in-command, preferring the company of legionaries to mingling with the other officers. Now suddenly he had been handed the burden of command, and the weight of it as he made his way back to his quarters felt like a pair of heavy marching yokes on his shoulders. The success or failure of the looming mission rested entirely with him, and hinged on whether he could prove himself a good leader of men as well as a fearless soldier. For the sake of the men under his command, and the prisoners held in the village, Figulus knew he could not afford to fail.

CHAPTER SIX

'Load of bollocks if you ask me,' Rullus grumbled as Figulus joined him on the outer perimeter of the tent lines. A gap of sixty feet separated the neatly ordered tents from the rampart, the distance carefully measured in order to ensure that the men in the marching camp were well out of range of any missiles thrown by the enemy. Beyond the sentries manning the main gate Figulus could see precious little except a mute dense blackness.

'We shouldn't be making deals with the Britons,' Rullus went on. 'That grain's for us, not some grubby villagers.'

'What would you suggest, Rullus?'

'Attack 'em.' He slammed a fist into the palm of his hand. 'Hit 'em with everything we've got. Take no prisoners.'

Figulus rolled his tongue around his teeth before flashing a toothy grin. 'It's a nice thought, I'll give you that. But they've got our lads. They could kill them at any moment. It's less risky to give them what they want.'

'Afraid you're wrong, sir. The only reason we're not destroying the village is because it benefits the legate.'

'How so?'

'Think about it,' he said, tapping the side of his nose. 'The legate returns the prisoners to Rome, he gets all the plaudits and puts a smile on the faces of those Greek freedmen running the imperial palace. That's all Celer gives a shit about. He doesn't care that by negotiating with the enemy and giving them a reward we're encouraging them to kidnap more soldiers. Next time, it could be us.'

Figulus craned his neck at the sky, eyeing the thin wisps of fog lurking over the coast. 'Could be worse, I suppose.'

35

'Oh?' Rullus remarked tersely. 'How'd you figure that one?'

'At least it's not raining. The weather gods favour us.'

'There's that famous Gallic sense of humour again,' Rullus remarked wryly.

Figulus smiled back. 'Take it from me. When you grow up in Lutetia, you can't take life too seriously. We're an amphora-half-full lot, my people.'

Rullus grunted and Figulus turned his attention to the soldiers standing in a line in front of the perimeter. As soon as he'd left the legate's tent he'd briefed Rullus on the mission, instructing him to round up the fighting men in the century who were in the best physical shape – men still capable of holding a sword and marching a dozen or more miles without dropping out, even after the strain of the day's battle. Now Figulus examined the faces of the men in front of him and realised that only a handful of the men chosen for the task were veterans. The years of waging war in Britannia had thinned the ranks. Most of the soldiers standing in line were young soldiers, new to the Sixth Century and the province. Quite a few were younger than Figulus himself; and even though he was only nineteen years of age, he was painfully aware that his experience made him one of the century's veterans. He recognised most of the faces, although a few were unfamiliar since he'd not yet had the time to get to know each ranker.

His eyes settled on an unfamiliar soldier standing at the end of the line. The man had a thick beard and his burly frame swayed heavily on the spot. Judging from the glazed look in his eyes the man was inebriated. Figulus marched over to him.

'You. Name?'

'Sextus Porcius Blaesus,' the soldier slurred. He made a half-comical, half-pitiful salute. He let out a loud belch and wiped his mouth with the back of his hand. Figulus gritted his teeth, a hot rage sweeping through his veins at the sight of the drunken legionary. As he glowered at Blaesus, Figulus dimly recalled seeing his face before but he couldn't quite place him.

'You're drunk,' he said.

Blaesus raised his hands in protest. 'I had a little drop after the evening meal,' he replied defensively. 'That's all.'

36

'It's "sir" to you,' Figulus responded sharply, balling his hand into a tight fist. 'I'm acting centurion for the time being, so you'll address me as "sir" like every other man in the century. Got it?'

Blaesus mock-bowed. 'My humble apologies . . . sir.'

Suddenly Figulus remembered where he'd seen the man before. He clenched his jaws in rage. 'It's you . . .'

Blaesus grinned. 'What's that, sir?'

Figulus stepped closer and jabbed a finger at the man's chest. 'I thought I recognised you from somewhere. The Thirsty Greek tavern. In Calleva. You're the bastard who cheated me at dice! I want my money back!'

There was a glimmer of recognition in the legionary's glazed eyes. Blaesus quickly composed his face and flashed a weak smile. 'Forgive me, sir, but I'm afraid you are mistaken. I can assure you I wasn't cheating. Never have done.'

'I lost twenty games straight,' Figulus thundered. 'No one's that unlucky. You owe me a hundred and fifty sestertii.'

Blaesus fixed his smile. 'What can I say, sir? I won that money fair and square. When it comes to the dice I've got the magic touch. I didn't cheat.' He placed a hand on his heart, adding, 'I swear on my mother's grave.'

'Your mother was a whore!' a scrawny soldier joked from down the line. Several other soldiers chuckled. Figulus saw Blaesus's expression instantly darken. In a raging blur of movement he spun away and lunged at the soldier, charging into him with his head forward like an enraged bull. His opponent gasped in pain as Blaesus's shabby pate slammed into his stomach, knocking him off his feet and badly winding him. The man landed on his back with a grunt and before he could scramble to his feet Blaesus pinned him to the ground and lashed out at his face with his fists. The other soldiers now formed a rough circle round the two men, yelling their support for whichever of the two they favoured.

'What did you say?' Blaesus snarled as he clamped his hands round his opponent's throat and squeezed. 'WHAT DID YOU FUCKING SAY?'

'Get off me, you drunk!' the man yelled, thrusting a hand into Blaesus's face in an attempt to gouge his eyes out.

'All right, that's enough!' Figulus boomed, barging past the circle of cheering soldiers and wrestling Blaesus away from the stunned soldier on the ground. But Blaesus was powerfully built, even bigger than the Gaul, and Figulus struggled to control him as Blaesus roared in anger and tried to break free. Rullus raced into view and grabbed Blaesus by his other arm, and together he and Figulus managed to drag the fuming man away from his dazed opponent.

'He's an animal,' the soldier sputtered nasally as he tried to staunch the blood streaming out of his nostrils. 'Bloody Germans.'

Rullus spoke to Figulus in a low voice. 'Manius Silo. He's a troublemaker, sir.'

'I swear on Jupiter's cock,' Blaesus growled at Silo, his broad chest heaving, 'I'll make you sorry you were ever born.'

Figulus looked at Blaesus and arched his eyebrows. 'You're a German?'

Blaesus clenched his jaws. 'Half, sir,' he replied, quickly sobering up. 'I was born in Argentoratum. In the village next to the Second Legion's fort.' Then he lowered his eyes in shame. 'My mother was a tart, sir. She did a brisk trade with the soldiers at the fort. When she died, I was adopted by a centurion and raised with his family. As soon as I was old enough, I enlisted in the Second.'

Figulus nodded sympathetically. Now he understood why Blaesus had snapped at the other soldier in a blind rage. It didn't excuse his behaviour, but Figulus knew all too well what it felt like to be an outsider in the legion. He was aware of the insults muttered behind his back, the disparaging remarks about Gauls and the distrustful looks of comrades who questioned where his loyalties truly lay. For a brief moment he even forgot about the small fortune Blaesus had cheated him out of.

'Half German I may be,' Blaesus added, 'but I've spent my whole life surrounded by the army. Got a centurion for a father and the Second Legion in my blood. Sir.' He puffed out his chest in pride and cocked his chin at Silo. 'More than some of this lot, I'll wager.'

Figulus bit his lip. Strictly speaking he knew he ought to put Blaesus on a charge. Fighting between soldiers was prohibited in the legions, and as an officer he was expected to enforce the stringent rules. But his soldierly instincts told him that Blaesus was a good fighting man and would be handy if they ran into trouble. There were precious few such men left in the century; if he disciplined Blaesus, booting him out of the detachment, he would be replaced by a less experienced soldier. On the other hand, if Figulus forgot the issue for the moment and only dealt with it on their return, he risked looking weak in front of the men. Besides, it would not be good to go into the mission with tension simmering under the surface. Figulus made a decision, cleared his throat and looked sternly at Blaesus and Silo in turn.

'One more word from either of you and I'll have you both on a charge. Got it?'

'Yes, sir,' both men mumbled quietly before resuming their places in the line. Satisfied that he'd dealt with the situation, Figulus turned to the other men. 'That goes for all of you. The next man who steps out of line will be on fatigues for the next month with no pay. Am I clear?'

'Yes, sir!'

'I can't hear you!' Figulus bellowed.

'YES, SIR!'

'Better.' Figulus fixed his gaze on the soldiers. In spite of the hardships they had endured and the treacherous mission they were about to undertake, none of them displayed a trace of nerves, and Figulus felt a surge of confidence at the sight of these brave fighting men. He took a deep breath and prepared to address them for the first time as their commanding officer.

'Right then, lads. As you've probably heard, Ocella is currently laid up in the field hospital. That means I'm your acting centurion for the time being. Titus Rullus here will be acting optio. We'll be marching through the night. If I catch anyone slacking off you'll be in a world of shit.' He paused, scratching his backside as he tried to think of something else to say. 'There'll be absolute silence. We're heading into enemy territory and we don't want any unwelcome attention. The scout will steer us clear of any trouble but I don't want you lot taking any chances.' He paused again. 'And, er, watch yourself. Your average Durotrigan might look as thick as cow shit, but they're crafty buggers. There's plenty of dead Romans who've underestimated them in battle.' He stopped and shrugged. 'Anyone got a question?'

An awkward silence hung over the detachment. A soldier coughed loudly. Rullus shifted on his feet. Stiffening his neck, Figulus filled his lungs, 'Sixth Century, fall out!'

At his command each legionary grabbed his grounded javelin and trooped towards the main gates, where three ox-driven wagons, weighed down with baskets from the grain stores, waited to set off. Beside the wagons stood a spindly, bald-headed man dressed in woollen breeches: Magadubnus, the native scout who would be accompanying the soldiers on the march. As Figulus watched the men file past him, he noticed Helva lagging behind. The legionary's sidebag had fallen from his belt, spilling its contents over the ground.

'Get a bloody move on, soldier!' Figulus barked.

Helva frantically shoved his rations back inside the sidebag and hurried along. 'Yes, sir.' He grinned at Figulus before adding, 'Can't wait to get stuck in, sir. Kill me a Briton or two. That'll impress the girls back home.'

Figulus cocked his head at the legionary. 'You've not killed anyone before?'

Helva shook his head. 'But I used to do plenty of hunting on my father's farm in Campania, sir. I hunted all sorts: hares, wild boar and deer. Slaying Britons can't be much different.'

'If you say so, lad,' Figulus replied flatly, reminded of his own misguided enthusiasm when he'd first signed up to life with the Second Legion. 'Now, how about you focus on keeping pace with the march and worry about killing Britons later.'

Helva nodded and hurried on to take his place alongside his comrades. As the small column of men and wagons filed beyond the picket lines, Figulus noticed Blaesus and Silo exchanging vengeful stares. There would be bad blood between the two men for a while. He made a mental note to himself to keep an eye on both soldiers during the operation. With a final glance past his shoulder, Figulus watched the flickering lights of the marching camp fade into the darkness. Then he faced forward and led the soldiers into the dark shroud of the night.

CHAPTER SEVEN

As the soldiers marched through the marsh, a thin fog descended over the isle, covering the ground in a fine cobwebbed mist. Gradually Figulus's eyes adjusted to the dark, and what had previously been a shapeless dark mass now betrayed the faintest of details: a sloping hill fractionally lighter than the night sky, the waters of a distant bay softly gleaming under the wan moonlight. In an effort to lighten the load, Figulus had decided that the soldiers would not carry the usual marching yokes or apron belts. Instead they were equipped with only their shields, swords, spears and armour. Their meagre rations, consisting of chunks of leavened bread and vinegared water, were packed in their sidebags and waterskins respectively. Magadubnus led the way, moving a few paces ahead of the foremost soldier with a deftness that belied his years, periodically stopping to assess his surroundings, his eyes studying the natural dips and rises of the land. Although he trusted the scout's instincts, Figulus worried that they were veering hopelessly off course. If the detachment found itself on open ground when dawn broke, they would be horribly exposed to the Durotrigan scouts combing the land.

As well as the ever-present fear of attack, the men had to contend with the treacherous nature of the terrain. Figulus kept his eyes fixed to the ground, watching out for any obstacles that could trip up the unsuspecting soldier. On a march through hostile territory, far from the comfort of the marching camp and the field hospital, a twisted ankle could be just as fatal as a stab wound from an unseen Briton. The pace of the march was unsteady and every so often one of the wagons would get stuck in the waterlogged ground. Then the entire column had to stop while teams of men set down their weapons and toiled to prise the wheels free from the quagmire.

Figulus was acutely aware of every sound in the night air: the thick squelch of sodden mud beneath his boots and the hoots of distant owls. From time to time he would glance to the side, straining his eyes at some distant scrub or gloomy copse, convinced that he'd seen a figure moving among the endlessly shifting shapes of the dark. Figulus knew that it was simply his eyes playing cruel tricks on him, painting silhouettes where there were none. But he could not quite shake off the disturbing sense that the small column of Roman soldiers was being watched. As they ventured deeper into the heartland, he grew certain that the enemy was lurking nearby.

A few hours later the sky lightened close to the horizon and the twinkling stars began to fade. Figulus stifled a yawn. His eyes felt heavy, as if they were filled with sand. Remembering an old trick, he reached for the leather waterskin hanging from his belt, removed the cork stopper and tilted his head back, tipping a few drops of vinegared water into both his eyes. The liquid stung sharply and his eyes ran from the burning pain. But it had the desired effect and snapped him out of his weary stupor.

'What do you reckon, sir?' Rullus said quietly as he narrowed his eyes at Magadubnus a short distance in front of the column. 'Do you trust him?'

'Magadubnus?' Figulus rubbed his eyes. 'Don't see any reason why not.'

Rullus grunted. 'Wish I could say the same, sir. Don't forget he's a native. Backstabbing is a way of life for these scum. All the tribes and factions they have, sir, forever fighting each other over land and women.' He lowered his voice, careful to make sure that the scout could not overhear them. 'You grow up surrounded by enemies, you learn to have eyes in the back of your head. That's what makes the Britons worse than the Germans. Take it from me, I've fought plenty of both.'

Figulus considered the veteran. 'You used to be on the Rhine frontier?'

'I joined not long after the legion transferred there. Tribune Vitellius's uncle was the legate back then. Used to see his nephew running around the legionary camp as a boy. Now he's in charge of

42

the whole bloody legion. Or what's left of it on the mainland, anyway.' He shook his head. 'I've spent twenty-two years in the legions, all told. More than half my life, sir. One more campaign, then I'm due for retirement.'

'What'll you do then?'

Rullus considered for a moment. 'To be honest I haven't really thought about it, sir. The legion's all I've known since I stepped into the recruiting office in Tusculum as a fresh-faced young lad. Maybe I'll buy a plot of land somewhere. Settle down with a nice tart and a vineyard of my own. Who knows?'

'Here in Britannia?' Figulus asked.

'Gods, no!' Rullus looked horrified. 'Who'd want to live in this hole?'

'Ah, it's not all that bad,' Figulus replied cheerfully. 'The weather's shite, I'll grant you. But there's plenty of good meat and decent beer to be had, and the women may be ugly but they aren't half bad in the sack.'

'Spoken like a true Gaul.'

Figulus grinned. Before he could respond, the column abruptly drew to a halt and he looked ahead to see Magadubnus had stopped. Figulus moved stiffly down the line, his legs feeling twice as heavy as they had done at the start of the march. He had no idea how much further they had to go.

'What the hell have we stopped for this time?' Silo complained to the man next to him as Figulus brushed past. Figulus shot the legionary a cold look before moving to join Magadubnus a short distance to the side of the column. The scout stared ahead, scanning the dense forest in front of the Romans.

'Thought I saw something,' Magadubnus said in thickly accented Latin, turning to meet the Gaul's questioning gaze.

Figulus felt a stab of anxiety in his chest. 'Where?'

'Ahead.'

Figulus squinted at the darkness and grunted. 'Can't see anything.'

'Evil spirits here, *sa*,' Magadubnus cautioned. 'We must move on, quickly.'

Figulus sheathed his sword, forcing his tensed muscles to relax. He gave the order for the men to resume the march and strode a few paces ahead of the column, with Magadubnus at his side.

'You look more like one of us than a Roman,' the scout observed as they trudged through the dense forest. 'You're not from Italia, are you?'

Figulus shook his head. 'I was born in Lutetia.'

'A Celt from the Aedui tribe?' There was a note of surprise in the scout's voice and he stared at Figulus curiously. 'If I may ask, how did you end up in the service of Rome and her legions?'

Figulus pursed his lips and stared ahead. 'My grandfather, Parisiacus, was a warrior in the tribe. He took part in the revolt against Rome. But they were beaten and . . .' His voice faded and he closed his eyes for a moment.

'What happened?' Magadubnus asked.

Figulus turned to the scout and exhaled deeply. 'He spent years hiding in the forest.' He waved a hand at the surrounding woods. 'Similar to this one, come to think of it. I only saw him once, just before he died at my parents' home. Sickly pale and close to death, he was, lying on a bedroll. He cursed Rome with his last draw of breath.'

'I'm sorry,' Magadubnus said quietly.

'After that, most of the men in our town sided with Rome. They knew they had been defeated, and there would be no going back to the old ways. My father served in the auxiliary cavalry. Saw action in Moesia and on the Rhine. Did his twenty-five years and got his Roman citizenship. He raised me to be the same. Other children grew up on stories of Vercingetorix, but I heard stories about the great soldiers in the legions.' He shrugged. 'It sounded like a good life. You get a decent pay – more than I'd earn back home, at least – and you get to see the world. The day I turned eighteen, I enlisted.' Figulus glanced at Magadubnus. 'What about you?'

Magadubnus feigned puzzlement. 'What about me?'

'Why are you helping us fight your own kind?'

Magadubnus thought for a moment before replying. 'I used to be a farmer,' he said. 'Lived in a village, not far from Vindocladia. It was a hard life, but an honest one. Then one day a nobleman came to our village, rounded up every young, able-bodied man and pressed them into service. To fight the Romans, they said. They took my firstborn. I never saw him again. There was no one left to pick our crops. They withered and died, and many people in the village starved. One year later, the nobleman returned. This time he took my youngest son. He died too. Now our village is gone. Our people are left with nothing.' His voice quivered as he added, 'The Durotrigans blame the Romans for bringing war to our land. But they are the ones who chose to fight, who refuse to sue for peace. Rome did not take my sons from me, my crops, my wife. The Durotrigans took these things. Many times I have been asked, why do I fight for Rome? I do not care for Rome, Gaul. I fight because I despise the Durotrigans.'

He looked quickly away and Figulus felt a sudden pang of pity for Magadubnus. Through no fault of his own, the scout found himself in an impossible position, forced to choose between working for the men who had invaded his land and the warriors who had killed his family. Even if the Second Legion did eventually succeed in subduing the Durotrigans, Magadubnus would have to live the rest of his days in fear of reprisal from the warriors he had betrayed. And yet Rome relied on such men for victory, the disparate network of informants, scouts, spies and interpreters who were instrumental in providing the legions with vital intelligence on the strengths and weaknesses of their enemies.

They followed a rough track through the forest, twisting between dense thickets of ash trees and hawthorns. By now the fog had settled into a dense veil and took on a luminous glow in the pre-dawn light. Figulus ordered the men to keep silent, fearful that any sudden noise might reveal their presence to any nearby Durotrigan forces. No one said a word as they marched on through the forest. The silence was broken only by the cracking of twigs underfoot and the snorting of the oxen to the rear of the column as they pulled the creaking wagons along the trail.

A short while later the column emerged from the forest. It was past dawn now and the fog gradually lifted to reveal a wide plain nestled between a series of gently sloping hills. Magadubnus drew to a halt and pointed towards a minor settlement two hundred paces away.

'Here,' he said. 'The village, *sa.*'

Figulus ran his eyes over the place. A shoddily constructed palisade encircled the settlement, with scores of the cone-like thatched roofs of Celtic huts visible above the sharpened wooden stakes. A rough track ran directly from the edge of the forest to the village gate. Thick palls of woodsmoke drifted lazily up from fires burning within.

Rullus joined Figulus. 'What now, sir?' he whispered.

'This way,' Magadubnus said, gesturing for them to continue towards the gates. 'We meet the chief. He is waiting for us, *sa*.'

Rullus pulled a face and spat on the ground. He glanced at Figulus, a deep frown creasing his brow. 'Bollocks to that. We should make the exchange out here in the open, sir. It should be on our terms, not his.'

Magadubnus shook his head. 'I'm afraid that is not what was agreed with Legate Celer. Grain first. Then prisoners.'

'I don't like it, sir,' Rullus protested.

Figulus considered for a moment. As far as he could tell, there was only one gate leading in and out of the village. If he agreed to enter the settlement, once his men were gathered inside they could easily be trapped. Then Figulus reminded himself that these people were hungry and desperate, driven to negotiating a deal with their hated enemy in order to fend off starvation. He doubted such people would pose much threat to forty armed Roman soldiers.

'Very well,' he told Magadubnus.

'But, sir,' Rullus began.

Figulus cut him off. 'We don't have any choice. Their chief has the prisoners. He can set whatever demands he wants.' He turned back to Magadubnus. 'Send for the chief. Tell him we'll move the grain wagons into the village as soon as he gives the word.'

With a quick smile, Magadubnus turned and scurried down the track. Figulus watched him as he darted inside the village. Several moments passed. Then he reappeared at the gates alongside a frail-looking man with flowing grey hair and a wispy beard, accompanied by a pair of bodyguards. He waited hesitantly by the gates while Magadubnus signalled for the Roman column to approach. At once Figulus turned to his men and gave the order to proceed towards the village, and the still early morning silence was broken by the soft thud of boots on grass and the rumble of the wagons' wheels. When Figulus reached the gates, Magadubnus stepped forward and gestured to the man at his side.

46

'This is Brigotinus, chief of this village.'

Figulus acknowledged the chief with a curt nod. 'Acting Centurion Horatius Figulus of the Sixth Century, Fifth Cohort. These are my men. I've been sent by the legate, Lucius Aelianus Celer, to fulfil our side of the bargain.'

Brigotinus raised an eyebrow in surprise at Figulus's command of his native tongue. 'You speak the language of my people. I'm impressed. I was led to believe that the Romans do not bother to learn the tongues of the people they wish to rule over.'

'Not all of us are the same,' Figulus replied.

The chief grunted. With his stooped posture and sunken cheekbones, the chief cut a pathetic figure. From the numerous scars on his torso Figulus reasoned that Brigotinus had once been a proud warrior. But age and years of hardship had reduced the chief to a pale shadow of his former self. Brigotinus smiled at Figulus, parting his lips to reveal a set of crooked yellow teeth which reminded the Gaul of the gravestones he'd seen in the native burial sites scattered across the mainland. The chief muttered something to Magadubnus in his native dialect.

'What'd he say, sir?' Rullus asked.

Magadubnus replied for the chief. 'Brigotinus wishes to reassure you that the Roman prisoners are in good health. He says they have been treated well. He hopes this will convince your legate to protect his people from the Durotrigan warriors.' Magadubnus leaned towards the Romans and lowered his voice as he spoke in Latin. 'Between ourselves, the chief is worried about reprisals. Should the warriors learn of this exchange, they will surely punish these people and raze the village to the ground.'

'Why in the hell would the Durotrigans do that?' Rullus spluttered.

'We are not a single tribe, but many smaller tribes based around blood ties. The refugees from the mainland belong to a different tribe to the villagers.'

'But you're all fighting Rome,' Rullus replied tartly.

'True,' the scout conceded. 'But I assure you, Roman, our peoples have been fighting each other for much longer than your men have been on our shores. It is true that the invasion has united the tribes in

47

opposition to Rome. But if the warriors discover that the prisoners have been traded for food, they will spare no one. They will treat the villagers as harshly as if they were Roman soldiers. Perhaps worse.'

Rullus grunted sceptically.

'Magadubnus is right,' Figulus put in. 'The Durotrigans loathe traitors even more than they hate us. If they find out what Brigotinus has done, they'll torture and kill every one of the villagers.'

'That's not our problem, though, is it?' Rullus retorted. 'Our mission is to oversee the exchange and bring home the prisoners safe and sound.'

Figulus nodded reluctantly and shouted the order for the column to march into the village. He posted Silo and another soldier, Postumus, on watch beyond the entrance, reasoning that the two soldiers could send for help if there was any sign of danger. And by putting Silo on sentry duty, Figulus could keep him away from Blaesus and avoid the bad blood between the two men spilling over into a physical confrontation. Figulus followed Magadubnus through the village, keeping his palm rested on the pommel of his sword. Magadubnus seemed agitated, Figulus thought. His eyes were constantly darting left and right as he scanned the hills flanking the village, as if looking for something.

A crowd of hungry-eyed men and women gathered outside their wattle and daub huts to greet the Romans with suspicious stares. Figulus noted that many of the villagers were even thinner than the warriors he'd encountered on the beach the previous day. Children stood close to their parents and stared. Several villagers cast their hungry eyes over the grain wagons at the rear of the column and for a moment Figulus feared that the column might find itself besieged by the starving crowd. As he picked his way through the natives it suddenly occurred to him that there was none of the usual bleating of livestock common to Celtic villages. Then he caught sight of a dog being spit-roasted over an open fire and his stomach churned. The people had been reduced to slaughtering their domestic animals for food. No wonder the chief had been so willing to negotiate for the release of the prisoners, Figulus thought. His people were on the cusp of starving to death.

Magadubnus stopped in the middle of the village in front of a large roundhouse with a cattle pen to the east. To the side of the settlement stood a dozen storage huts, where the grain supply was traditionally kept during the harsh winter months. These huts now stood empty, attesting to the desperate situation the villagers found themselves in. Brigotinus turned to Figulus and nodded at the wagons.

'Tell your men to unload the grain here. Once my men have checked that every modius of grain is accounted for, we will hand over the prisoners.'

Figulus shook his head. 'I want to see the prisoners first.'

Brigotinus's wizened face folded into a deep frown. 'That was not what was agreed, Roman. I suggest you do as I say.'

Figulus replied in the chief's native tongue. 'I take orders from my centurion, my legate and the Emperor of Rome. Not the likes of you. And I won't allow my men to begin unloading the grain until I've seen proof that the prisoners are alive.'

The chief sighed wearily. 'Very well. As you wish.'

The chief gestured to one of his men. As the villager trudged towards the cattle pen, Figulus allowed himself a slight sigh of relief. The exchange was almost complete. Once his men had finished unloading the grain and the prisoners were fully accounted for, his detachment could begin the long journey back to the marching camp. He licked his lips at the thought of his warm tent and the hot evening meal waiting for him upon his return.

The bodyguard had almost reached the pen when a shout pierced the air.

Figulus snapped his gaze towards the entrance. He saw Silo and Postumus scrambling past the huts and sprinting towards him, their eyes wide with terror and their faces drained of colour. Postumus reached him a few steps ahead of his comrade, sweat running down his brow.

'What is it?' Figulus demanded.

'Must be a hundred of them, sir,' he said between sharp intakes of air.

'Who?' Figulus barked, suddenly furious with this man. His flustered demeanour was spreading panic amongst his fellow soldiers. 'What the hell are you talking about?'

Postumus caught his breath. 'Durotrigans, sir. Armed.' He pointed to the hill beyond the walls of the settlement. 'Came out of nowhere. They're heading right for us.'

Figulus felt the hairs on the nape of his neck stand on end. Beside him Brigotinus visibly trembled, the colour draining from his face. 'Betrayed!' the chief whispered icily. 'We have been betrayed!' He glowered at Magadubnus.

The scout shifted on the spot. Figulus was about to question him when a shrill cry split the air and he swivelled his gaze back to the entrance just in time to see several javelins launch over the palisades and rain down over the village. A javelin impaled Silo through the back. The legionary spasmed and let out an almost inhuman cry of agony. His cries were swiftly drowned out by a throated roar coming from beyond the entrance. The men of the Sixth Century simultaneously looked up from the stricken legionary and saw a teeming mass of Durotrigan warriors a short distance from the settlement, charging towards the entrance.

'Where the fuck did they come from?' Figulus growled as he unsheathed his sword.

Brigotinus balled his hands into tight fists at his side. 'Someone must have told them about our plan. They have come to punish us.' There was a look of terror in his eyes. 'They're going to kill us all . . .'

CHAPTER EIGHT

There was no time for Figulus to form up the men. The Durotrigans were only a few paces short of the entrance. Then they were sweeping into the village in a frenzied blur of movement: thickset men wearing homespun trousers and spiked-up hair. Some of them were armed with thrusting spears, others wielded long swords or broadaxes. One of the warriors surged ahead of his comrades and brought his broadaxe down on the nearest villager in a heavy swinging motion. The man let out a hideous shriek of pain as the axe head slammed into his skull with a dull, wet crunch. The man fell away, blood squirting out of his skull as the warriors stormed past his lifeless body and fanned out across the settlement, their faces twisted into raging snarls.

'On me!' Figulus shouted to his men at the top of his voice. 'NOW!'

His words were drowned out by the screams and shouts coming from the panicked villagers as the Durotrigan warriors set upon them, cutting them down in a mad flurry of hacks and slashes. Terrified women grabbed their children and ducked into their huts in a desperate attempt to hide from the enemy. At the same time the main body of Durotrigans charged directly at the Roman column forming up in the middle of the settlement. Steeling his muscles, Figulus trained his sword point towards the swarm of onrushing Britons and filled his lungs.

'Sixth Century!' he bellowed. 'Charge!'

He raced towards the enemy, tensing his grip on the handle of his shield, his men charging alongside him. As Figulus drew closer to the seething horde of warriors he could feel his heart thumping inside his chest. Gripping his sword firmly in his right hand, he lunged at a heavyset Briton with an iron torc wrapped round his thick neck. The warrior brought his sword down towards the Gaul's neck with a snarling roar. Figulus quickly hunched behind his shield, blocking the attack. A shudder travelled up his forearm as his opponent's blade hammered against the iron rim of his shield. Now Figulus pushed forward, stabbing up at the Briton's throat with his short sword. The warrior saw the gleaming sword point driving towards him at the last moment and deftly sidestepped the blow, hissing through gritted teeth as the blade nicked his shoulder, slicing through muscle and grating against his shoulder bone. The man fell back a step, clasping a hand to his wound and cursing Figulus in his native tongue.

Shaking his head clear, the warrior launched himself at Figulus again, this time aiming a kick at the bottom edge of Figulus's shield, tipping it forward so that the Gaul's upper torso was exposed to the enemy. The warrior angled his blade towards his opponent's neck. Figulus quickly dropped to his haunches and avoided the thrusting blade by just a few inches. As momentum carried the warrior forward half a step, Figulus sprang up on the balls of his feet and plunged the tip of his blade into the man's groin. The warrior gasped. Blood instantly stained his breeches. Then Figulus gave the blade a twist, carving up the man's internals and drawing a keening sound from his throat. The Gaul wrenched his weapon free with a loud grunt. He felt a hot thrill run through his veins as the Durotrigan keeled over.

Sweating heavily, Figulus glanced around at the battle raging inside the village. The Roman soldiers had by now formed a solid formation either side of him and were attacking the Durotrigans with a concerted series of shield thrusts and sword stabs. At that instant a panicked shout came from the right flank and Figulus glanced across his shoulder to see another band of Durotrigans charging out from behind the grain huts. With a feeling of dread tingling down his spine, Figulus realised the warriors had crept round the edge of the settlement unseen. Now they fell upon the Roman soldiers with savage intent, cutting the closest men down with lightning-quick hacks and wild thrusts. Amid the confusion Figulus spotted one soldier being struck down by a Briton with a wolfskin draped round his neck. The Briton rolled the legionary on to his back and raised his long sword above his head before jamming the blade down with a throated roar. The Roman screamed for help. His cries were instantly silenced as the sword tip plunged into his gaping mouth.

Seized by a sudden rage, Figulus immediately charged at the Briton, skewering him in the flank. Figulus could feel the tip glancing off his ribs as it punched through his lower chest. As he watched the warrior fall away, he heard a faint low hiss behind him and glimpsed a dull glint out of the corner of his eye. Figulus half turned to see a giant of a man clasping a broadaxe in a two-handed grip. At the last possible moment he deflected the blow with his shield, and there was a violent crack as the axe head split open the shield and buried itself in the wooden surface. With a snarled grunt, the Durotrigan wrenched his broadaxe away, ripping the shield from the Gaul's stunned grip in the same brutal motion. Deprived of his shield, Figulus swiftly stabbed his opponent in the thigh. The Briton showed no sign of pain. Instead he kicked Figulus in the stomach, knocking him off his feet. He felt the air push out of his chest in a painful rush as he landed on his back, his sword tumbling from his hand.

He looked up to see the warrior looming over him and caught a whiff of his foul breath as the man bared his crooked teeth. His scarred lips formed a twisted, sinister smile. The Durotrigan slowly raised the heavy broadaxe above his head to deliver the fatal blow. A cold fear ran through Figulus. He was going to die here, in this pitiful corner of the empire.

Then he heard a growl from behind the warrior. The Briton heard it too and began to turn. Figulus glimpsed a flash of steel driving towards the man's broad shoulders and saw Blaesus plunge his sword into the warrior's neck. The Durotrigan convulsed as the sword punched out of his throat in a single brutal thrust. He wavered on the spot for a moment, blood spewing out of his mouth while his dimming eyes lowered to the steel tip protruding from his throat. He pawed uselessly at his wound. Then Blaesus pulled his sword free and the Durotrigan's legs buckled. The man collapsed in a bloodied heap beside Figulus. Blaesus loomed over the fallen Briton, his chest heaving as he searched for the next enemy to kill.

'Come on!' he thundered at the top of his voice. 'Which one of you bastards wants it?'

Another warrior set upon the legionary but Blaesus reacted in a fast flicker of movement, tearing into the Briton and slashing open his belly. Then he charged at a third Durotrigan, head-butting the man before he could thrust at him with his sword. Blaesus was seemingly Hades-bent on defeating the flank attack by himself. The Durotrigans, accustomed to the Roman tactics of a solid wall of men crouching behind their shields, were stunned by the sight of Blaesus tearing into their ranks and they scattered. Figulus grabbed his sword and shield and scraped himself off the ground. He charged forward to join Blaesus and the two burly soldiers fought side by side to repel the enemy attack.

'Hot work, sir!' Blaesus said with a grin.

'Going to get hotter.' Figulus cut down another warrior. He looked up, searching for another enemy. An icy grip of fear clamped round his neck as he looked back at the roundhouse. 'Shit! The prisoners!'

Three Durotrigans had managed to slip through the melee and were now racing towards the pen. Figulus grabbed the nearest soldiers in the line, Helva and Postumus, and gestured towards the pen. 'You two. With me! Now!'

A putrid stench emanated from the willow-weave walls of the cattle pen as the three men drew close. Fighting the impulse to gag, Figulus wrenched the gate open and stormed inside. He saw the burly Durotrigans charging towards the manacled prisoners, their sword points glinting in the murky light as they shaped to execute the stricken Romans. While Blaesus and Helva fell upon the others, Figulus sprang forward on the balls of his feet and slammed his shield into the closest warrior's back. There was a satisfying crunch as the shield crashed against the base of his spine. The Durotrigan let out an anguished grunt as the force of the blow knocked him to the hay-strewn floor. Figulus leapt forward before the man could reach for his fallen sword, stabbing him between the shoulder blades.

Past his right shoulder he caught sight of Helva locked in a desperate struggle with another Durotrigan. The Briton had kicked away the Roman's shield and sword and his scarred hands were clamped round his enemy's neck. Helva struggled for breath as the Durotrigan pushed him back against the pen wall. In a flash the young legionary reached a hand down to his belt and, snatching at his dagger, stabbed the warrior several times in his flank. The Durotrigan kept on trying to strangle his enemy, even as blood gushed out of his stomach. Helva continued stabbing the man repeatedly. After a couple more breaths the Durotrigan fell away, snarling and cursing at the Roman, his teeth stained with blood. Figulus raced over and ended the warrior's life with a quick thrust to the neck. Helva stood rooted to the spot, staring down at his shaking hands.

'I killed him,' Helva said quietly. 'I killed a man.'

It was then that Figulus noticed the terrible state of the prisoners. Their frayed army-issue tunics hung like rags from their skeletal frames, their skin was thinly stretched across their gaunt faces. The squalid pen reeked of urine, shit and sweat. Merely drawing breath within these walls was enough to make Figulus want to retch. The straw was soiled with blood and faecal matter. Iron chains bound each prisoner's scrawny ankles and wrists, with a long chain linking the men together. Some of the prisoners were missing teeth, Figulus noted grimly. One man had several stumps in place of his fingers. The Gaul shuddered at the thought of the unimaginable suffering these men had endured over the past few months. He quickly counted the number of prisoners – twelve – and turned to Helva.

'Looks like all the prisoners are here. Help these men outside, lad.'

Helva nodded distantly.

'Now, Helva!' Figulus thundered.

While the two legionaries helped the captives to their feet, Figulus turned and hurried outside of the pen. He spotted the bloodied bodies of several villagers nearby and a fist clenched his heart at their needless suffering for their betrayal of the wider Durotrigan cause. He raced past the sprawled bodies and charged towards the fighting. By now the men of the Sixth Century, spurred on by the actions of Rullus and Blaesus, were pushing back the Durotrigans, who were beginning to tire as the ferocious opposition to their attack began to take its toll. The ground underfoot was slick with blood and Figulus almost slipped on the greasy surface as he took his place in the formation alongside Rullus, thrusting his sword into the eye of a Durotrigan a few inches opposite his shield.

To the rear of the warrior ranks Figulus spied a man riding up and down on horseback. He was dressed in a long black robe with a hood pulled low over his pale face, shading his features. A Druid, Figulus realised with a shudder. The Druid appeared to be in command of the Durotrigan troops, urging them on. Despite his repeated exhortations the warriors were giving ground, weary and terrified by the ferocity of their Roman opponents. Figulus felt his chest swell as the Romans edged ever closer to victory. He bellowed orders for his men to hold formation as they continued to push the enemy back. As yet more of their companions were cut down, the Durotrigans to the rear started to turn away from the fight, fleeing the village.

'Come on, lads!' Figulus roared, struggling to make himself heard above the rasping clash of steel on steel. 'We've got 'em on the back foot! Let's finish the job!'

Seeing their companions retreating, the main body of the Durotrigans finally broke and ran. The skirmish turned into a chaotic free-for-all as the Roman soldiers swiftly descended on the fleeing Durotrigans, killing many before they could escape. The Druid defiantly held his ground by the entrance, ordering his men to stand and fight. But his orders were largely ignored. The remaining warriors were torn between obeying their Druid commander and dying an honourable death in a flicker of Roman sword points, or fleeing for their lives. Most chose the former, and Figulus and his men eagerly gave the warriors their wish and cut them down. Realising that all was lost, the Druid jabbed his heels into the flank of his mount and raced away from the battle with a handful of warriors running at his side.

Figulus felt his forearm muscles ache from the strain of battle. He turned to Rullus. 'You're in charge here. Kill any wounded. We can't afford to take any prisoners back with us. Once you're done, order the column to form up and prepare to fall out.'

Rullus blinked sweat out of his eyes. 'Where are you going, sir?'

Figulus tipped his head towards the men retreating alongside the Druid. 'Some of those bastards are escaping. Can't have that now, can we?'

Rullus grinned. Figulus gathered a handful of soldiers and set off in the direction of the Druid. He was sweating profusely in spite of the chill weather and as he hurried along he could feel his leg muscles aching from the exertions of the past several hours. He willed his weary body on, gripped by a compulsive desire to catch up with the Druid and kill him, spurred on by the image of the slaughtered women and infants. A short distance ahead the warriors jogging alongside the Druid abruptly stopped, turning to confront the pursuing Romans while their commander bolted up the hill on his black mount.

'You're mine!' a stocky Durotrigan wielding a wooden club barked at Figulus.

He lunged at the Gaul with surprising speed, dodging a quick stab from Figulus before kicking his shield away and swinging his club against the side of the Gaul's helmet in a glancing blow. Figulus saw white for a brief moment and a jarring pain rattled through his skull. He barely had time to regain his balance before the Durotrigan clubbed him again. A sharp pain exploded through his skull as the iron band wrapped round the end of the club struck his cheekguard and Figulus stumbled backwards.

He shook his groggy head clear. He tasted something warm and salty in his mouth. Spitting out blood, Figulus thrust his sword at his opponent. But his movement was slow and clumsy and the Durotrigan easily sidestepped his tired attack before shaping to club him a third time. This time, though, Figulus anticipated the move and, summoning one last shred of energy, he managed to deflect the blow with his shield before bringing it crashing down on top of his opponent's bare feet. The man howled in pain and anger as the iron shield edge crushed his toes. Figulus followed up, launching a powerful thrust at the warrior's midriff and sinking his blade into his stomach, plunging it in all the way to the handle. The man spasmed. Figulus ripped out the blade. Blood gushed down his front and splashed his toes. Figulus looked around for another enemy. But there were none left to kill. The other soldiers had made short work of the Durotrigans, killing them with ruthless efficiency. Only the Druid was left.

The sound of hooves clomping on wet earth reached Figulus's ears. He snapped his gaze forward just in time to see the Druid galloping towards the crest of the hill. Anger burned inside him. The

Druid was already too far away. He was going to escape, and there was nothing Figulus could do about it. At the top of the hill the Druid abruptly reined in his mount, drawing the horse to a halt. He pivoted in his saddle and looked back at the Gaul, smirking as if taunting him. His cloak hood had fallen from his head, revealing a hideously disfigured face with a crop of hair the colour of chalk. Then Figulus noticed a mark on his pale forehead: a dark ink tattoo of a crescent moon. The Druid scowled at Figulus before twisting back round in his saddle and jabbing his heel into his horse's flank. He promptly disappeared from view down the other side of the hill. A pair of soldiers started to run after the Druid but Figulus thrust out a hand and shook his head.

'Too late, lads,' he panted. 'We're too late. He's gone.'

He trudged back towards the settlement, a leaden feeling weighing heavily in his chest. He should have been basking in the warm glow of victory. After all, his men had survived an ambush, the prisoners had been rescued and he'd saved most of the villagers from certain death. But instead he felt only a sharp pang of disappointment. The Druid had escaped. Dozens of the villagers had been slain. His own men had sustained numerous casualties. They had been lured into a trap and had paid a terrible price.

Reaching the entrance, he sought out Rullus and found the veteran by the main roundhouse, busy organising the surviving soldiers into a marching column. Several of the men had sustained wounds in the battle, and Figulus ordered those men who were fit enough to stand to take their place in the line. Those who were too badly maimed to continue on foot were carried on makeshift stretchers to the rear wagon. Figulus issued instructions for the grain baskets to be unloaded in order to make space for the injured soldiers. Some of them were in such a poor state he privately doubted whether they would survive the journey back through the marshes.

'We should leave now, sir,' said Rullus once the wounded soldiers had been lifted on to the wagon. He pointed to the hills. 'It won't be long before the ones who legged it send for reinforcements.'

Figulus nodded. He scanned the village, frowning. 'Where's Magadubnus?'

Rullus cocked his head at two soldiers manhandling the scout between them. 'One of our lads caught the bastard trying to escape, sir. Grabbed him before he could get away.'

Figulus scratched his cheek. 'Why was he running?'

'Obvious, isn't it?' Rullus snorted. 'He was the one who led us into this trap, sir.'

'Liar!' Magadubnus raged as he overheard the veteran. The soldiers steered him towards the rear of the column. 'I swear upon all the gods, I'm not working for anyone except your legate!'

Rullus spat. 'Someone told that lot we'd be here. And it wasn't the chief who sold us out.' He glowered at the scout and turned to Figulus. 'I'm telling you, sir. This one's working for the enemy.'

Magadubnus trembled. He looked at Figulus, his eyes wide and pleading. 'Please. I beg of you. I had no idea it was a trap. You must believe me—'

'Lying scum,' Rullus interrupted. 'We should kill him now. Get it over and done with.'

Figulus considered. Despite his suspicions, there was no tangible proof that Magadubnus had conspired with the Durotrigans. After all, the man was one of the legate's trusted scouts. Could he afford to kill the scout on a mere suspicion? He shook his head briskly.

'We'll let the legate decide what to do with him when we get back,' Figulus said. Then he cocked his chin at a soldier whom he knew to be the most sadistic in the century. 'Tiberius Culleo.'

'Sir?'

Figulus gestured to the scout. 'Keep a close eye on this one.'

Culleo grinned. 'With pleasure, sir.'

Brigotinus approached. 'What about my people?' He waved a hand at the huddle of shivering villagers. 'You can't just abandon us here, Roman. You know that the warriors will come back after you leave. We gave you the prisoners as agreed. Now you must help us in return.'

Figulus stared coldly at the village chief. 'I'm sorry, but there's nothing else for us to do here. I have my orders. I must return to the camp with the prisoners at once. We can't stay here and defend your people.'

Brigotinus looked aghast. 'But when the Durotrigans return, they'll kill every last one of us. No one will be spared.'

'The deal was for the grain,' Figulus replied.

Brigotinus laughed weakly. 'Grain is no use to us if we are dead, Roman.'

Figulus clenched his jaws shut and glanced at the villagers, their expressions blank with mute horror at the carnage they had just witnessed. In his heart he knew he couldn't just leave these people behind to their grim fate. Sighing, he turned back to the chief.

'You can accompany us back to the camp. I can't say what will happen to you and your people when you arrive there, but at least that way you'll be safe from reprisals from the Durotrigans.'

'And leave our village? But . . . this is our home. Our livelihood.' Brigotinus pointed towards the grief-stricken villagers. 'What will my people do? Where will we go?'

Figulus shrugged. 'It's better than being carved up by the enemy. If you don't believe me, ask them.' He nodded at the dead villagers slumped across the muddied ground.

The chief shook his head bitterly. Then he swallowed his pride and said, 'Very well. I will tell my people. We will come with you.'

Then Brigotinus turned his back on Figulus and returned to the villagers, ordering them to take whatever meagre possessions they owned and prepare to quit the village at once. Figulus felt his tensed muscles relax, knowing that he had done the right thing. He anticipated that the legate might reprimand him for bringing civilians back to the army camp. But he could live with that.

Once the villagers were ready and the grain had been loaded on to one of the native wagons, Figulus sounded the order for the party to move out of the settlement. The Roman column led the way, with the native tribespeople following in close file behind. They marched at a good pace, eager to put as much distance between themselves and the enemy as possible. Soon the abandoned village was shrinking from view.

As the column approached the forest, Figulus glanced back at the hill. He'd seen the Druid's tattoo of the crescent moon before. He knew it was the mark of the Dark Moon Lodge, a secretive sect of Druids who peddled a fanatical hatred of Rome and inspired amongst their followers an unbelievable fanaticism in battle, teaching that they would be reincarnated if they fell to a Roman sword. The

Druids of the Dark Moon had inspired a defiance unlike anything else Rome had encountered in the province. Most members of the religious order were believed to have been killed during the campaign across the south-west the previous summer. But if the Druids of the Dark Moon were thriving once more on Vectis, Figulus thought grimly, then the men of the Second Legion were in grave danger.

CHAPTER NINE

A wash of desolate grey clouds hung low in the sky as the detachment approached the marching camp in the late afternoon. It had started to rain not long after the men had left the native settlement and they had trudged on in grim silence through the forest and the marshes, their feet slithering in the freshly churned mud, the rain tapping against their helmets and spattering their faces in a relentless icy blast. As the skies darkened, the weary men of the Sixth Century dragged their aching bodies past the earthworks surrounding the camp.

A short while later the detachment, accompanied by the villagers and the captive scout, crossed the picket lines. Palls of dark grey smoke drifted lazily up from fires burning inside the camp and Figulus licked his lips at the prospect of a hot meal followed by the warm embrace of sleep in the modest warmth of his goatskin tent. At the main gates he identified himself to the officious duty centurion, who waved the men through. Magadubnus was handed over to the legate's bodyguards, and the duty centurion ordered Figulus to present himself to the legate's tent immediately. Meanwhile the soldiers rescued from the village were taken to the field hospital to be fed and clothed, and the villagers were ushered into a guarded compound normally used to hold prisoners of war awaiting interrogation. Many of the villagers cut despondent figures as they trudged into the compound under the stern gaze of the Roman guards. Their livelihoods had been destroyed and they now faced the harsh prospect of rebuilding their lives from scratch. With a sad shake of his head Figulus reminded himself that the invasion had affected countless thousands of villagers just like the ones before him, all because of the ruinous decision of their tribal leaders to wage an unwinnable war against the legions of Rome.

He marched up the main thoroughfare towards the legate's tent. The sun was beginning to set, silhouetting the tent lines against the purple wash of the sky. The bodyguards posted outside saw Figulus approach and promptly stepped aside. The Gaul brushed past them and entered through the tent flap.

'Have a seat,' Celer announced sharply from behind his trestle table. Figulus sat stiffly down on the stool and watched Celer drip wax from a heated wick on to a scroll. An acrid stench lingered in the air as he pressed his ring finger into the melted wax, sealing the document with the insignia of the Second Legion. Then he blew cool air on the wax to harden it and handed the sealed document to a clerk waiting patiently to one side.

'Fetch me the Falernian,' Celer said. 'The good stuff.'

His beady eyes followed the clerk as he hastily marched out of the tent. Then he turned to Figulus, leaning back in his chair and placing his slender hands behind his head. He nodded at a waxed slate on his desk.

'The duty centurion has just informed me of the success of your mission. I understand that the prisoners have been returned safe and sound.'

Figulus nodded tentatively. 'Yes, sir.'

'Splendid.' Celer flashed a broad grin. 'I'd say this rather calls for a celebration, don't you think?' He cleared his throat. 'Although I understand that you ran into some trouble at the village.'

Figulus nodded. 'It was all going to plan until a party of Durotrigan warriors showed up just as we were about to complete the exchange, sir. It's clear the enemy got wind of the chief's plan and showed up to put a stop to it.'

He related to Celer the Durotrigan ambush in as much detail as possible. The legate listened without interrupting once, still as a Greek statue. When Figulus had finished, Celer nodded.

'I see. Thank you for that vivid account, Optio.' Celer placed his hands flat on the oak table surface and sighed heavily through his long sharp nose. 'As for our, ah, friend Magadubnus, the interrogators are going to work on him as we speak. They're good at their job and he'll tell us the truth soon enough.' He drummed his fingers on the desk and frowned. 'At least the native's apparent betrayal explains one particular mystery.'

'What's that, sir?'

'How the enemy came to learn about our plans for the invasion of Vectis. We've been searching for the culprit high and low. We never suspected it would be a scout who'd served us so well in the past. But it makes sense. If Magadubnus has indeed been betraying us to the Durotrigans all along, he would have known the precise spot where we intended to land the men.'

Figulus gritted his teeth. 'That's why there were so many of the bastards on the beach yesterday.'

'Once Magadubnus has confessed, and mark my words he will, we'll crucify them. Tomorrow at dawn. All of the scouts.'

'All of them, sir?' Figulus repeated in disbelief.

Celer's facial muscles twitched with anger. 'We must send a warning to anyone who dares betray us to the enemy.' There was an unsettling calm and coldness to the legate's voice as he spoke. 'This bloody province. Traitors everywhere you look. You can't trust anyone. Not even your own scouts, it seems.'

'But what will we do without scouts, sir?'

Celer smoothed out his features and smiled faintly. 'We'll recruit some replacements from the villagers. You insisted on bringing them back with you, so we may as well find some use for them. They know the territory well enough; they ought to be able to do a reasonable job. As for the others, we'll question them for further information on the enemy. Any intelligence would be helpful at this juncture, considering that we can't trust any of the intelligence provided to us by Magadubnus or any other traitors.'

Two orderlies entered the tent, one bearing a silver tray with a brass jug and a silver goblet, the other carrying a platter of cold meats and honeyed figs which he laid down on the side table. Figulus cast a wistful look at the food, his hollow stomach rumbling with hunger. It had been almost a full day since he'd last eaten a proper meal. As the orderlies exited the tent, Celer rose from his chair and poured a generous measure of wine into his goblet. Then he raised his cup and toasted Figulus.

'To the successful return of the prisoners.' He took a swig of his Falernian and smacked his lips. 'You have proved yourself an excellent soldier once again. It's a shame there are precious few men of your quality left in the legion, or we might already have conquered Vectis.' Celer paused, toying with the cup in his hand for a long moment. Then he smiled and went on, 'Not that you will be here for much longer. Since you clearly have a taste for such tasks, I've chosen you for a special mission.'

Figulus felt his pulse quicken as he stared at the legate. 'What do you want of me, sir?'

Celer set down the wine goblet. 'First, I would like to know something. How well do you speak the native tongue?'

'Well enough,' Figulus replied with a shrug. 'Most of the local dialects are fairly close to Gallic, sir. I can understand most of what's being said. May I ask why, sir?'

A curious smile played out across the legate's face. 'An ability to communicate with the locals will prove useful in this particular instance. In fact, it makes you the ideal man for the task.'

'What task, sir?' Figulus asked.

'I received a letter yesterday, shortly before we departed from Noviomagus. From one of Emperor Claudius's imperial envoys. Fellow by the name of Numerius Scylla. He's recently arrived in Britannia in the company of an exiled Durotrigan king. Trenagasus, I believe his name is. Heard of him?'

Figulus shook his head.

The legate clicked his tongue as he rummaged through the paperwork on his desk, locating the papyrus scroll buried amidst a pile of official documents. He quickly scanned the text. 'According to Scylla, Trenagasus has been living in exile for several years. Courting friends in high places in Rome. Apparently he's return-ing to this island in order to stake his claim as the rightful ruler of the Durotrigans. Quite why a man would wish to forgo the pleasures of Rome for the deprivations of Britannia is beyond me, but there you have it.'

'Sorry, sir, but I doubt the Durotrigans will accept our man as their rightful king.' Figulus sucked his teeth. 'They're a proud people, and they'll not willingly take to Rome's placeman. Not without a struggle.'

Celer squirmed at this uncomfortable truth. 'Be that as it may, Scylla is planning to travel west to Lindinis with Trenagasus, with a view to installing him as king before the year is out. The idea, I gather, is to begin the process of Romanisation of the inhabitants of the tribal capital at Lindinis, thus warding off the threat of the natives rising up against us in any great numbers. Or something like that.' He waved the document at Figulus. 'It's all here in the letter, though I can't say I see much point in trying to civilise these drunken, hairy-arsed locals.'

'What's all this got to do with me, sir?'

Celer slid out of his chair and paced over to the side table. He grazed casually on the food. Figulus felt his stomach growl with hunger. 'The envoy has requested that I send him a small detachment of men to accompany them,' Celer said, popping a honeyed fig into his mouth. 'Given his imperial connections, it's vital I send him good men who are up to the task. I can't fob him off with a few wet-behind-the-ears recruits. Especially with Vitellius watching my every move.'

'Vitellius, sir?' Figulus repeated.

Celer nodded irritably. 'The tribune is extremely well connected. My every move, no doubt, is being reported back to the imperial palace. So you can appreciate that I need the best men for the task. This is where you come in. Given your background, your knowledge of these people and the land, I'd say you're the right man to lead the detachment. Wouldn't you?'

There was a long pause as Figulus took this all in. Celer scoffed down a few more figs. 'Escort duty, sir?' Figulus asked, struggling to conceal his disappointment.

'Escorting a representative of the Emperor, no less,' the legate corrected. 'It won't be easy, of course. Far from it. As I'm sure you're aware, the land west of Calleva is rife with bandits, and our ports have been coming under increasing attack. You will have to keep your wits about you and above all protect the envoy and the king at all costs. If either of them comes to any harm, I'll earn the displeasure of the Emperor. And you know what that means for you in turn, don't you?'

Figulus swallowed. 'Sir?'

Celer tightened his smooth features into a menacing look. 'I will personally see to it that your career in the Second Legion will be finished. I'll have you thrown into the nearest mine with the slaves. Am I understood?'

'Yes, sir.'

'Good.' Returning to his desk, Celer sat down and tapped the waxed slates in front of him. 'I've already seen to the necessary details. You'll leave first thing tomorrow morning and sail back on one of the galleys to Noviomagus. From the port you'll make your way to the estate of the local king, Cogidubnus. Scylla and Trenagasus are currently guests of his. I believe Cogidubnus has a large, if rather modestly furnished, dwelling. Although not for much longer.' He chuckled. 'I gather we're building him some extravagant palace, at great cost, as a reward for his unswerving loyalty to Rome.'

'What about Ocella?'

'Your centurion will remain behind on Vectis. He'll resume command of the century once he's fully recovered from his injuries. I dare say he'll kick up a fuss about losing some of his men to what amounts to a glorified bodyguarding detail, but I'll arrange for some of the new recruits to be transferred to the Sixth. That ought to shut him up, at least for a while.'

Celer ate the last of the figs as he went on. 'You'll take two sections with you. You'll need to source some supplies in Noviomagus for your journey, since Lindinis is several days' march to the west. Upon your arrival, you'll present yourself to the commander of Batavian auxiliaries manning the vexillation fort there. Prefect Cosconianus. Any questions?'

Figulus thought for a moment then shook his head firmly.

'Good.' There was a long pause as Celer fell silent and drummed his hands on the edge of the trestle table. 'You are aware, are you not, that Ocella has put in for a transfer back to the Praetorian Guard?'

Figulus cocked an eyebrow. 'I had no idea, sir.'

Celer shrugged expressively. 'He'll probably get his wish, too. I'm told he has plenty of friends in the imperial palace. No doubt they will pull a few strings. But his request, should it be approved, means there will be an opening for the position of centurion.' The legate leaned forward. 'I can tell that you're a promising soldier. Your success in retrieving the prisoners is ample evidence of that. Prove to me that you're equally capable of carrying out this new task and you never know. Perhaps a promotion will await you on your return to the Second Legion.'

Figulus drew up sharply. The mere thought of being a commanding officer of his own century filled him with dread. Leading the detachment on Vectis had done little to dispel his fears that he was not up to the task of being a centurion, that he was a better soldier than an officer. He'd assumed his current leadership duties safe in the knowledge that in a day or two Ocella would be fit to resume his command. Now he was being ordered to lead another detachment for an indefinite period. He quickly composed his features and nodded dutifully.

'Yes, sir. I won't let you down.'

Celer eased back in his chair and smiled broadly. 'Glad to hear it. You may leave now, Figulus. Best of luck.'

With a stiff salute Figulus turned on his heel and ducked out of the tent. The sun had almost fully set by now, leaving a faint pink glow on the horizon. The moon shone starkly in the dark sky. A team of soldiers were cutting up blocks of wood in preparation for tomorrow's crucifixions. Figulus shuddered and looked away. Past the baggage train he saw the guards posted outside the compound where the villagers were being held. A pair of clerks were interviewing each villager in turn while a bodyguard from the legate's staff selected the fittest men for scout duties. As Figulus paced back down the main thoroughfare towards his century's tent lines, he spotted Rullus, Helva and Blaesus seated round a camp fire. The air was filled with the aroma of cooked meat as the legionaries sat in a semicircle and greedily ate their evening meal.

'Here, sir. Saved you some,' Rullus said, handing the Gaul a mess tin filled with steaming sliced sausage mixed with hunks of bread.

Figulus stared at his meal for a moment, his belly aching with hunger. 'We're leaving Vectis.'

Rullus looked surprised. 'So soon?'

'First thing tomorrow.' Figulus scooped a chunk of soaked bread from the mess tin and swallowed it hungrily. Soon the warm food in his belly began to revive his tired spirits and between mouthfuls of food he recounted the details of the assignment: bodyguarding the imperial envoy and the exiled king on their journey west.

Rullus pursed his lips. 'Lindinis,' he mused in his gruff voice, before shaking his head wearily. 'I heard that place is in a bad way. A friend of mine served there a few months back. He said the natives were causing no end of trouble. Cavalry scouts going missing, convoys ambushed . . . all sorts, sir.'

'Great,' Figulus muttered. 'Bloody great.'

The four men fell into a comfortable silence for a moment before Blaesus spoke up. 'Well, sir,' he said, clearing his throat, 'I don't give a shit about the envoy or some exiled king, but you can count me in.'

Helva straightened his back. 'Me too, sir.'

Rullus remained tight-lipped. Figulus turned to him, smiling grimly. 'What about you, Rullus? You can stay here on Vectis if you wish.'

'And put up with Ocella?' Rullus scoffed. 'With all due respect, sir, fuck off.'

Figulus grinned. 'Spoken like a true Gaul.'

The four men laughed easily. Then the veteran's expression turned serious and he looked past the men towards the crucifixes being assembled in the middle of the camp. 'I'll tell you one thing, though. This isn't going to be an easy task. Not the way things are going with the Durotrigans.' He glanced back at Figulus with a glint of anxiety in his eyes. 'Something tells me we're in for a long, hard winter, sir.'

CHAPTER TEN

As the Roman galley steered through the unsettled grey sea the following day, Figulus stood on the aft deck and gazed out towards the naval base ahead of them. The facility had been built into the large natural harbour that stretched out around the galley beneath the cold, pale sky. A line of slaves edged along the quayside to the docks, carrying supplies to be loaded on to several moored ships. To the east of the naval base Figulus spied a teeming native settlement: Noviomagus, capital of the Regni tribe and one of Rome's staunchest allies in Britannia.

'We'll be landing shortly,' the trierarch announced, shouting to make himself heard above the fierce wind battering the ship.

'Thank the gods,' Rullus muttered under his breath. 'Bloody sea! I'd sooner learn Greek than spend another moment on this fucking boat.'

Figulus glanced at the veteran legionary. Rullus had a queasy look on his face as he gripped hold of the side of the deck to steady himself against the constant pitching of the *Proteus*. 'With the seaborne operations you've experienced in the Second Legion, I'm surprised you haven't become used to it by now.'

Rullus made a face. 'I joined the Second to get away from the sea, Optio. My old man was a fisherman down in Genua, years back. Used to take me out on trips now and then. I couldn't stand the smell of all them fish guts. When I turned sixteen, I enlisted in the legions and swore I'd never set foot on a boat again. Now look at me.' He shook his head bitterly. 'Seem to spend more time afloat than I do on dry land these days.'

The trierarch overheard their conversation.

'You landlubbers are always complaining. You think this is bad? Wait until we get to the depths of winter; the sea's rougher than an Aventine tart then.'

'Hang about. Isn't the fleet going to be docked for the winter?' Figulus asked, turning back to the trierarch. The biting chill in the air served as a sharp reminder that the present campaigning season in Britannia would shortly be drawing to a close. Once it became too cold to march and fight, the soldiers would spend the winter months bottled up in the legionary fortress at Calleva, with nothing but wine and dice to stave off the boredom of endless training drills and kit inspections.

The trierarch clicked his tongue. 'We should be so fortunate. The fleet's to maintain operations over the winter. Legate's orders.'

Figulus frowned. 'What for? The campaign on Vectis will be over by then, surely.'

'Aye, this campaign might be over soon enough for you lot,' the trierarch conceded. 'But these storms we've been having have wreaked havoc with the convoys coming over from Gaul. Half the supply ships were battered or lost at sea and as a result the whole bloody province is in danger of starving unless we can make up the shortfall.' He squinted at the horizon. 'We'll be sailing right through to the spring, I reckon. It's going to be a long winter for us poor bastards. Just remember that when you're tucked up in your cosy barracks with a mug of heated wine and a warm meal to fill your bellies.'

With a final sigh, the trierarch paced to the stern to speak to one of his deck hands, leaving Figulus and Rullus alone. Rullus stared at the trierarch for a moment before shaking his head. 'I fear things aren't going to be much better for us this winter, sir.'

'How d'you mean?'

'Where we're headed, I mean. You know what the lads have been saying about Lindinis. The arsehole of the empire, they call it. That place is supposed to be one of the most primitive settlements in all of Britannia, and that's saying something.'

'Bollocks!' Blaesus scoffed. 'The lads say that about everywhere on this bloody island. In fact, I'm beginning to wonder if any-where *isn't* completely shit round here.'

Rullus shook his head. 'I think it's different with Lindinis. You know what the Durotrigans are like. Hate our guts more than any other tribe in Britannia. Can't see that lot being ruled over by us and not kicking up a fuss.'

'All the more reason to get the drinks in when we're on dry land,' Blaesus declared, rubbing his hands together. 'I hear there's plenty of good cunny and cheap wine to be found in Noviomagus. And I plan on sampling a bit of both tonight.'

Rullus laughed. 'You Germans are all the same. All you care about is where your next drink is coming from.'

'There'll be plenty of time for tarts later,' Figulus said. 'We've got to get through this mission first.'

An icy dread squirmed through his guts as he turned his thoughts back to the mission. Escorting his charges through the territory of the Durotrigans would be far from easy. There was a good chance of Figulus's detachment being ambushed, he anticipated. Worse still, if any harm came to the envoy or his Durotrigan companion, Figulus knew that his career in the military would be finished. Pushing aside his unease, he looked back to Rullus. The veteran narrowed his gaze beyond the prow and spat over the side of the deck.

'We should've stayed on Vectis,' Rullus muttered under his breath. 'Bodyguarding some exiled noble and his imperial lackey is no task for real soldiers, sir. At least if we were still on Vectis we'd be doing some proper soldiering, getting stuck into the enemy.' He flashed a yellow-toothed grin at Figulus. 'Not to mention getting our share of the loot. That extra coin would've come in handy for my retirement fund,' he added ruefully.

Figulus shrugged. 'The legate said he wanted his best men for the job. That happens to be us. So here we are.'

Blaesus shook his head and laughed cynically.

'Best men, you say?' Rullus cocked his chin at Helva. 'Even that idiot?'

Figulus turned to the young legionary. Helva was bent over the side of the deck, retching violently as he emptied the contents of his stomach into the churning waters below. He spat out the bitter dregs of vomit and groaned loudly above the hiss and suck of the sea, to the general amusement of the other soldiers gathered on the deck. New recruits were regarded with little compassion by their battle-hardened fellow soldiers who knew from experience that there was a sharp difference between the rigours of legionary training and fighting in actual battle. But so far Helva had managed to hold his own among the rankers, despite his occasional naivety and youthful recklessness, traits that Figulus recognised from his own early days as a new legionary. Figulus had sensed a steely determination in Helva to prove his worth to his comrades. His enthusiasm and breezy character were good for morale, and he had a natural skill with any weapon, so Figulus had chosen him for the mission. But now he was beginning to regret his decision.

'Fuck Neptune!' Helva croaked as he stood up straight and turned away from the sea. The colour had visibly drained from his face and there was a look of utter despair in his eyes. 'I swear to the gods, I'm never going to set foot on another boat as long as I live.'

The men laughed. Even Rullus joined in, temporarily forgetting his own discomfort at being at sea. 'You thick bastard,' he barked. 'If you never board a boat again then how the hell are you ever going to get home?'

Helva wiped his mouth with the back of his hand and thought about this for a moment. Then his eyes widened. 'Oh, shit . . .'

Figulus chuckled heartily as he nodded towards the quay. 'Your suffering's almost over, lad. We'll be ashore soon.'

Proteus eased her way through the harbour waters and the crew used her sweep oars to navigate towards an empty berth between two moored transport galleys. Figulus spotted a pair of supply ships beached close by so that repairs could be made to the damage caused by the recent storms. Just then an abrupt shout went up from one of the deck hands and the trierarch began aligning the ship's bow. The deck hands scrambled into action, grabbing hold of the mooring ropes stowed at both ends of the ship and tossing them to the dock workers gathered on the quayside. Once the workers caught the ropes, they quickly secured them to the sturdy posts along the edge of the dock. With the ropes fastened, the trierarch filled his lungs and gave the order for the gangway to be lowered. Then Figulus called out for the two sections of men under his command to disembark.

One by one, the sixteen soldiers trudged down the narrow wooden gangway and formed up a short distance along the quay. Helva stumbled off the boat a few steps ahead of Figulus, whispering thanks to the gods that his misery was finally over.

Figulus glanced around him. Sentries patrolled the battlements above the main gate to the north, watching over the naval base as overseers drove on the slaves, the sharp cracks of their short whips echoing violently across the wharf while the shivering wretches carried baskets to each of the moored ships in preparation for their return journey to Vectis. The constant flow of ships in and out of the port would become a familiar sight for the next few weeks, Figulus thought to himself. The Durotrigans believed it was better to fall in battle than suffer the humiliation of surrender and, for the soldiers who remained on Vectis, it would be a long and bloody campaign to conquer the isle, mile by mile, day by day, until every last drop of native blood had been shed.

Rullus caught his attention and nodded towards the parade ground. 'Over there, sir.'

Figulus looked round. The naval headquarters building stood at the far end of the quay, flanked on either side by barracks blocks. A pair of soldiers marched briskly towards him from the headquarters building. One wore a helmet with a distinctive transverse crest atop it, denoting his rank of centurion. As the two soldiers passed down the wharf, the slaves hurriedly stepped aside to make way. The centurion stopped in front of Figulus and glanced briefly at the optio's staff he carried, before clearing his throat.

'I take it you're the lads I was told to expect?' he snapped impatiently. He directed the question at Figulus.

'If you're looking for the escort detachment, then yes, sir.'

'I'm Centurion Lucius Ovidius Scrofa, officer in command of the garrison here.'

Figulus nodded and puffed out his chest and formally introduced himself. 'Optio Horatius Figulus of the Sixth Century, Fifth Cohort, sir. I've orders to meet with the imperial envoy, Numerius Scylla.'

The centurion paused and cast his critical eye over the other soldiers in the detachment. Then he looked back to Figulus. 'I hear you lot ran into some heavy resistance on the beach at Vectis.'

'Nothing the Sixth Century couldn't handle, sir,' Rullus replied. 'Pity your men weren't there to enjoy the show.'

The centurion glared at Rullus for a moment. Then he looked to Figulus and thrust out his hand. 'Your authorisation, Optio?'

Figulus reached a hand into his sidebag and quickly produced the waxed tablet containing the authorisation one of the legate's clerks had drawn up the previous evening at the marching camp on Vectis. 'It's all in here, sir,' he said, handing it to the centurion.

Scrofa flipped open the lid and began reading. At length, Scrofa looked up at Figulus, his brow furrowed. 'Says here you're headed to Lindinis. We're to provide you with whatever assistance you require.'

Figulus nodded. 'That's right, sir.'

The centurion sucked the air between his teeth and raised an eyebrow. 'Rather you than me, Optio. No Roman in his right mind would volunteer to go to that soldiers' graveyard.' He lifted his gaze to Figulus, his lips parting slightly into a grin. 'Who'd you piss off to get sent there?'

'No one, sir,' Rullus replied angrily. 'The legate wanted his best men for the task. That's us.'

Scrofa suppressed his smile. 'If you say so.' He thrust the authorisation back to Figulus and sighed. 'Right, then. The envoy's waiting to see you. He's staying as a guest at Cogidubnus's estate, a mile or so from here. Him and that Durotrigan friend of his, Trenagasus. Follow me.'

Figulus returned the waxed slate to his leather sidebag and started after Scrofa. Rullus shaped to follow but Scrofa abruptly stopped and shook his head. 'Just the optio,' he said tonelessly. 'Orders of the envoy. Your men can stay here. This officer will show them to the barracks. Plenty of room at the moment, given that half my men were drafted into the ranks for the assault on Vectis. Clear? Good. Hurry up, then. I don't have all bloody day.'

Without waiting for a response, the centurion turned swiftly on his heels and began marching towards the gates at the far end of the naval base, while his second-in-command led the other men in the detachment towards the nearest barracks block. As Figulus turned to follow the centurion, Rullus leaned in close.

'Word to the wise, sir. Be careful around that envoy. You know what those imperial types are like. Can't trust 'em further than you can piss.'

Figulus tried not to show his anxiety. It was well known that the coterie of advisers who served under Emperor Claudius were the true wielders of power inside the imperial palace. Since the day-to-day running of the vast Roman Empire was too onerous a task for one man, the Emperor relied heavily on his staff for guidance and their authority had grown steadily ever since Claudius had been declared Emperor. They disposed of their enemies with ruthless efficiency and were known to be some of the most dangerous men in the empire. The very thought of having to report to the envoy unsettled Figulus more than any enemies who might be lurking on the road to Lindinis. He nodded to Rullus then set off after Centurion Scrofa as he headed towards the main gate, a heavy feeling building in the pit of his stomach. He was about to undertake a mission quite unlike anything he'd done before in the Second Legion, away from the field of battle and the comfort of fighting alongside hundreds of his comrades. Now there were just sixteen men, and he was going to lead them into certain danger. As he hurried after Scrofa, Figulus sensed that this mission was going to be far tougher than anything he'd faced on Vectis.

CHAPTER ELEVEN

Figulus and Scrofa emerged from the naval base onto a wide thoroughfare covered with filth. The optio's first impression of Noviomagus was that not much had changed since he'd last set foot in the settlement a couple of years ago. Back then, Noviomagus had been a minor collection of roundhouses and cattle pens, but the construction of a major military base had raised hopes that the settlement would quickly transform into a Roman town. Glancing around at the assortment of modestly furnished wine shops and empty market stalls, Figulus could see little sign of improvement in the settlement's fortunes. A few rowdy bars lined the various alleys, their rooms filled with the peals of hoarse laughter from off-duty sailors enjoying cheap wine. As the two soldiers carried on, they passed a large warehouse situated to the west of the main thoroughfare. Figulus noticed that the warehouse was closely guarded by a handful of stern-faced soldiers watching over the slaves as they dutifully carried baskets of grain back towards the wharf. Scrofa noticed Figulus staring at the warehouse and grunted.

'The local grain supply,' he said with a snort. 'Or what's left of it. I've orders to send what grain I can to the cohorts on Vectis, but it won't amount to much. We're already stretched here, what with the storms holding up supplies from Gaul. With things going the way they are, I'm going to have to order my men to subsist on half rations, at least until our stocks are replenished.'

Figulus frowned and turned to meet the centurion's gaze. 'Can't you buy more grain from the locals?' he asked. 'Most of this lot are skilled farmers. Surely they've got plenty of grain stored away for the winter?'

Scrofa laughed. 'Most of the farmers from these part were drafted into the ranks under Caratacus. Without the men around, there was no one to harvest the crops and most of 'em were left to rot in the fields. There's now a shortage of wheat and barley across the region. As for the locals, those pinch-faced bastards are tightening their belts in preparation for the winter, and they won't sell us what little they've got to go around.' He spat in the gutter and gave a slow shake of his head. 'As it stands, this warehouse is all there is between the people of Noviomagus and starvation over the winter months. Another reason for the locals to despise us.'

Figulus pursed his lips as he glanced around and saw a young boy smiling shyly at him from the side of the street. 'The locals look friendly enough to me, sir.'

'Don't be fooled, Optio. Some of them may have taken to our ways, wearing the toga and drinking wine and what have you, but underneath it all they're British scum, and the only reason they're not ransacking the warehouse and attacking my men is because Cogidubnus keeps them firmly in check.'

Figulus nodded sagely. Cogidubnus, the chief of the Regni tribe, had been one of the first native kings to seek terms with Rome almost as soon as legionary boots hit the shore of Britannia. He had sold himself out to Emperor Claudius, body and soul, in exchange for the protection of the Roman invaders.

Scrofa went on, 'As long as Cogidubnus remains king, these ungrateful bastards will behave themselves. But if it wasn't for him, this lot would be tearing us limb from limb.' He grinned. 'That, and the fact that there's a Roman legion breathing down their necks. Take it from me, Optio, civilisation sits very lightly on the Britons.'

Figulus rubbed his stubbly cheeks and frowned. Would the natives remain forever opposed to Rome? He wasn't quite so sure. Although he'd been born a Roman citizen, and his allegiance was never in any doubt, Figulus sometimes found his natural sympathies lying with those whom Rome considered its sworn enemies. His ancestors, brave Celts, had defied Rome for many years before finally surrendering. Now men like Figulus fought its wars, spoke its tongue, worshipped its gods. To the optio's mind, the Britons were in a similar situation to his Gallic ancestors, and while the older generation would carry its hatred of Rome to the grave, the subsequent generations would gradually be absorbed into the empire, until the day arrived when the natives would consider themselves proud subjects of the Emperor.

But any attempt to integrate Britannia into the empire was doomed to fail unless their basic needs could be met, Figulus knew. As long as the threat of starvation hung over the natives there was a chance they might rebel against their Roman conquerors. The sooner the supply lines were secure and the grain stores replenished, the quicker any unrest within the native settlements could be swiftly dealt with. Then Rome could turn its attention to the remaining enemies to the north and west of the island.

At the end of the thoroughfare Scrofa led the Gaul down a rutted track between bare fields. After a brief walk they arrived at the entrance to Cogidubnus's residence. A pair of native guards stood on watch at the front gate, brandishing their spears with their leaf-shaped tips. Beyond them Figulus could see a large building, set into the grounds of a sprawling enclosure built on the bank of a small inlet off the harbour. Further inland, but still within the confines of the estate, Figulus caught sight of a vast building site. Slaves worked in teams, grunting under the strain of the foundation stones they hauled across the site, while others dug up soil into heaped mounds. The sheer scale of the building site was astonishing and, to judge from the layout, the finished building would dwarf even the governor's palace back in Lutetia.

While Figulus cast his eye over the grounds, Scrofa nodded curtly to the guards and they promptly lowered their spears and stepped aside. The centurion led the optio through the gates and into the estate. At the same time, a portly servant rose from his stool and approached, the bulge of his belly visible beneath his Roman-style tunic. His small black eyes were pressed like buttons into the thick folds of his face and his lips were formed into a welcoming smile.

'May I help you, sirs?' he inquired in faintly accented Latin.

Scrofa gestured to Figulus. 'Optio Figulus here to see Numerius Scylla. The envoy's expecting him.'

'But of course. *Sa.* You must be the leader of the escort His Majesty, Trenagasus, has been expecting?'

'That's me,' Figulus responded.

'The imperial envoy is waiting for you, sir. I'll escort you to his quarters.' The servant turned to Centurion Scrofa and cocked an eyebrow.

'Right,' Scrofa nodded. 'I'll be off.'

He turned and quickly departed while the servant led Figulus towards the large building in the middle of the estate. Aside from the main building, there were several small structures within the enclosure for receiving guests, as well as a sprawl of cattle byres and animal pens and a large stable. Figulus found his eye being drawn back to the construction site and he tried to imagine what the palace would look like when it was finished. The servant noticed him staring at the site and smiled.

'Cogidubnus's palace will be quite the sight to behold once it's finished. I've seen the plans, you know. When it's finished, the palace will have more than fifty rooms, floor mosaics commissioned by the best artists in the empire, gardens filled with exotic plants and rare animals, colonnades quarried from the finest Dacian marble. Not to mention the very latest in hypocaust heating.'

Figulus whistled. 'Sounds expensive.'

'*Sa*, it is not cheap. Everything has to be imported, naturally. And the plans are changing all the time. Cogidubnus says he wants the palace to be the grandest building outside of Rome. It's important to keep up with the latest trends in the capital.'

'Who's paying for it all?'

The servant laughed. 'You are, of course. Or, more correctly, your Emperor. It is a gift from him to Cogidubnus's people, something every Regni man and woman can take great pride in. Actually, Trenagasus was very impressed with the plans. He's even considering something similar in Lindinis.' He smirked. 'Once he's established his rule, of course.'

'Is that wise?'

'Why not? I think it's a wonderful idea. What better way for a king to announce his triumphant return than to commission a new palace?'

Figulus pursed his lips but didn't reply. It was one thing to build a lavish palace in a peaceful settlement like Noviomagus, but the locals here were reasonably tame. The natives to the west were much poorer, however, and even Figulus could see that building a palace while ordinary men and women starved would not go down well. He pushed this unsettling thought to one side as they arrived in front of a smaller timber-framed building to the side of the much larger structure in the middle of the enclosure. The servant yanked the studded wooden door and ushered Figulus inside. He led Figulus down a high-ceilinged corridor with a packed-dirt floor and drew to a halt at the far end, outside a room. Gesturing to Figulus to stop, the servant cleared his throat and, after a moment's silence, a haughty voice called out from inside the room, 'Who is it?'

'Optio Figulus to see you, sir. The soldier in charge of the detachment you requested.'

There was a long pause. Then the voice said, 'Send him in.'

The servant nodded at Figulus and stepped aside. Figulus stood for a moment in the doorway. Then he took a deep breath and stepped inside.

CHAPTER TWELVE

Figulus entered the room, the servant's footsteps echoing in the corridor as he turned on his heels and marched swiftly out of the building. The optio found himself in a sparsely furnished room with a hearth fire flickering to one side, providing some modest warmth against the draughty chill inside the villa. A slender, grey-haired figure sat behind a large desk, his head lowered in concentration as he worked his way through the tablets and scrolls before him. The man was well into his middle years and wore an expensive woollen tunic. Thin tendrils of steam drifted up from a jug resting in front of him on the desk. He reached for the jug and, without acknowledging Figulus, began filling an ornate silver goblet with hot red wine. When he had filled the goblet he finally lifted his eyes and scrutinised the burly Gaul in front of him.

'So . . . *Optio* Figulus, is it?' Numerius Scylla asked in an aloof tone of voice.

Figulus nodded stiffly as he watched Scylla carefully set the jug back down on the desk. Then he leaned back in his chair and stared at Figulus for what felt like a very long time. The look on the envoy's wrinkled face suggested he did not like what he saw. 'Well, I must say this comes as a bit of a surprise.'

Figulus shifted. 'How do you mean?'

'I asked the legate to send me his very best men for this task. Not competent men or merely good, but the best. I must admit I was rather expecting a junior tribune or a centurion at the very least. Instead Celer has sent you.' He narrowed his eyes to knife slits.

'The legate saw fit to place me in charge of the detachment.'

Scylla sat in thoughtful silence for a few moments, drumming his

82

fingers on the desk. 'You can see why this looks a little odd from my end. I explicitly requested the legion's finest soldiers, because this is no ordinary escort duty. Instead, Celer sends me a junior officer, and a rather young looking one at that. Tell me, how old are you?'

'Nineteen.'

'I see.' The envoy looked disappointed. 'You can't have much experience of battle, then?'

Figulus bristled. Despite his relative youth, he'd been involved in many battles during his time in the Second Legion. Almost from the day he'd set foot in Britannia he'd been thrust into the front line of the action and although his youthful complexion and easy-going manner suggested a novice soldier, the pinkish scar running just above his right eye hinted at a close scrape with death at the hands of a Druid. Good soldiers were not born, they were made, but Figulus felt he'd always been a natural at fighting, from his early days fending off bullies in the backstreets of his village. He was fearless in battle, unfailingly loyal and one of the few soldiers who had survived the hard campaigning since the early days of the invasion of Britannia.

'I'm a match for any man, inside the legion or out of it,' he said. 'I may be young, but I've earned my rank the hard way.'

'Bold words, Optio. Let us hope you live up to them. There's nothing worse than a man who cannot keep his word.' He cocked his chin at the optio and furrowed his brow. 'Tell me, where are you from? You don't look very Roman to me, not with that wild hair of yours. Nor do you sound like one, come to think of it.'

'I was born in Gaul, sir.'

The envoy frowned heavily. 'Aren't you people only supposed to serve in the auxiliaries? Or have the recruiting offices become so desperate they're now letting anyone join these days?'

Figulus bit his tongue, startled by the envoy's lack of knowledge about the rules for military service for non-Roman citizens. 'My father served as an auxiliary cavalryman. He did his twenty-five years and earned his citizenship when he retired, along with a small gratuity, as was his due. I was born a Roman, and raised as such.'

Satisfied at this, Scylla leaned back in his chair and reached for the silver goblet. He took a sip of the wine and promptly curled up his features in disgust. 'This godsforsaken island,' he muttered as he set the goblet back down on the desk with a shake of his head. 'One cannot find a decent wine here, no matter how much one is willing to pay.' He stared at the foul brew and sighed. 'Well, you and your men will have to do, Optio Figulus. I've been in this province for a week already and I've no intention of wasting a moment longer than necessary here. My place is not here, but back in Rome where the weather is agreeably warm most of the year and one is never short of a good wine, which is more than can be said of this benighted island. The sooner my work here is done, the sooner I can return to Rome and resume my duties at the imperial palace. And the sooner you can go back to doing whatever it is you soldiers normally do. Scrapping in the streets and getting drunk, I suppose.'

Figulus listened in silence as Scylla leaned forward in his chair and went on.

'Now I know about you, I suppose I ought to tell you a little about myself. My name is Numerius Scylla, although you probably already knew that.'

Figulus nodded.

There was a note of bitterness in the envoy's voice as he continued. 'I'm the Emperor's official representative in Britannia. My reward, apparently, for twenty years of unstinting service to Rome. Although, at the present time, it feels more like a punishment. But the reason for my presence here is because of the deteriorating situation to the west of the province.' He hesitated. 'I presume that, as you're in the ranks of the Second Legion, you fought under Vespasian when he conquered the Durotrigans?'

'That's right, sir.'

An image flashed briefly in his mind's eye of the siege warfare the legion had conducted against the hill forts the previous summer. Onagers and ballistas had been used to devastating effect against the native defences, smashing apart the palisades and impaling warriors as they stood on the battlements. Once the defences had been shattered, the legionary columns had moved in for the kill, keeping their shields hefted above their heads to protect themselves against any missiles being hurled down at them. The Durotrigans had built their hill forts in the belief that they were impregnable to attack, but they had no answer to Roman siege weapons and had fallen in quick succession, to the despair of the native warriors.

Scylla set down the wine cup and said, 'No doubt you're aware that the Durotrigans, having seen their warriors defeated in battle, are in the throes of deciding whether to assist or resist us.' The Gaul nodded and he went on. 'However, negotiations have been complicated by the fact that there are various tribal factions with no clear ruler among them.'

Figulus grunted. 'I can guess which path that lot will choose. Even if the natives want peace, many of the noblemen will be opposed to it.'

'Sadly, you are right. The Durotrigan warriors may have been crushed on the battlefield but the hostility to our presence, even among the common tribespeople, is a cause of concern. Especially when one considers that our control over their territory is tenuous at best, thanks to Vespasian leaving behind only a scratch force to administer the various tribal areas. Should they revolt, our control of their land would come under immediate threat. Moreover, the Emperor is keen not to get dragged into another prolonged conflict coming so soon after the defeat of Caratacus and his army. That campaign cost the imperial treasury dearly, not to mention the accompanying losses in the ranks. To that end we have decided to steal a march on the enemy by appointing our own man as king to rule over the Durotrigans. Namely, Trenagasus. Once he's put on the throne he'll persuade the natives to adopt Roman customs and laws. In time they'll learn to worship our gods, pay our taxes and – who knows? – perhaps even fight in our auxiliary units one day. Eventually our deadliest enemies will become trusted allies.' He smiled again before adding, 'Much like the Regni under Cogidubnus, in fact.'

'And that will work?' Figulus asked sceptically.

'It must, Optio. The situation in the kingdom is getting worse with each passing day and the reports coming in from General Plautius make for disturbing reading. Our forts in the west are under-strength, our supply lines stretched, our control over the local villages practically non-existent. I'm told that morale is pitifully low amongst those soldiers serving on the frontier due to the constant fear of attack.'

Figulus shook his head. 'But that's why we're invading Vectis, isn't it? To put a stop to the Durotrigan forces based there. They're the ones carrying out the attacks on the mainland.'

Scylla made a pained face. 'The few hundred Durotrigans on Vectis are a nuisance but nothing more. Wiping them out will provide an ample boost to morale and send a message to our enemies that resistance will not be tolerated. However, the greater threat lies to the west. Conquering the Durotrigan warriors has not brought the rest of that tribe into line, as we had hoped. The settlements are densely populated because we drove the natives out of the hill forts where many of them lived. Moreover, the ongoing campaign has resulted in most of the island's crops being left unharvested to rot in the fields. As a result, we now have many thousands of hungry and hostile natives overseen by a handful of undermanned forts. We cannot dismiss the possibility that Durotrigans could unite under a new leader and turn on our forces in a mass uprising. If that happens, we'd be forced into an embarrassing retreat, to say nothing of the damage to our military prestige among the other tribes.'

'We'd beat them eventually,' Figulus replied. 'We always do. The Britons are tough fighters, as tough as they come, but we have the better training, equipment and experience.'

'I wish I could agree with you. But the truth is our resources have been stretched to breaking point. Both the Ninth and Twentieth Legions are preoccupied with the push north of the legionary fortress at Cornoviorum. Meanwhile the Fourteenth is busy chasing Caratacus's shadow across the mountainous region to the west of Glevum, and gods only know how long the Second will be camped on Vectis. We are down to the bare bones, Optio, and if the Durotrigans somehow managed to organise themselves, they'd be able to overrun our forts before our troops could finish breakfast. I shouldn't have to tell you that any such defeat would be a disaster for our newest province. Our enemies to the west and north would be emboldened by the Durotrigans' success and redouble their efforts to resist us. Our forces would come under increasing attack. Even our strongholds to the east at Camulodunum and Londinium would not be safe. Needless to say, our alliances with those tribes under our protection would collapse.' He swallowed hard. 'And any hope of victory in Britannia would be gone.'

A bitter rage gripped Figulus. He didn't really care about the political or economic arguments for invading Britannia, or the benefits of civilising the natives. He was a junior officer and he followed his orders without question. But the thought of all his comrades who'd perished on this island filled him with anger. 'We can't lose here, sir,' he said firmly. 'We've paid for the province with our blood.'

'A reasonable point, Optio. But equally the Emperor cannot afford to lose thousands more men at this time.' He hesitated to go on. 'Particularly with the growing disquiet back home.'

'How do you mean?'

Scylla sighed. 'It's been almost two years since the Emperor held his triumph in Rome, declaring the invasion of Britannia to be over. But this cursed island has proved far more difficult to tame than we assumed. First Caratacus defied us. Now the Durotrigans are causing us problems. Some of these reports reach Rome, despite our best efforts to prevent this information from being used against us, and the Emperor's critics are growing more vocal with every passing day. Some, gods forbid, are openly calling for a complete withdrawal of our forces from Britannia.'

Figulus grunted. 'I doubt that will happen.'

Scylla sucked the air between his teeth. 'An unthinkable prospect, I agree. At the moment, it's only the view of a handful of trouble-makers, but there is a real danger of those calls becoming more widespread should our difficulties in this province persist. That's why it's vital that we succeed in establishing Trenagasus as king. It's the only way to stop the Durotrigans from overrunning us without drafting in more cohorts from one of the other provinces. Our future in Britannia depends on Trenagasus uniting the Durotrigans under his rule before the entire region explodes into a full-blown rebellion.' Scylla stared hard at Figulus and there was a steely glint in his pale eyes as he continued. 'And you and your men are going to help.'

'How?' Figulus asked.

'First, by escorting us to Lindinis. The party will be myself and Trenagasus along with his personal retinue of advisers and servants.' Scylla shifted uncomfortably in his chair. 'I gather from General Plautius that the route to Lindinis is not terribly safe?'

Figulus grunted. 'There's plenty of trouble on those roads, that's for sure. Raiders and brigands, that sort of thing.'

'I see.'

The optio saw a flicker of anxiety in the envoy's eyes and moved to allay his fears. 'Don't worry. The lads under my command are good soldiers. If any bastard tries it on with us, we'll cut them down quicker than boiled asparagus.'

His words hardly seemed to reassure Scylla but, after a pause, the envoy cleared his throat and continued, 'Escorting us to Lindinis is the first task I require of you.'

'What's the second?' Figulus asked.

'Once we arrive in Lindinis, I will need your assistance in removing the incumbent tribal ruler.'

'Who is he?'

'A troublesome fellow by the name of Quenatacus. According to the report I have from the general, he's a former noble who once professed his loyalty to the Druids. Although Quenatacus denounced the Druids shortly after the invasion, his loyalty to our cause remains somewhat questionable. Indeed, we suspect he's been providing reinforcements to a roaming band of warriors, behind our backs.'

'Why is he still in charge, then?'

'Quenatacus is the ruler only under sufferance. He assumed power five years ago, when he usurped Trenagasus, thanks in no small part to Druid backing. Trenagasus was given the choice of death or exile. He subsequently fled to Narbonensis and pleaded his case with the governor there.'

'Why wait this long to install him as king?'

'At the time it was felt that, while Trenagasus had the right credentials to be an effective client king, it was too risky to impose a change of ruler on the Durotrigans while we were still busy dealing with Caratacus. We couldn't afford any further strife among the Durotrigans with the legions busy campaigning elsewhere.' Scylla folded his arms in front of his chest and smirked. 'Now Caratacus is out of the way we can deal with Quenatacus.'

Figulus jammed his thumbs in his belt and thought for a moment. 'Knocking the existing ruler on the head is going to piss off the locals. Especially if he's got their support.'

'Perhaps. But a few disgruntled farmers are preferable to allowing the present situation to continue. We need to create a pro-Roman stronghold among the Durotrigans, and Quenatacus is clearly not up to the task. His former Druid sympathies mean we can't be certain where his loyalties lie, Optio. You understand our position.'

'Fair enough. But I've only got two sections of men under my command.' Seeing the quizzical look on the envoy's face Figulus quickly added, 'Sixteen men. What happens if Quenatacus puts up a fight when we attempt to force him out?'

'Doubtful. Quenatacus was permitted only a handful of body-guards by Vespasian after the conquest. He needed some men in order to gain credibility among the outlying settlements he theor-etically rules, of course, and by all accounts his bodyguards are ferociously loyal. But they're poorly trained and shouldn't pose much of a problem for your men. Besides, the auxiliaries stationed at the nearby fort will be on hand to provide support and discourage the natives from doing something foolish.'

'What's the strength of the garrison there?' asked Figulus.

'One cohort of Batavian auxiliaries under the command of Prefect Titus Cosconianus. Ordinarily I'd entrust the task of arresting Quenatacus to the garrison, but in this instance I don't think that's a particularly good idea. The prefect is quite new to his position and is still learning the ropes.' He paused. 'It's imperative that we remove Quenatacus and replace him with our own man before the situation deteriorates.'

'We'll need supplies for the journey.'

Scylla nodded. 'Have your men help themselves to whatever they need from the naval-base stores. If Centurion Scrofa kicks up a fuss refer him to me. Which reminds me . . . How far is it to Lindinis from here?'

'Five days, by my reckoning.' Figulus had studied a map of the route from Noviomagus the night before. He'd stayed awake until late in the evening, trying to work out the safest way to reach the settlement. He'd gone to bed late, and had little sleep. But the tiredness had not yet caught up with him.

'We leave tomorrow,' Scylla announced. 'At the first hour. I've given instructions that your men are to be provided with mounts from the local stables. Now, if that's everything . . . ?'

Figulus could think of nothing else, so he took a deep breath and nodded as Scylla slid out from behind the desk. The envoy turned away from the optio and gazed silently out of the small window on the far wall overlooking the inlet, lost in his thoughts for several moments.

'The politics on this island are a nightmare,' Scylla grumbled as he stared out of the window. 'Blood feuds, tribal elders, family squabbles. Not to mention those Druids forever meddling in political affairs.' He half-turned back to Figulus. 'By comparison, Rome is almost a paragon of stability.'

The Gaul didn't know what to say to any of this. He felt distinctly uncomfortable discussing weighty matters and was much more at home swapping jokes in the soldiers' quarters or learning a magic trick from some Phoenician magician. He stood still and waited for Scylla to continue.

'We have defeated our enemy in pitched battles, Optio. We have laid siege to their precious hill forts and driven their leaders into hiding. Normally that would be enough to achieve an overwhelming victory. But our enemies in Britannia have not surrendered. Far from it. They have retreated into the shadows to wage a new kind of war against us. They have abandoned the Celtic tradition of open warfare in favour of a prolonged campaign of raids and ambushes. The British think they can beat us this way, Optio. They are sorely mistaken. And you and I are going to play our part in their defeat.'

Scylla spun away from the window. He stared hard at Figulus as he spoke.

'We must not fail. Britannia may be a depressing backwater of little material worth, but it threatens to do great harm to the Emperor. We have pinned our hopes on a decisive victory here. If we fail to protect Trenagasus and install him on the throne, then our hopes of peacefully securing the south-west of the island will be dashed. Worse, our supply lines to all the rest of the army will be endangered. If that happens, then, before we know it, the entire province will be under threat.'

CHAPTER THIRTEEN

That evening, Figulus joined Blaesus, Rullus and Helva at the naval-base gates and the four soldiers made their way up beyond the thoroughfare and climbed a small rise towards a quiet drinking spot overlooking the centre of town. The Golden Dolphin was silhouetted against the setting sun and, from a short distance, Figulus could hear the faint hubbub of conversation from within. A dense fog had started to settle behind his eyes and, as they trudged past the numerous roundhouses and cattle byres, he felt tired. After quitting Cogidubnus's estate, he'd returned to the naval base to make his preparations for the coming mission. Meanwhile, he sent Rullus to get the necessary rations and feed from the garrison's quartermaster. Later, Figulus had briefed the men on the mission, ordering them to present themselves at the parade ground at first light to leave for the town gates.

After the briefing, Blaesus had mentioned that he knew a friend in Noviomagus, a comrade from his old century who'd been invalided out of the Second not long ago and had sunk his modest savings into a nearby tavern. The former soldier heard all the local gossip and Blaesus suggested that he might be able to give them some further intelligence on Lindinis, since he had been based in a fort in that region before his discharge. Figulus agreed, and Rullus and Helva both offered to come along, curious to see what was on offer in a friendly native settlement. So, their swords hanging from their belts, the four men had left the base as the sun sank towards the horizon and the air turned frosty with the cold. Centurion Scrofa had explained to Figulus that there had been several attacks on Roman soldiers around Noviomagus recently. As a consequence, every off-duty soldier was to carry his weapon.

As the four men drew near to the tavern, the door flung open and a pair of sailors stumbled out of the wan orange glow of the room, drunkenly singing as they staggered down the rise towards the naval base. Figulus brushed past the sailors and ducked under the low doorframe, entering the tavern. A thick smell of sweat and roast meat greeted him inside. A mix of natives and off-duty guards and sailors were packed around the trestle tables while a hearth fire burned brightly in one corner of the room. A harassed-looking bar woman shuffled back and forth between the main counter and the tables as she topped up the customers' drinks. As a rule, most natives tended to avoid the drinking spots frequented by the soldiers and Figulus was surprised to see the two groups mingling freely. Three other soldiers from the detachment sat at one of the tables. Figulus had given the men permission to go out drinking tonight, reasoning that they had a long journey ahead of them tomorrow and this would be their last chance to indulge themselves for a while.

Helva rubbed his hands as he tried to work some warmth back into them. 'Fuck, it's cold tonight!' he exclaimed.

Rullus chuckled. 'You think this is bad, wait until it's the depths of winter. It'll get so cold then you won't feel anything from your waist down. Even your balls will freeze up. You get a proper winter in Britannia, lad, not like those mild ones back home in Campania, or wherever it is you're from.'

'Atella,' Helva said quietly. 'I'm from Atella.'

Just then, Blaesus spied his friend seated alone at a trestle table in the far corner of the tavern. The ex-soldier waved the four men over and they promptly threaded their way past the other drinkers and drew up at the table, sitting down on the rickety wooden bench. Blaesus nodded at the grizzled man sitting opposite.

'This is Cethegus,' he said by way of introduction. 'Good friend of mine from the glory days back in the Eighth, my old century.'

The other man grinned. His cheeks were streaked with fine purple veins and his eyes heavily glazed from an extended bout of drinking, his thickset frame run to fat in early retirement. As Cethegus clasped arms, Figulus noticed that three of his fingers on his right hand were missing.

'Best days of my life,' he said above the general hubbub of conversation around them. 'Remember that last summer in Vindocladia when we were busy kicking the Durotrigans' arses? Hot work, that!'

'Is that how you got injured?' Helva asked.

'What? This?' Cethegus waved his maimed hand at the young legionary. 'I bloody wish! I lost my fingers lifting a wagon out of a quagmire. The bastard next to me let go and my fingers were crushed under the wheel. Had to cut the buggers off before the wound went bad.' He looked back to Blaesus. 'How's the Sixth treating you, then? Still cheating soldiers out of their hard-earned pay with those weighted dice of yours?'

'Er, still winning fair and square, you mean,' he replied awkwardly.

Figulus glared at his comrade while Cethegus signalled to the waitress for her to bring over five cups. His heavily lidded eyes lingered on her shapely frame for a moment before he turned back to his guests, the grin now wider than ever. 'My wife, Conwenna. Wed her right after I settled down here. Proper native lass, and a right goer in the sack, I can tell you. She's good for business too. Keeps the locals coming back, if you know what I mean,' he added, winking at Figulus.

The waitress, Cethegus's wife, swiftly brought over a jug of heated wine and five chipped clay mugs, which she laid out in front of them. Cethegus half-filled the cups and handed one to each of the soldiers, filling his own almost to the brim and splashing a few drops on the table. After a toast to old times, the five men clinked their mugs and Figulus took a sip of his drink. The sweetened wine burned the back of his throat. Cethegus necked half his cup of wine in one gulp and then hastily refilled his mug.

'Blaesus tells me you lads are heading to Lindinis.'

Figulus nodded. 'What have you heard?'

Cethegus puffed out his cheeks. 'Only what some of the locals have been saying. A few of the more peaceful Durotrigans have been resettling here lately, which always gets under this lot's skin.' He laughed and shook his head. 'Britons – they never cease to amaze me. They hate us, they hate the other tribes, and they can't stand their neighbours. They'll only be happy when everyone else buggers off and leaves them to it.'

'What are they saying about Lindinis?' Figulus insisted.

'Just that the settlement is in a seriously bad way. Food is in short supply and, with the winter coming, things are only going to get worse. Of course, in the usual run of things the local fort would make up the shortfall with provisions from their own stores to keep the natives happy. But, from what I hear, the garrison's grain supplies are running low and the few convoys that are sent that way are getting hit by raiding parties on a regular basis. The auxiliaries barely have enough to feed themselves, let alone the natives. Quenatacus has been coming under pressure from his own people to do something about it. Some say he's even been providing men to local brigands in exchange for a share of the spoils.'

'Why hasn't the garrison stopped 'em?' Rullus wondered aloud.

'Same story as every other fort in that kingdom. The garrison's under-strength and cut off from the rest of the army. Supplies are low, and morale's rock bottom.' He pressed his lips shut. 'Then there are the rumours that have been doing the rounds, unnerving the men.'

Figulus frowned. 'What rumours?'

Cethegus shifted his eyes left and right to make sure none of the natives could overhear. Then he leaned across the table and lowered his voice. 'The word is there are Druids at work in that part of the island. They're stirring up the locals, preparing them to fight us once more.'

'Bollocks!' Rullus spat. 'We cut most of them down last summer.'

Cethegus stared at the veteran. 'Most, but not all.'

'It's true,' Figulus put in. 'The Druids have got more heads than a bloody hydra. Every time you kill one, another crops up in its place.'

Rullus dismissed his concerns with a wave. 'It'll take more than a few decrepit old Druids to scare us, sir. And it's hardly cause for the auxiliaries to get their loincloths in a twist.'

Cethegus shook his head. 'Then I fear you don't understand the hold the Druids have over the natives, friend. There are many who cling to the old beliefs. The Druids have wielded power over these people for hundreds of years and they won't give up without a fight. If they're on the rise again, there are plenty among the natives who'll support them against us.'

No sooner had Cethegus finished speaking than the tavern door crashed open and a thickset native man appeared in the doorway, his eyes wide with panic and his chest heaving up and down with exertion from having run a fair distance. He instantly began shouting and pointing frantically outside, in the direction of the main settlement lower down the rise.

'What's he saying, sir?' Rullus asked.

Figulus listened and quickly formed his features into a deep frown. 'Durotrigans!' he translated breathlessly as he shot up from the bench. 'He says they're raiding the settlement!'

The other three soldiers instantly bolted upright and followed Figulus as he charged out of the tavern. They were swiftly followed by Cethegus and the few off-duty soldiers from the detachment who'd been drinking inside the establishment, along with several worried local patrons who abandoned their tables and rushed outside to see what was going on. The sun had fully set by now and Figulus had to squint in the speckled gloom as he scanned the settlement before him, searching for signs of the fracas. At first he could see nothing except the faint warm glow of hearth fires visible through the entrances of native huts, and the thin trails of smoke rising into the darkening sky. Then his eyes centred on the naval base, and Figulus felt a chill slither down his spine.

A large party of Durotrigan raiders was swarming through the settlement, the pointed tips of their spears gleaming dully in the blue hue of twilight. Terrified natives screamed and ran for their lives as chaos spread. Families grabbed their children and fled their roundhouses towards the gates. Livestock bleated and snorted wildly as the animals sensed danger, responding to the panicked shouts all around them. But the raiders ignored the locals and instead charged directly across the settlement. Their intention was immediately obvious to Figulus.

'The enemy are attacking the naval base!' he exclaimed. 'We've got to stop them!'

'That lot don't stand a chance, sir,' Rullus retorted gruffly. 'They don't even have a sodding battering ram.'

As the veteran spoke, the main party of Durotrigan raiders reached the naval base gate and began hurling their spears at the sentries atop the battlements. The Romans were well protected behind their defences and the guards swiftly answered with a volley of well-aimed light javelins and slingshots. Distant cries pierced the cold night air as the javelins impaled several of the Durotrigans massed outside the gate. The raiders defiantly stood their ground beside their fallen comrades and continued to hurl their spears at the Romans. But Figulus could see that their attack was doomed to fail. The Durotrigans were heavily outnumbered by the better-equipped guards the other side of the main gate, and once Centurion Scrofa's men had depleted the enemy ranks with their missile attacks it would simply be a matter of lowering the gate and cutting down the surviving raiders before they could escape. Why, Figulus wondered, had the Durotrigans decided to launch such a reckless attack?

'Sir!' Helva suddenly cried. 'Over there! Look!'

Figulus quickly followed Helva's pointing finger. To the west of the naval base he spied a small party of raiders sneaking around the edge of the settlement, their faces lit by the flickering flames from the torch each man carried in place of a shield. As he narrowed his gaze on the raiders, Figulus felt his blood turn cold with dread. The enemy's true intention was suddenly clear. The main body of Durotrigans attacking the naval base was a distraction, diverting the garrison's attention while the second party of raiders made for their real objective: the grain warehouse. The few lightly armed Roman guards defending the warehouse would be cut down soon enough, Figulus realised. By the time Scrofa and the men under his command understood what was happening, it would be too late. The grain warehouse would already be ablaze.

There was only one thing for it. He turned to his fellow soldiers and jabbed a thumb in the direction of the warehouse.

'Those bastards are going after the grain,' Figulus said, forming a plan in his mind as he spoke. 'That's all that stands between this settlement and starvation. We've got to stop them. If we head down this side of the hill we'll be screened by the roundhouses so they won't see us coming.' He grinned. 'Not until it's too late, anyway. They're not carrying shields so it should be an even fight. Stay quiet until we're breathing down their necks. If anyone makes too much noise, I'll see to it that they're on latrine duty for the next month.

And as anyone who's ever shared a tent with Blaesus knows, that's a punishment worse than death.'

The other men laughed uneasily at his poor joke. Rullus simply rolled his eyes. Then Figulus unsheathed his sword and pointed the gleaming tip towards the warehouse. 'All right, lads. On me!'

He broke into a quick run as he started descending the low rise towards the settlement, the other half-dozen soldiers scrambling after him. Without shields or heavy armour weighing them down, Figulus and his men ran easily down the gentle slope, keeping their noise to a minimum. A short distance ahead, he could see the Durotrigans charging at the warehouse, their bare torsos inked with striking tattoos, their hair washed stiff with lime. They descended upon the few guards and thrust at them with their spear points, cutting the defenders down. Then they began encircling the warehouse and holding their torches to its thick timber frame. Several sections of timber simultaneously burst into flames, and Figulus quickened his stride as he reached the bottom of the rise.

'Come on!' He implored the other soldiers. 'Let's get 'em!'

He broke into a sprint and charged past a cluster of roundhouses, his chest heaving, his face drenched with sweat despite the chill evening air. The Durotrigans were busy watching the flames lick at the warehouse and blissfully ignorant of the Roman soldiers charging towards them. As he drew closer, Figulus tightened his grip around the pommel of his sword and experienced a hot thrill at the thought of engaging enemy. Then one of the raiders looked up and caught sight of the Romans emerging from the crowded nest of roundhouses. He spun around to alert his comrades. They immediately turned as one to face the onrushing Romans, dropping their torches and shaping to attack their enemy.

'Charge!' Figulus roared at his men.

One of the raiders singled out Figulus, lunging at him with a furious thrust of his spear. The optio sidestepped the attack then charged at the man, knocking his spear aside before driving the tip of his sword up into the Durotrigan's bowels, cutting up into his stomach. The man collapsed to his knees, blood gushing out of his wound, pooling between his legs. At the same time, the rest of the soldiers fell upon the other raiders, sword points and spear tips flashing as they caught the light of the rising flames. The air was by now choked with fumes as the fire quickly spread across the warehouse structure, churning acrid smoke into the night sky. Figulus bolted towards a raider setting light to another section of the timber and slashed at the man's back, kicking him to the ground then thrusting the point of his sword through the native's throat.

'Sir, look out!' Rullus boomed above the brittle clash of steel.

Figulus spun around just in time to see a raider thrusting his spear towards his neck. He jerked back a step, ducking to evade the blow. The raider snarled and thrust at him again, forcing Figulus to retreat another step until his back was almost against the burning timber and he could feel the heat from the flames singeing the bristles on the nape of his neck. His opponent's scarred features were illuminated by the flickering light of the fire and a cruel smile played out on his lips as he grasped that Figulus was trapped. With a throated roar the raider stabbed at Figulus, driving the spear tip at his throat. Figulus quickly ducked low and to his left and heard the tip clatter as it struck against the timber post. The raider growled as he tried wresting his spear free from the post. Figulus booted the man backwards and then drove home with his sword point, thrusting at the raider's midriff. He felt the blade connect with tendon and muscle. The raider spasmed and his hands fell limp by his sides as dark red blood leaked out of the corners of his slack mouth. Figulus pulled his sword free and blood sprayed over the huge Gaul, spattering his forearms as the raider fell away. He turned towards Rullus.

'That's the lot of 'em driven back, sir,' Rullus explained between sharp intakes of breath. Figulus looked around him. Several raiders were sprawled on the bloodstained ground outside the warehouse. A few of the Durotrigans had managed to escape the skirmish, Figulus saw. They were now fleeing the settlement, heading for the darkness. But there was no need to give chase. Over at the naval base, Centurion Scrofa had read the situation perfectly and ordered the gates to open so that his men could charge out and cut down the retreating Durotrigans, and Figulus was filled with joy at the sight of the routed enemy being picked off at will. Then his joy turned to dread as he remembered the fire. He turned to the others.

'Fetch some water,' he barked. 'Grab whatever you can. We've got to put out the fire before the grain goes up in flames. Do it now!'

The Romans sprang into action. By now a small crowd had formed at the nearest group of roundhouses and the soldiers raced towards the onlooking natives and gestured frantically to the fire. The locals grasped their meaning at once and darted inside their homes, emerging moments later with clay jugs or woven baskets sealed with pitch and filled them with water from the troughs in the street. Talking to them in the native tongue, Figulus ordered the locals to form a chain leading from the troughs to the warehouse where his men hurled the water on the raging fire. There was a violent hiss as the water doused the flames, smothering the smoke eddying into the night sky. Moments later, Cethegus arrived with several locals in tow and Figulus ordered more chains to be formed in order to tackle the various pockets of fire threatening to consume the warehouse.

Gradually the flames petered out. The air was heavy with the smell of damp wood and burnt ash. Figulus breathed a sigh of relief. Although the warehouse itself was damaged beyond repair, nearly all of the grain was salvageable. The garrison and the people of Noviomagus would not starve. With the fire put out, he at last slumped to the ground in exhaustion beside Rullus. The veteran wiped sweat from his brow and shook his head at the smouldering warehouse ruins.

'We've not even left for Lindinis yet and the bloody Durotrigans are already causing us problems,' he grumbled. 'Gods only know what's in store for us when we get there.'

CHAPTER FOURTEEN

The following morning, Figulus and his companions headed out of the naval base under a bleak wintry sky. The men were weary and aching from a fitful night's rest. On Centurion Scrofa's orders, every soldier had worked late into the evening, some transferring the grain stores to the naval base in case the Durotrigans returned, while the others took turns to keep watch around the settlement. Once the dead raiders had been cleared away and their equipment confiscated, the tired soldiers had at last returned to their barracks. Even then, sleep had been impossible. Throughout the night, a crowd of angry locals had gathered outside the base gates, protesting loudly at the Romans' failure to prevent their town from being raided. At dawn, the soldiers had risen from their troubled sleep and taken a small breakfast before receiving their steeds from the local stables. Now the sound of horse hoofs echoed through the deserted streets as the men made their way towards the town gates.

Figulus led his horse at the front of the column as they passed the burnt and blackened ruins of the empty warehouse. Rullus moved alongside the optio and formed his features into a scowl as he lifted his eyes to the dark clouds.

'This weather ain't looking good,' he grumbled. 'Better pray there's no snow before we reach Lindinis.'

'What's wrong with snow?' Figulus responded. 'I love a bit of snow, me.'

'What's wrong with it?' Rullus repeated apoplectically. 'It's cold, it'll slow us down and there's always some joker tossing snowballs at you.' He screwed up his face at the thought of it. 'Still, one more campaign and then I'm finished. I'll collect my military discharge and my gratuity and sod off to somewhere nice and warm.' He grinned at Figulus. 'I hear the weather's good in Syria. Good fleshpots there too. Make a change from this shithole, anyway.'

Figulus laughed easily, but he would be sorry to see Rullus retire. He was a hard man, often grumpy and belligerent, but he'd also looked out for Figulus on several occasions since he'd joined the Sixth Century, offering support or a quiet word of advice to the young optio. A lesser soldier would have resented having to take orders from a man half his age, but Rullus had gone about his duties without complaint. Without the veteran by his side, leading the detachment would have been a much more daunting task.

Scylla stood at the town gates, waiting for the soldiers. The envoy was accompanied by a dark-haired man, well into his later years, tall and with a neatly trimmed grey beard and hair cut short in the Roman style. There was no sign of a stoop in the way the man carried himself, his back rigidly straight and his stride arrogant and assured, his greying eyes conveying just the right amount of grace and steely coldness becoming to a tribal king. An expensive cloak was draped across his shoulders, beneath which he wore a tunic and a pair of brightly coloured breeches. The envoy stared coldly at Figulus.

'Optio,' he began, 'Centurion Scrofa tells me that your men helped save the grain supply during last night's raid.'

Figulus shrugged. 'We just happened to be in the right place at the right time. Any other soldier would've done the same, in our place.'

The envoy feigned a smile. 'Spoken with the humility of a true Roman, I see. Still, the fact remains that, but for your actions at the warehouse, the good people of Noviomagus would be facing a winter of famine. King Cogidubnus asked me to pass on his thanks.'

'A nice reward would've been better,' Rullus muttered under his breath.

Scylla glared at the veteran. 'What was that, soldier?'

'Nothing,' Rullus replied stiffly. 'Just saying it's nice to be thanked once in a while.'

Scylla studied the legionary for a moment before gesturing to the man at his side. 'May I introduce King Trenagasus, rightful ruler of the Durotriges.' He turned to Trenagasus and bowed slightly. 'Your

Majesty, this is the soldier I was telling you about: Optio Figulus, of the Second Legion. He's the officer in charge of your escort detail.'

Trenagasus narrowed his eyes and regarded Figulus as if contemplating an unfamiliar dish at supper. Gold rings gleamed on each of his fingers. 'Scylla tells me you're a Gaul.' He spoke with a slight trace of a native accent.

Figulus nodded. 'My family's from the Aedui tribe, Your Majesty.'

'Ancestors of ours,' Trenagasus replied airily. 'We Durotrigans are descendants of the first Celts who crossed the sea, you know. Two hundred years ago, our forefathers came to these shores, established villages, built temples and set up trading posts. Now our Roman friends wish to do the same, albeit on a grander scale, and a fringe minority is outraged. Hypocritical of us, don't you think?'

Figulus hesitated, wary about getting drawn into a political debate with Trenagasus about the finer points of imperial policy, but not wanting to offend the king. 'I suppose so.'

Crow's lines formed at the corners of Trenagasus's narrow eyes. 'We have turned our back on civilisation for too long now. Men like Quenatacus are leading us down a path that will end in utter disaster. They must be removed.' His expression hardened as he went on. 'I swear upon all the gods, Quenatacus will live to regret the day he forced me to flee my people. I spent five years in exile at the governor's palace in Narbonensis. Five long years as a king without a land, while that treacherous dog turned my people against me. Now Quenatacus is going to know what it's like to be cast out of your own home.'

The anger in his voice took Figulus by surprise and he privately wondered whether Trenagasus was motivated more by a deep hatred of the current ruler than any burning desire to lead his people to a peaceful future. He shook the thought aside as the Briton's mood brightened and his thin lips parted into a smile.

'I learned Latin during my time in exile. I read a great deal, too, and spoke frequently with the governor. It occurred to me then that our native culture is woefully inferior and unless we follow the ways of our Roman betters, our people are doomed. Quenatacus understands nothing of this, of course. He's a simple brute who thinks resistance is preferable to change. But once he's out of the way, I'll introduce my loyal subjects to the benefits of Roman culture, for the good of my people. I shall start by building a palace of my own.'

They were interrupted by the faint sound of hoofs approaching from the direction of the town and Scylla turned towards the gates to see a slight figure approaching them. The figure rode atop a sleek white mount with a fur-lined hood pulled down low over their face to protect against the cold. Figulus watched the figure trot past the soldiers, riding in the confident manner of someone who had received plenty of instruction.

'Ah!' Trenagasus said, beaming with pride. 'Here she is. My daughter.'

The rider tugged gently on the reins, easing the horse to a stop next to Trenagasus and pulling back the hood on her winter coat to reveal the face of an elegant young woman with a gleaming silver Celtic torc wrapped around her neck and long brown hair running down past her shoulders. She smiled at Trenagasus, her light blue eyes glowing softly above her smooth round cheeks. Trenagasus gestured to her as she dismounted.

'Allow me to introduce my daughter, Ancasta. My child, this is Optio Figulus of the Second Legion.'

Ancasta nodded at the Gaul, her lips forming a slight smile as her eyes met his. Figulus was momentarily lost for words, ruffled by the unexpected sight of a beautiful woman among them. He quickly regained his composure. 'Pleasure to meet you, miss.'

Ancasta glared at him. 'That's "my lady" to you,' she scolded, although unlike her father her voice carried no hint of a native accent. 'I'm the daughter of a king, not some common wench, and you'll address me as such.'

'Of course, my lady,' Figulus replied falteringly. 'My apologies.' Then he looked to Trenagasus. 'Is she, er, supposed to be coming with us?'

'Of course! She's my flesh and blood. I'm hardly going to leave her here in Noviomagus.' He frowned heavily at Figulus. 'Is there a problem?'

Figulus shook his head. 'It's just . . . there may be some danger. Fighting. There's no place for a woman.'

Ancasta placed her hands on her hips and glowered at Figulus.

103

'Is that so, Optio? Perhaps you'd prefer it if I stayed at home to cook and clean, like a good Roman wench?'

'I meant no offence, my lady. But this is a dangerous journey. The route we're taking is under constant attack from brigands. Any soldiers unlucky enough to get captured alive are taken prisoner and treated as slaves. Those are the fortunate ones. The rest are tortured and killed. Gods only know what they'd do if they captured you.'

'Isn't that your job?' Ancasta responded icily. 'To protect us from attack?'

The Gaul lowered his head slightly. 'My men will defend to the last, my lady. But there are no guarantees.'

'I've heard enough,' Trenagasus cut in. 'My daughter can handle herself in a fight. She's been using a sword practically from the day she learned to walk, as is expected of all women of the warrior caste. She practised under a retired gladiator daily at our residence in Narbonensis. No mere gladiator, I might add, but a man who once fought the great Hermes and lived to tell the tale. I can assure you, Ancasta will not be a burden to us.'

Figulus opened his mouth to reply but Trenagasus cut him off with a raised hand.

'The matter is not up for debate, Optio. My daughter will accompany me to Lindinis. One day I'll be too old and weary to reign. Since I have no sons, I'm going to need Ancasta to marry one of the trusted young chiefs in order to continue my legacy.'

There was a hint of irritation in his voice and Figulus sensed it would be pointless to argue any further. He shrugged in resignation and bowed. 'As you wish, Your Majesty.'

'Good!' Scylla declared, clapping his hands. 'Now, if that's all, we really should be on our way.'

While the king and his personal retinue mounted their horses, Figulus gave the order for his men to do likewise and he climbed awkwardly up into his saddle. Like all Roman soldiers, he'd been taught to ride as a recruit, but it had been two years since his training and now he struggled to remember the riding lessons taught to him by the training centurion back in Argentoratum. His bulky frame meant that he sat awkwardly in the saddle and, as he gripped the reins, he trotted to the front of the column with some difficulty, his horse stopping for no apparent reason. Rullus rode alongside him, glancing back at the Britons behind them.

'The benefits of Roman culture . . .' he muttered under his breath so that no one overheard. 'What a load of bollocks.'

Figulus twisted in his saddle and winked at the veteran. 'I take it you don't believe him?'

'Of course I bloody don't. Trenagasus doesn't give a toss about the natives, sir. It's obvious he's only doing this to get his own back on Quenatacus.' He shook his head. 'I'm no politician, but even I can see that this is a recipe for disaster. A king aping our ways and coming across as more Roman than Briton, booting out a local chief who's no doubt got most of the people behind him. I can't think of a better way to piss off the natives. Can you?'

Figulus pressed his lips shut but did not reply. Rullus was right. It wasn't hard to see why Scylla was convinced of Trenagasus's claim as king of the Durotrigans. His aloof manner and enthusiasm for everything Roman would have gone down well in the imperial household. Privately he dreaded to think what the Durotrigans would make of the exile with the Latin accent and the grand plans for Romanising their way of life. Then Figulus shook his head angrily. It wasn't his place to worry about the likely success or failure of the men under his protection. All he could do was obey his orders to the best of his abilities, like the good soldier he was. With a sharp tug on his horse's reins, Figulus urged his mount on as they began the journey west to Lindinis.

CHAPTER FIFTEEN

As the detachment travelled west along the rutted track, the clouds lifted and the sun shone starkly over the land, warming the frozen mud. Brown leaves rotted beneath the trees and, as they passed through a pleasant valley of undulating hills and forests alive with birdsong, it was briefly possible to forget they were still at war in Britannia. The two sections of men under Figulus's command rode at the front of the column, with Helva acting as a scout a short distance ahead. Helva was a natural rider and had a sharp eye and a keen ear, honed by hunting on his father's farm as a child, and he had the makings of a talented scout. Behind the legionaries rode Trenagasus and his entourage. The king-in-waiting was closely followed by his quartet of personal bodyguards: maimed ex-gladiators he'd recruited to his cause during his stay in Narbonensis. Bringing up the rear of the column were the baggage mules, weighed down with saddlebags and feed nets bulging with hay.

As the morning wore on, Figulus gradually began to master his horse, remembering the correct position in his saddle and how to properly cue his mount. By the early afternoon, his horse was obedient, responding to his prompts, and the optio rode on confidently at the head of the column as they journeyed towards Clausentum, a flourishing coastal village where they would put up for the night at the fort. The clear skies helped lighten the mood among the soldiers and Blaesus entertained a few of his comrades by recounting stories of his various drunken nights out.

'You should've seen the size of her tits,' he said hoarsely. 'Out to here, I tell you. And then her sister walked into the room . . .'

The other soldiers laughed. Figulus glanced back just in time to

106

see Blaesus taking a swig from his wineskin. The legionary wiped his lips with the back of his hairy hand and grinned.

'Hair of the dog, sir. It's the local brew. Cethegus gave me some supplies before we parted ways. Got a real kick to it.' He offered the wineskin to Figulus. 'Care for a drop?'

Figulus shook his head. 'We're on escort duty. Best put it away.'

'Come on, sir. We're just having a drink, is all. No harm in that.' Blaesus swept his arm in a broad arc in front of him. 'Besides, we're in friendly territory. Who's going to bother us here? The local farmers? The sheep are in more danger than us!' He laughed at his own joke and took another sip from the wineskin.

Figulus considered. 'Fair enough, lads. Just keep it down, eh?'

With a knowing nod of his head, he turned in the saddle and faced forward. In the corner of his eye he noticed Rullus staring at him disapprovingly. He shook his head and waited until Blaesus had resumed telling his story. Then he leaned over to Figulus and said under his breath, 'You shouldn't go easy on the men, sir.'

'Why's that?'

Rullus chose his words carefully. 'You're a fine soldier, sir. And one day you'll make a fine centurion. But if these lads think you're a light touch, how do you think you're going to discipline them when one of 'em steps out of line?'

Figulus suddenly realised his mistake. In his private moments he admitted to himself that he was finding the step up from optio to commanding officer much more testing than he'd imagined. Leading others did not come naturally to the giant Gaul. Some men in the legions were born to be officer material, but Figulus was happier as a second-in-command, acting as a vital buffer between the rankers and the centurion. His cheerful character had served him well in this regard, with the legionaries comfortable airing their grievances to the easygoing Gaul, who in turn relayed them to the centurion. But now he was in charge of these men, and that same affable manner was working against him. It didn't help that he was several years younger than most of the other soldiers, who still regarded Figulus as more of a youthful brother-in-arms than a superior officer. If he really wanted to realise his ambition of one day becoming a centurion, Figulus decided he would have to start acting more like one.

As darkness settled over the land, the detachment stopped for the night at Clausentum. The garrison commander there was quick to offer Scylla and Trenagasus his quarters for the night when he learned of the envoy's imperial connections, while Figulus and his men were left to sleep on straw bedding in the storeroom.

The following day, they set off towards Sorviodunum, the last major settlement before they would cross the border into Durotrigan territory. That morning, the weather turned foul. Thick banks of leaden cloud pressed low in the sky, bulging as if they were poised to burst apart. An icy cold wind blasted in from the south, buffeting the men, who pulled their cloaks tight across their chests in an effort to keep themselves warm.

Every three or four miles, the escort column passed a military signal station: small timber-walled structures encircled by earthen ramparts and sharpened wooden palisades, garrisoned by a handful of soldiers from one of the auxiliary cohorts. The fortlets were a powerful reminder of how Rome won its wars: not through reckless charges on the field of battle, but through a campaign of steady and continuous advance. As the legions pushed further and further into the land of the enemy, they set down networks of roads and earthworks and legionary bases, until their enemies had nowhere left to run. The scale of the invasion had never occurred to Figulus before but, as they continued along the rough track, he was a little in awe of what he and his fellow soldiers had accomplished on this island – and what they stood to lose should the Durotriges succeed in driving them out of their land.

On the afternoon of the third day, the detachment passed through a village situated on the border between the Regni and the Durotriges. Even here, far from the cosmopolitan surroundings of Noviomagus, there were signs of Rome's growing influence; some of the men had shaved their beards or cut their hair short in the fashion of the men from across the sea. One enterprising native had even scraped together a few sestertii and opened a small inn to serve thirsty soldiers passing through. Villagers emerged from their roundhouses to greet the soldiers, and Figulus ordered the detachment to dismount and give their horses a chance to eat and rest before continuing their journey west.

Trenagasus pulled his hood low over his head in order to disguise his identity. His arrival in Britannia was a closely guarded secret and Scylla was worried about the would-be king being recognised by any villagers who might be loyal to Quenatacus. His bodyguards clasped their hands around their sheathed sword handles as they stayed close by his side, searching the crowd for any obvious threat. But most of the villagers did not seem to notice or care about the hooded figure in their midst.

Figulus's men took the opportunity to stretch their legs, climbing down from their mounts and chewing on their rations of strips of dried beef. A few of the children waved shyly at the soldiers. The warm welcome from the locals made a pleasant change to the rancorous mood Figulus and his men had been expecting and he found himself relaxing slightly. He noticed one child watching from afar and gestured for him to approach. Then Figulus reached into his mess tin and removed a single copper coin as he dropped to a knee and prepared to play a magic trick he'd learned back in Calleva. Holding the coin between his thumb and forefinger, Figulus brought his other hand over the top of the coin and said a few magic words in Phoenician. Then he removed his hand. To his puzzlement, the single coin had failed to magically turn into a pair of bigger sestertius coins. Figulus tried the trick again, taking extra care with the magic words this time. Still the trick didn't work. After a third failed attempt, Ancasta noticed him struggling and drew alongside him.

'Here,' she said. 'Allow me.'

Taking the coin from him, Ancasta delicately placed it between her slender thumb and forefinger. The child leaned in close to get a better look. So did a clearly puzzled Figulus. Then Ancasta waved her other hand over the coin a couple of times and, without saying a single word, opened her hands to reveal a sestertius nestled in each palm. Both Figulus and the native child stared at the two coins in open-mouthed amazement. Ancasta tossed one of the coins to the delighted boy. His wide eyes instantly lit up and he clamped his hand tightly shut around the coin and raced back to his parents. Figulus looked back to Ancasta.

'But . . . how did you do that?'

'I travelled to Rome with my father when he petitioned the

Emperor to restore him to power. In the mornings, I'd head down to the forum and learn magic tricks from a Cyrenacian perfume seller. It's a city full of characters, Rome. A very . . . interesting place. Have you ever been?'

'To Rome?' Figulus shook his head. 'Afraid not, my lady. Been too busy cutting down the enemy.'

Her expression suddenly hardened. 'You mean my fellow Britons.'

'Sorry,' he spluttered, suddenly realising his mistake. 'My lady, I only meant—'

Ancasta smiled sadly. 'Don't worry, Optio. I'm perfectly aware of how Romans see my people. I know how they view natives like me, the insults they whisper behind my back when they see this.' Her fingers lightly touched the torc wrapped around her neck. 'The truth is that we Britons have done ourselves no favours.'

'How do you mean?'

'We've spent generations fighting petty wars against each other. Our rulers preferred to settle ridiculous blood feuds rather than trying to work together, so when your precious legions invaded, there was no great army to defy them, no massed ranks to stop Rome from claiming this land as its own. Our kings were too busy indulging in self-preservation to react to the threat, while our brave warriors hurled themselves at your spears and swords, choosing a glorious defeat over an ugly victory. It was ever thus in our land. So you see, Optio, I don't blame the Romans for our predicament. The blame lies squarely with our own people. We were too selfish to unify against our common foe. If I were Roman, I would have invaded too.'

Figulus shook his head firmly. 'I disagree, my lady. Caratacus opposed us, didn't he? Even came close to beating us at one point, as I recall, and he had thousands flocking to his cause from all over the island.'

'Many of whom were recruited by Catuvellaunian thugs who went from village to village, rounding up every fit young man of fighting age and forcing him to fight against his will,' Ancasta countered. 'Snatched from villages such as this one and thrown into battle with little or no training. And where is Caratacus now, do you think? Shivering on some remote mountain with those wild Silurians, his army destroyed, his titles turned to dust.' She watched the child showing his treasured coin to his mother. 'We Britons used to pride ourselves on resisting foreigners. Now we're overrun with them. It's like Father says: there's nothing we can do except try to make the best of it.'

'Rome isn't all that bad, you know.'

'Not to you, perhaps. But we are on the other side of the divide. Rome protects those it is in its best interest to protect. Everyone else must bargain – as my father has done, in exile.'

Figulus formed a deep frown. 'I'm not sure I follow.'

She smiled sympathetically, her eyes softening. 'My father is like you, in a way. He rather admires Rome and quaintly thinks Rome is here to support him, not the other way round. But the Emperor only agreed to help in return for a favour.'

'A favour?' Figulus repeated.

'Of a sort.' Ancasta fixed her smile, but her eyes were narrow and cold and reminded the optio of the gleaming tip of a knife. 'In return for helping my father become king, Rome expects his full and complete cooperation on all matters, without exception. It is what you might call a marriage of convenience, but one for which I fear my father will pay a high price. I have no wish to see him become another one of the Emperor's lap dogs, but sadly that is what he will become, eventually.'

'Why have you come back, then? If you don't agree with his decision, I mean.'

Ancasta sighed. 'Because the truth is, my father is the Durotriges' only hope. He knows that our people cannot win a war against Rome. He wants peace, as we all do, even if it must be achieved with Roman weapons. I just wish there was some other way.'

Ancasta fell silent for a few moments. She suddenly remembered the spare sestertius coin in her hand and chucked it to Figulus.

'Keep it, Optio. Perhaps one day I'll teach you a trick or two of my own.'

Their eyes met for a brief moment and she smiled softly at him. Figulus felt a hot sensation through his veins, his cheeks burning red. He quickly averted his gaze, gripped by an acute sense of embarrassment. Figulus had precious little experience of the fairer sex. There'd been an awkward fumble with a local girl the night before he joined the

Second Legion, and thereafter the occasional dalliance with a tart at a cheap brothel whenever the opportunity arose. But generally Figulus was a novice in the ways of women and he was painfully aware of his shyness in front of Ancasta. He tucked the coin into his purse for safekeeping.

A short while later, the men climbed back into their saddles and continued west. Past the village, they crossed the border into Durotrigan territory. The rough track was soon devoid of traffic and the column passed isolated farmsteads interspersed with bleak woodland, the trees bare of leaves and jutting out of the dark earth in twisted skeins against the pale sky. Dark grey clouds rumbled ominously overhead and on the fourth day the rain fell. The skies opened up in a torrential downpour, casting a veil of freezing cold raindrops over the party of Romans and Britons, soaking through their winter clothing and turning the rough track into a slithering trail of mud. The soldiers trotted on in dismal silence, the metallic patter of raindrops against their helmets and shields accompanied by the dull sloshing of horse hoofs on the puddled track. It rained all day, and ferocious storms battered the fort at Durnovaria, where they stayed overnight.

On the fifth morning, the column set off on the final leg of their journey. Every so often, they passed signs of the attacks that had blighted this troubled region: the charred remains of burnt-out supply wagons to the side of the road, and abandoned fortlets and signal stations which had been unable to defend themselves against the constant native threat. They followed the track through a gloomy valley floor, the ground underfoot slick with churned mud from the stormy weather. Trees had been uprooted and twice the men had to stop to clear the road, slowing the pace of the march. To the right of the column stood a low, forested hill, the treeline screened by a nest of birch trees and prickly gorse bushes. To the left was a narrow stream. As they trudged on, a brisk breeze picked up, rustling the long grass on the hill slope like a thousand hissing snakes. Figulus lifted his gaze to the hill and squinted at the forested crest, wondering if he had seen some glimmer of shadowed movement.

'How much further to Lindinis, do you think?' Scylla asked, drawing his horse alongside.

Figulus twisted back around in his saddle and gazed at the horizon. 'Another seven or eight miles, by my reckoning. With a bit of luck, we should reach the fort before nightfall.'

The envoy glanced nervously up at the crest of the low hill Figulus had just been gazing at. 'Are we in any danger here, Optio?'

'Hard to say. This territory is supposed to be under our control, but the area's crawling with raiding parties.'

Scylla swallowed nervously. 'What sort of raiders, exactly?'

Figulus shrugged. 'Some of them are just desperate groups of warriors who don't want to admit they're beaten. Most of 'em fled into the forests after we conquered their land. Then there are the brigands who raid for a share of the spoils. Some of the other tribes have been getting in on the act too. The Silurians and the Dumnonii have been known to launch the odd cross-border raid lately.'

Scylla's eyes went wide with alarm. 'I see.'

Their conversation was suddenly interrupted as Helva pulled back on his reins a short distance ahead of the column, drawing his mount to a halt. Figulus threw up a hand and signalled for the column to stop, then trotted forward several paces to see what had caused Helva to halt.

'Well?' Figulus asked. 'What is it, lad?'

'Think I heard something, sir,' he replied with a strained expression. 'A voice, maybe.'

Figulus steadied his mount and pricked his ears, listening intently. At first, he could hear nothing but the gentle trickle of flowing water in the river, the wind rustling the dead leaves and his horse snorting through its nostrils. Figulus frowned.

'You must be mistaken. I can't hear a bloody—'

Then a sound split the air, one that was instantly familiar to the Gaul from the battlefields of Britannia. A sound that always sent a shiver running down his spine.

The distinct braying of a Celtic war horn.

CHAPTER SIXTEEN

The men of the Sixth Century sat frozen in their saddles as the war horns sounded their strident blast once more, their horses snorting and whinnying in an agitated manner as they sensed imminent danger. In the next instant, a rasping native battle cry split the air and a line of figures appeared on the crest of the low hill to the column's right flank. Figulus counted at least a dozen of them. They brandished their Celtic long swords and spears. A handful of the natives were armed with short bows, Figulus noticed.

'Shields up and keep moving!' Figulus shouted to the column, jabbing his heels into his mount. 'Don't stop!'

Just then the Durotrigan archers unleashed their shafts at the column and there was a rattling din as several missiles smashed against hastily raised Roman shields, stopping the escort column in its tracks. As the enemy closed, the first spears were launched at the Romans and Figulus heard an agonised shriek from the rear of the column. He glanced back down the tracks to see Trenagasus's horse rear up in pain, a spear shaft protruding from its wounded flank. With a cry of fear, Trenagasus lost his grip on his reins and fell from the saddle, crashing to the muddied earth. His bodyguards leapt down from their horses and rushed to the king's side while Scylla looked on from his horse, stunned with horror. Grasping that flight was no longer possible, Figulus reined in, unsheathed his sword and shouted for the column to halt.

'Form up!' he bellowed. 'NOW!'

There was a collective rasping hiss as the men wrenched their swords free from their scabbards and turned their mounts to face the enemy rushing down the slope towards them. Figulus felt his muscles constrict with tension. Now they were closer, he saw that some of the natives wore Roman armour and gripped auxilary shields and swords looted from previous raids. They let out a savage roar as they charged out from beyond the treeline and fell upon the Romans in a frenzy of flickering sword points, weaving between the horsemen and dodging the soldiers' desperate thrusts and stabs. The legionary shields of the Roman escort were wholly unsuitable for mounted fighting, forcing the soldiers to adapt their tactics. Figulus's men slashed repeatedly at the Britons, some using their shields as weapons and hammering the metal rims down on the skulls of their nearest attackers.

A gaunt and grey-haired raider charged at Figulus, driving his thrusting Celtic sword at the optio's throat. Figulus adjusted his stance and parried the blow, deflecting the gleaming tip away from his head. With his opponent exposed, Figulus aimed a thrust towards the man's neck. But the raider easily evaded his attack and Figulus silently cursed the fact that he and his men were equipped with legionary short swords rather than the longer spatha and spear favoured by Roman cavalry. He thrust at the raider again, this time bending forward in his saddle, leaning low to maximise the range of his attack. The raider cried out in agony as the blade punched through his flesh. His weapon clattered to the ground before he fell away. Then Figulus twisted in his saddle and searched for his next enemy.

'Shit!' Rullus exclaimed. 'To the rear, sir!'

Figulus swung around and looked up towards the crest of the hill. A loose line of archers occupied the slope, but Rullus was pointing further along. Then the Gaul felt the blood turn to ice in his veins as he saw a second band of Britons streaming out of the wood further back in the direction they had ridden. They were heading directly towards Trenagasus and his entourage, pouring down the slope at a good pace as they roared their battle cries. In a matter of moments, the enemy would be on top of the king unless Figulus could stop them. He gritted his teeth and kicked his heels and galloped, grim-faced, along the side of the track towards the Britons. A man blocked his path, thrusting his sword up at an angle towards Figulus. The optio immediately jerked on the reins, parrying the blow with his sword. The Briton stumbled forward with the momentum of his attack. Now Figulus leaned low in the saddle and slashed his sword point across his enemy's stomach. The man let out a deep grunt as his bowels spewed out. He fell away and Figulus now saw that the second group of Durotrigans was descending upon Trenagasus's bodyguards. They had formed a loose circle around their king, but they were hopelessly outnumbered and three of them were cut down in quick succession. Now only a single bodyguard stood between the raiders and the king.

Figulus willed his mount on. The enemy on the hill continued blowing their war horns for all they were worth in an effort to inspire their men to victory. Arrows whirred past Figulus as the archers dotted along the slope tried to stop him before he could reach Trenagasus. He could feel the sweat prickle beneath his tunic. Ahead of him, Ancasta jumped down from her horse and grabbed a sword from one of the fallen bodyguards, then charged towards the nearest enemy, deftly evading his ragged attack before plunging the sword into his groin with the speed and precision of a trained fighter. The Durotrigan gasped in shock at being defeated by a woman. Then Ancasta gave the blade a good twist before wrenching it free.

Figulus fixed his sights on a raider making for Trenagasus. The man heard the rumbling of hoofs pounding towards him and stopped in his tracks, spinning around to see the terrifying Gaul bear down on him. Figulus aimed his sword at a point just below the man's chin and punched out with his weapon before the man could react. The blade sliced cleanly through his opponent's neck, his head snapping back with the violent impact of the blow. Figulus yanked his weapon free, a pang of satisfaction flowing through him as he watched the native fold at the waist.

The other half-dozen raiders simultaneously turned to face Figulus and he felt sure he was going to die, but he had to buy time if Trenagasus was to stand any chance of escaping the ambush. He smiled grimly to himself at that thought as he headed into the sea of enemies. With a deep roar, Figulus attacked with a frenzy of stabs and thrusts that took the Durotrigans by surprise. One native managed to break free and sprinted towards Trenagasus as he lay dazed on the ground beside his wounded horse. Ancasta lunged at the man, stabbing him in the ribs before he could attack her father. The raiders had surrounded Figulus but, just then, he heard the pounding of hoofs from behind. In the next instant, Blaesus burst forward and set upon the nearest enemy with an angry thrust, sinking his sword deep into the man's chest before tearing his blade free and slashing another native in the throat.

'Come on, then!' Blaesus rasped at the stunned attackers. 'Come and get it, you bastards!'

Figulus glanced back down the track and saw that the first band of Durotrigan raiders had been driven off, the Romans having repelled their attack. A few enemies stood their ground, picked off at will by a handful of Figulus's men. The remainder promptly turned and fled back up the hill, abandoning their stricken comrades as they realised that the ambush had failed. With the first group in retreat, several others were now free to follow Blaesus and Figulus in attacking the second band of raiders. Confusion and panic spread through their ranks and they were quickly cut down. The Romans set about routing the last of the raiders, hunting them down as if they were rats in a storehouse, and the melee quickly descended into a killing frenzy.

They set upon the retreating enemy in pell-mell fashion. Figulus swung his gaze back to Ancasta, who was tending to her stricken father. He stared at his slaughtered bodyguards, shaking his head in disbelief. A thick pool of blood had formed beneath the flank of the king's dying horse.

'Get your father up on the back of your mount,' Figulus barked at Ancasta. 'Do it now!'

The daughter wiped blood from her brow as she nodded and called for the surviving bodyguard to help Trenagasus climb on to the back of her saddle. Then Figulus turned back to search for the next enemy. But the raiders were in retreat, scrambling frantically back up the hill to shouts of anger from their leader, a shadowed figure perched on his steed atop the crest of the hill.

'Bastards are getting away!' Blaesus growled, pointing to several dark shapes hurrying towards their leader. 'We should go after them, sir!'

Figulus stood there for a moment, torn between the powerful urge to go after the surviving raiders and the need to reach the fort at

Lindinis as soon as possible. After a brief pause he shook his head. 'No. Leave them.'

Blaesus frowned. 'But, sir—'

'There's nothing more we can do,' Figulus replied forcefully. 'We're still miles from the fort. We have to leave before more of them show up.' He turned to Rullus. 'Call the men back. That's an order.'

Blaesus bit his tongue and nodded sullenly. Figulus gave the order for the column to form back up on the track. A few Durotrigans briefly stopped at a safe distance from the Romans, near the top of the slope, and resorted to hurling defiant shouts after them. Their leader shook his fist at his sworn enemy before kicking his mount and he promptly disappeared from view over the other side of the hill. The few Durotrigans left followed him. Figulus watched them go. Then he swivelled his gaze to Helva.

'Pick up our dead,' he barked. 'Secure them over the backs of the baggage mules. We'll bury them once we get to Lindinis.'

Helva nodded dutifully and set off with another soldier drawn from the ranks. Figulus took a deep breath, his chest muscles heaving with exertion. How long had the ambush lasted? It had seemed to pass in a blur of vivid impressions. His muscles ached with the stress of the fight and his blood was still pounding in his veins. He watched as the lifeless corpses of the bodyguards, servants and three soldiers were slumped over the backs of the baggage mules. They would be given proper funeral pyres later. The enemy dead would be left to rot along the track. In a day or two, the survivors would return for their fallen comrades and inter them in the earth, one of the more barbaric native customs.

As Figulus ordered the soldiers to form up, he glimpsed Scylla trembling visibly as he ran his eyes over the hilltop, fearful of a repeat attack. But Figulus knew the Durotrigans would not return, at least not for a while. Years of fighting the legions had turned the Britons into masters of the ambush and their lightning-fast attacks were followed by swift retreats into the surrounding forests before Roman reinforcements could arrive. A strategy that had proved crudely effective, Figulus reminded himself. But they could not stop the advance of the Romans through their land.

'Who did we lose in the end?' He asked Rullus as the column pushed on at a quick pace towards Lindinis.

Rullus cleared his throat. 'Laterensis, Buteo and Paetus.'

Figulus nodded quietly. 'Good lads, all of them.' He fell silent for a moment, lost in thought. Then he turned back to the veteran. 'The others?'

'A couple of the lads have got flesh wounds. Nothing serious, sir.'

'The gods were kind.'

Rullus made a face. 'The gods had nothing to do with it, sir. We fought hard and we kept our discipline, and that's the only reason we're still drawing breath instead of those bastards.'

Figulus pursed his lips. A bitter fury gripped the optio as he gave the order for the escort column to push on. He had lost three men and they had not even ousted Quenatacus yet. As he headed to the front of the column, he set a quick pace despite the risk of blowing their horses before they reached Lindinis. The light was already fading and they would have to hurry if they were to reach the fort before darkness fell.

CHAPTER SEVENTEEN

The column arrived at Lindinis in the late afternoon. Figulus experienced a palpable feeling of relief as he sighted the fort in the distance. Their horses were blown from the stress of racing away from the raiders and the pace of their journey had slowed noticeably for the last two or three miles. Here, the forested valleys gave way to a wide expanse of land set by the banks of a narrow river. The ground was waterlogged in places from where the banks had burst during the recent seasonal storms. To the sides of the track stood several abandoned farmsteads flanked by fields of unharvested crops. The weather had turned bitingly cold and Figulus could see his breath misting in front of his lips as he set his sights on the fort a mile or so further along the track to the west.

The fort had been constructed on low ground south of the river, with a bridge linking it to the opposite bank, where a road led north, paved with logs for a short distance. Observing the terrain with his keen soldier's eye, Figulus now grasped the strategic importance of Lindinis to the overall campaign. The fort provided a vital link between the new trading posts at Corinium and Aquae Sulis to the north, as well as Sorviodunum and Calleva to the east, and its location would allow it to serve as a key supply depot for the legion's planned push west in the spring. Moreover, strengthening Rome's grip on Lindinis and the surrounding region would confine Caratacus to the mountainous lands of the Silures and the Ordovices.

'Optio!' Scylla exclaimed. 'What's that over there?'

Figulus followed the envoy's pointed finger. He spotted a huge mound rising dramatically up from the plain several miles away. The earthwork extended nearly a quarter of a mile and, even at this distance, it was possible to discern the overlapping ramps and tiered earthworks encircling the vast structure. It was a breathtaking sight, one that never failed to stir mixed feelings of awe and pity in the Gaul's heart.

'That's a hill fort.' He frowned before adding, 'What's left of it, anyway.'

Scylla snorted. 'After all the stories I'd heard about them, I rather expected something more . . . grandiose.' He laughed and shook his head. 'It's a wonder their warriors held out for so long behind such crude fortifications.'

Looking at the hill fort, it was easy for Figulus to see why the natives had grown so disaffected with life under Roman rule. The once-proud fort now stood abandoned, the blackened ruins serving as a painful reminder of the Durotrigans' humiliating defeat against the men of the Second Legion.

Three shadowed figures rode towards the escort column from the fort. As they drew closer, Figulus readily identified the men as auxiliary soldiers: thickly-bearded Batavians equipped with their distinctive oval shields. The optio tugged gently on his reins, slowing his weary horse to a halt. The Batavians flicked their eyes warily from one soldier to the next, resting their palms on the pommels of their swords, ready to draw their weapons at the slightest provocation. Given that the enemy had taken to looting Roman equipment, their suspicion was well founded, Figulus conceded. The men who hailed from the northern banks of the River Rhine were renowned as fearless warriors who were without equal on the field of battle, but these soldiers appeared quite anxious. The middle rider wore plumed feathers in his helmet crest and Figulus stiffened to attention at the sight of a superior officer. The two men at the officer's shoulders kept glancing to either side, as if expecting an ambush at any moment.

'Who are you?' the officer demanded. He directed the question at Figulus.

'Optio Horatius Figulus, sir!' the big Gaul snapped and saluted, briefly explaining his mission and introducing the imperial envoy and Trenagasus. The officer eyed the latter suspiciously.

'Centurion Gaius Vibius Tuditanus,' he replied, looking back to the optio. 'Our sentries saw you approaching. Prefect Cosconianus sent me out here to escort you and your men back to the fort.'

'Bit late for that, sir,' Rullus grumbled. 'We got caught in an ambush a few miles back. Nearly did for the lot of us.'

There was no surprise on the centurion's careworn face. 'I figured as much. That road is treacherous enough without everything else that's been going on.'

'Why?' Figulus asked, frowning heavily. 'What do you mean, sir?'

Centurion Tuditanus cocked an eyebrow at the optio. 'You haven't heard, then? Quenatacus has been up to his old tricks again, stirring up trouble. Whole bloody place has gone to shit.' He shook his head. 'Prefect Cosconianus will fill you in on the details. Now, if you'll follow me, please. Best not to stay out here any longer than necessary.'

Blaesus looked startled. 'Surely you can't be under fear of attack here, sir? We're right under the noses of the fort's garrison.'

Tuditanus stared at the legionary. 'Then you don't know the Durotrigans very well. They have no fear of us, or our armies. Even our own kind are not as brave as these people.'

The centurion abruptly turned and steered his horse back down the track leading towards the fort. Figulus led the column after Tuditanus and, as they trotted along the muddy track, he turned his attention to the native settlement less than a quarter of a mile south of the fort. The embanked enclosure was surrounded by a turf rampart and an outer ditch, the familiar thatched roofs of the Celtic wattle-and-daub roundhouses faintly discernible above the rampart. Columns of dark grey smoke eddied from the rooftops into the darkening skies above. The settlement looked to be almost the same size as the hill fort, Figulus thought – except on lower ground and without the doglegged system of defences.

A short ride brought them to the main gate on the eastern side of the fort. An outer ditch and inner earthen rampart staked with sharpened wooden palisades provided defence against enemy attack, and a narrow ramp led over the ditch, up to the gate. Engineers worked at the defences, repairing shattered palisades. Figulus looked to the centurion and cocked his chin at the engineers. 'Had some trouble here?'

Tuditanus chuckled. 'A storm, Optio. It wreaked merry havoc on our defences last night. The natives got the worst of it, though. Battered quite a few of their roundhouses.'

Sentries peered cautiously down at the approaching column from the gatehouse overlooking the thick timbered gate with two auxiliaries standing guard outside. They lowered their spears at the sight of Tuditanus and there was a slight delay while one of the sentries called out to the watch commander. Figulus cast his eye around for signs of the local vicus, the bustling arrangement of wine taverns and brothels that set up for business just beyond bowshot of every fort by resourceful traders eager to make a living off the soldiers. There was nothing here but the local settlement – a sure sign that the surrounding kingdom was far from peaceful.

The gates opened. Tuditanus led the escort column into the fort and Figulus walked his horse up the ramp a few steps and through the gates, taking in his new surroundings. The neatly ordered layout was instantly familiar, as all Roman forts were constructed along the same basic principles. Just inside the gates stood the horse stables and barracks for the cavalry squadron, along with the hay-stacks to provide feed for the horses. In the middle of the fort stood the headquarters building and the infirmary, along with the granaries where the garrison's supplies would be stored for the approaching winter. On the far side of the fort were the infantry barracks. Figulus counted several barrack blocks – enough to house at least two standard cohorts. The fort was much bigger than he'd been expecting and it was clear that a larger force had previously been stationed at Lindinis.

The auxiliaries sat in small groups around the barracks. Some of them shared jugs of wine. Others played games of dice or went through the motions of cleaning their equipment. There was little sense of the usual easy ambience enjoyed by off-duty soldiers; Figulus could not help wondering at that. The Batavians, the loudest and most raucous of Rome's auxiliaries, were strangely quiet to a man. They were in a sombre mood and it was plain to see that their morale had suffered badly.

While the duty optio sent for a clerk to arrange accommodation for Trenagasus and his retinue, the soldiers were left to unpack their saddlebags and were assigned quarters in one of the empty barrack blocks. Figulus put Helva in charge of tending to the horses and ordered Rullus to oversee the men. Then he joined Scylla and followed Tuditanus to the prefect's quarters, his muscles aching dully with tiredness and his belly growling with hunger. He'd hoped for a brief rest upon reaching Lindinis, spurred on those last few miles by the prospect of a hot meal and a warm bed. But now those simple pleasures would have to wait.

Tuditanus led the men across the parade ground towards the headquarters building. They were shown into a cramped room, dimly lit by tallow lamps, with wooden planks covering the dirt floor. A cleanly shaven man wearing an embroidered cloak sat moodily behind a desk overflowing with scrolls and wax tablets. Tuditanus cleared his throat, announcing the arrival of his two guests, and the prefect arose stiffly from his chair. A gold signet ring gleamed on one of his fingers, Figulus noted. Unlike most of the men under his command, Cosconianus was a Roman citizen by birth, as was the case with most senior officers in charge of auxiliary regiments. The prefect formed a tired smile at the imperial envoy, ignoring Figulus.

'A pleasure to make your acquaintance, sir,' he said. 'I understand you ran into a spot of bother on the road.'

'A few raiders,' Figulus replied first, puffing out his chest. 'Nothing me and the lads couldn't handle, sir.'

'The optio saved our lives,' Scylla pointed out. 'As well as that of King Trenagasus. It's safe to say, if it hadn't been for his efforts, we wouldn't have escaped. We owe him a great debt.'

Cosconianus forced a smile. 'Good job, Optio.'

Figulus started to explain the purpose of their mission but Cosconianus threw up a slender hand and gestured for him to be silent.

'I know why you're here. You've come to oust that troublesome wretch Quenatacus and install your own man in his place.'

Scylla frowned. 'How did you come to know of this, Prefect? Trenagasus's arrival in Britannia is a secret, privy to only a select few, and I'm certain your name was not among them.'

Cosconianus stopped smiling. 'It's a secret no more, I'm afraid.'

Scylla stared coldly at the prefect. 'Please go on.'

The prefect straightened his back. 'I have bad news, gentlemen.

124

Quenatacus has learned that he's to be replaced as king – by the man he ousted from power, no less.'

'From who?' Scylla demanded.

'Not from anyone inside this fort,' Cosconianus countered defensively. 'We didn't even know about the plan until this morning, when Quenatacus kicked up a bloody great fuss.'

The envoy screwed up his face into a scowl. 'Someone must have passed word to Quenatacus. Someone from within our camp.' He shook his head. 'Tell me exactly what happened, Prefect.'

Cosconianus shifted. 'I dispatched a team of engineers into Lindinis to repair the damages done to the settlement during the storm. One of those acts of building good relations that General Plautius is always going on about,' he sniffed. 'My engineers happened to be trapped inside right at the moment Quenatacus learned of your man's arrival. His supporters surrounded the engineers and herded them into a cattle byre, which they set fire to. Poor bastards burned alive. Quenatacus has publicly denounced Trenagasus as a puppet ruler and is inciting the whole settlement to rise up against us. He's even trying to drum up support in some of the outlying settlements under his rule.'

Scylla stroked his chin. 'I see. And where is Quenatacus in all this?'

The prefect shrugged. 'Bottled up in his enclosure with his loyal bodyguards, I imagine.'

'You're quite certain he hasn't fled?'

Cosconianus shook his head. 'My scouts are patrolling the area, arresting any warriors from other settlements who might try to join his cause. They would've seen Quenatacus if he tried to leg it. Anyway, that's not his style, apparently. He's one of those bloody-minded natives who would much prefer to fight, regardless of the odds stacked against him.'

Scylla narrowed his gaze at the prefect. 'Why have you done nothing to prevent this unfortunate chain of events?'

Cosconianus visibly bristled at the envoy's remark. 'I had no idea if the rumours about a king to replace Quenatacus were true, until you showed up. If I'd gone and arrested Quenatacus before there was someone to replace him, it would have caused chaos. The natives are restless enough as it is.'

'Fine,' Scylla conceded. 'But if his opposition to Rome has won him support from further afield, as you suggest, then any move to unseat him will be much riskier.'

'The other chiefs could throw their weight behind him,' Figulus offered, his mind racing with thoughts. 'The tribal factions normally can't stand each other, but they set aside their differences when it comes to Rome. They hate us all the same. Once they hear that we've tried to knock Quenatacus on the head, they might respond to his calls for help.'

'Then it's clear what we must do,' Scylla declared. 'Since Quenatacus has been forewarned, we must remove him before he has an opportunity to further entrench his position. There's no time to lose. Trenagasus must be installed as the new king this evening.' He turned to Figulus. 'Optio, you and your men will accompany Trenagasus to Lindinis at once. You'll enter through the gates, escort him to the royal hall at the heart of the settlement and forcibly remove Quenatacus from power. Cosconianus will accompany you with a century of men.'

The prefect tried not to look alarmed. He cleared his throat uneasily. 'Are you mad?' he asked anxiously. 'Going in with just a century of men . . . There's thousands of angry natives in that settlement.'

'Farmers and women, mostly, I believe,' the envoy responded dismissively. He flashed a thin smile at Cosconianus. 'Hardly a match for the battle-hardened Batavians under your command, I should think. Besides, we must refrain from any heavy-handed tactics around the natives. The people of Lindinis are already hostile to our presence and we must be careful not to do anything that might tip them into outright rebellion. A heavy show of force could provoke the chief's supporters into doing something foolish.'

The prefect opened his mouth to protest but Scylla cut him off.

'I am giving you an order in my capacity as the official representative of His Majesty, Emperor Claudius, and you will obey me.'

The prefect stood there in stunned silence for a moment, burning with outrage at being ordered about by a freedman. Then he remembered who he was talking to and the damage he could do to

126

his future political career by crossing the Emperor's trusted freedman. He lowered his head. 'As you wish.'

'Glad to hear it. Your rules of engagement are to attack only those who attack you first, and then only using appropriate force. I don't want your men provoking a reaction from the natives.' Scylla looked to Figulus. A cruel smile formed on his thin lips. 'Capture Quenatacus alive, if you can. A very public execution of the deposed chief would serve as a highly effective warning to any other tribal leaders considering rising up against Rome.'

'And if he refuses?' Figulus asked.

'Then kill him,' Scylla responded flatly. He clasped his hands together. 'Now, if that's everything, I suggest you both prepare your men. It's time we got rid of Quenatacus once and for all.'

CHAPTER EIGHTEEN

As the light began to fade, the soldiers left the fort and marched across the sodden ground towards Lindinis. Figulus and the thirteen surviving men of the Sixth Century detachment were joined by the century of Batavians led by Prefect Cosconianus. A compromise had been reached with Scylla, and the rest of the garrison was under arms and ready to intervene if called on. Trenagasus marched behind Figulus and his men. The king was accompanied by his remaining bodyguard, as well as Ancasta, who had been steadfast in her insistence that she accompany her father on his return to Lindinis. Scylla had elected to remain at the fort, claiming that he needed time to compose the king's speech for the following day and tend to preparations for his banquet, although Figulus suspected that the envoy was eager to stay at a safe distance from the settlement in case the Romans encountered fierce opposition when they tried to remove Quenatacus.

The ground underfoot was sodden, making it difficult for the soldiers to maintain a brisk marching pace and, as they headed for the native settlement, their breath steamed in front of their faces. A soft orange orb glowed dully in the overcast sky and the air was perfectly still and silent apart from the soft squelch of boots and the faint metallic clink of each man's kit.

Rullus noticed Figulus frowning. 'What are you thinking, sir?'

'Should've eaten a bite back at the fort,' came the optio's reply. 'I'm starving.'

Rullus threw back his head and laughed. 'We're about to enter a town full of Durotrigans, who'd like nothing better than to cut us up, and all you can think about is food.'

Figulus shrugged. 'Nothing worse than going into a fight on an empty stomach.'

He fixed his gaze on the settlement to the south. A hundred or so paces away stood the main gate, flanked by a pair of stone towers. As they drew closer, a Briton stationed in one of the towers sighted the soldiers and raised the alarm. Cosconianus halted and threw up a hand a few short steps from the entrance, signalling for the men to stop. Then he sent forward an auxiliary, well versed in the local dialect, to speak to the Briton in the watchtower and demand that the gate be opened, or the people of the settlement would be forced to face the consequences of defying the order of a Roman officer. After a terse exchange, the Briton shouted for the gate to be opened and Figulus stood in line behind the auxiliaries, grasping his shield handle tightly. In the corner of his eye, he glimpsed Helva staring, grim-faced, at the main gate, his hand shaking. He tried to think of a few words of encouragement to put the recruit's mind at ease.

'Easy there, lad. Just remember, they're more scared of you than you are of them.'

'Really?' Helva tried to steady his trembling voice as a series of shouts rang out from deep inside the settlement. 'Doesn't sound that way to me, sir.'

Figulus shook his head. 'Don't forget, we're the ones who kicked their arses last summer. The Durotrigans might hate our guts, but to them we're bad news. They can shout and make all the fuss they want, they won't dare try it on.'

Helva nodded uncertainly. 'I hope you're right, sir.'

The gate groaned open on its hinges and Cosconianus gave the order for the men to enter the settlement. The auxiliaries entered first, followed by Trenagasus and his escort, with Figulus and his men bringing up the rear of the column. The soldiers stared ahead with grim determination as they advanced into a teeming wide thorough-fare, a sprawl of native roundhouses, barns and cattle byres on either side. Heaped mounds of animal dung were stacked outside the wattle-and-daub houses, the foul stench hanging in the air. Geese and chickens freely roamed the streets, pecking at the dirt. Some of the locals did their best to ignore the soldiers, their eyes rooted firmly to the ground as they hurried back to their huts and slammed their doors shut. Others simply stared at Trenagasus. A few natives hurled abuse at the new king from the shadows and Figulus could feel the tension, thick as a blanket.

At the end of the crude street stretching through the native settlement, Figulus glimpsed a larger building with a conical roof, set into a separate enclosure: the hall of the tribe's king. A small crowd of enraged Durotrigans had gathered in front of the royal hall, glaring at the soldiers with undisguised hatred.

'Looks like Quenatacus's lot have come to give us a nice, friendly welcome,' Rullus remarked. He pricked his ears as the Durotrigans hurled abuse at the soldiers in their native tongue. 'What're they saying, sir?'

Figulus frowned. 'Something about us being dogs . . . or sons . . . No, that's not it. We're the sons of dogs, I think.'

Rullus looked at him. 'You mean "sons of bitches"?'

'Scum!' Blaesus spat. 'I'll soon show 'em.'

He went to unsheathe his sword but Figulus thrust out a hand and shook his head. 'Don't, Blaesus! We're not to do anything that might piss off the locals, remember.'

Blaesus reluctantly took his hand away from his sword and spat on the ground. 'Load of bollocks, if you ask me, sir. This lot could do with being roughed up a bit. Put them in their place.'

Figulus clamped his lips shut. He fully agreed with the legionary, but the rules of engagement had been set by the envoy and the men were under orders to follow them. The mood among the natives was even more poisonous than Figulus had imagined. A few rasped curses at the prefect and his men while others called on their foreign gods to smite the Romans down where they stood. Someone in the crowd tossed a clay jug at the soldiers and the drinking vessel shattered against an auxiliary's bronze helmet, prompting a full-throated cheer from the crowd. The Batavian stumbled backwards from his comrades, stunned. Cosconianus yelled for his auxiliaries to push on towards the royal hall and not to give in to provocation from the crowd. Figulus and Rullus now closed ranks around Trenagasus, their shields raised to protect the king from the objects being hurled at the party. Trenagusus stared ahead, stony-faced, wilfully ignoring the cries from the natives for him to return to Narbonensis, his daughter marching faithfully by his side.

The men stopped in front of the royal hall at the end of the street. As they drew near, several broad-shouldered figures emerged from the compound, their naked torsos rippling with taut muscle. They wielded spears in two-handed grips and Figulus quickly identified these men as the chief's bodyguards. They stared with silent menace at the soldiers before them, then parted in the middle. A taller man now stepped forward. A dark cloak was draped over his shoulders, fastened at the shoulder with a golden brooch, and a Celtic long sword with an intricately decorated hilt hung from his belt. Quenatacus. Trenagasus stepped forward with Figulus and the rest of his men to greet Quenatacus while the auxiliaries spread out across the street, flanking the king and his party. The present ruler of the Durotrigan nation folded his arms across his chest and glowered at Trenagasus, his green eyes glowing brightly, as if a fire raged behind them.

'Trenagasus! You dare to show your face in my kingdom?' he said in his guttural native tongue. Then he narrowed his eyes at Figulus. 'You've made some new friends, I see. I should've known you would have gone begging to our enemies like a dog. It is all that can be expected of a traitor.'

Trenagasus cleared his throat. He tried to steady his voice as he addressed his rival. 'Quenatacus, I have come to reclaim what is mine. As the true ruler of my people, I command you to stand down at once. Order your bodyguards to surrender their arms and I promise no harm will come to you or your men.'

Quenatacus chuckled meanly and spat on the ground. 'Promises are worthless when they are uttered by a Roman lap dog.' He cocked his head at the crowd. 'Look around you, Trenagasus. I am the true leader of these people now. They answer to my word, not yours. You should've stayed in exile, studying your precious Greek poetry. You do not belong here anymore.'

'I am the king!' Trenagasus intoned, shaking his fist at Quenatacus. 'It is my birthright. My ancestors have ruled over this kingdom for centuries. Your claim is baseless. You forced me out at the point of a sword . . . you and those scheming Druids.'

Quenatacus formed his features into a wicked snarl. 'And how is

131

that different to your new friends, Trenagasus? The Romans have invaded our lands, captured or killed our rulers and imposed their ways upon us. Those who resist, such as Caratacus, are hunted like dogs. Those who choose to side with Rome become pathetic lackeys, stripped of all power and dignity, like that fool Cogidubnus.'

Trenagasus shook his head. 'The Romans bring order, and a better way of life. I have seen with my own eyes in Narbonensis what they have done for the people there. Our tribe will be better off with Rome's influence.'

Quenatacus suddenly exploded with rage. 'Lies! All of it! You're a traitor to your people, Trenagasus, no better than the Roman scum you choose to do business with, and yet you dare to come marching in here with our sworn enemies, demanding to be returned to power. As Cruach is my witness, these people will never accept you as their ruler, just as I will never surrender to you!'

The king looked momentarily lost for words. Ancasta stepped forward and addressed Quenatacus on his behalf. 'Stand down now,' she urged, throwing a hand in the direction of Figulus, 'or I swear by all the gods, these men will remove you by force.'

Quenatacus quickly composed his features and stared at the daughter with a mixture of amusement and hatred. 'I don't think so, woman.'

'I am your king!' Trenagasus snapped. His cheeks flushed with colour, and Figulus saw that the king was losing his patience. 'I carry the backing of the imperial authority of His Majesty, Emperor Claudius. Who do you have, Quenatacus? A few ignorant supporters!'

Quenatacus smirked at the king but did not reply. At that moment, a shadowed figure emerged from the royal hall and moved towards the native chief. This man was dressed in long dark robes and he wore a thick matted beard, with his wild hair tied in a ponytail at the back. Figulus felt a thrill of terror as he realised this man was a Druid. He stopped next to the native chief and glared at Figulus with his stony grey eyes. The Druid abruptly turned and whispered a few words to the chief. Quenatacus nodded, then unsheathed his sword and thrust it at the sky, shouting a Durotrigan battle cry at the top of his voice.

Rullus frowned. 'What the fuck is he up to?'

Before Figulus could answer, a vast throng of native Britons streamed out from between the clusters of roundhouses on both sides of the street and charged at the soldiers, responding to their chief's signal. Figulus spun to face the onrushing enemy. The Durotrigans were armed with a mixture of weapons and farm tools and they screamed ferociously as they attacked the stunned auxiliaries; Figulus realised with a jolt of horror that the soldiers had walked into a deadly trap.

'Stand firm!' Cosconianus bellowed. 'Shields up and close ranks!'

The Batavians hurriedly split into two lines, forming up into shield walls either side of the street to confront the onrushing natives. One man launched at Trenagasus, thrusting his sword towards the king. The bodyguard stepped into the way, taking the blow to his chest and saving the man he'd been sworn to protect with his dying breath. Trenagasus stared at his bodyguard in horror before Cosconianus pulled him back between the two shielded lines of auxiliaries. At the same time, another man hacked and slashed at Ancasta, who neatly evaded his attacks. Figulus bolted over and knocked the native down with a punch of his shield. Then he grabbed Ancasta by the arm and hauled her towards the ranks of auxiliaries. She stopped for a moment and stooped down to pick up the unconscious native's sword.

A seemingly endless stream of attackers poured forward from the shadows, launching themselves at the auxiliaries. Cosconianus's men hunched low behind their shields, keeping the Durotrigans at bay with the occasional stab or thrust. The air was filled with the brittle clatter of the natives' crude weapons clashing against sturdy Roman shields. Above the noise, Figulus heard the Druid loudly imploring the Durotrigans not to stop until every Roman in sight was dead. The auxiliary shield walls were holding firm but the sheer weight of numbers pressing down on them meant they were unable to extricate themselves from the attack. Figulus saw one Briton wrenching a shield from a wounded auxiliary. Several natives reached out and dragged the despairing soldier away from his comrades, the man screaming for help before he disappeared under a flurry of blows.

'Shit!' Blaesus cried out to Figulus, pointing back down the street. 'Sir, the gate!'

Figulus spun around. His muscles constricted with dread as

he saw a band of natives heaving the gate shut and fastening the locking bar in place, trapping the soldiers inside the settlement. Cosconianus and his men had failed to notice the trap being set for them: they were occupied with attackers hurling themselves at their lines. Figulus gritted his teeth. With the gate shut, the reinforcements at the garrison would be unable to reach their comrades inside the settlement. Unless the gate was opened, the entire party of soldiers was in danger of being overrun. He turned to Rullus.

'We've got to get back to the gate,' he said in as calm a voice as possible. 'Otherwise, we're dead. If we stay here, we'll be cut down soon enough.'

Rullus nodded. Both men knew that reinforcements would already be on the way. The sentries at the fort were under orders to observe the goings-on at the settlement and they would have sounded the warning to the rest of the garrison as soon as the gates had been slammed shut. Rullus smiled grimly.

'It's about time we taught these bastards a lesson.'

Figulus rounded up his men. Once he'd made sure that Trenagasus and Ancasta were protected behind the auxiliary ranks, he turned and led the way back along the thoroughfare, trotting down the street in close formation with his legionary comrades. He was determined to reach the gate before those in command of the native mob grasped what was happening. The lives of his men, and the fate of the province, depended on it.

A heavyset native, covered in tattoos, spotted the optio and moved to block his path. He was gripping a club studded with iron spikes and he swung it at Figulus. In a blur of movement, the optio sprang forward and punched his shield boss into the man's face, shattering his nose. The native man howled in pain as he fell away, the club clattering to the ground as he pawed at his bloodied face. Figulus stabbed him through the neck before he could pick himself up off the ground.

One of the Britons by the gates heard his fellow native's anguished cry and looked up. Spotting Figulus and the other soldiers, he alerted his companions. They turned to face the Romans bearing down on them. Those who had swords hefted them up. The rest grabbed their scythes and sickles and clubs.

134

'On me!' the Gaul thundered as he raced towards the gate.

The men of the Sixth Century followed his lead and charged at the Durotrigans, shields hefted up, stabbing at exposed flesh with the points of their legionary swords. The enemy was pinned between the gate and the Romans and they answered by attacking with even more fervour than usual, despite their inferior weaponry. Figulus heard a gasp of pain to his right and he glanced across his shoulder to see a Briton driving his long sword down behind a legionary shield and piercing the neck of the man hunched behind it. The soldier shuddered wildly as the blade punched through his throat and he fell to his knees, mouthing a silent curse to the Briton as blood spewed out of the deep gash in his neck and splattered down his chest armour and tunic.

Figulus pressed on, cutting his way through the natives standing guard in front of the gate. A Briton armed with a scythe stood in front of the heavy bracket securing the locking bar in place. The man bared his teeth at Figulus then swept the long curved blade low in front of him in a sudden, violent blur. The Gaul saw the blade glinting beneath the blue hue of winter twilight and lowered his shield, deflecting the blow. His shield shuddered as the cutting edge slammed against the metal rim. The Briton grunted and swung again, aiming the blade towards the optio's neck. Figulus dropped to his haunches and ducked the blow. The blade narrowly missed his head by a couple of inches, the metal swooshing as it sliced through his helmet crest. Then Figulus sprung forward, crashing into the native with his shield and knocking him down. The optio shot to his feet and plunged his sword into the Briton's stomach. The man let out a deep grunt of pain as the blade tip tore deep into his guts, slicing the man's intestines. Figulus looked around him and saw that his fellow soldiers had rapidly overpowered the other natives, for the loss of two men.

'Get the fucking gate open!' he bellowed.

To his left, Helva dropped his shield and raced towards the locking bar. There was a deep groan as the young legionary slid it out of its heavy bracket. Blaesus and Rullus then grabbed hold of the gate and the heavy timbers made a loud grumbling noise as the gate began to swing inwards. Figulus could hear the voices of the approaching Batavians outside the town, urging their comrades within to open the

135

gate at once so they could get stuck into the enemy. As soon as a narrow opening appeared the first reinforcements streamed through, racing down the street towards Cosconianus. The reinforcements slashed mercilessly at the first natives they encountered. Those who had been attacking Cosconianus's men suddenly found themselves caught between two bands of auxiliaries, and they stood little chance against the Batavians keen to avenge their butchered treachery.

As the tide of battle turned in their favour, Figulus spied Quenatacus looking on from his position in front of the tall oak doors guarding the entrance to the royal hall. His bodyguards tried pulling him back, begging for him to retreat from the action. But Quenatacus shrugged off their attempts to spirit him away and defiantly stood his ground alongside his Druid ally.

'The enemy chief!' Figulus pointed him out to his fellow soldiers. 'Get the chief!'

Drawing in a deep lungful of air, Figulus raced forward, making for the royal hall. The Britons were in disarray by this time, fighting for their lives in desperate clusters across the settlement, and he swept past them and pushed on past the maze of native huts, his heart beating inside his chest. He glimpsed Ancasta by her father's side, sinking her blade into a wounded Briton as the battle turned into a decisive rout. Beads of sweat lined Figulus's brow, drenching the felt lining of his helmet. Behind him he could hear the erratic breathing of the surviving men of the Sixth Century, the pounding of their boots on the frozen street, the clinking of their scabbards against their kit.

The bodyguards instantly turned and charged at the Romans in a last, desperate effort to protect their chief. Quenatacus lunged at Figulus, the veins bulging on his thick forearm muscles as his body trembled with rage, the light from the torches in front of the hall faintly revealing the scowl on his scarred face. Quenatacus let out a savage roar. Then he drove his long sword at the optio's throat with a brutal combination of strength and speed. Figulus parried the blow with an upward heft of his shield, deflecting the thrust at the last possible instant then shrinking back behind his shield. The chief roared as the bodyguards engaged the other soldiers in single combat, thrusting their spears at the legionaries and keeping them pegged back, out of sword range. Quenatacus ripped off his cloak to reveal a muscular chest. Then he snarled and spat on the ground in front of Figulus.

'Roman scum!' he hissed in his own tongue.

'Come and get me . . .' Figulus answered in the same dialect.

The chief stood up straight and narrowed his beady eyes at Figulus in surprise. Then he shook his head and charged at the Gaul once more, this time angling his thrust low, towards his opponent's groin. Figulus read the attack and deflected it by sweeping his shield in a broad arc in front of his chest. The sword point clanged as it glanced off the shield boss and veered to the left of the optio, the momentum of the thrust carrying Quenatacus forward half a step and exposing his torso to attack. Figulus dropped low and aimed at the chief's leg, not wanting to kill the man but just disable him. Quenatacus hissed sharply between gritted teeth as his opponent's sword point slashed open a deep, bloody wound on his thigh.

To the optio's disbelief, the chief stayed on his feet and fought through the pain, launching a vicious drive at Figulus, slamming his blade against the Gaul's shield with such fury the latter felt the handle shudder in his sturdy grip. Quick as a striking snake, Quenatacus lashed out again, kicking his good leg at the base of Figulus's shield and tipping it forward. Figulus felt his grip loosen. Now Quenatacus clamped a thick hand down on the metal rim of the shield and pulled it further forward, following through with a sharp blow to the side of the optio's helmet with the base of his sword. Figulus briefly saw white and tasted blood in his mouth. His sword fell uselessly from his hand. Then he felt the handle slide free of his grip as Quenatacus wrenched the shield away from him.

'Now you're mine!' he rasped, twisting his features into a savage grin at his defenceless opponent.

He lunged at Figulus but, in the same movement, the optio dived to the left, rolling out of the line of attack and reaching for his dropped sword. Clasping his hand firmly around the pommel, Figulus sprang up and slammed the sword handle against the chief's spine. There was a sharp sound like a branch snapping in two and Quenatacus groaned, reflexively letting go of his long sword. The chief doubled over and Figulus kicked him to the ground, rolling him on to his front. Quenatacus looked up at the Gaul, blinking.

'Lights out for you,' Figulus said.

He slammed the pommel of his sword into the chief's face. Quenatacus groaned, his eyes rolling into the back of his head as his body went limp. Around Figulus, the last bodyguards now surrendered, seeing that the man they had sworn to protect had been felled. One or two tried to flee, but Blaesus led the men after them and they were hacked down before they could escape through the royal hall. Figulus got slowly to his feet and caught his breath. The fighting began to stop as word of Quenatacus's capture spread through the settlement and even the most blindly faithful of the natives could see that the game was up. Most dropped whatever makeshift weapons they were holding and surrendered to the Batavians. A few foolhardy individuals turned and ran, hoping to hide amid the roundhouses. The rest were cut down without mercy. As the last man fell, there was a fleeting sense of stillness in the narrow streets of Lindinis and the pounding in Figulus's ears drowned out the moans of the wounded and the soft sigh of the evening breeze.

It was over, Figulus told himself. Quenatacus's attempted revolt had been crushed.

He blinked the salty sweat from his eyes and looked to Rullus. The two men exchanged a knowing glance, both thinking exactly the same thing. But only Figulus said it out loud.

'Bloody Hades, that was close.'

CHAPTER NINETEEN

Later that evening, Figulus was summoned to the imperial envoy's quarters. The sun had set and the horizon was a burning orange hue, highlighting the bare limbs of distant trees. The Roman wounded men were carried by stretcher bearers, or made their own way, to the fort's infirmary to be treated by the physician and his small staff of assistants. They struggled to keep pace with the number of men requiring their attention and did their best to treat the injuries of those who would live and ease the passing of the mortally wounded. An orderly went along the line of the wounded, stooping down to examine the severity of each man's injuries and making notes on a waxed slate of whether the man was a priority case for treatment or if he could wait a little longer.

As Figulus left his quarters in the barracks block, he spotted the prisoners they had taken, on their knees in the street outside the headquarters block. Their wrists and ankles had been bound tightly with rope and their faces hung low, their shoulders sagging despondently. There had to be at least forty of them, Figulus noted – too many to accommodate within the small guardhouse inside the fort. Quenatacus himself was being held in a private cell adjacent to the headquarters building, away from his faithful followers.

Figulus found Scylla in a comfortably furnished room at headquarters. A bearskin rug provided modest warmth against the shivering evening cold and Figulus looked enviously at the steaming bowl of stew resting on the envoy's study table. Scylla gestured to a stool opposite his table. He seemed in good spirits and poured two cups of wine, one of which he handed to Figulus.

'From Campania,' he said. 'The good stuff. From the prefect's own stocks.' He smiled broadly and proposed a toast. 'Congratulations are in order, Optio. Quenatacus is deposed and in our custody. We're now free to install Trenagasus as king. It's all gone to plan, in the end.'

'I suppose so,' Figulus replied moodily, staring at the wine in his cup and thinking of the men he'd lost in a single day of combat. Three had perished at the ambush outside Lindinis. A further two had died retaking the gates. He tried to console himself with the knowledge that, if he and his men hadn't reopened the gate, their losses would have been significantly higher. He looked up at the envoy sampling a taste of the wine.

'Does this mean we're free to return to the Second?' he asked.

Scylla set down his wine cup and winced. 'I'm afraid not. You and your men are needed here, for a while at least.' He met the optio's puzzled gaze and smiled again. 'Trenagasus is in need of a bodyguard, since his own men were killed during the ambush. I've decided you fit the bill.'

'Why me?' Figulus asked.

'Why you?' Scylla cocked an eyebrow. 'You saved the king's life today, that's why! Not once, but twice! Who better to provide a reassuring presence at his side? I'm sure you will make a fine job of it.'

'There are natives who can be trained for that,' Figulus responded.

'Ah, but none we can trust quite as well as you, Optio. It's a bit like the German bodyguards who stick close to the side of the Emperor. Ironic how many leaders dare not trust their compatriots to protect them.' Scylla twisted the cup in his hands, savouring its warmth as he studied the Gaul. Figulus tried to mask his irritation. He had been looking forward to a few days of rest in Lindinis before rejoining the Second Legion. Now he was facing the prospect of an entire winter cooped up in this miserable little corner of the province. The envoy continued, 'There is, however, a more pressing reason for keeping you on.'

'What's that?'

Scylla took another sip of the wine, savouring its taste. Figulus just swigged from his cup indifferently as the freedman continued.

'We captured that Druid accompanying Quenatacus. One of the

auxiliaries caught him trying to sneak out of the settlement during the skirmish. I've had one of Cosconianus's men loosen his tongue. He's provided us with some valuable information.'

Figulus waited for him to continue. Scylla folded his spindly arms across his chest.

'The Druid has informed us of a plot to assassinate Trenagasus. According to this Druid, a secretive sect called the Dark Moon Lodge is planning the death of our man. I don't suppose you've heard of them, Optio?'

Figulus pursed his lips as he cast his mind back to Vectis and the Druid commander who'd led the attack on the village. He remembered the tattoo he'd seen on the Druid's forehead – a distinct black crescent moon. He nodded and listened as Scylla went on.

'We had previously assumed that the Dark Moon Lodge had been eliminated during Vespasian's march through the kingdom. But according to our prisoner, the surviving Druids are presently uniting around a new leader. A young priest by the name of Calumus. His followers call him the Blood Priest. Something to do with offering his enemies to the gods by ritual sacrifice.'

As he stood in the envoy's quarters, Figulus felt a growing sense of unease twisting like a knife inside his guts. First the Druid they'd captured in Lindinis. Now this talk of the Dark Moon Lodge sect on the rise again, and the mention of a young new Druid priest. There seemed to be no end of trouble caused by the Druids in the new province. He shook his head clear of the troubling thought as Scylla continued, sniffing his wine.

'Apparently, Calumus has been quietly building up his influence in the region. That explains why our Batavian friends are so nervy. They've been on edge these past few months, swapping horror stories about the Druids. In particular, their penchant for horrifically torturing those soldiers unfortunate enough to be taken alive.'

'The auxiliaries might be unnerved,' Figulus responded gruffly, 'but the Druids don't scare me.'

The envoy responded with a delicately raised eyebrow. 'A few wild-eyed barbarians peddling their obscure beliefs? I should hope not. Nevertheless, we must take any threats to our interests seriously. Calumus has apparently foretold the death of our ambitions on British soil and to that end he's calling on his followers to murder Trenagasus.'

Figulus scratched his cheek as he thought back to earlier in the day. 'Those raiders who ambushed us this morning – were they following the Druid's orders?'

'According to the prisoner, yes. From what he's told me, however, their failed attempt won't deter them from trying again. Indeed, he claims they're already plotting their next attack on Trenagasus.'

'So the king's never going to be safe?'

'Not for a while,' Scylla conceded. 'Until then, we must take the threat of assassination seriously. The Druids are fanatics who will go to any lengths to achieve their aims.'

'Sounds about right,' Figulus mused.

'Which is why I am assigning you and your men to be bodyguards to the king. The nature of the threat, and the importance of the target, means we need skilled men to protect him, not the usual tired old warriors or retired gladiators looking for a quick pay. You will have to protect Trenagasus and stay by his side at all times. At least until we can find out where Calumus and his army of Druid followers are hiding themelves, and then crush them.'

Figulus felt his heart sink. Winter in the barren fringes of the province, far removed from the pleasure houses and drinking holes of Calleva, was a grim prospect. Worse, he'd have to spend his every waking moment shadowing an aloof puppet leader despised by all those natives who'd supported Quenatacus. He couldn't think of anything worse. But nor could he refuse an order from the imperial envoy. With a heavy sigh, he nodded at Scylla and resigned himself to a brutal winter in Lindinis.

'What about my men?' he asked.

'They will stay too, if that's what you mean. Three watches of four men will guard Trenagasus day and night. We'll train the locals to act as his permanent bodyguard, once we know who among them we can trust. That will also be a good way of keeping an eye on the natives. Even after our arrests, there will inevitably be some of Quenatacus's supporters who have slipped away. They'll be planning revenge, and I imagine volunteering for a spot on the king's bodyguard. That would be as good a way as any to get close enough to Trenagasus to kill him.'

Figulus nodded briskly. 'When do we start?'

'Tomorrow. I'll brief you in more detail in the morning. However, your first task will be to guard Trenagasus when he addresses the natives as their new ruler. The speech will be followed by a banquet to celebrate his new regime, attended by the chiefs from the outlying settlements. Trenagasus is hoping to find a suitable young noble to marry his daughter and extend his influence. You and your men will be by the king's side throughout the ceremony.' A thought flickered behind his eyes. 'That reminds me. We shall have to get rid of all the signs of this evening's struggle first.'

Figulus listened but said nothing. He could already foresee that this would not be an easy task. Protecting a hated new king on his supposedly celebrated return, less than a day after the natives had fiercely resisted the removal of the previous ruler . . . There would be threats from every direction, not just the Dark Moon Druids. Protecting Trenagasus from attack was a nightmare prospect. He sighed and waited for Scylla to dismiss him.

'I'll send for you in the morning, once I've gone through the programme of events with Trenagasus. Tomorrow we begin the task of turning this truculent tribe into Rome's newest British ally,' the envoy said as he reached for his cup of wine. 'I expect you to protect the king at all costs, Optio. The future of this province is not yet safe, nor will it be until Lindinis is successfully Romanised. That requires Trenagasus to make sweeping changes. Some of those will not be popular and he will inevitably make enemies. But should you fail to protect him, our bid to secure the Durotrigan people will be in tatters. We will lose control of their lands and hand the initiative back to Caratacus. He'll drive a wedge through the heart of the province and that is the kind of blow from which Rome is unlikely to recover. Do you understand?'

Figulus nodded.

'Good, because if you let me down, then I can assure you that you will not live to see your precious Second Legion ever again.'

CHAPTER TWENTY

'Three sixes!' Blaesus exclaimed at breakfast the following day, punching a fist in the air in celebration. 'Yes!'

Figulus stared down in dismay at the three dice lying on the trestle table in the soldiers' mess. The optio shook his head and muttered a curse to the gods at his bad luck. Around the table the ten other legionaries from the detachment looked on in hushed concentration as they waited for Figulus to take his turn. On the next roll of the dice rested a hundred sestertii, equivalent to almost a month's salary for a junior officer in the ranks of the Second Legion.

The previous evening had passed without incident. After Figulus had left the headquarters building he'd returned to the barracks and quickly briefed his men, before falling into a troubled sleep. He'd awoken early that morning and headed over to the mess with his comrades for a hot breakfast. The mess was unusually quiet. The majority of the Batavian cohort garrisoned at the fort had departed for the settlement at first light, under orders from Scylla to police the natives ahead of the day's planned instalment of the new ruler of the Durotriges. All evidence of the struggle to remove the previous incumbent had to be cleared away before the celebrations could begin and only a single depleted century now remained inside the fort.

With nothing further to do until the briefing with Scylla, Figulus had decided to pass the time with a few games of dice against the Sixth Century's unofficial gambling champion. He'd insisted on inspecting the dice before the game began, in case Blaesus tried to cheat him by using weighted ones. And now Figulus was on the cusp of defeat.

Blaesus leaned back and gestured to the playing dice, grinning through his straggly beard. 'Your turn, sir.'

Clenching his teeth in frustration, Figulus scooped up the dice and dropped them into the clay cup shaker. A tense silence descended over the legionaries as Figulus clamped a hand over the mouth of the cup.

Silently whispering a prayer to Fortuna, the optio rattled the shaker for a few moments before he removed his hand and released the dice. They clattered against each other as they tumbled out of the shaker and rolled to an abrupt halt on the table. The legionaries leaned in closer to inspect the numbers carved on to the surface of the ivory dice. Figulus craned his neck, the tension rising in his chest. Then he caught sight of the numbers. He had scored a pair of ones and a three. A much lower total than the three sixes Blaesus had just thrown.

'Blaesus wins!' one of the legionaries cried out.

Figulus's opponent sucked in air between his teeth and tried to control his pleasure. 'Never mind, sir. And, oh, yes . . . you owe me a hundred sestertii.'

'Bollocks!' Figulus thundered, slamming a fist on the table as the painful extent of his heavy losses began to sink in. 'But that's impossible! No one's that lucky, for fuck's sake. Not even you.'

His opponent folded his thick arms across his broad chest and flashed a smug grin at Figulus. 'Luck has nothing to do with it, sir. There's a certain technique to it, you see. It's all in the wrist.' A thought occurred to him and he smiled at the downcast optio. 'Another game, perhaps? Winner takes all . . .'

Figulus clamped his lips shut. Despite his losses, he was sorely tempted to accept Blaesus's offer of another bet. He felt certain the legionary's luck had to run out eventually. He was about to take up the challenge when a distant shout sounded from the other side of the fort. A few moments later an icy blast swept through the mess and the handful of Batavian auxiliaries taking breakfast swung their gazes towards the entrance. An auxiliary stood in the doorway, struggling to catch his breath and wearing a panicked look on his face.

'Stand to!' he shouted at his comrades. 'Everyone at the gates, now!'

At once the Batavian auxiliaries shot to their feet, as they grabbed their kit and hurried out of the mess after their comrade. The shouts outside grew louder with each passing moment, accompanied by the heavy thud of the soldiers' boots crunching on the frozen ground.

'What the hell's that all about?' Rullus wondered aloud.

Figulus shrugged. Then he abruptly rose from the bench and turned to his comrades, temporarily forgetting about his punishing losses at the dice. 'Only one way to find out. Move yourselves!'

He led the way out of the mess on to the main thoroughfare. A bitterly cold wind lashed across the fort, burning his bristly cheeks. The mild weather of recent weeks now seemed like nothing more than a fanciful memory. The first snow of winter had arrived during the night, drifting down from the bleak grey clouds and settling on the roofs of the buildings and coating the tips of the wooden palisades enclosing the fort. Across the thoroughfare several auxiliaries were staggering out of one of the timber barracks blocks to see what the fuss was about, fiddling awkwardly with the fastenings of their armour and scuffed helmets. Figulus and his men followed the auxiliaries, stopping off at their barracks to seize their equipment and weaponry in case they were needed.

The snow crunched softly under their boots as they carried on towards the hubbub. The familiar strident note of a Celtic war horn reached their ears from the far side of the gate and Figulus felt his pulse quicken.

'Looks like the Britons are up to their old tricks again.'

Rullus spat. 'Bastards never learn, do they?'

Figulus smiled grimly at his comrade. They passed several more empty barracks blocks as they approached the smaller gate built on the northern side of the fort. Twenty or so auxiliaries stood around in the falling snow, muttering anxiously amongst themselves. A few more were climbing the gatehouse armed with javelins and bows, taking up their positions on the ramparts overlooking the ground beyond the fort.

'What's going on here?' Figulus demanded.

'Convoy's under attack, sir!' an auxiliary replied, struggling to control the anxiety in his voice. 'Durotrigan raiders hit 'em just across the bridge. Escort column's almost done for.'

146

Rullus stared accusingly at the auxiliary. 'And you lot thought you'd just stand around doing fuck all?'

The auxiliary was momentarily stunned by the veteran's savage tone. Figulus forced himself to stay calm as he searched the faces of the men outside the gates. No one was ordering the men to form up, he realised. He looked back to the young auxiliary and gritted his teeth.

'Who's in charge here?'

'Centurion Ambustus, sir.' The auxiliary pointed in the direction of the gatehouse.

Figulus immediately headed towards the wooden structure, his comrades following close behind. Rullus growled and said, 'Durotrigans have got some brass fucking balls on 'em, hitting the supply lines this close to the fort.'

'Bit of a coincidence that they knew to attack now,' Figulus replied, furrowing his brow. 'Just when most of the garrison is in Linidinis.'

'Maybe one of the locals tipped them off.' Rullus shrugged. 'Either way, they're getting a bit too ambitious for my liking, sir. Any more of these raids and we're going to be on starvation rations.'

Figulus grunted and climbed the rickety ladder to the main platform along the turf rampart. A loose throng of auxiliaries stood crowded on the creaking deck, ready to hurl their missiles at the enemy in case they launched a bold attack on the fort. The optio gazed out across the winter landscape. A small bridge connected the fort to the road on the far side of the river, leading north towards the new trading post at Aquae Sulis. A track led directly from the gate to the bridge. Bracing himself against the wind, Figulus narrowed his gaze at the track beyond the bridge. Then he saw them.

Clusters of British warriors were tearing down the tree-lined slope, many armed with spears and wicker shields. Most of them wore no armour and their dark hair flowed freely as they unleashed a relentless stream of slingshot and arrows at the stricken Roman convoy. Several auxiliaries from the escort lay slumped on the ground, their lifeless bodies pierced with arrows. The survivors guarded the six wagons as they trundled on towards the bridge, the drivers lashing their whips for all they were worth as they urged their terrified oxen on.

Dozens of Britons instantly swarmed over the handful of auxiliaries protecting the rear wagon. The natives were urged on by their Druid leader. He stood mounted on horseback further up the slope. The auxiliary commander tried to rally his men but he was quickly surrounded by native raiders and disappeared beneath their savage blows. Then the native warriors set upon the driver of the rear wagon, cutting him down in a mad frenzy of hacks and slashes. The driver's screams carried across the air as he begged his enemies for mercy. His panicked cries were cut off as a Durotrigan warrior drove his spear at the man, impaling him through the back.

Figulus knew they had to act at once before the convoy was done for. The fort could ill afford to lose any more supplies. And yet there was no sign of anyone rallying the troops. Figulus spotted Centurion Ambustus standing further along the wooden walkway. The officer stood rooted to the spot, his vine staff clenched in his fist as he stared out at the unfolding carnage across the bridge. He seemed too young for his rank – almost as young as Figulus.

'Shit, shit!' Ambustus hissed, his lips beginning to tremble. 'Druids . . .'

The Batavians regarded the Druids with a mixture of fear and awe, and it was obvious that the centurion was terrified by the prospect of fighting them. But Figulus knew that something had to be done if they were to rescue the remnants of the endangered convoy. He grasped the unnerved centurion by his shoulder and pointed at the unfolding raid below. With the last few soldiers in the escort column being cut down, the convoy was now in complete disarray.

'Sir! We've got to rescue the convoy before those bastards seize all the grain!' he said harshly.

There was a risk that the centurion might take offence at his presumption, but there was simply no time to worry about that now. Ambustus blinked then suddenly shook himself out of his terrified stupor.

'Yes, yes,' he said, nodding quickly at Figulus. He raised his head and called out to his men gathered behind the gate. 'Form up and get ready to move out!'

CHAPTER TWENTY-ONE

The auxiliaries hurried to form up according to Centurion Ambustus's barked order. Figulus and his men followed quickly behind. In a matter of moments the optio and the remaining eleven legionaries under his command had assembled in front of the gate along with the Batavians, four deep. Figulus and his men took their place in the front rank in an attempt to inspire confidence among the anxious Batavian auxiliaries. Their morale was desperately low and Figulus decided that the sight of a Roman officer leading from the front would help to settle their nerves. As a centurion, Ambustus was obliged to lead from the front. He nervously took his place alongside Figulus.

The Gaul looked around him. The scratch force amounted to a little over forty men, roughly equal to the enemy force assaulting the wagons. Ambustus ordered a few guards to remain on duty inside the fort. Then he bellowed for the gate to be opened and at once the pair of auxiliaries manning the gate slid the locking bar free and pushed the gates aside. Beyond the walls Figulus could hear the war cries of the enemy as they tore enthusiastically into the convoy. There was a loud scraping as Ambustus shouted for his men to draw swords and the auxiliaries wrenched their weapons free from their scabbards. Figulus clasped his hand tightly round his horizontal shield grip. He could feel his heart thumping in his chest, as it always did in the moments before a fight.

The gate opened with a reverberating groan. Ambustus yelled for his men to march out of the fort at the double. They paced towards the bridge, their weapons glinting in the early-morning light. A hundred paces ahead Figulus could see the native warriors swarming over the bridge. Some of them were armed with slings and bows. Others brandished the traditional Celtic long swords. Less than a dozen auxiliaries now remained from the escort and they were hopelessly outnumbered by the Britons. Figulus saw several warriors setting upon the nearest wagon on the bridge, as the driver toppled from his bench. With a collective grunt the Britons lifted up the wagon and tipped it over the side of the bridge. The vehicle fell into the river with a deafening splash, spilling its contents into the water and dragging with it the oxen still yoked and harnessed. The animals bellowed in terror as they crashed into the icy water, wildly thrashing about.

Figulus turned to his comrades and pointed towards the Durotrigans. 'We've got to stop them ditching the wagons! On me!'

The warriors attacking the convoy became aware of the approaching soldiers and those by the nearest wagons now turned away from the shattered convoy and began hurling missiles at the advancing men. The soldiers swiftly hefted their shields and there was a series of sharp cracks as the slings and arrows clattered uselessly off the curved shield surfaces. With a defiant roar the Britons brandished their swords then charged Figulus and his companions.

The two sides met in a shimmering flicker of sword points, spear thrusts and the dull thud of shields. The Britons hurled themselves singly at their Roman opponents, swinging with their long swords. In response the Romans closed ranks, responding with the defensive parries and measured stabs they had practised in endless parade-ground drills, and the air was quickly filled with the rasping clang of clashing steel. It was a desperate attack, Figulus knew. Their best hope was to cut down as many of the enemy as possible and buy some time for the surviving wagons to reach the safety of the fort.

The warrior directly opposite Figulus lunged at him, his neck muscles bulging, his expression twisted into a raging snarl. The Durotrigan drove his sword towards Figulus's throat. The optio neatly parried the attack with an upward jerk of his shield and then immediately dropped his shield before his opponent could recover his stance and stabbed out at the man. His blade tore into the warrior's side, punching through his flesh, and the Briton let out a gasp as Figulus ripped his sword free. The warrior crumpled to the ground, cursing his enemy through gritted teeth.

Figulus turned to find his next opponent. By now the air was thick with the tang of blood and sweat. A scrawny older warrior bore down on Figulus, the tip of his sword glinting as he drove it towards the Gaul's face. Figulus jerked to the side and felt a searing pain as the blade grazed his neck. The optio clenched his jaws and jerked back a step. He felt warm blood trickling down from the flesh wound. The Durotrigan stood out of thrusting range and worked his features into a cruel grin.

'You're bleeding, Roman,' the Briton hissed. 'Now you're mine!'

In a blur of motion the warrior hurled himself at Figulus, hacking at the latter's shield. But the Briton was old, like so many of the veteran warriors who had retreated to the forests to continue their stubborn resistance to Roman rule. Ignoring the hot throbbing pain from his wound, Figulus punched out with his shield then drove his weapon towards his enemy's throat. The Briton grunted as the blade punched into him. He swayed on his feet for a moment, lowering his eyes dumbly as Figulus ripped his sword free and the warrior slumped to his knees, blood spraying hot and bright onto the snow.

The optio glanced around. Although they were equal in number, the Britons were no match for the better equipped auxiliaries and, inspired by Figulus's example, the Batavians were making short work of the enemy. Half of the convoy wagons had been toppled into the river. The remaining three were in no immediate danger but it was vital that the soldiers seized the initiative and pushed back the enemy for long enough to get the wagons across to the other side of the bridge.

He swivelled his gaze back to the bridge just in time to see a warrior charging at him, screaming manically. Figulus reacted in an instant, slamming his sword through the warrior's groin. The Briton stumbled back a step before falling over the side of the bridge and landing in the river amid the smashed wagons and the drowning oxen, thrashing about desperately in the current. Figulus urged his men on and the Britons began falling back from the bridge as they realised the tide of the battle was turning decisively against them.

'Get 'em!' Figulus roared, pointing his sword at the retreating Britons. 'Kill them all!'

A chorus of enthusiastic shouts sounded as the auxiliaries followed his lead and streamed forward across the bridge, cutting down the fleeing Britons as they tried to escape. Despairing cries split the air as the wounded Durotrigans were killed where they lay. At the crest of the hill the Druid leader shouted at his followers, ordering them to keep up the fight. But his warriors, faced by a determined and organised foe, had lost heart and most of them now spun away from the bridge and fled up the forested slope.

'Get your men to clear the bridge, sir!' Figulus shouted to Ambustus. 'We need to get these wagons into the fort!'

The centurion nodded then barked an order to one of his sections and the men sheathed their swords and downed their shields before clearing away the dead bodies blocking the wagons. With a rough path cleared through the carnage, the remaining drivers urged the oxen across the bridge, the loud snorting of the beasts accompanied by the groaning squeak of the transport carts' poorly greased axles. Pockets of native warriors held their ground at a safe distance from the soldiers. Some still hurled slingshots and shot arrows, but their aim was wild and most of the missiles fell short of their intended targets. A few of the auxiliaries raced forward, intending to give chase to the Britons fleeing up the slopes, but Figulus shouted for them to stay back and provide cover for the surviving wagons as they trundled across the bridge.

Once the last of the wagons had crossed, Ambustus recalled his men. The soldiers turned and escorted the wagons to the fort, leaving behind the wrecked wagons half-submerged in the icy waters along with the last of the oxen still bellowing pitifully as its strength gave out. Figulus trotted alongside his comrades, sweating heavily; his thick winter tunic was pasted to his skin beneath his armour. He paused, gasping, and glanced over his shoulder to see a few Britons giving chase across the bridge in a final attempt to cut down more of their hated foes. The handful of auxiliaries who'd remained in the fort launched a volley of arrows from the battlements over the heads of their comrades and struck down one of the warriors, and the rest scrambled back out of range.

A few moments later Figulus and his men entered the fort behind the last of the wagons. The auxiliaries on the battlements loudly cheered them and their Batavian comrades as the gate shut. The men slumped to the ground, overcome with exhaustion. Figulus tore off his helmet, his muscles aching from the physical strain of battle, his heart still pounding inside his chest. In the distance he could hear the angry shouts of the Britons growing fainter by the moment as they retreated back into the forest. Catching his breath, he watched three pairs of orderlies hurry over to the gate from the direction of the hospital, bearing stretchers to carry those who had suffered wounds during the fight. A quick head count told the optio that all of his men had survived. Several auxiliaries were missing, however. Their comrades sat on the ground, their faces and kit spattered with blood.

Rullus wiped sweat from his brow and grunted. 'Hot work, sir.'

Figulus nodded. 'At least we saved the grain.'

'What's left of it,' the veteran replied tersely.

The men fell silent as Centurion Ambustus gave the order for the remaining wagons to be taken to the granary and unloaded. Half of the convoy supplies had been lost. Only three wagons had made it to the fort unscathed. Figulus swallowed hard. Three wagons, at the price of the lives of dozens of auxiliaries from the garrison and almost all the escorts. The supplies would keep the men at the fort fed for perhaps another month. But with the food supply already strained, the prefect would have little choice but to reduce the natives' pitiful rations.

A bitter anger seized Figulus. The prospects for the natives in Lindinis were bleak. Many would starve to death in the coming winter. Unless more grain convoys managed to reach Lindinis, the already restless population would be tipped ever closer to open rebellion. As he watched the wounded soldiers being carried away, Figulus was suddenly conscious of a burning pain on his neck. He touched a hand to his wound and winced. Rullus was looking at him.

'You should take yourself down to the infirmary and get that checked out, sir.' Rullus grinned. 'Can't have you dying on us and missing out on all the fun now, can we?'

'No,' Figulus replied glumly. 'I suppose not.'

He left Rullus in charge of his men and trudged towards the infirmary, his mind swirling with grim thoughts. The Durotriges had put up a firm resistance out there on the bridge. And they had been bold. The Roman hold over the Durotrigan kingdom was as tenuous as ever it seemed.

CHAPTER TWENTY-TWO

'Hold still, Optio. This is going to hurt.'

Figulus was sitting on a stool in the small hospital, watching the surgeon dipping a bloodstained rag in a bowl of stained water. Pained groans echoed through the hospital as orderlies treated the men injured in the skirmish in front of the fort.

'It's just a flesh wound,' he responded, clenching his jaws in frustration. A soldier lay prone on the bed opposite, his face drained of colour as he waited for treatment. Figulus felt ashamed at receiving attention when there were others who were clearly more in need of help.

The surgeon wagged a bony finger at him. 'Ah, but even the slightest wound can become infected if not treated properly. This won't take a moment. I'll wash it out and stitch it up and you'll be back on your feet before you know it.'

'Just get it bloody over with,' Figulus growled. He had a fear of needles and the prospect of stitches unnerved him. But he said nothing and instead clamped his lips shut as the surgeon dabbed the damp rag on his cheek. Then he reached for a needle and twine, and Figulus felt a sharp prick of pain as the needle tip pierced his skin.

'I don't believe I've seen your face around the fort before,' the surgeon said casually as he stitched up the wound with his long, bony hands. 'New to these parts, I presume?'

'I'm with the Sixth Century, Fifth Cohort, Second Legion,' Figulus responded. 'My men and I only just arrived. From what I've seen so far, the sooner we leave the better.'

The surgeon smiled slightly. 'A sentiment shared by many in this place, I'm afraid. The ones who are left, anyway. This cohort has lost

154

too many men. Now we are down to the bare bones of the garrison.'

'What happened to the rest of the men?'

'You haven't heard the full story?' The surgeon clicked his tongue. 'A few weeks ago another convoy came under attack close to the fort. A hot-headed centurion took it upon himself to pursue the enemy into the marshes to the west. His men became bogged down in the mud and were ambushed. Only a handful managed to escape the trap.'

Figulus looked up at the man, trying hard not to look at his hands efficiently working the needle. 'And the rest?'

'Most were cut down. A few surrendered, only to be tortured and executed,' the surgeon responded simply. 'Their bodies were flayed and tied to stakes outside the marshes. As a warning to the others. Since then, no auxiliary patrol has dared enter the marshes.'

Figulus grunted derisively. 'You wouldn't get the Sixth Century shitting themselves like that.'

'If you say so, Optio. Almost done.'

The surgeon sewed the lips of the wound together and then tied the remaining twine up with a tight knot. He stood back and wiped down his bloodstained hands, admiring his handiwork.

'There you go. Good as new.'

At that moment the door opened and Figulus lifted his head to see an orderly enter. 'Optio Horatius Figulus?'

The Gaul nodded. 'That's me.'

'Imperial envoy requests your presence, sir.'

'Now?' Figulus asked, touching a hand to his stitches. 'Right bloody now?'

The orderly gave a stiff nod of his head. 'That's what he said, sir.'

Without waiting for a reply he turned swiftly on his heels and stepped out into the corridor. With a weary sigh Figulus stood up and followed the soldier out into the central corridor of the infirmary.

The moans of the injured soldiers faded as Figulus stepped outside and marched towards the headquarters building. The orderly ushered Figulus through the entrance and down the draughty hall. He stopped outside the envoy's private quarters and cleared his throat. Scylla looked up from a scroll on the desk in front of him and fixed his piercing gaze on Figulus.

155

'Leave us,' he said, waving the orderly away.

The man turned and left. Scylla pushed the document to one side then leaned forward across the table. A wooden platter of grilled mutton and bread was laid out on the desk in front of him, along with a cup of vinegared wine and a bowl of fish sauce. Evidently reduced rations did not apply to senior officials within the Emperor's administration.

Scylla frowned at Figulus's stitches. 'That's a nasty-looking wound.'

'It'll heal.'

Scylla grimaced. 'A pity your efforts were largely in vain. I understand from Centurion Ambustus that half of the grain was lost, along with nearly all of the auxiliary escort. Now the natives will suffer yet more misery, thanks to those Druids.'

Figulus bit down on his anger. 'There was nothing else we could do. The Britons hit the convoy before it reached the fort. By the time we rallied the lads, it was too late.'

Scylla glared at him for a moment before giving a firm shake of his head. 'Never mind. I didn't call you here to listen to excuses. I need you to begin your bodyguard duties at once. Report directly to the royal hall. Trenagasus is expecting you. You'll be billeted in accommodation inside the royal enclosure. Far preferable to having your men troop back and forth from the fort, as I'm sure you'll agree.'

'I suppose so,' Figulus replied, gloomily resigning himself to spending the next few days bottled up in the crude native settlement, surrounded by locals, many of whom would like nothing more than to gut him.

'The king has a busy day,' Scylla went on. 'First, he's due to meet with the native nobles.' He gave a cold laugh. 'Those we haven't arrested, anyway. The rest have been quick to offer their grovelling support to Trenagasus now that he enjoys Rome's backing. After the meeting the king will address the natives. He'll give a speech on the sweeping changes he intends to make to his barbarian realm. Of which there will be many. Clearly it's going to require a great effort to lift these feckless savages on to the first rung of civilisation and turn them into valuable allies.'

Figulus clamped his jaws to contain his anger at the envoy's withering assessment of the natives. Time and again the generals and imperial administrators demonstrated a stunning disregard for the Britons and their way of life. To the Romans the inhabitants of this island were little more than bog-hopping barbarians with no discernible culture or civilisation. It sometimes made Figulus wonder why Rome had bothered to invade the island in the first place.

'Of course, a public appearance is not without risk,' Scylla continued. 'You and your men will have to be vigilant, especially now that we know the Dark Moon Druids are plotting against the king.'

'If we're worried about the Druids, why not just cancel the king's address?' Figulus suggested.

Scylla glared at him. 'Trenagasus is attempting to Romanise the most hostile tribal capital in the province. He can only do that from a position of strength. If he suddenly postpones his public engagements the locals will think he's running scared of the Druids. He will look weak, Optio. You of all people should know that these Celts will only respect a strong man as their ruler.' He paused and took a sip of his wine. 'As a precaution, however, I've instructed Prefect Cosconianus to have some of his men remain in the capital for the day's festivities and watch over the natives. Three centuries, to be precise.'

'Are we expecting trouble?'

'Trouble?' Scylla repeated, arching an eyebrow. He laughed cynically. 'We already have plenty of that, Optio. The Durotrigans' old king has been deposed and is currently in our custody, along with almost fifty of his loyal supporters. Those fanatical Druids are denouncing his successor as a Roman puppet and are plotting to butcher him. To make matters worse we must now contend with this troubling business of the grain ration.'

Scylla sighed and sank back in his chair. The imperial envoy suddenly looked old and tired, thought Figulus.

'This latest attack is going to put an even greater strain on our resources,' he continued. 'I'm afraid we will have no choice but to stop supplying grain to the natives altogether.'

Figulus's stomach tightened into an anxious knot. 'But if we cut their rations again, some of the locals won't have enough food to last through the winter, surely?'

'Which is why it's imperative that you protect the king at all costs. If Trenagasus succeeds in holding off the Druid threat then we'll be free to secure our supply lines. That'll allow us to quell any lingering unrest among the natives and expand our operations in this area. Otherwise our position in this kingdom is in peril.'

'How do you mean?' Figulus asked.

Scylla explained. 'General Plautius intends to use Lindinis as the forward base for a full-scale advance west in the spring, crushing those tribes who continue to defy us and ending the last dregs of resistance in this benighted land. But if the Dark Moon Druids succeed in assassinating Trenagasus then our ambitions here will be dealt a fatal blow. Without our man on the throne to pacify the Durotriges, our operations would be delayed. In all likelihood we'd be forced into a humiliating retreat from Lindinis.' He leaned forward across the desk and stared hard at Figulus. 'I don't need to tell you how that would go down back at the imperial palace. The Emperor would show no mercy to those who are perceived to have failed him.'

The threat hung in the air like a knife. Figulus swallowed hard and tried his best to sound bullish. 'You can rely on us. Me and the lads will do our best to protect the king.'

'Then you had better hope that your best is good enough, for all our sakes.'

The envoy turned his attention back to the scroll as he continued speaking.

'You will leave at once for the settlement. I will join you later, when the king gives his public speech. In the meantime I have to write up my report to send back to Rome. You may go.'

Figulus ducked out of the envoy's quarters and left the headquarters block. He strode down the main thoroughfare feeling as if an immense weight was pressing down on his young shoulders. Assuming the responsibility for guarding the new native king filled Figulus with dread. He was a skilled soldier, but this task was unlike anything he had faced before.

He entered the barracks block assigned to his detachment. His men had returned there after the earlier skirmish. They were sitting around talking in low voices and cleaning their kit. Blaesus was teaching another legionary how to play at dice. Figulus sought out

Rullus and ordered him to summon the soldiers. They quickly formed up inside the barracks, standing stiffly to attention.

'Right, then. We're starting our bodyguard duties today,' he began awkwardly, struggling to sound authoritative. 'Four of us will take the watch in turn. That means three watches in total, each watch lasting eight hours. I'll lead the first watch. Rullus, Helva, Blaesus, you're with me. Vatia, Scaeva, Quadratus, Pulcher, you're second. Habitus, Albinus, Naso, Sura, you'll take the third watch.'

Figulus paused and ran his eyes over his men, looking each legionary in the eye.

'A word of warning. We'll be staying in Lindinis throughout, so make sure you pack all your kit. If I catch anyone slacking on the job, they'll find themselves knee deep in the shit. Literally. Latrine duty for the next month.'

It was a cheap joke and a few of the soldiers rolled their eyes, but it had the required effect of easing their apprehensive mood.

'It goes without saying that Trenagasus isn't exactly popular with the locals, what with all the changes he's planning to make. There'll be some who will be itching to have a crack at their new king. It's our job to make sure they don't get close enough to attack him. Do your job and we'll return to the Second Legion before long.' He grinned. 'Then we can get back to what we do best. Which in Blaesus's case means shagging as many ugly tarts as possible.'

The men chuckled. Figulus glanced across the line of soldiers, satisfied that his men were ready for the task ahead of them. 'Sixth Century! Form up and prepare to move out!'

CHAPTER TWENTY-THREE

It had stopped snowing by the time Figulus and his comrades emerged from the main gate on the eastern side of the fort to begin the short march towards the settlement. West of the fort stood a vast expanse of barren marshes stretching as far as the eye could see. Figulus felt his guts twist with anxiety as he surveyed the surrounding landscape. He and his men were at the very edge of Roman-controlled territory in Britannia. Beyond the fort lay the great swathes of land that the legions had yet to conquer, populated by those tribes still opposed to their rule.

A fetid odour hung in the air as the soldiers trudged through the thick timber gate at the entrance to the native settlement. Sewage puddled the streets, adding to the stench emanating from the stacked piles of animal manure outside the wattle and daub roundhouses. The snow on the ground mixed with the excrement to form a slippery brownish sludge, and Figulus and his men had to watch their step to avoid slipping. Smoke eddied from the small openings in the roofs of each roundhouse and a thin skein of woodsmoke hung low over the settlement, darkening the grey sky above.

The scrawny natives, their faces gaunt from months of surviving on shrinking rations of barley gruel, stared with open hostility at the Romans as they made their way up the main thoroughfare. A few bold Britons shouted lewd insults at Figulus and his men from the gloom of the side streets.

'Back in this stinking pit,' Blaesus moaned. 'We must have really pissed off the gods, I tell you.'

'Why are the locals so angry with us, sir?' Helva asked. 'I thought the Druids were the ones nicking all the grain?'

'Because we're getting properly fed, lad,' Rullus said. 'And because life's gotten worse for this lot under us, not better. It's more convenient for the Brits to blame us for their ills rather than their own kind.'

Blaesus snorted loudly through his flared nostrils. 'Bloody politics. We should be back in Calleva right now enjoying a jug of cheap wine with the lads down at the Drunken Boar. Not spending the winter in this arse end of the empire among these barbarians.'

Figulus glared at the soldier. 'Keep your voice down,' he said as he glanced anxiously at the Britons lining the street.

'What, in case any of this lot overhear, sir?' Blaesus nodded at a small group of scrawny native youths, all of them bearing the sullen looks of resentment of a defeated people. 'There's more chance of Mount Vesuvius erupting than there is of these scum speaking Latin.'

'For now, maybe,' Figulus replied quietly.

'You really think the king will succeed in Romanising these people, sir?' Helva asked.

'It depends,' Figulus replied with a shrug. 'The Durotriges are stubborn bastards but even they must realise that there's no point resisting us now that we've kicked their arses. If the king can persuade them of the benefits of being on our side, he might be in with a chance.'

Blaesus grunted and shook his head. 'Sorry, sir. But this lot hate our guts. More than any other tribe in Britannia, I'd say.'

'It doesn't matter what the locals think,' Rullus countered. 'The king has the backing of that old goat Claudius. An attack on Trenagasus is an attack on the Emperor. As long he's got the Second Legion watching his back, Trenagasus will keep his arse firmly planted on the throne.'

'If he doesn't push the locals too far,' Figulus added.

Rullus shook his head. 'The envoy will rein him in. If he's wise the king will keep a low profile until the mood's lifted. Take it from me, sir. A year or so from now this lot will be watching gladiator fights and worshipping Neptune and Minerva with the best of 'em.'

'As long as the king's changes include a few decent drinking holes, I couldn't care less what he does,' Blaesus said. 'I could do with a nice cup of Falernian right now, as a matter of fact.'

Rullus laughed. 'Since when did you ever have just the one drink? Or the one tart, for that matter.'

Blaesus looked back at the veteran and pulled a face. 'Are you honestly suggesting that I'm a whoremongering drunkard who only cares where his next drink is coming from?'

'I'm suggesting exactly that.'

Blaesus nodded at him and smiled. 'Good. Just checking.'

Figulus and his men arrived at the heavily guarded royal compound. Dozens of auxiliaries were patrolling the main thoroughfare in front of the compound, their hands resting lightly on the pommels of their sheathed swords. Teams of ragged natives swept through the streets, cleaning up the shattered weaponry and discarded equipment from the previous day's struggle. A tall timber gateway was guarded by a pair of auxiliaries standing with their spears crossed. More soldiers were patrolling the surrounding streets, keeping away any curious locals who tried to get too close to the compound. As Figulus approached the gate one of the guards advanced his spear and stepped forward.

'State your business,' he demanded.

'Optio Horatius Figulus.' He gestured to his comrades. 'And these are my men. Imperial envoy's sent us to be the king's new bodyguard.'

The auxiliary nodded, lowered his spear and stepped aside. 'You're expected. In you go.'

Figulus swept through the gateway and led his men into the enclosure. They entered a wide space with a large building at the far end. To the right of the royal hall stood a ramshackle arrangement of storage sheds for food supplies and a few smaller timber-framed structures for receiving guests. To the left of the hall Figulus saw an animal pen filled with bleating livestock. As the soldiers drew near to the royal hall a servant emerged from the gloom and approached them. He stopped in front of Figulus and bowed slightly.

'You must be his majesty's new bodyguards,' he said in Latin.

Figulus nodded. 'That's us.'

The servant straightened his back and smiled faintly. 'Please. Follow me.'

He turned and marched promptly back inside. Figulus and his men followed the servant down a gloomy hall supported by timber beams carved with images of the native gods. Narrow openings high on the daubed walls admitted weak shafts of light which formed grey pools on the dirt floor. Figulus saw that the walls were adorned with animal skins, as well as ornate Celtic swords and oval shields decorated with native symbols. The air was thick with the smell of stale beer and roast meat from the previous inhabitant's occasional feasts.

At the far end of the hall stood a raised dais with an empty throne in the middle. An iron brazier flickered to one side of the throne, throwing long shadows across the walls. In front of the dais Figulus saw a long table at which several well-dressed Britons sat, with jugs of steaming hot wine and silver goblets and platters of cold meat and bread. Trenagasus sat at the head of the table, grazing on a selection of pastries. Ancasta sat to his right. At the sound of the soldiers' echoing footsteps the king lifted his head towards the approaching party.

The servant drew to a halt in front of the table and began to speak in his native tongue until the king stopped him. 'In Latin, if you please.'

The servant cleared his throat and began again. 'Your bodyguards are here, Your Majesty.'

Trenagasus wiped crumbs from his tunic and nodded slowly as he turned his gaze on the four Romans standing next to the Briton. He waved a bony hand at his surroundings. 'Please excuse the rather frugal living arrangements, Optio. I'm afraid the previous occupant lacked any sort of taste for refinement. Regrettably, my fellow Durotrigans are not known for their appreciation of the finer things. We have no equivalent of Vitruvius, or Catullus. Not yet, anyway.'

'Yes, Your Majesty,' Figulus said, wondering who or what the king was talking about.

'Roman bodyguards, Your Majesty?' another man seated at the table queried in a gruff voice. 'Is that, ah, wise?'

Figulus turned his attention to the handful of native nobles seated around the table. The tribal elders and notable warriors from the most ancient and respected Durotrigan families had been quick to ingratiate themselves with the new king now that he had been restored to the throne at the point of a Roman sword. They were dressed more elegantly than the moody Britons Figulus had seen in the streets, with thick woollen cloaks over their colourful check-weave leggings. Trenagasus set his cold grey eyes on the man who had spoken.

'A threat has been made against my life, Sediacus. A king must take such threats seriously, particularly when it has been made by those perverted extremists, the Druids of the Dark Moon.'

'A wicked cult, Your Majesty.' Sediacus nodded in agreement. 'One that has blighted our land for too long.' He coughed. 'We are, of course, deeply grateful that you have reclaimed the throne from that wretch Quenatacus. Most of us suffered terribly under his reign. But your people will take this as a grave insult. There are many proud warriors among our own tribe. Why not draw up a bodyguard from your subjects?'

Trenagasus fixed his gaze on the aristocratic Briton. 'And I shall. Once I can be certain who among my people I can trust.'

Silence descended over the hall. No one spoke for a few moments and the other men seated around the table shifted uncomfortably. Sediacus cleared his throat.

'You are the king. Your subjects are loyal to you, Your Majesty.'

Trenagasus chuckled. 'Loyal, you say? I am old, not blind. I know some of my subjects are opposed to my return. All those who cheered when I was sent into exile, fleeing into the night while my entire family was slaughtered, save for my daughter.' His voice was shaking with rage and his facial muscles twitched with anger. 'I trusted my people once before, and they betrayed me. I do not intend to make the same mistake twice.'

'But your opponents are under arrest at the fort, are they not?'

'Some. But there are many more I suspect of collaborating with the old regime.' The king shook his head. 'No. Until I can be sure that the loyalty of all my subjects is beyond doubt, I must keep Romans as my bodyguards.'

'Father is right,' Ancasta said. 'It is better to be protected by Romans than not at all. Besides, Rome is no longer our enemy. What better way to demonstrate our new alliance than by Father placing his life in their hands?'

All eyes turned to the king's daughter.

Trenagasus smiled softly at her. 'An excellent point, my dear

Ancasta. A most excellent point.'

Ancasta looked round the table, searching the eyes of the nobles. 'I can't speak for the others at this meeting but I know this much: Optio Figulus is a brave man and will do his utmost to protect my father from those who would try to harm him. He saved Father's life once. His loyalty is not in question . . . which is more than can be said for some.'

She smiled brightly at Figulus as she spoke, and he felt something warm flutter inside his chest.

'Even Claudius is protected by foreigners, I believe. By Germans, no less. Is that correct?' Ancasta directed the question at him.

'Yes, my lady,' Figulus replied.

Ancasta looked back to her father. 'Then if it is good enough for the most powerful man in the world, Father . . .'

Trenagasus beamed with pride. 'As ever, my dear, you are wise beyond your years. What a great pity it is that you were not born a boy. Otherwise I would have no concerns over who to choose as my successor.'

'You honour me by seeking my counsel, Father.'

Trenagasus yawned as he rose stiffly from his chair. 'Now, gentlemen, if you'll forgive me, it has been a long few days and I wish to rest awhile before I address my people.' He looked to Figulus. 'One of my servants will show you and your men to your accommodation, Optio.'

Sediacus stood and bowed. 'Your subjects will be excited to hear from you, Your Majesty, now that you are back on the throne.'

'Most will be welcoming, I expect. Some will be sorry to see me, no doubt. Especially since that unfortunate business with the convoy means we shall have to cut their rations again.' The king's eyes seemed to glow bright orange as they reflected the flickering flames from the iron brazier and a cruel smile parted his lips. 'But my enemies will not be vocal for very much longer.'

CHAPTER TWENTY-FOUR

A stony silence descended over the settlement as Trenagasus emerged from the royal hall flanked by his Roman bodyguards. A heaving throng of natives had gathered in an open market area a short distance from the royal compound, braving the bitter cold to hear from their restored king. Trenagasus and his entourage paced towards a wagon that had been placed in the middle of the market-place to act as a temporary speaking platform. The snow had been trampled into an icy slush. A line of auxiliary soldiers stood guard in front of the wagon while the rest remained inside the royal compound prepared to react if there was any trouble. The Batavians stood impassively in front of the crowd, their shields raised and ready to thrust back any of the natives who came too close.

There was a dangerous tension in the air as the king approached the wagon. Many of the locals stood with their arms crossed, their expressions surly and their threadbare clothes hanging loosely from their undernourished frames. Those further back from the wagon craned their necks, straining to catch a glimpse of their new ruler. Several angry shouts went up from pockets of the crowd but Trenagasus ignored them as he climbed atop the wagon with the help of a pair of servants, his purple cloak fluttering in the icy breeze. Figulus and the other men on the first watch took up their positions either side of the wagon. The optio stood to the left with Blaesus, while Rullus and Helva guarded the opposite flank. The king's retinue of advisers stood between the wagon and the compound gate, watching Trenagasus expectantly. Figulus spotted Scylla among them. The imperial envoy was next to Ancasta, his hands folded behind his back and a fixed smile on his thin lips.

'Let's hope he keeps his speech nice and short, sir,' Blaesus moaned under his breath. 'Otherwise we'll end up freezing our bollocks off out here.'

'At least it's stopped snowing.' Figulus tipped his head in the direction of the crowd. 'It looks like we're not the only ones who'd rather be somewhere else. That lot don't look too happy either.'

'Can't really blame 'em, sir,' Blaesus responded, keeping his voice low so that no one overheard him. 'Their king's been knocked on the head and now they've got a Roman puppet sitting on the throne. They're bound to be unhappy. The only surprise is that they're not rebelling already.'

'Hopefully the king won't do anything to piss them off.'

Figulus felt a deep sense of unease as he scanned the sea of faces. There was none of the adulation that might be expected to accompany the return of an exiled king, no cheers or shouts of welcome. It was obvious to the optio that Trenagasus had his work cut out if he was to persuade the stubborn locals to abandon their simmering hatred for Rome and all that the empire stood for.

Up on the wagon Trenagasus waited for the crowd to settle down. After a few moments the murmurs died away. The king drew a deep breath and began addressing his people in the native tongue.

'My fellow Durotrigans,' he said, his eloquent voice carrying clearly across the market area. 'You all honour me with your presence here on this glorious day. I stand before you now as your rightful king once more. After five long years of misery, the wicked reign of Quenatacus and his henchmen is over.' He raised a clenched fist as if expecting a cheer from the natives, but none came. The king remained composed as he went on, 'No longer will we be divided, fighting amongst ourselves. Today marks the start of a new era for our tribe . . . as allies of Emperor Claudius!

'From today, there will be no more costly wars against the might of the legions. Never again will our sons perish in futile battles while our crops are left to rot unharvested in our fields. Never again will the Druids peddle their depraved philosophies among our villages, enticing our brothers into a conflict they cannot win. Under my rule I shall usher in a new era of peace and prosperity for all in my kingdom. From this moment on, my friends, we shall throw off the shackles of humiliation and defeat!'

The Britons stared back at Trenagasus in silence before several among the throng voiced their disapproval. One or two heckled him with abuse. Trenagasus stared defiantly back at his subjects then continued.

'During my time in Narbonensis I saw with my own eyes the benefits of Roman rule: the splendid towns, the markets filled with exotic goods drawn from the remotest parts of the empire. The marvels only made possible by Roman civilisation. Above all, I saw order. Order is what makes Rome strong. For centuries we Britons have been squabbling amongst ourselves, waging petty wars against our neighbours while our settlements fell into neglect and our wealth was needlessly squandered. Under Rome, and her great Emperor Claudius, there will be no more conflict between our tribes. There will instead be order and a common purpose.'

Rumbles of discontent erupted from pockets of natives every time the king mentioned Rome. Figulus spotted some of the crowd shaking their heads in disbelief. Others muttered in low voices to one another and he sensed the hostility towards the new king beginning to spread.

'Seems like this lot aren't too happy about the new arrangement with Rome,' he muttered.

Blaesus grunted. 'What a fucking surprise.'

'We Durotriges do not like change,' Trenagasus went on. 'That is understandable. We are a proud tribe, descended from the greatest warriors in Britannia. It is natural that we seek to cling to our glorious past, but we must look to the future now. For too long our people have wallowed in filth, turning their backs on culture and civilisation. No more, my friends. Today, our kingdom will embrace an alliance with the coming power in this land . . . Rome!'

Trenagasus paused and glanced at Scylla, as if looking for approval. The envoy gave a slight nod of his head and the king turned to face his subjects again, a steely look in his eyes.

'There are going to be significant changes to our way of life. Changes that must be made.' Trenagasus searched the faces of his subjects as his lips quivered nervously. 'First, I am imposing a ban on the possession of weapons within the settlement walls. All weapons are to be confiscated immediately. Those who disobey will be punished severely.'

Loud boos rang out across the throng. Figulus looked on uneasily. Many of the Durotrigans were proud warriors and any order to disarm them would be perceived as a grave insult to their honour. Trenagasus raised a hand for silence. When that failed the auxiliaries began roughing up a few of the noisier Britons at the front of the crowd, striking them with their shield bosses. A few Britons fell to the filthy ground to cries of anger from their companions. At length the king was able to continue his speech.

'That is not all, my friends. In addition, the Druid influence is to be wiped from our lands. Any cult that promotes human sacrifice and consults the gods by examining the victim's entrails has no place in civilised society. The Druids' shrine and offering pits will be obliterated and the sacred oak tree cut down.'

There was a collective stunned gasp from the crowd. The attack on their beliefs was a step too far for many of the Durotriges and their despair quickly turned to anger. Figulus's right hand slid down to his legionary sword, ready to wrench it free if the Britons' anger suddenly exploded into violence.

'This doesn't look good,' Figulus said.

'Even I can see that, sir,' Blaesus responded. 'And I don't understand a word anyone is saying.'

'Moreover,' Trenagasus continued, 'I am imposing the imperial cult. Each and every one of my subjects will be required to worship the divine Julius and Augustus. A new temple dedicated to the divine Emperor Claudius will be built in place of the existing Druid shrine. It will be paid for through a new system of taxes that will be collected from our people—'

'Oi, Trenagasus! What about our fucking grain?' a Briton near the front of the crowd shouted, interrupting the king.

Figulus fixed his gaze on this man. He was solidly built, his neck and face were heavily scarred. His hair was noticeably thinned from years of washing it with lime in the ancient warrior tradition.

'You talk of Roman gods and Roman customs. What good are such things to us when we cannot feed our children?' he yelled, his guttural voice filled with rage. He pointed to Figulus and his comrades.

169

'We're living on scraps while these fucking foreigners hoard all the grain for themselves! If these bastards want us as allies then they should start sharing their grain!'

A throaty cheer of support rang out from sections of the crowd. Figulus heard one or two jeers directed at the Romans. Up on the wagon Trenagasus glared at the warrior, momentarily thrown by the interruption to his carefully rehearsed speech. He quickly recovered his composure and tried to go on, but the man continued shouting over him. The other Britons cheered again. The king's expression abruptly hardened. He turned towards Cosconianus.

'Prefect! Arrest this man.'

Cosconianus nodded and shouted the order to his men. At once a pair of auxiliaries stepped forward from the line and grasped the old warrior's arms before dragging him clear of the crowd, to howls of protest from his fellow Britons. At first the warrior tried to resist but one of the auxiliaries punched him in his guts and he keeled over, gasping. The soldiers hauled the stricken man towards the wagon then threw him to the ground. Trenagasus stared at the warrior with a mix of pity and contempt. Then he looked back to the crowd.

'I am your king. I shall brook no opposition. None! All those who dare to defy my authority will suffer a terrible penalty. This I swear!' Trenagasus turned back to the auxiliaries standing over the warrior. 'Kill this pathetic wretch. We shall make an example of him. Put his head on a stake above the gate and dump his body in the midden for the wild dogs and rats to feast on. That will serve as a lesson to anyone who thinks they can oppose my rule.'

The angry grumbles from the crowd instantly increased and were joined by cries of dismay. A woman rushed forward from the crowd before her companions could pull her back, screaming shrilly and clutching an infant close to her chest. She fell to her knees in front of the auxiliary soldiers. Tears streamed down her cheeks as she pleaded with Trenagasus in a high-pitched voice.

'What's she saying, sir?' Blaesus asked out of the corner of his mouth.

Figulus swallowed. 'She's begging the king to spare her father. She says if he is to be killed then she won't have any way of supporting her child. Her son is already sick and he won't survive the winter otherwise.'

Trenagasus stared coldly at the woman, utterly unmoved by her desperate pleas. Slowly it dawned on the woman that there was nothing she could say or do that would spare the old man. Increasingly frantic, she began pleading with Trenagasus to at least give her father the dignity of a proper burial in accordance with the native customs. But Trenagasus merely glared at her with cold indifference before calmly turning to the auxiliaries.

'Seize this woman,' he commanded. 'She can join her father in the midden. The child can die too, so that the scum's treacherous bloodline is wiped from this earth.'

At once the soldiers moved to snatch the infant from its mother. Suddenly the whole crowd roared with anger. Even the nobles standing obediently beside the king appeared shocked by his command. One Briton stepped forward and moved towards the auxiliaries, his face twisted into an angry snarl and his huge hands clenched into fists, but he was swiftly restrained by his companions before the soldiers could strike out at him with their shields. A wild-haired woman screamed at the top of her voice and hurled colourful curses at the auxiliaries. Figulus sensed the mood in the crowd turning fatally against Trenagasus. He glimpsed Ancasta moving quickly towards the king.

'Father, there's no need for this.' She waved a hand at the crowd. 'Your subjects have learned their lesson. There's no need to punish them needlessly. It'll do more harm than good.'

Trenagasus stared at his daughter for a moment and then smiled faintly. 'Very well, my dear.' He turned back to the auxiliaries. 'Release the woman. She's free to go with her child.' He paused. 'But her father must still die. I will not tolerate dissent from such insolent scum.'

The auxiliaries lifted the woman to her feet and shoved her back into the crowd, still clutching her infant to her chest. The mood remained tense as the woman cried out to her father. The Briton was forced to his knees. He clamped his eyes shut as he resigned himself to his grim death. One of the auxiliaries brought his boot crashing down against the old warrior's spine. The Briton let out a pained grunt as he fell forward and landed face down in the mud. Before he could scrape himself off the ground the auxiliary stepped towards him and unsheathed his sword with a grating rasp.

The pointed sword tip glinted dully in the pale winter light as the auxiliary hefted the weapon above his head. Figulus forced himself not to look away as the auxiliary plunged the gleaming point into the nape of the Briton's neck. The man jerked as the blade tore through his flesh and punched out of his throat. The woman in the crowd let out an anguished shriek at her father as he lay dying on the ground, making a deep groaning hiss in his throat. The auxiliary began hacking through his neck in a methodical fashion, severing tendons and bone. Finally his head became detached from his body and rolled aside. Figulus looked away, feeling sick.

The king nodded with satisfaction. He signalled to Cosconianus. 'Prefect, disperse the crowd. You are to confiscate all weapons and begin destroying the Druid shrine immediately. Do not let anyone stand in your way. Is that clear?'

'Yes, Your Majesty.'

Cosconianus bowed his head, clearly irritated at having to address a native as a superior. The prefect spun away from the king and in a booming voice ordered his men in the royal compound to join the rest of his command and clear the market. The auxiliaries formed up and advanced, pushing the crowd back with their shields. Some reluctantly trudged back to their huts. Others stopped at the side streets, pausing to glance back at the soldiers with barely disguised hatred. A few Britons tried to stand their ground but after a token show of defiance they turned and retreated down the crude alleys between the dense sprawl of roundhouses. Soon the market was empty except for the old warrior slumped lifelessly on the ground, the blood still disgorging from the stump of his neck in a steady flow. Trenagasus curled his lips in disgust.

'Someone clear that miserable wretch away.'

Two auxiliaries snapped into action as the king stepped gracefully down from the wagon. One soldier grabbed the dead Briton's legs and dragged the corpse away while the second man picked up his severed head. The prefect shouted for his men to begin sweeping through the settlement and the auxiliaries were promptly divided into eight-man sections. They moved from hut to hut, seizing whatever weapons they could find, while another group of Batavians headed towards the settlement gates and set off for the Druid shrine located in a nearby sacred grove. Pockets of native men glared darkly at the foreign soldiers, their hands balled into fists and their expressions stitched with rage.

'Perhaps we could run through the details for the festivities again,' Trenagasus said to Scylla. He smiled. 'I'm afraid my memory is not quite what it used to be.'

Scylla bowed. 'Of course, Your Majesty. This afternoon you will dedicate an altar to the imperial cult, on the site of the proposed temple in honour of Emperor Claudius. Following the dedication we will return to the hall for the banquet celebrating your glorious return to the throne.'

'Ah, yes. I trust that all the chiefs from the outlying settlements will be present?'

The envoy nodded. 'They're due to arrive later today, Your Majesty.'

Figulus saw a wicked gleam in the king's slit-like eyes. 'And what of the gladiator fights? We are having them, aren't we? I'm very sure we discussed the possibility of some light entertainment for my guests later on in the evening.'

Scylla gave a false smile. 'I have already attended to the necessary details, Your Majesty. I propose that we use some of the prisoners currently being held at the fort for the purpose of the spectacle.'

The king's face lit up with excitement. 'A truly marvellous idea. Let the treacherous dogs cut each other's throats!'

With that he spun away from the market and returned through the gateway at the front of the royal compound, flanked by his four Roman bodyguards and followed by his large retinue. Figulus marched alongside the king, gripped by a sudden sense of revulsion. Trenagasus's reign had got off to the worst possible start. If he continued executing and imprisoning his own subjects, then it wouldn't be long before the natives rebelled. And when that happened, Figulus and his comrades would be caught right in the middle of it.

CHAPTER TWENTY-FIVE

As dusk closed over the winter landscape the royal hall was filled with the hubbub of conversation and laughter as the king's guests arrived. The hall had been transformed for the purposes of the evening's entertainment, with trestle tables laid out across the floor space and oil lamps and tallow candles creating a soft amber glow, throwing flickering shadows across the walls. Dozens of tribal chiefs and their families sat at the various tables, along with some of the more prominent native warriors and nobles. The guests were tearing into their meat while the king sat at the high table on the dais surrounded by his most trusted advisers, including Scylla and Ancasta. They were joined by Prefect Cosconianus, resplendent in an exquisite tunic.

A steady stream of house slaves flowed in and out of the large open kitchen at the back of the hall, bearing plates of roast pork and jugs filled with wine. A mouth-watering aroma of spices and cooked meats wafted in from the kitchen, teasing Figulus's nostrils as he stood guard in front of the dais alongside his comrades.

'Nice to see that the well-heeled half of Lindinis isn't going hungry,' Rullus muttered. 'Look at all this bloody food. There's enough here to keep the Second fed for a whole campaign.'

'It's a long way from how the other half lives, that's for sure,' Figulus replied.

Rullus frowned deeply. He lowered his voice and said, 'This isn't going to go down well with the locals, sir. Especially when the prefect is cutting their rations yet again.'

Figulus shared Rullus's opinion. The mood in Lindinis had gradually worsened as the day wore on. After his speech Trenagasus had ordered the arrest of every native who had openly supported the previous king. Throughout the day soldiers had moved from hut to hut in the settlement, dragging suspects from their homes while crowds of angry Britons looked on. The men were separated from their wives and children and taken away to be executed, while their anguished relatives were tethered together by their necks and marched to the fort, where they would be held prisoner until they could be sold into slavery.

In the late afternoon the king insisted on witnessing the destruction of the Druids' sacred shrine. The grove was situated in a dense forest a few miles beyond the settlement and Figulus and his men had looked on as teams of auxiliaries torched the Druids' huts, pulling down the stone altars and filling in the pits piled high with offerings to their gods. In the dying light thick columns of smoke rose from the shrine into the grey wintry sky. As the native prisoners were marched out of the settlement, the air filled with the cries of defiance from the men about to be executed, Figulus realised that he was protecting a man filled with bloodlust. A man who had the backing of the Emperor.

At the end of his watch Scylla had pulled Figulus aside and explained that the optio and his men were to remain on duty during the banquet. The chiefs from the outlying settlements had seen which way the wind was blowing and were hoping to win favour with the new king, but many had openly defied Rome in the past and Scylla feared that if any of them still had an allegiance to the Druids they might make an attempt on Trenagasus's life. Figulus had posted the legionaries of the second watch at the entrance to search the arriving guests for weapons, while the men of the third watch patrolled the outer enclosure looking for any sign of intruders. That left Figulus and his three comrades guarding the king inside the royal hall. The optio and Rullus stood guard over the dais while Blaesus and Helva moved around the hall, keeping a close eye on the guests.

No expense had been spared in an effort to win the chiefs' favour. As well as traditional native fare, Trenagasus provided samples of Roman cuisine, serving cuts of venison marinated in fish sauce and bowls of garlic mushrooms, along with a selection of potent-smelling cheeses imported from Gaul. Servants moved from table to table, topping up the chiefs' drinking horns with dark, frothy beer or, for those with a more refined palate, cups of heated wine. Figulus licked his lips as another servant passed bearing a platter of rich delicacies.

'What d'you reckon?' he asked, nudging Rullus. 'Think we'll get the leftovers once the banquet's finished?'

Rullus laughed heartily. 'You must be joking, sir! We're soldiers, not high-born officers. There's more chance of those pigs flying away than there is of us eating 'em.'

'Pity.' Figulus sighed, staring mournfully at the food. 'I'm starving. I could eat a horse right now.'

Rullus chuckled. 'You're always bloody hungry. Must be that Celtic blood of yours.'

Figulus smiled at his companion. Although Rullus would gently tease the young officer from time to time, he never took it to the bullying extremes of some of Figulus's superiors in the Second. Most senior officers looked down on him, regarding him as an inferior even though he had proved his worth in battle on countless occasions. He steeled his muscles and tightened his hand into a fist, reminding himself that should he succeed in helping to establish Trenagasus on the throne, he might have a chance of a swift promotion to centurion. It suddenly occurred to Figulus that, given the high-ranking prejudice against his ancestry, saving the king from an assassin's blade might be his best chance of advancing through the ranks. Perhaps his only chance.

He tried to take his mind off his growling stomach by searching the faces of the guests. Any one of the Durotrigans seated in the hall could be an assassin, he thought to himself. He was surprised by the demeanour of some of these Britons. The older chiefs were in good spirits, eager to please the new man on the throne. But the younger men seated further back from the dais wore severe expressions, making no attempt to hide their displeasure with the new king. If anyone was going to try and kill Trenagasus this evening, Figulus decided, it was likely to be one of them.

'Optio!' the king called out, waving him over.

Figulus reluctantly turned away from Rullus and approached the high table. The conversation had turned to politics and everyone was keenly involved in the discussion. Trenagasus was in high spirits and Figulus noticed dribbles of wine on his chin. One of the guests at the high table sat in glum silence as he picked at his food. He was an older man with thinning hair and a wizened face. Figulus recognised him as Sediacus, one of the tribal elders who'd attended the meeting with the king that morning. He appeared distracted.

'We were just discussing the benefits of Romanisation,' the king said to Figulus between chewing mouthfuls of tasty morsels. 'As a Gaul, someone who has seen their own lands transformed under Rome's guiding hand, perhaps you would care to share with us your thoughts on the matter. What's your opinion on the subject?' He furrowed his brow at Sediacus. 'It would appear that some of my advisers are yet to be fully convinced.'

'Well?' Scylla urged. 'What do you think?'

Figulus panicked. This was precisely the sort of moment he secretly dreaded. The question required a carefully phrased answer, crafted with diplomacy and tact, and he was severely lacking in both qualities. Out of the corner of his eye he noticed Ancasta staring curiously at him. Figulus cleared his throat.

'I'm just a soldier, Your Majesty. I don't really know, to be perfectly honest.'

Trenagasus smiled drunkenly. 'A simple answer from a simple mind. No doubt you'd rather be debasing yourself with endless drinking and whoring than debating the important topics of the day. But you must have some opinion on the subject, surely?'

Figulus shifted uneasily. Every time he looked at the king, he kept seeing the faces of the women and children he'd condemned to slavery. It was hard to believe that this well-spoken native aristocrat with his fondness for Greek poetry and fine art was the same man who had ordered the merciless slaughter of dozens of his own subjects and the enslavement of many more. Figulus tried again.

'Rome is far from perfect, Your Majesty. We have our faults, like any other, but being part of the empire is better than the alternative, in my humble opinion. My people used to spend their days fighting against the Sequani and the Arverni. Now we have peace, and opportunities that our forefathers could only dream of.'

'Britannia is not Gaul, Your Majesty,' Sediacus responded warily as he gently swirled his wine cup. 'I do not doubt that change is necessary. But it is not so easy to achieve with our people, I fear.'

'Nonsense!' Trenagasus declared. 'A few obstinate farmers and warriors will not deter us from doing what is necessary.'

Sediacus chose his words carefully. 'But surely it might be wise to listen to the views of your people, Your Majesty?'

'That is your grave mistake, my dear Sediacus. You actually believe my subjects' opinions carry any weight? Why, most of these people lack any sort of education. They cannot read, they cannot write. Gods, they can barely count the fingers on their hands! How are such brutes supposed to know what's best for them? Hmm? Answer me that!' Smiling, he turned to Scylla. 'Why, next you'll be suggesting that we let the people decide their own future!'

The envoy and the king both chuckled meanly. Sediacus glowered at Trenagasus. 'But what of the grain situation, Your Majesty? Your subjects are upset that our allies are hoarding most of the grain while they go hungry. Something must be done before you have no subjects left to rule.'

'That is not the fault of Rome!' Trenagasus snapped irritably. 'Blame those vile Druids. Their constant raids are driving my people to starvation.' He shook his head. 'And yet there was outrage when I gave the order for their sacred grove to be destroyed.'

Sediacus forced a smile. 'Forgive me, but your subjects do not see it that way, Your Majesty. On the one hand they sympathise with the Druids' continued resistance. On the other hand, they are tired of broken promises from Rome. They were led to believe that life would be better under the Emperor. That there would be order and food and wealth. Instead your people are starving to death.'

'What would you suggest I do, Sediacus?'

'Perhaps a more equal distribution of the grain, Your Majesty? That would at least quell the deep-rooted suspicion among your subjects that our allies are receiving preferential treatment.'

Cosconianus interjected. 'Absolutely out of the question, I'm afraid. I've already made it perfectly clear that our soldiers must be properly fed if they are to keep order in the kingdom, and defeat the Druids.'

The king smiled apologetically at Sediacus. 'It is unfortunate that my people must go hungry. But we will crush the dregs of the Druid resistance soon enough. In the meantime, I'm afraid, we must all suffer.'

He said this as a pair of servants set down another platter of delicious-looking pastries, and not for the first time Figulus wondered whether it wouldn't be so bad if the king fell on an assassin's blade after all. The king popped one of the pastries into his mouth and his mood suddenly brightened.

'Things will improve now that my enemies have been purged. We're free to open up my realm to all the traders from the empire. Soon the markets will be filled with merchants hawking every luxury imaginable. Before long this backward settlement will be transformed into a thriving town and a shining example of Rome's civilising influence.'

'His most gracious majesty Emperor Claudius will be delighted to hear of the progress you are making,' Scylla responded. 'I'm sure he will reward your majesty accordingly.'

Trenagasus smiled then rose to receive some newly arrived tribal chiefs. Blaesus and Rullus stood close by the king's side as each chief in turn approached the dais and bowed while their servants presented him with gifts of jewellery and fine cloth in a public demonstration of fealty to the new king. Ancasta remained at the high table, closely watching Trenagasus.

'It pains me to see Father like this,' she said to Figulus.

'My lady?'

Ancasta turned towards him. Figulus caught a whiff of the sweet perfume she was wearing. 'My father was very different before he was exiled. He could be warm-hearted and caring. Then we were cast out of the kingdom. Mother died not long after, and Father became obsessed with reclaiming his throne. It's all he ever talked about, day and night, in Narbonensis.' She pursed her lips. 'Now he's back, he'll do whatever it takes to stay on the throne.'

'You wish he'd never returned, my lady?'

'*Sa.* Sometimes.'

Ancasta fell silent for a few moments, her eyes fixed on Trenagasus as he warmly greeted another chief. 'Father is old and tired, Optio. Much more so than he looks.' She turned back to face Figulus and there was something like sadness in her eyes. 'I worry he will not be able to carry on much longer. Do you know what will happen to our people then?'

'The next in line will assume the throne?'

'No. Rome will take over the administration of our territory, as they have done with the other tribes. We'll be annexed, and there will be no more Durotrigan kings or chiefs. Our heritage will turn to dust.'

Figulus did not know what to say to that. In truth he sympathised with the plight of the Durotriges. Their stubborn refusal to accept the puppet leader Rome had imposed on them contrasted starkly with the meek surrender of his own people. The Durotriges deserved a better leader than Trenagasus. Instead they were at the mercy of men who took decisions far away in Rome. Figulus shook his head angrily. Rome would make few friends in this part of the empire until she realised that you could not rule at the point of a sword alone. One day, he reflected gloomily, the people of Britannia would be pushed too far. Then there would be a terrible price to pay for those who were associated with the invaders.

At length Trenagasus finished receiving his guests' offerings and returned to the table. He drained his wine cup, spilling drops on the table and down his front to the barely concealed disgust of the imperial envoy. Then he set his cup down with a burp. 'That's enough ceremony for one night!' he declared to his advisers. 'Bring out the gladiators. It's time we showed our guests some true Roman entertainment!'

CHAPTER TWENTY-SIX

At the king's command the servants cleared away the remains of the feast and moved the trestle tables away from the centre of the hall. The guests stood to the sides while the king took up his place on the throne atop the dais, flanked by his daughter and Sediacus and the imperial envoy. The household slaves continued to top up the guests' cups with beer and several of the Britons were already roaring drunk, punching each other in the stomach in tests of strength or rushing outside to vomit.

At the king's command the hall door swung open and the rowdy guests hushed as a line of eight bedraggled men shuffled inside, accompanied by several auxiliaries. Figulus recognised one of the Britons. These men were native prisoners who had been captured during the struggle to remove the previous king. They were naked except for loincloths and their necks were tethered together and their ankles manacled. The auxiliaries shoved the defeated Britons roughly towards the cleared space in the middle of the hall, to loud cheers from the inebriated audience. There was some aggressive jostling as the Britons fought to get the best view of proceedings while the auxiliaries formed a loose circle round the hall, creating a makeshift ring. The soldiers looked disgruntled at having to act as attendants for the occasion while their comrades remained at the fort enjoying a well-earned rest.

Blaesus rubbed his hands together expectantly as he stood next to Figulus. He and Helva had joined their two comrades in front of the dais, with the other eight legionaries spread out around the hall.

'At last! Been ages since I last saw a gladiator fight. Let's hope it's a good one.'

'Waste of good prisoners if you ask me,' Rullus rasped. 'This lot would've made us a tidy profit. I hear that the slaves are fetching a good price in the markets in Gaul these days.'

The practice of selling prisoners into slavery was well established among the legions, and one of the few ways in which the soldiers could supplement their modest pay. Each legionary received a share of the profit from the sale, with officers receiving considerably more than the rankers. These prisoners had been part of the soldiers' booty and many of the rankers had expected them to be sold on to the slave dealers in Calleva. Instead they would be slaughtered for the amusement of the king and his guests, to the evident displeasure of Rullus.

'Who cares about a few sestertii?' Blaesus responded. 'This is much more fun!'

'Easy for you to say, lad. I've got my retirement to think about. I need every sestertius I can get.' Rullus tipped his head at the prisoners. 'Selling this lot would've made a nice supplement to my savings.'

The first two prisoners were released from their shackles and ushered towards the middle of the circle by a pair of auxiliaries wielding heated iron rods which they prodded at the downcast fighters, spurring them on. An auxiliary centurion assumed the role of master of ceremonies. As he introduced the two fighters, his two assistants stepped forward and handed each prisoner a weapon. One of the Britons was given a legionary sword while his much larger opponent was handed a broadaxe. Neither man had a shield.

The drink continued to flow as the natives cast bets amongst themselves over the outcome of the first bout. Most of the audience appeared to favour the heavyset Briton with the broadaxe over his rival.

'What do you reckon, sir?' Blaesus said. 'How about a wager? A hundred sestertii says the big fucker loses.'

Figulus shot a look at the legionary, burning with the memory of the small fortune he'd lost that morning in the mess. He didn't trust himself to beat Blaesus at the dice, but Figulus considered himself a good judge of gladiators. He'd spent his childhood in Lutetia sneaking into spectacles at the local amphitheatre, watching some of the biggest draws from across the empire take to the sand in front of an enthralled crowd. This was an excellent chance to claw back his losses, he thought as he weighed up the two fighters. The prisoner with the broadaxe stood several inches taller than his opponent and his torso rippled with taut muscle. The swordsman was thin and sinewy but handled his weapon in the practised manner of a veteran fighter. Figulus reasoned that the bigger man would prove too strong for his smaller foe. He turned back to Blaesus and nodded briskly.

'Deal! A hundred sestertii it is!'

'You seem confident your man will win, sir,' Helva said.

'Why not? Look at the size of him. He's almost as big as me. He's bound to win. Trust me, this is the easiest money I'll ever make.'

Blaesus grinned at him, revealing a set of crooked teeth. 'We'll see, sir.'

'Gladiators!' the centurion shouted above the drunken cheers from the rowdy audience. 'To your marks!'

The auxiliaries marched the two fighters to a pair of chalk marks scored at either side of the circle. The centurion called for the crowd to fall silent. Then the Britons were turned to face each other and the centurion roared, 'Ready . . . Fight!'

At first neither prisoner showed any inclination to attack. Boos rang out as it became clear that the fighters did not understand the orders shouted at them in Latin. One of the auxiliaries booted the swordsman in the back and he stumbled towards the centre of the circle. A cheer went up as the bulkier Durotrigan instantly charged forward at his opponent, swinging his broadaxe with a savage roar. His opponent recovered his stance just in time and jerked backwards on his nimble feet, dodging the attack. The bigger Durotrigan snarled at the swordsman and lunged again at his opponent, bringing his broadaxe crashing down at his opponent, as if chopping wood. The swordsman crouched low and parried the strike with his weapon, a metallic ring sounding above the excited cheers of the guests. The swordsman was moving deftly on his feet, using his speed to evade his opponent's slow attacks and Figulus suddenly began to worry that he had backed the wrong man. After a few more attacks the larger Briton began to tire. Beads of sweat glistened on his heavily scarred face.

'Your one's making heavy work of it, sir,' Helva noted.

'It's still early,' Figulus replied, clenching his fists. 'He'll come good. You'll see.'

The broadaxe attacked again to roars of drunken delight. The man was clearly enjoying the status of crowd favourite. Spurred on by the support from the audience, he brought his weapon crashing down through the air towards the slighter man's skull. The latter raised his sword at the last moment and deflected the attack. The axeman was breathing heavily, the mass of muscle on his chest heaving up and down with exertion as he struck out again at his foe. The swordsman kept retreating around the edge of the circle, deftly parrying each attack as the two fighters exchanged an increasingly frenzied series of blows and thrusts. But the axeman was fighting on the front foot against a much weaker opponent and Figulus decided that it was only a matter of time before he won. He experienced a quick thrill at the prospect of winning back a substantial sum of his hard-earned pay from Blaesus.

The heavyset Briton swung again. This time the swordsman deflected the attack then stabbed out, piking his foe through his trunk-like thigh. The axeman let out a pained grunt and stepped back, hissing sharply between his clenched jaws as he reached down and clamped a hand over his wound. The swordsman was proving surprisingly skilled with his weapon.

Now the broadaxe let out a manic roar of anger as he charged forward, swinging his weapon in an wide arc. The swordsman had backed up to the very edge of the circle and had no room left to manoeuvre. He dropped to his haunches, narrowly avoiding the blade as it cut through the air with a violent swoosh, forcing the closest members of the audience to scramble backwards to safety. In the same fluid motion the swordsman thrust out, punching his sword through the other man's guts. The fighter's mouth fell open in shock as the blade tore through his vitals. There were gasps of disbelief from the audience as the swordsman wrenched his weapon free. His stunned opponent sank to his knees, blood and intestines spilling out of the wide gash across his stomach. He wavered a moment before collapsing.

'The swordsman wins!' the centurion declared, raising the arm of the victor.

'Bollocks!' Figulus cursed.

Angry shouts erupted from those in the audience who had heavily backed the axeman. Several heated arguments broke out among the guests at the outcome of the fight and one or two of them hurled abuse at the slain Briton for not putting up a better fight as a pair of auxiliaries dragged his still breathing body away. Blaesus placed a consoling hand on Figulus's shoulder, grinning smugly.

'Unlucky, sir.'

Figulus glowered at the legionary then thumped a fist against his thigh in bitter frustration at losing yet more of his meagre savings. 'How did you know your man would win?'

'First rule of the arena, sir. Speed beats strength, every time. The one with the axe was too big for his own good.'

There was a short break as the auxiliaries prepared for the next fight. The victorious prisoner was disarmed and once more placed in chains. Figulus turned his attention back to the king. Trenagasus appeared to be enthralled by the contest, his eyes alight with excitement as he signalled for one of his slaves to refill his silver wine goblet.

'A splendid contest!' he remarked to Scylla. 'Strictly speaking a man of my high standing ought not to indulge in the barbaric pleasures of the arena, I suppose. But one can see the usefulness of such fights. They're a wonderful means of increasing a sponsor's popularity.'

The imperial envoy gave a deferential nod of his head. 'As ever, Your Majesty, your insight is remarkable.'

Sediacus leaned close to Trenagasus and pointed out a spot at the front of the circle around the arena. 'Perhaps your majesty would care to have a closer view of the action?'

A drunken smile formed on the king's lips. 'An excellent idea, my friend. One doesn't quite have the best view from up here.' He sought out Figulus and beckoned to him. 'Guards!'

The order was given and the king's servants hastily cleared away a space directly beside the makeshift arena, while two more slaves carted a chair over to the spot. Then the king stood up from his throne and moved down from the dais, accompanied by his bodyguards. He took up his seat, with his advisers standing on either side. Figulus and the other Roman bodyguards closed ranks around

185

Trenagasus, warily eyeing the surrounding chiefs. The king drained the rest of his wine in a single gulp.

'On with the next fight!' he roared excitedly.

Two more prisoners were shoved into the circle. More bets were taken among the audience. More drink was poured. Above the raucous din the centurion shouted, 'For our next fight, we have a secutor against a retiarius.'

'A net fighter?' Figulus spluttered. 'He's got no chance.'

Blaesus made a face. 'I'm with you on this one, sir.' He tipped his head in the direction of the net fighter. A large wound on his left shoulder had been stitched up. 'This one's in no bloody condition to fight. Anyone who bets on him is asking for trouble.'

'The fight won't last long, then?' Helva wondered.

'About as long as it takes to boil asparagus,' Blaesus responded.

'Waste of money, if you ask me,' Rullus added sourly. 'At this rate there won't be anyone left to sell. So much for spending my retirement getting pissed in Damascus with a nice tart on my lap.'

The auxiliaries handed out the weapons to the second set of gladiators. The injured Briton accepted his trident and a casting net weighted with lead pellets fixed to the ends. His squat, dark-haired opponent wielded a short sword and carried a small shield. Figulus was surprised by the latter's composure. He seemed very calm and showed no sign of fear or uncertainty as he stood in his corner, tightly gripping his weapon and staring intently at his opponent, his muscles tensed. With a sharp rap of his vine cane the centurion marked the start of the second bout of the evening. Accompanied by a cheer from the audience, the fighters engaged.

The guests jostled for a good view of the contest, looking on with a mix of excitement and macabre fascination. The net fighter was a new type of gladiator who had only recently been introduced into the arena in Rome and those present were eager to see how he would match up against the more traditionally equipped secutor. As far as Figulus could tell, the intention of the net fighter was to snare his opponent in the throwing net before applying the killer blow with the trident. But the injured man was clearly struggling under the weight of the net and, using his left hand, he instead jabbed the tips of the trident at the secutor's throat, before quickly backtracking.

He stuck rigidly to this routine, keeping his distance and constantly shifting around the ring, his face a picture of anxious concentration. The audience grew increasingly frustrated as the two fighters continued circling each other, exchanging tentative blows. Figulus sensed the mood in the crowd turning ugly. From his position at the front of the circle Trenagasus watched the contest unfold with obvious irritation.

'Get at him, for fuck's sake!' someone yelled at the secutor.

'Stop dancing around!' another intoned. 'Let's see some bloody fighting!'

The net fighter grew tired of this seemingly endless pursuit. With a gruff roar he threw himself into a furious attack on the secutor. His opponent ducked the thrust of the trident and then knocked the butt of the weapon aside with his blade. Then he charged at the net fighter, plunging the short sword into the man's thigh and giving the blade a twist, drawing a howl of pain from his wounded foe. He tore the blade free as the net fighter lashed out with his heavy net. The secutor neatly sidestepped the attack and the net fighter cursed. He was struggling to remain on his feet as blood pumped steadily out of the large wound on his leg. Sensing his opportunity, the secutor stabbed at his opponent, sinking his blade deep into his shoulder and opening up his old wound. With an agonised curse the net fighter stumbled backwards then sank to his knees as his trident and net fell from his grip. The secutor kicked out at the net fighter. He fell backwards and crashed to the ground as the audience broke out into contemptuous jeers.

'That didn't last long, then,' Blaesus remarked drily.

The roars from the guests grew louder as the secutor stood over his fallen opponent. Breathing hard, the secutor slowly lifted his sword and aimed the tip at the net fighter's neck. His foe lay on the ground, his muscles tense and eyes wide with fear as he waited for the secutor to apply the killer blow. The latter hesitated for a moment. All around the hall the bloodthirsty onlookers shouted for the secutor to slay the defeated fighter.

'Finish him!' a drunken Briton roared at the top of his voice.

The secutor spun away from the net fighter, a slight smile playing out on his lips as he turned to face the crowd. Figulus caught a glimpse of his expression. His features were twisted into a snarl of rage. With his back to his fallen opponent the secutor sprang forward and launched himself at the figure seated a few paces away from where he was standing. Figulus looked on in horror as he realised that the gladiator was charging directly at Trenagasus.

'Your Majesty!' the optio shouted. 'Look out!'

The Briton was a couple of steps away from the king and several more away from Figulus. Trenagasus sat frozen with fear as the bloodied tip of the short sword drove towards his neck. The auxiliaries looked on, too stunned to react and too far away to stop the assassin. Without thinking Figulus hurled himself at the Briton, slamming into the man before he could cut down the king and the two crashed to the ground to cries of panic from the nearest guests. The fighter let out an explosive grunt as the sword clattered to the ground. He reached for his weapon but Figulus grabbed him by the shoulder, pulling him back before he could seize the sword handle. With a roar the Briton drove his elbow back, striking Figulus square in the face. His grip weakened and Figulus felt the assassin scrabbling away from him. His vision returned just in time to see the man scraping himself off the floor and reaching for the sword, a couple of paces from Trenagasus.

At that moment Blaesus surged into view. The legionary kicked away the sword and launched his boot at the man's face. There was a sharp crack as his foot connected with the fighter's jaw. The Briton fell away. Before he could pick himself up, Blaesus unsheathed his own weapon and aimed the blade at the assassin's throat. The Briton froze. He looked up at Blaesus, his eyes burning with an intense hatred. The legionary grinned back at him as he prepared to plunge the blade down into his neck.

'No!' Figulus thundered, fighting the jarring pain in his skull. 'We need him alive.'

'What the fuck for? This bastard tried to kill the king.'

'We need to question him.'

With a sigh, Blaesus lowered his weapon but kept the assassin pinned to the ground with a boot pressing down on his chest. At the same time Helva and Rullus and the other bodyguards swarmed forward to form a protective circle around the stunned king.

Pandemonium erupted across the hall as the guests scrambled towards the doors, fearing that they too might be in danger. In their rush to escape several benches were knocked over. Some of the older Britons lost their footing amid the melee and were crushed beneath the feet of the panicking crowd.

As the guests stumbled outside Figulus could hear distant shouts coming from the direction of the main gateway. Beyond the gates he glimpsed a crowd of natives gathering to see what all the fuss was about. Word about the failed attempt on the king's life quickly spread and it seemed to embolden the crowd to express their contempt for Trenagasus. Rocks and clumps of animal dung were hurled at the soldiers standing guard outside and chants broke out.

'Down with the king!' a voice shouted. 'Down with Rome!'

More missiles showered down on the guards. The guests, caught between the chaos inside the hall and the anger outside the compound, stopped in their tracks and shrank back from the gateway.

'You there!' Cosconianus shouted at one of the auxiliaries. 'Return to the fort. I want every man available sent here at once, before the entire settlement turns against us!'

'Yes, sir!' The auxiliary nodded then spun away and hurried out of the hall, rushing towards a horse tied to a post just inside the compound. He untied the rope, mounted the horse and jabbed his heels into the animal's flank. Then he bolted out of the gates and rode through the crowd, the horse's hooves pounding the frosted ground.

Soon the hall had emptied of its guests. Large puddles of spilt beer and wine glistened in the flickering orange light. The floor was strewn with discarded food and the shattered shards of clay amphoras. Scylla was staring out at the main gateway, his expression somewhere between shock and fear. After a few moments he turned away.

'Optio!' he shouted above the ugly chants of the native throng outside. 'Post every spare man you've got at the gate. We'll need to keep these scum pushed back until the reinforcements arrive.' He glanced at the king. Trenagasus stared in horror at the assassin. Ancasta was comforting him. 'And for gods' sakes get the king out of here.'

Figulus ordered two of his men to accompany the king to his private quarters. The rest of his legionaries hurried outside to the gateway, where the crowd was becoming ever more vocal. Then Figulus pointed to the would-be assassin.

'What about him?'

Blaesus still had his sword drawn and aimed at the Briton, ready to cut him down if he tried to escape. The man glared angrily at his captors.

Scylla paused and took a breath. Then he said, 'Take this wretch to the servants' quarters. Once things have calmed down here we'll question him and find out what he knows.'

CHAPTER TWENTY-SEVEN

The distant roar of the crowd rumbled softly through the walls of the servants' quarters as Centurion Vespillo stepped back from the prisoner and admired his handiwork. He wiped his scarred fist with a bloodied rag and turned to the imperial envoy.

'That ought to have loosened his tongue a bit, sir.'

Scylla nodded slowly. A length of rope bound the prisoner's wrists, with one end of it fastened round a ceiling timber so that the man hung from it with his arms above his head, his feet dangling a few inches above the floor. As soon as the auxiliary reinforcements had arrived at the tribal capital, Scylla had sought out Centurion Vespillo, the garrison's specialist interrogator, to question the captured assassin. Figulus had been ordered to act as a translator during the interrogation. It was immediately obvious that Vespillo had long experience of plying his grim trade. The centurion had started beating the prisoner with a series of hard punches to the stomach, followed by several vicious lashes to the kneecap with his vine stick. Figulus had looked on as the man's cries of pain echoed through the modest quarters.

'Very good, Centurion,' Scylla said as he approached the prisoner.

The envoy regarded the Briton with a withering look of contempt. His legs were visibly swollen and blood trickled out of his slack mouth. Groaning in agony, the prisoner slowly lifted his head to look directly at Scylla. One of his eyes had swollen shut and his lips were purpled with bruises. He croaked a few words in his rasping native tongue.

'What's he saying, Optio?'

Figulus hesitated. 'He says you can get fucked. Something you should be used to, as a Greek.'

The Briton smirked, revealing a set of bloodstained teeth. Scylla glowered at the prisoner, his lips twitching with rage.

'And there I was thinking that the Britons were more than just a bunch of hairy-arsed barbarians utterly lacking in sophistication.' Clearing his throat, the envoy turned to Vespillo. 'I think our friend here needs another lesson in Roman manners, Centurion.'

Vespillo grinned. 'As you wish, sir.'

The centurion stepped forward, his hand balled into a fist, the knuckles shading white. He was still grinning as he slammed his fist into the prisoner's stomach. The Briton grunted in agony, gasping as the air rushed out of his mouth. Figulus heard something crack. Vespillo slapped the Briton across the face so hard the man's cheek shaded bright red. The Briton coughed violently and made a horrible retching noise. Then he spat at the centurion. A gobbet of phlegm landed on Vespillo's breastplate. He looked down, then stepped forward and repeatedly punched the prisoner in the stomach. The Briton moaned, thrashing about in pain as he recoiled from each blow and the timber beam above his head began to creak under the strain.

'That's enough for now, Centurion,' Scylla commanded. 'We don't want to kill him.' He chuckled. 'Not yet, anyway.'

Vespillo took a step back and wiped the spittle from his front with the bloodied rag. The prisoner hung limp from the cross-beam, moaning softly.

'Let's try again, shall we?' Scylla nodded at Figulus. 'Optio, tell this man that it would be wise if he cooperates. I wish to know if there are any other conspirators. If so, I want their names. Kindly explain to him that Centurion Vespillo has much practice in the interrogation of prisoners, and sooner or later we shall find out what he knows. It is simply a question of how much suffering he chooses to endure first. If he speaks now, he has my word that he will have a quick death.'

Figulus translated as best he could. When he had finished, the prisoner took a ragged draw of breath and lifted his eyes to his interrogators. Then he said a few hoarse words in his native tongue. Figulus looked at the envoy.

'He says he swears upon Cruach that he was acting alone. He says you can inflict any torture on him, it will make no difference.'

'He's lying, sir,' Vespillo stated flatly. 'I can tell. I've been in this line of work long enough to know when someone's holding something back. This one definitely knows something.'

Scylla smiled cruelly. 'He will tell us what he knows, or I will see him crucified on the town gates. It can take a man up to three days before he dies. His suffering will be unimaginable. Tell him, Optio.'

Figulus translated the threat. Slowly the Briton lifted his head a few inches and looked at the envoy as he spoke through his parched lips. His voice was so weak that Figulus had to lean in close to hear. When the prisoner had finished speaking Figulus turned to the envoy.

'He says that he is not afraid of death. He says that none of his people fear death, unlike the cowardly Romans. That is why they will defeat Rome in the end, even if it takes a hundred years. They are not afraid to die. They will not rest until every last drop of Roman blood has been spilled.'

Scylla let out a derisive snort. 'Astonishing how they still cling to such laughable sentiments even after we've crushed their armies. One almost admires their deluded thinking.'

'He's a stubborn one, that's for sure,' Vespillo observed, shaking his head. 'I could try something else, sir. Beat him with a hot iron? Or gouge out his eyes with a heated sword tip? That usually does the trick, in my experience.'

'Later, perhaps,' Scylla replied. 'Centurion, perhaps you could fetch some bread and water for our guest. We don't want him fainting before he tells us what he knows.'

'Very well,' Vespillo replied gruffly.

He turned and marched out of the room, calling out to a nearby servant. The prisoner glared at the departing centurion with a mix of resentment and fear. 'Your friend is an animal,' he mumbled once the door had shut.

Figulus shook his head. 'He's not my friend. But I've seen a fair few interrogations in my time and I can promise you one thing. He won't stop torturing you until you start talking.'

The prisoner drew in a breath. There was a flicker of hesitation in his eyes and for a brief moment Figulus thought he might finally be prepared to talk. But the prisoner kept his lips clamped shut and began mouthing silent prayers to his gods. Vespillo returned to the room just then. Scylla turned to him.

'This isn't getting us anywhere. Centurion, perhaps it's time to cut out our guest's tongue, since he obviously has no use for it.'

'Yes, sir.'

The Briton followed Vespillo with his eyes as he reached for a series of surgical instruments and blades laid out on a side table next to a bowl of bloodied water and several rags. The centurion picked up a small dagger. A sudden look of panic flashed in the Briton's eyes and he started convulsing as Vespillo approached him, his muscles tensing up with fear. The centurion teased him with the blade and the prisoner tried jerking his head away, pleading with his captors in a frantic voice.

'Before he talks,' Figulus said, 'he says he wants an assurance that you will keep his family from harm. He wants us to swear it.'

Scylla smirked. 'First he must tell us what he knows. Tell him if he is not honest with me, I will see his family nailed to the town wall alongside him. He can listen to their agonised cries as he dies.'

Figulus looked back to the prisoner. His eyes were shifting left and right, as if he was trying to decide whether to trust the Gaul. Vespillo was still holding the blade close to his face. Finally the Briton took a breath and spoke.

'He says he was approached by an agent of the Dark Moon Druids,' Figulus translated for the envoy. 'They promised him they would rescue his family from slavery if he killed the king. They told him he had nothing to lose, since he was going to die either way. He agreed for the sake of his family. He doesn't know anything else, he swears upon all of the gods. He begs you to spare his wife and son.'

'What did this agent look like?' Scylla asked.

'He can't be sure,' the optio said. 'It was dark and the man was wearing a hood over his head.'

'Bastard's lying, sir,' Vespillo hissed. 'I can see it in his eyes.'

Scylla sniffed. At that instant the door swung open and a serving girl entered bearing a cup of vinegared water and a crust of stale bread. The prisoner stared at her intently as she set down both the cup and bread on the side table.

194

Scylla said, 'Ask him about the Dark Moon Druids. I want to know where they are hiding.'

Figulus translated. The prisoner mumbled under his breath.

'Well?' the envoy demanded. 'What did he say?'

'He swears upon his gods that he doesn't know. All he has heard is that there's a place somewhere in the marshes.' The prisoner said something else, and Figulus paused, not sure if he'd heard the man correctly. He told the man to repeat himself before turning to the envoy. 'He says the Druids keep the stolen grain there.'

That caught Scylla by surprise. The envoy straightened his back, frowning at the prisoner. He signalled for Vespillo to step back and the centurion lowered the dagger, scowling at the prisoner.

'Where, exactly?' Scylla demanded.

Figulus listened, struggling to keep up with the prisoner as he spoke quickly. 'Near the Druids' lodge. They keep it there because none of the locals would dare approach the lodge out of fear. They've been stockpiling the captured grain since the end of the summer.'

As he finished speaking the servant quietly left the room. Scylla waited for her to depart then narrowed his eyes at the prisoner. 'How does our friend know all this, Optio?'

Figulus put the question to the assassin. The Briton struggled to reply. He was delirious with pain, his eyes dancing wildly in their sockets, and he could hardly open his mouth to speak.

'Before he was taken prisoner he says he was a bodyguard to Quenatacus,' Figulus said. 'One of his duties was to escort the stolen grain convoys to the Druids.'

The Briton could say no more. He let out a light gasp as his eyes dimmed and clamped shut. Then he suddenly went limp and his battered head hung low. Scylla snapped his fingers and Vespillo promptly grabbed the cup of water and pressed it to the Briton's lips. But he was losing consciousness and most of the water spilled down his front.

'Keep this scum alive,' Scylla ordered, stroking his chin. 'We'll need to question him further once he's regained his strength. It's imperative we find out more about this.' Then he looked at Figulus. 'I'll need you and your men to locate and retrieve the grain before the Druids realise that we have discovered its location.'

Figulus reacted with a jolt. 'Why us? We're supposed to guard the king.'

'I'd have thought that was perfectly obvious. Prefect Cosconianus and his auxiliaries are needed here, in order to keep the locals in check.'

'What about our bodyguard duties?'

'We'll post a few of the auxiliaries by the king's side. Before you ask, Optio, sending the auxiliaries to rescue the grain is out of the question. I understand that our Batavian friends are afraid of the Druids. This mission is too vital to risk sending a bunch of jumpy soldiers into enemy territory. We need someone with leadership and experience. You have plenty of both. Need I say more?'

Figulus's guts squirmed with dread. Meandering through the marshes at night, in the depths of a bitingly cold winter, was a grim prospect. All this to save the reign of a cruel and merciless tyrant. For a moment he wondered if perhaps it would have been better if he had failed to stop the assassin. Then he clamped his jaws shut and checked himself. No. If Trenagasus had fallen, the kingdom would have been thrown into bitter violence, provoking a renewed war with Rome.

'You'll leave at once,' Scylla added. 'There's no time to lose. It's critical that you retrieve the grain hoard. It's our only chance to placate the natives and secure Trenagasus's position on the throne. If we fail, then this capital will fall to the Dark Moon Druids and our hopes of securing a lasting peace among the Durotriges will be finished. Now hurry!'

CHAPTER TWENTY-EIGHT

It was still dark when Figulus and his comrades trudged out of the settlement and headed towards the marshes. The first streaks of light were tingeing the horizon but the silvery crescent moon still shone brightly in the sky amid the stars and scattered clouds. Figulus marched in silence in front of his men, staring anxiously ahead at the vast tract of dull marsh six or seven miles away. A thin mist hung over the fringe of the marshes, clinging to the dips and folds in the land, and a shiver ran down his spine as he ran his eyes across that impenetrable mass of bogs and clumps of gorse. Figulus was acutely aware of the fact that they were moving beyond the territory under Roman control. He alone was responsible for the lives of his men, and the success or failure of Rome's fate in the Durotrigan kingdom. He tried very hard to ignore the knot of fear tightening in his stomach as he marched steadily on.

Their departure from Lindinis had been delayed after a fire had broken out in one of the animal pens inside the royal compound. With the auxiliary ranks preoccupied by the angry crowd in the streets, Figulus and his men had been forced to put out the flames before they spread to the royal hall. The soldiers toiled hard, carrying buckets filled with water from the kitchen to the pen, and by the time the fire had died out most of the structure had been razed to the ground, leaving only a few blackened piles of timber and the charred remains of the cattle and sheep. Several men suspected of torching the structure had been arrested and by the time Figulus and his legionaries swept out of the timber gates, the restless natives had retreated to the warmth of their homes.

The legionaries were accompanied by four sections of auxiliaries

197

provided by Scylla in case they ran into trouble. At the rear of the column were half a dozen military carts borrowed from the depot at the fort, on to which the men would load the grain stores. Trenagasus had also provided Figulus with a guide for the mission. One of the king's slaves claimed he was familiar with the routes leading into the marshes. Now he led the way a few paces ahead of the main column while behind him the soldiers marched as quietly as possible through the darkened landscape, the frigid silence broken only by the soft crunch of the snow beneath their boots and the gruff snorting of the oxen pulling the carts.

'Fucking great,' Blaesus grumbled. 'The marshes in the middle of bloody winter.' He shook his head bitterly. 'And there I was thinking things couldn't get any more crap around here.'

'Could be worse,' Figulus responded with a shrug.

Blaesus stopped in his tracks briefly. 'Really, sir? How's that, then? We're stuck in the arsehole of the empire, the natives hate our guts for saving the king's life and now we've got to slog for miles in the freezing cold to find this grain, just so the king can stay on the throne and butcher a few more of his own people. How can it possibly get any worse than that?'

'We could be listening to another one of your crap jokes,' Rullus remarked.

Blaesus glanced darkly at the veteran and snorted. Figulus and the other soldiers shared a laugh, lightening the tense mood among them. After five miles the sun crept over the horizon, casting a pallid glow over the marsh, and the mist began to thin. Snow tumbled down from the band of grey clouds as the column reached the fringe of the marshes. Amid the settling snow Figulus noticed a narrow rutted track leading from the open ground into the heart of the marshes, twisting between the dense gorse thickets and stunted bare trees. A foul odour of rotting vegetation hit the optio as he followed the guide down the gorse-choked track.

They were approaching the fringe of the marshes now, and the soldiers had to take care to avoid tripping up on the tangled under-growth partially concealed beneath the snow. In places the snow had turned into a thick, greasy sludge which impaired the progress of the carts and the column kept having to stop in order to prise the wheels free from the quagmire. Then the wind came, a low howling moan that blasted the snow at them in wild flurries, clinging to their uniforms and faces and making it impossible for them to see more than twenty or so paces ahead.

Figulus was shivering despite the military cloak draped over his shoulders and the woollen tunic under his armour. The cold stabbed viciously at his face and before long his hands and feet were almost numb. He hated this rank place. He could think of nothing more he'd love to do at that moment than warm his frozen hands at the crackling fire in his quarters at the barracks. Then Figulus reminded himself that as an officer in the Roman army he couldn't afford to show any hint of weakness. Not if he wanted to command the respect of his men. He had to appear fearless despite the anxieties and doubts troubling his mind. So he forced himself to push on through the marshes, cold and grim-faced.

After another half a mile the track began to disappear beneath the snow and the guide slowed the pace as it became increasingly difficult to pick his way through the vile marshland. Figulus glanced back down the column to check on his men. All of them were frozen to the bone and marching on with their heads down to shield their faces from the biting cold. The Batavian auxiliaries to the rear appeared anxious, constantly directing worried glances left and right of the track, as if they half expected the enemy to come charging out of the gorse thickets.

'How much further?' Figulus asked the guide.

'Not far, Roman,' the scrawny Briton replied in coarse Latin. 'A mile or so. Don't worry. We will be there soon enough.'

'Don't worry, he says!' Blaesus moaned as he marched just behind the optio. 'Bollocks to that! At this rate it'll be Saturnalia by the time we reach the bloody stash.'

Rullus chuckled and glanced back at Helva. 'Bet you don't get winters like this in Campania, lad.'

'G-g-gods, no!' the young legionary gasped, his teeth chattering as he shivered beneath his uniform in the wet and slimy cold. 'How by Jupiter's cock do these people survive here?'

'Beer,' Rullus replied. 'They drink a lot of beer, lad. And they're forever fighting each other. Keeps 'em warm.'

Figulus swept his eyes to left and right but he could see no sign of enemy movement, only the shifting shadows of the marshes in the cold gloomy light of winter. He swivelled his gaze back to the track.

Rullus shivered. 'This place gives me the fucking horrors, sir.'

'That makes two of us,' Figulus replied.

A mile or so further along, the column veered close to the edge of the marshes and reached a sharp bend in the track. Suddenly the guide froze on the spot. Figulus immediately threw up his hand and the entire column lumbered to a halt. He edged forward and moved alongside the guide. The Briton glanced at Figulus then pointed out a series of deep impressions in the snow, continuing round the bend and up the track towards a slight rise. At first Figulus thought they were animal tracks. Then he shook his head. No. These were bigger.

'Footprints,' the guide hissed.

Figulus nodded slowly, counting the impressions. There were several sets of footprints, all leading in the same direction. They were still fresh in the snow and Figulus realised they had to have been very recent. He looked back at Rullus and spoke quietly.

'Wait here with the lads. Have them stand to.'

'Right you are, sir,' Rullus said in a hushed tone. 'Where are you going?'

Figulus pointed to a drumlin to the side of the marsh, running parallel to the track. 'I'm going to have a closer look from up there. Helva, follow me.'

The young legionary nodded firmly. 'Yes, sir.'

The two soldiers made their way up the slope in silence, the sound of their breathing and the faint metallic chinking of their armour muted by the snow. Here and there grassy tussocks poked out of the snow, patches of green in an otherwise blank white vista. It was a short climb to the top of the drumlin but the gradient was steep and by the time Figulus reached the snow-capped crest he had worked up a sweat beneath his winter layers. With Helva at his side, Figulus moved in a low stoop towards the far side of the drumlin overlooking the marshes. Down below he could see the track skirting the wetlands as it headed towards a clearing on a slight rise a short distance away. In the middle of the rising ground stood a simple timber-framed structure that Figulus presumed was the Druids' lodge. Mounds of snow-covered turf were heaped to one side of the lodge, he noticed.

'Shit!' Helva said in an excited whisper. 'Sir, look!'

Figulus followed his pointing finger, squinting in the early-morning gloom. A line of figures stood close to the lodge. They had rested their oval bronze shields and javelins against the side of the lodge and were busy lifting amphoras out of several large pits. Each pit was several feet wide and big enough to store a large hoard of grain. The Britons worked quickly, carrying the amphoras from the pits over to a dozen native chariots fitted with wooden side panels and converted into crude transport carts. They appeared to be in a hurry. Several more armed Britons stood guard over the chariots. These men wore armour and helmets and looked to be more of a challenge than the men Figulus had encountered on the bridge. He tightened his grip on the handle of his shield.

'They're removing the grain hoard,' he hissed, forcing himself not to display any hint of anxiety in front of Helva. 'We've got to stop them before it's too late.'

He sent Helva back down the drumlin with orders to bring the men forward, leaving the grain wagons behind on the track with a pair of auxiliaries and the native guide to guard them. After what felt like a very long time Rullus and the rest of the soldiers manoeuvred up the slope to join the optio, taking care to make as little noise as possible. Fighting the rising tension in his chest, Figulus took a deep breath and addressed the men in a low, calm voice.

'The enemy's emptying the grain pits,' he explained, pointing down at the clearing. 'There's no time to lose if we're to stop them. On my command we'll move down the slope. Until I give the word, everyone stays quiet. Anyone who makes a fucking noise will find themselves on a charge.'

'At bloody last,' Blaesus said with a grim smile. 'Some proper soldiering.'

Rullus scratched his chin, wearing a puzzled expression. 'Why are those bastards in such a rush to move the grain, I wonder?'

Figulus shrugged. 'There's no time to worry about that. They're busy loading up their chariots, so they won't see us coming until it's too late. Hit them hard and don't stop until we've cut every one of them down. We'll have 'em trapped between us and the marsh. All clear?'

Every man nodded. Gripping his shield, Figulus crept towards the edge of the drumlin. He slowly drew his sword, the blade scraping quietly against the scabbard. He was suddenly gripped by a moment of self-doubt. If he failed to prevent the Britons escaping with the grain, his efforts to protect the king would have been in vain and the settlement would be plunged into chaos. Figulus steeled his muscles, suddenly conscious of the dull ache from the stitched wound on his neck. Then he filled his lungs with cold air.

'At the trot . . . advance!' he called down the line.

On his command the men pounded down the side of the drumlin, towards the clearing. Figulus led the way, the wind moaning in his ears. Over at the pits the Britons stopped what they were doing and turned as one towards the snow-covered slope. Those nearest to the lodge immediately ditched the amphoras in the deep snow and seized their spears and shields. Several hurled their javelins at the advancing Romans. A shrill scream cut through the freezing air as a javelin punched through an auxiliary to the right of Figulus. A second auxiliary was struck down by a javelin and Figulus saw the man sink to his knees, clutching the wooden shaft. Other javelins clattered into the soldiers' raised shields or stabbed into the snow. Figulus kept his head low and raced on.

'Get 'em!' he roared.

The soldiers reached the clearing and closed on the Britons in a tight-knit formation, their armour and sword points glinting dully under the overcast sky. They were close enough now for Figulus to make out the Britons' features and the mysterious tattoos on their forearms. The snow had drifted in places, slowing the pace of the Romans' advance. The rest of the Britons grabbed their swords and spears and charged towards the Romans, falling upon them and lunging and stabbing. The strength and skill of these warriors took Figulus by surprise. A couple of auxiliaries were swiftly cut down by the Britons, and the fight quickly deteriorated into a desperate melee.

Figulus realised that his men were in imminent danger of being overrun. Hefting up his shield, he pounded through the snow and raced towards the nearest Briton, training his sword point at the man and yelling at the top of his voice in an effort to inspire his men to victory. The squat warrior drove his spear at Figulus with a vicious thrust. The Gaul dropped low and evaded the blow then pushed up and struck out at the shaft of his opponent's spear with an outward swipe of his sword, knocking the man off balance. Before he could recover Figulus sprang forward with his shoulders hunched and his elbow tucked tight to his side, investing all of his forward momentum into thrusting his sword at his foe's guts. The Briton's eyes went wide with shock as the blade slammed into his stomach. Figulus drove his weapon up under the man's ribcage, lacerating his vital organs. The man grimaced with pain and slumped forward, the sword still embedded in him up to the handle.

Kneeling down, Figulus ripped his blade free from the dying Briton with a grisly sucking noise. He spun round to face his next enemy, the blood rushing in his ears above the brittle clattering sounds of the skirmish. Figulus punched out with his shield at a powerfully built Briton bearing down on him, knocking him back a couple of steps. Then he hacked open the man's throat with a violent slash of his sword. A gout of blood sprayed out of the man's wound and he sank to his knees and clamped his hands round his neck in a futile attempt to staunch the hot flow of blood.

Glancing around, Figulus glimpsed the bodies of three auxiliaries slumped on the ground, their blood spattering the pristine snow. The enemy was better armed than the usual ragtag native armies Figulus had fought against elsewhere in Britannia and they attacked with an almost unbelievable ferocity, forcing the Romans to shrink behind their shields in order to block the steady stream of blows raining down on them. These warriors would not surrender easily, Figulus knew. Their fanatic Druid priests taught them that great rewards awaited the Durotrigans in the afterlife if they died in battle against the Romans. The only thing for it was to stay disciplined and hit the enemy hard. Filling his lungs, Figulus bellowed for his men to hold their ranks and push back the enemy.

'Sir!' Helva cried. 'Look there!'

Figulus swung his gaze across the clearing, his eyes chasing the direction the young legionary was pointing. He caught sight of several Britons beyond the melee. They had finished loading the amphoras on to the converted chariots and were now driving the horses in a bid to make their escape from the clearing with the stolen grain. Figulus felt a sharp stab of anxiety as he looked on. Any moment now the chariots would disappear down the track into the vast unmapped sprawl of the marshes, taking the grain with them. The fate of Lindinis, and the wider Roman invasion, hung in the balance. There was no time to formulate a plan. He simply had to act. He looked to the men on his immediate left and right, his heart thumping erratically.

'We've got to get to the horses, lads!' Figulus shouted above the thud and clatter all around him. He turned to Rullus. 'Stay here with the men. Kill every last one of these scum.'

Rullus smiled grimly. 'With pleasure, sir.'

Then Figulus bolted forward, moving across the open ground as fast as he could under the heavy weight of his armour and equipment. Blaesus and Helva and a trio of auxiliaries rushed alongside him. Up ahead the chariots had steered down the clearing and were now drawing close to the snow-covered track. For a moment Figulus feared that they were going to escape. But, weighed down by their heavy grain loads, the normally light and fast chariots sank into the churned mud and melting snow of the track and ground to a halt.

'Now we've got 'em, lads!' Figulus roared, increasing his stride as the snow thinned out towards the track. 'On me!'

In a few more strides the Romans reached the stricken chariots. They hacked at the horses' hamstrings in the manner they had been taught in training, preventing the animals from pulling the chariots free of the filthy quagmire. The horses shrieked in agony as Figulus and his comrades slashed at their limbs causing their legs to collapse beneath them One mount kicked out at the nearest auxiliary, knocking him to the ground. Before the soldier could rise to his feet the wounded horse fell on its flank, toppling the overloaded cart on to its side and the auxiliary screamed as the wheel came crashing down on him, crushing his ribcage. At the same time the drivers jumped down from their chariots and tried to flee down the track but Figulus and his men instantly fell upon them, before they could escape into the marshes.

Several shouts rang out above the metallic ringing of blades and the solid crack of weapons clattering against shields. Figulus spun away from the chariots and spied a few Britons charging towards them. They had seen what was happening to their imperilled companions and were now coming to their aid.

'Turn and face!' Figulus shouted throatily at his comrades. 'Whatever you do, don't let them get to the grain!'

The men turned simultaneously towards the onrushing Britons and stood firm in the mire as the warriors launched themselves at them in an attempt to salvage the grain, thrusting their long swords against their opponents' shields. In the periphery of his vision Figulus saw Blaesus stumbling backwards as an enormous Briton wrenched his shield free from his grip. With a menacing snarl the Briton drove the point of his spear at Blaesus's neck. The legionary reacted in an instant, deflecting the blow with an upward jerk of his sword. The warrior feinted, thrusting his weapon at his opponent's midriff. Blaesus saw the attack too late to react. The spear punched into his groin and he grunted in pain, folding at the waist. Then the Briton tore his weapon free with a savage grunt. Figulus looked on in horror as Blaesus crumpled to the ground.

'Over here!' he screamed at the Briton. 'Come on, you bastard!'

The warrior spun away from the stricken legionary. Figulus rushed at the man, gripped by a compulsive desire to avenge his fallen comrade. The Briton stood his ground, wielding his heavy spear in a two-handed grip. He was the biggest man Figulus had ever seen, with bulging biceps and legs wide as tree trunks. His weapon looked tiny in his huge grip and his face was fixed into a savage snarl as he swung the point of his weapon round. Figulus jerked up his shield at the last possible moment. It shuddered violently as the spear tip clattered against the metallic boss. The Briton stayed at more than a sword's length from his opponent so Figulus aimed for the spear shaft instead, intending to strike it down. In a lightning-fast motion the warrior swung his weapon round then thrust the butt of his spear at Figulus, striking him in the chest. The blow was vicious and almost toppled him.

Figulus quickly regained his balance and smashed his shield into the Briton's face. Then he dropped his shield and jabbed his short sword into the gap above it. He felt the blade shudder as it glanced off bone and Figulus rammed his weapon home, giving it a vicious twist and drawing a gasp of pain from his stunned opponent. The optio wrenched his sword back but to his surprise the wounded Britain was still standing. The warrior came again, blood staining his mangled teeth as he bellowed in anger. He kicked out at Figulus, booting him in the stomach and winding him. Figulus lost his grip on his sword and shield and stumbled backwards as he struggled to avoid slipping in the soft mud and animal blood.

The Briton threw himself at Figulus, knocking him to the ground and clamping his huge hands around the optio's throat and squeezing tight, crushing his windpipe. Figulus rocked left and right in a desperate attempt to throw his opponent off but the man was too heavy even for the burly Gaul and slowly Figulus could feel the world turning dim and dark and he knew he was close to blacking out. He heard a distant shout and several legionaries descended upon the powerfully built Briton, thrusting their swords into his back to try to finish him off. But the blows seemed to have little effect on the man's strength and Figulus felt himself starting to lose consciousness. Then Rullus swept forwards and there was a brief flash of steel as he punched his blade into the Briton's throat. The enormous tribesman spasmed, making a gasping sound in his throat. Blood leaked out of the wound as Rullus wrenched the blade free, and soaked Figulus. The optio rolled the dying Briton off him and lifted his eyes to see Rullus standing over him, blood dripping from the glistening tip of his lowered sword.

'That's the last of 'em, sir. Need a hand?'

Figulus accepted Rullus's hand and climbed unsteadily to his feet. He scooped up his weapon and then turned towards the clearing. The Britons had been pushed back towards the marsh, pursued by the soldiers, who finished off any warriors still drawing breath. Some of the remaining enemy plunged into the marsh in a blind panic, preferring to chance their luck in the freezing marshes rather than accept capture or death at the hands of their Roman enemies. Those soldiers who were armed with javelins threw them at the retreating Britons, and agonised screams rang out as the javelins struck their targets, impaling the warriors before they could escape. Their lifeless bodies slowly sank into the mire.

The fight was over. Both sides had suffered heavy losses. The pained cries of the wounded rose up from the clearing into the frosty sky as they lay bleeding in the snow. Figulus spotted several of his own men slumped on the ground, the white flakes gently settling on their still bodies. Blood pooled out from beneath them, staining the snow dark red.

Figulus hurried over to Blaesus. The legionary lay on his back, shaking horribly as his body convulsed with shock at the severe loss of blood. Figulus examined his injuries. Blood was pumping steadily out of his wound, slicking his tunic and spilling across the greasy brown slush around him. With a great effort Blaesus lifted his eyes to Figulus and swallowed painfully.

'Did we win, sir?' he asked in a barely audible croak.

Figulus placed a hand on his shoulder and nodded. 'We won,' he replied softly. 'We beat the lot of 'em.'

Blaesus smiled. 'It was a good fight, sir.' He winced in pain and shivered. 'It's cold . . .'

'Easy, there,' Figulus said. 'Save your energy. We'll get you back to the fort as quick as we can.'

But his eyes were already dimming, like the flames of a dying fire. There was nothing that could be done for him. Figulus watched helplessly as the legionary closed his eyes for the last time.

'Yes, sir,' Blaesus whispered. 'It was a good fight . . .'

Then he stopped shivering. The breath no longer misted in front of his parted lips. His body went rigid. Figulus watched him for a moment and whispered a final goodbye to his comrade. He was lost for a moment in his thoughts. Then one of the legionaries called out.

'Some of 'em are escaping that way, sir!' Vatia announced breathlessly, pointing at the drumlin. A few shadowed figures were climbing up the slope. Figulus stood up and nodded vaguely.

'Go after them. Take a few of the lads with you. But be careful. No heroics.' He lowered his eyes to Blaesus and swallowed hard. 'We've lost enough good men for one day.'

Vatia nodded and set off towards the drumlin with a handful of legionaries. It did not take long to cut down the fleeing Britons. Once the last of them had been killed, Figulus gave the order for the wagons to be brought up through the quagmire and he organised the exhausted men into eight-man teams to begin the arduous task of loading up the carts with the grain amphoras, transferring them from the chariots. The native dead were left where they lay, slowly covered by the falling snow. Figulus assigned a pair of auxiliaries to collect the Roman dead and wounded and load them on to the last of the carts. Blaesus was among them. Rullus stood alongside the optio, watching in silence as their comrade's body was placed on the cart.

'Poor bastard,' Rullus said at last, lowering his head. 'They don't come any braver than Blaesus, sir. If we had a hundred men like him in the Second, this war would be over tomorrow.'

Figulus looked down. His hand was trembling. He balled it into a tight fist. He turned away, suddenly feeling very tired.

In the grey light Figulus forced himself to focus on the mission at hand. He knew he had to return to the settlement as soon as possible. With the supplies they had rescued, there would be enough grain to allow the locals to eke out their lives for the next month at least. That would go some way towards assuaging their hatred of their king and give him a chance to to establish his authority. Disaster had narrowly been averted, but it felt like no kind of victory to Figulus. He was about to give the order for the shattered remnants of the column to thread their way out of the marsh when a cry went up from across the clearing.

'Sir!' Helva shouted. 'Look at this.'

Figulus paced wearily over to the legionary. He saw several faint sets of footprints leading from the lodge to thick tangles of gorse at the edge of the clearing. Helva was standing over several more deep pits dug into the loose soil. He'd scraped off the snow and drawn back the leather covers.

Then Figulus saw something gleaming dully in the bottom of the pit. A sword, he realised. He set down his equipment and dropped down into the pit. It was deep as a man and wide enough to accommodate a wagon. He reached down and picked up the sword lying on the ground. From the length and the ivory ridged handle he recognised it as a legionary weapon. In one corner of the pit Figulus spotted a helmet and a dagger and a pair of leg greaves. They were sprinkled with loose dirt. Figulus stood in the pit for a moment, his mind racing.

'What is it, sir?' Helva asked anxiously.

'This was a weapons haul,' Figulus replied, gulping as the dread implication of the discovery sank in. 'I've seen 'em before. The Druids nick whatever kit they can from our dead soldiers and store it away until it's needed. But whoever emptied this haul did it in a hurry. And that means only one thing.'

'What's that, sir?'

Figulus looked up at Helva and paused. 'They knew we were coming.'

CHAPTER TWENTY-NINE

'Well, I must say that is unfortunate,' Scylla tutted. 'We badly needed a prisoner.'

Figulus stood in the royal hall, caked in mud as he finished making his report to the imperial envoy. Scylla sat at the table in front of the dais, grazing on some of the leftovers from the previous night's feast. Around him the king's house slaves were hard at work cleaning up the mess from the failed assassination attempt, soaking up the dried bloodstains and puddles of beer on the floor while others moved from table to table, collecting the discarded drinking horns and shattered clay cups strewn across the open space.

The optio and his remaining men had returned to the settlement earlier that morning as the sun finally broke through the grey clouds. Five of his men had perished in the fight, along with thirteen auxiliaries. Nearly all the Britons who they had engaged had been killed, except for a few stragglers who managed to escape into the marshes. As they marched through the streets, Figulus couldn't help noticing how quiet the settlement was. There had been no sign of the angry protests of the night before. Once the wagons had returned, the king had announced that there would be an ample grain ration to every man, woman and child, silencing the tongues of those who opposed his reign. After the soldiers had unloaded the grain and returned the wagons to the fort, Figulus dismissed his men. They quietly headed off to mourn their brothers in arms with a jug of wine in their quarters. Figulus was tempted to join them. But he had to make his report to Scylla, including the discovery of the emptied pit where the natives had stored their wepaons.

'You are to be commended on the rescue of the stolen grain, I suppose,' Scylla continued as he chewed on a mouthful of pastry. 'Now that the natives have food the immediate threat to the king's regime is over. But the failure to capture any of the enemy alive is a mistake on your part.'

Figulus bit his tongue, bristling with rage at the thought of Blaesus and the others who had died during the skirmish. There was no point trying to explain that the fight for the grain had been a close run thing, that the soldiers' blood had been up and giving an order to take the men alive in such circumstances was likely to be ignored in the blood and sweat of battle. There was no point saying any of this, because Scylla wouldn't understand.

'A prisoner would have proved highly useful to us,' Scylla went on. 'They may have been able to provide intelligence about these damned Druids.'

'But we still have the assassin. We can try questioning him again. He obviously knows more than he's letting on.'

'Sadly we cannot.' Scylla stared blankly at the optio.

Figulus frowned. 'Why?'

'The assassin is dead,' Scylla responded tonelessly. 'He took his own life in his cell. He had a small blade secreted in his loincloth. The guards think he must have smuggled it in and then used it to cut his throat when no one was looking. Apparently no one thought to search him thoroughly. Any lingering hopes we had of discovering the whereabouts of the Druids' lair have been dashed. Now we must consider the unpleasant likelihood that your discovery of their weapons cache means that there are more of the enemy out there in the marshes. Well-armed men sworn to serve the Dark Moon Druids.'

'It seems so,' Figulus replied. He had roughly estimated the number of swords, shields and armour that might have fitted into the weapons pits. If there was an army of enemy warriors lurking close by, the poorly trained Batavian cohort would be no match for them in a pitched battle.

Scylla nodded. 'Then I must write to Vitellius and request he sends us some reinforcements from Calleva at once.' He smiled wanly. 'I rather doubt the tribune will find the word of an imperial agent easy to ignore. In the meantime, you and your men will remain in Lindinis.'

211

Figulus did not attempt to hide his disappointment. 'What for?'

'We still need to train up some of the locals to provide Trenagasus with a royal bodyguard. I'd say you and your comrades are just the men to instruct the recruits.'

'What about the auxiliaries? Can't they do the job?'

'Cosconianus says he can't spare the men. His ranks are busy keeping order. And we need good soldiers to train the locals. Not those Batavian dogs.' He stiffened. 'I've already made arrangements with Trenagasus. He's agreed to the plan. Being protected by a complement of natives ought to silence those critics accusing the king of being a Roman puppet.'

'If we can trust 'em,' Figulus countered. 'What if the Druids try to sneak one of their agents onto the bodyguard? What then?'

'Taken care of, Optio. Every recruit will be personally vetted by the king and his advisers.' The envoy furrowed his brow. 'The few he still trusts, at least. Trenagasus is understandably rather nervous after the attempt on his life. He's keeping all but a few of his trusted advisers at arm's length.'

'Can't say I blame him. Not with half the locals baying for his blood.'

'You'll begin your duties next week. Once all the volunteers have been fully vetted.'

Scylla promptly stood up from the chair and stretched to his full height. The smile disappeared.

'There is something else that concerns me. Something has been playing on my mind ever since we arrived in Lindinis.' He glanced at a nearby pair of house slaves and waited until they had moved away before continuing. 'First, the enemy learned of our intention to install Trenagasus on the throne before we arrived here, when his return was supposed to be a closely guarded secret. We must also consider the fact that someone coerced the gladiator into making an attempt on the king's life.'

'The agent working for the Druids. The man with the hood.'

Scylla nodded. 'Rather conveniently, the assassin dies in captivity before we can get him to reveal the agent's identity. And then the Druids somehow learn that the location of the grain store has been compromised and very nearly manage to remove the hoard before we can prevent them. Worse still, they had already moved their weapons cache to a new hiding place.' He stopped dead in his tracks and looked at Figulus. 'There is only one conclusion we can possibly draw.'

'What's that?' Figulus asked.

'We have a traitor in our midst, Optio. Someone close to Trenagasus is working for the enemy.'

CHAPTER THIRTY

Six days later Figulus and Rullus marched towards the parade ground as the bleak winter sun struggled above the fort's palisade. Ahead of them stood a silent throng of Durotrigans, shivering in the icy breeze. The main thoroughfare was covered in a heavy fall of snow and some of the Britons stamped their feet in an attempt to stave off the numbing cold. The recruits for the king's new royal bodyguard were watched over by a handful of Batavian auxiliaries from the garrison, their armour and helmets gleaming dully in the thin morning light.

'Look at these sorry barbarian bastards,' Rullus muttered in a low voice. 'Hardly a decent specimen amongst 'em. Still can't believe we've got the job to train them, sir. Why us? Why not leave it to the Batavians?'

'It's not so bad a job,' Figulus said. 'Beats sitting around on our arses all day playing dice.'

'Speak for yourself, sir,' Rullus responded gruffly. 'Me, I'd rather be nursing a nice cheap jar of mulsum instead of teaching these idiots how to hold a bloody sword. Speaking of which, I hear there's a new wine merchant setting up business in the town. We should give it a try later.' He nodded his head in the direction of Lindinis. 'About bloody time there was a decent watering hole in this stinking pit.'

One of the Durotrigan king's first acts on his return to the throne had been to open the doors of the capital to all the Roman traders, pimps and slave dealers who followed the legions wherever they went, eager to exploit new opportunities. A few days earlier a handful of wine traders had arrived in Lindinis, looking to profit from the garrison's bored off-duty soldiers, as well as the locals. More merchants would surely follow once the Durotriges had been transformed into peaceful allies of Rome.

214

'Maybe another time,' Figulus replied distractedly.

'Don't tell me you're still pissed off over losing that lucky charm of yours?'

Figulus nodded but said nothing. His medallion had gone missing a few days earlier. He'd searched every inch of his quarters but so far he'd had no luck in finding it.

'It was a gift from my father. He earned it during his service as a cavalryman in the auxiliaries. He gave it to me the day I left for the camp at Gesoriacum. I've never fought a battle without it. Last time I had it was on the parade ground.'

Rullus clicked his tongue. 'I wouldn't get your hopes up of ever seeing it again. Especially if one of those grubby natives has got their hands on it. Anyway, luck doesn't keep you alive in the legions. It's skill and discipline that count. I didn't make it through twenty-two years of service relying on luck, sir.'

Figulus smiled briefly at his comrade as they approached the waiting tribesmen. The Durotrigans cast wary glances at the Roman soldiers as Prefect Cosconianus strode purposefully over, an irritable expression on his face. Figulus immediately stiffened to attention. Cosconianus nodded curtly.

'At ease, Optio,' he said, sweeping an arm towards the undisciplined natives. 'Your recruits. The imperial envoy sends his compliments, but says he's busy poring over plans for the king's new palace. Seems it's not enough that we put the king back on his throne, now we have to build him a lavish home to go with it.' He fixed Figulus with a stare as he went on. 'You're free to use this parade ground for training purposes, but I'll expect you to make sure your recruits don't get in the way of my men as they go about their duties. Am I clear?'

Figulus nodded keenly. 'Yes, sir.'

'Good.' Cosconianus frowned at the parade ground. 'You'll need training equipment. There's plenty in the fort's stores. It goes without saying that you're responsible for anything this lot break. The last thing I need right now is some nit-picking clerk on the imperial staff billing me for equipment that's been damaged by these halfwits.'

'What about accommodation for the men, sir?'

'We'll billet them in one of the empty barracks. It's not as if we are pressed for space.'

Cosconianus cleared his throat and gestured for one of the recruits to step forwards. A tall, broad-shouldered man approached. He was dressed in a dark woollen cloak, his hair cut short and his face cleanly shaven in the Roman style, unlike the unkempt beards of his wild-haired companions. He smiled at Figulus, revealing a set of small, stained teeth.

'This is Bellicanus,' Cosconianus explained. 'One of the king's inner circle. Trenagasus has appointed him as captain of the body-guard. He'll assist you in training the men.'

Bellicanus bowed slightly at Figulus. 'It's an honour to meet you, Optio,' he said in good Latin. 'I've been wanting to meet the man who saved my king's life.'

'I don't recall seeing you in the king's entourage.'

Bellicanus smiled. 'That is because I only returned to Lindinis a few days ago, Roman. For the past few years I have been living in Durnovaria. But I was born here. My father served on the king's wise council. Indeed, he was the king's most trusted adviser.'

'Was?'

The Durotrigan noble nodded. 'When the Dark Moon Druids forced my king into exile, all the men on his council were rounded up and put to death. I managed to escape before the Druids could kill me too. Once I heard that Trenagasus had returned to claim his throne, I came back as quickly as I could.' His voice carried a clear note of pride as he added, 'Now I am here to serve my king, as my father did before me.'

Cosconianus straightened his back and nodded briskly. 'If that's everything, I'll be off. If you have any problems, speak to my clerks.'

With that he turned and marched back down the main thorough-fare, accompanied by his auxiliaries. Figulus watched the prefect depart and then turned to Bellicanus. He jerked a thumb in the direction of the recruits, some thirty men in all.

'How many of this lot have any fighting experience?'

Bellicanus frowned. 'Six of us. Those who are from the warrior caste. They're reasonably fit and have been using weapons since childhood. Myself included.'

Figulus nodded. 'And the rest?'

'Farmers, mostly. A handful of hunters. The best of our tribesmen were killed last year in the fight against Rome,' he said solemnly. 'These men may not be a match for Roman soldiers, but they're as brave as any man.'

'Bravery didn't save 'em when we kicked their arses last summer, did it?' said Rullus.

Bellicanus scowled at the legionary and took half a step forwards before Figulus intervened.

'Right, then. Let's see what this lot's made of.'

Figulus called the men to attention in the native tongue. At his command the recruits slowly formed into a loose line two ranks deep. A jolt of awareness hit Figulus as he realised that many of the Durotrigans were badly out of shape; thin and gaunt. Others were old. Many of them wore sullen looks and glared at Figulus with obvious hostility – partly because they had been compelled to join the bodyguard, but mostly because he was a Roman. Earning the respect of these men was not going to be easy, he realised. He took a deep breath as he prepared to address the Durotrigans.

'My name is Horatius Figulus!' he called out clearly. 'Optio of the Second Legion, the toughest legion in the empire. Roman legionaries are the best trained soldiers in the known world, and you lot are going to train the same way. That means you'll address me as "sir" or "optio" from now on. Got it?'

A cold silence drifted across the parade ground. The recruits stared back at Figulus with a mixture of apprehension and resentment.

'I said, got it?' he shouted.

'Yes, sir,' the recruits replied weakly.

'LET ME BLOODY WELL HEAR IT!'

'YES, SIR!'

Figulus nodded. 'That's better.' He afforded himself a slight smile. 'Now, there's a good reason why the legions win more battles than anyone else. Someone want to tell me why?'

The recruits exchanged blank looks. Some simply blinked at Figulus with dull, bovine expressions.

'Training. You idiots!' He growled irritably. 'In the legions we train harder than anyone else. Endless training is why Rome wins its wars, and it's how you lot are going to become a royal bodyguard worthy of the name.'

217

He paused as he recalled the relentless drills he'd practised at Gesoriacum. On his first day of basic training Figulus had felt the full force of the drill centurion's vine cane after he'd failed to form up in the correct manner. After that painful introduction to discipline, Figulus had been forced to adapt quickly to the harsh standards required by the legions. There were times when the drill centurion despaired of the big Gaul's clumsy nature and his scruffy, wild-haired appearance. But Figulus had worked hard and refused to give up. Now he was a proud soldier of Rome, a junior officer at the tender age of nineteen. He turned to Bellicanus.

'May as well get started. We'll begin with a few sprints around the fort. Get the men nicely warmed up.'

Bellicanus frowned. 'Sprints? Shouldn't we be learning how to fight rather than run around in circles?'

'You'll learn how to fight once you are fit enough to fight.' Figulus leaned in close to the Briton and lowered his voice. 'And another thing. You'll address me in the proper fashion. Same as everyone else on the royal bodyguard.'

A look of surprise flared briefly on the Durotrigan noble's face and he opened his mouth to protest. Then he thought better of it and clamped his lips shut and nodded. 'Forgive me . . . sir.'

'Better. Helva!'

'The young legionary instantly sprang to attention. 'Yes, sir?'

'Take this lot for a run around the fort. Twenty laps. Set a steady pace, mind. Nothing too quick. I don't want 'em flat on their backs.' Figulus grinned. 'Not yet, anyway.'

'Yes, sir!'

Figulus barked his instructions at the Durotrigans. A few moments later they set off at a trot after Helva as the legionary followed a rough path that had been cleared through the snow. Soon the chasing pack of Britons were puffing and panting as they struggled to keep up with Helva and they fell further back. Figulus looked on anxiously as he watched the recruits staggering around the perimeter of the fort.

'This isn't going to be easy,' he muttered.

Rullus clicked his tongue. 'When is it ever, sir? One thing's for sure, we've got our work cut out getting this lot up to scratch.'

CHAPTER THIRTY-ONE

Over the following weeks, Figulus and his comrades worked the native recruits hard. At first light each morning the Durotrigans formed up on the parade ground in front of the legionary instructors and warmed up with several laps of the fort, followed by a series of sprints between sets of coloured markers. After a short break for a cup of vinegared water and a chunk of hard bread, Figulus led the men on a forced march beyond the walls of the fort. Each recruit was given a marching yoke weighed down with a bag of rocks and ordered to move at the same pace as the legionaries. After a while the column became stretched out as the less fit recruits fell further behind those drawn from the warrior caste. But none of the men dropped out, and even the weakest natives displayed a grim determination that impressed the young optio.

The new year dawned and, once he was satisfied with their fitness, Figulus moved on to basic swordplay. Rullus set up a series of wooden training posts staked along one side of the parade ground, each one as tall as a man. Wooden swords and wicker shields lay in a pair of transport carts at the edge of the ground, ready for distribution as the recruits assembled early that morning.

'There are two ways of cutting down a man in a fight,' Figulus announced to the recruits as he paced up and down the line. 'The first is the way you lot have been taught since birth – hacking and slashing at your opponent in single combat. That's all very well if you're a showboating gladiator or if you're seeking a glorious death in battle. But in the legions, we prefer to leave the dying to the enemy. That's why our main sword-fighting technique is to use the point of the sword rather than the edge.'

219

Figulus reached his hand down to his right side and drew his short sword with a casual flourish. Then he hefted the weapon above his head so that every recruit could see it. The sword tip glinted menacingly beneath the pale sun.

'This is a legionary sword,' he explained. 'As you can see it's much shorter than the long swords most of you have fought with. Used correctly, the Roman short sword is the perfect killing weapon.'

In a compromise between the king's enthusiasm for a Roman-style bodyguard and the need to appease his subjects, the imperial envoy had decided that in matters of uniform, the bodyguards would be free to dress according to their native custom, but their equipment should be the standard legionary sword and the same oval shield as the Batavian auxiliaries. The arrangement suited Figulus since he'd never used the longer Celtic sword before and was much more comfortable training the men with a weapon that had come to feel like an extension of his arm. He approached the nearest post and aimed the weapon's tip at a point roughly halfway up.

'Slashing at your opponent might look spectacular, but a nice, firm stab to the vitals is much more effective.' He tapped the tip of the sword against the post. 'A few inches of sharpened steel to the stomach is your best bet. Lots of organs, not much bone to deflect your thrust. Stab your enemy here and he'll be out of the fight, and as likely as not he'll die from the wound.'

The Durotrigans listened in uneasy silence. Figulus stepped away from the post and sheathed his weapon.

'Remember,' he continued. 'Thrust at your enemy, don't hack. Aim for the stomach or the throat, and for fuck's sake keep your shield up at all times. Stick to those basic rules and you'll have a much better chance of defending yourselves, and your king.'

Figulus turned to Rullus and signalled to him to begin handing out the training weapons. The legionary pulled back the leather cover from the transport cart and shouted at the other instructors, and they began distributing the wooden swords to the recruits. Many of the Britons regarded the weapons with disdain, arms folded across their chests. To a man they seemed unimpressed with the shorter Roman sword.

'What's up with this lot?' Figulus asked Bellicanus, nodding at the recruits. 'Don't they want to learn how to fight?'

Suddenly a throaty shout erupted from the ranks as a dark-haired Durotrigan threw his weapon to the ground in a fit of anger. His torso was thick with muscle and he wore a decorative silver torc with a pair of serpent's heads on either end. The man's name was Andocommius, the optio recalled. One of the warrior caste.

A tense silence fell over the other recruits as Figulus marched up to the Briton. He was aware that the other recruits were watching him intently, curious to see how he would deal with this flagrant breach of discipline. He halted in front of Andocommius and pointed to the sword lying at his feet.

'Pick it up.'

Andocommius sneered at him and folded his arms defiantly across his muscled chest. Figulus noticed that the Durotrigan warrior had a prominent scar running down the side of his face. A look of hatred glowed in his dark eyes.

'Why should I, Roman?' Andocommius rasped. 'You insult us!' He waved an arm at the other warriors among the recruits. 'We have been fighting wars since before you were born. Now you force us to practise with these wooden toys? We should be using proper weapons!'

The other warriors chorused his protest and Figulus sensed the dissent spreading through the ranks. He tensed his muscles and stepped into Andocommius's face.

'You'll train with that sword until I say otherwise,' he growled, jabbing a finger at the man's chest.

'Why? So you can teach me to fight like a child?' A ripple of laughter sounded among the other recruits. The warrior spat. 'There is no honour in the way you Romans fight.'

Figulus glowered at the warrior. 'Think you're too good to be trained, eh? Then prove it.'

The optio cast off his military cloak and picked up one of the spare training swords from the transport cart. The warrior formed a cruel smile on his lips as he dropped to a crouch, took up his weapon and prepared to fight. At the same time the other recruits and instructors shuffled back, forming a rough circle around the two men and giving them space. Figulus tightened his grip around the sword's wooden handle. The weapon was deliberately designed to be twice as heavy as the real thing. That way a recruit would develop the necessary strength in training to comfortably wield a proper sword in battle without tiring.

Andocommius hurled himself at Figulus, swinging his weapon in a broad arc towards his opponent's neck. Figulus quickly adjusted his posture and blocked the slash with an upward swipe of his sword. The wooden weapon shuddered with the stunning impact from the blow as the shock travelled down his arm. Andocommius came at him a second time, surprising Figulus with his speed of movement, and the optio found himself retreating several steps as his opponent rained down blow after savage blow, to cheers of support from the other warriors. Figulus blocked each attack, digging his heels into the dirt and watching his opponent carefully.

Andocommius drew a breath then charged again at Figulus, this time driving his sword up at an angle towards the latter's throat. The Gaul read the move and sidestepped the blow, then advanced towards his unsuspecting opponent, slamming the hilt of his sword into his face with a distinct crack. Andocommius stumbled backwards, groaning as blood gushed freely out of his nostrils and ran down his chin.

The warrior shook his head clear. His chest heaved up and down as his expression became enraged. He snarled and hacked at Figulus, but his blow was clumsy this time and the optio smoothly parried it with a deft swipe of his sword. Then Figulus stepped inside his opponent and slammed the blunt tip into Andocommius's midriff with a hard thud. The Briton's mouth went slack and he sank to his knees to audible gasps of disbelief from the aghast warriors, unable to grasp that the proud Durotrigan had been defeated with such apparent ease by the junior Roman officer.

Figulus turned away from the stunned Briton and held up the training sword, satisfied that he'd made his point.

'Anyone else got a problem using one of these?' His hoarse voice echoed across the parade ground. The recruits stared back in stunned silence. 'Good. Now get to work!'

The legionaries returned to their training groups to begin the sword drills. The warriors begrudgingly took up their weapons and soon the air was filled with a monotonous dull rapping sound as they landed their blows against their training posts.

'That was nicely done, sir,' Rullus commented as Figulus retreated towards the edge of the parade ground to oversee the training. 'That ought to keep the rest of the bastards in line. For a while, at least.'

'Let's hope so,' Figulus replied.

He sighed heavily. It was hard enough work to instruct these reluctant bodyguards. Now he would have to worry about Andocommius as well. Figulus knew the Celtic character better than most of his comrades. His public humiliation of Andocommius had been necessary to quell any dissent among the other recruits. But the warrior would surely look for revenge for his wounded pride, and Figulus made a mental note to watch his back.

For the rest of the month the recruits stuck to the same routine. In the mornings they worked on their swordplay drills, endlessly practising the basic types of thrust, parry and block under the watchful eye of the legionary instructors. In the afternoon the Durotrigans were given wicker shields and paired up as fighters, and Figulus and his legionaries trained the men in the principles of attack and defence in a skirmish, as well as mastering simple formations.

Training the natives was proving to be a frustrating experience for Figulus. Most of the Britons were tough enough, and possessed plenty of brute strength. But as soon as Figulus tried to drill them in any sort of disciplined and coordinated fighting, they were utterly hopeless. Only when it came to the sword drills did the recruits show any enthusiasm, but even then they were reluctant to practise in the style Figulus had taught them, instead hacking at their training posts as if they were wielding meat cleavers. The warriors among them were particularly recalcitrant. No matter how many times Figulus tried to instruct them that six inches of point was better than a length of blade, the warriors refused to listen. It was more than just an inability to wield a sword properly, Figulus thought. It was pure Celtic stubbornness.

As the weeks passed the winter loosened its grip on the land and the snow melted away as the weather became milder. A steady flow of merchants and traders began to arrive in Lindinis. There was still a long way to go, but for the first time since he'd set foot in the kingdom Figulus began to think there was a chance that peace might finally take hold in the new province. He redoubled his efforts to drill his men, determined that the king's plans to Romanise the kingdom would not be put at risk by an ineffective royal bodyguard. But he made little headway, and he began to despair that many of the recruits could ever be trained to an acceptable standard.

'For the hundredth bloody time, you're trying to kill your enemy, not tickle him!' Rullus shouted at one of the recruits as the Briton tamely struck his sword tip against the wooden post. 'Hit him again, and this time put some fucking effort into it!'

A passing group of off-duty auxiliaries had noticed the recruits toiling at their posts and stopped to observe the training. They looked on, smiling with amusement. Centurion Vespillo clapped as a recruit landed another lame blow against his post.

'Fine work, lads!' he called out to the instructors. 'These men will have the Druids shitting their breeches.'

'Wanker!' Figulus muttered under his breath as the other Batavians laughed before moving on. Rullus shook his head.

'But the centurion's right, sir. This lot are too thick by half. I wouldn't trust 'em to guard a seat at the Circus Maximus, let alone the king.'

Figulus nodded. 'This is going to take a lot longer than I'd hoped.'

'That's putting it mildly, sir. It'll be Saturnalia by the time we're finished training these big hairy idiots. I'll tell you something, though.'

'What's that?'

'If the Druids find out the king's got this lot looking after him, they'll be queuing up to stick a blade in him.'

At the end of the day's training the recruits were led on a quick march round the fort until the sun sank behind the palisade. Then they were issued with their rations for the evening meal before they dragged their weary bodies back to their barracks. Rullus and Helva headed into the settlement for a drink at one of the new drinking establishments while Figulus trudged towards the head-quarters block to make his report to the imperial envoy. The skies had darkened during the afternoon and the first drops of rain pattered off the wood shingle tiles of the headquarters building as he exchanged a salute with the sentry and entered the building.

Scylla sat at the table in his personal quarters, his brow furrowed in deep concentration as he hunched over the plans of a large building neatly inscribed on a sheet of vellum. After a pause the envoy lifted his eyes to Figulus and he smiled thinly.

'Tell me, Optio. How's the training coming along?'

Figulus pursed his lips. 'Some of the men are training well enough. They'll make decent bodyguards.'

'And the rest?'

'Hard to say. They're tough as they come, but getting them to accept our way of fighting is hard work.'

'I see.' Scylla stared at the optio. 'I suppose that will have to do then.'

'What do you mean?'

'Trenagasus is coming to the fort tomorrow morning to look over the recruits in person. Once the inspection is complete, we'll begin arrangements for the formal handover of duties to the new royal bodyguard. The auxiliaries currently guarding him will be returned to the garrison. I've already discussed the details with Prefect Cosconianus. He's going to provide the natives with weaponry from the fort's stores.'

Figulus shook his head. 'But the men aren't ready. Sure, we've made them fitter, but they barely know one end of a gladius from the other.'

'Nonetheless, it's vital that the bodyguards start work at once. As long as the king continues to be under Roman protection he's leaving himself open to accusations of being our puppet.' Scylla flashed a cold smile. 'And we wouldn't want that, now, would we?'

Figulus clamped his jaws shut in frustration. 'No,' he replied tersely.

'Anyway, how hard can it be? These fools are simply required to throw themselves in front of anyone who tries to cut down the king. Even they shouldn't find that too difficult. With any luck, the bodyguards won't be called upon to do that.' The situation in Lindinis is beginning to calm down now we've averted the grain crisis. Our food supplies are still a little stretched, but the locals aren't going to starve. That should buy us some time to implement the necessary changes to bring the natives into line.'

'What changes?' Figulus asked.

'We'll have the king introduce his subjects to the benefits of Roman civilisation. Nothing too heavy-handed, of course. We don't want to tip the natives over the edge. No, for now there will be a steady flow of Roman goods and culture into the kingdom. The native aristocracy will adopt our ways with the customary thirst, of course. And then there's the king's new palace. I've just approved the plans. It's going to be the crowning glory of his reign. A powerful symbol of the might and wealth bequeathed to those who ally themselves with Rome.'

'But what about the Dark Moon Druids? They're still a threat.'

Scylla popped a chunk of bread into his mouth, spilling crumbs over the plans. 'They've been quiet of late,' he responded airily as he chewed his food. 'There's been the odd raid on our supply lines. But nothing out of the ordinary.'

'Strange that the Druids have gone silent, don't you think?'

'Possibly. But it's more likely they've simply given up trying to undermine our regime. They've failed to kill Trenagasus twice, after all. Perhaps they've lost heart.'

'Doesn't sound like the Druids to me. They'd never give up. They'd rather die than admit defeat to Rome.'

Scylla dismissed the optio's concerns with a wave of his hand. 'Plenty of our enemies have set out with the same intentions. All have failed. The Dark Moon Druids are simply the latest to discover that one cannot defy the power of Rome.' He smiled faintly. 'Besides, the Druids won't pose a threat to the kingdom much longer.'

'How so?' Figulus asked.

'I received a despatch three days ago from the Second Legion garrison at Calleva. We can expect reinforcements within the next few days. Two cohorts from the Second, to be precise. Plus some replacements to bring the auxiliary cohort up to strength.' Scylla smiled contentedly. 'It appears that my requests have been heeded. Now we shall finally be able to crush the last pockets of resistance in Durotrigan territory.'

Figulus nodded. There were four hundred and eighty men in a

legionary cohort. The best part of a thousand of Rome's finest soldiers would easily be enough to defeat the dregs of the native resistance and pacify the Durotrigans for the foreseeable future. He smiled with relief. Once order was imposed he could finally return to his legionary comrades in Calleva. He was already looking forward to enjoying the pleasures to be found in the large vicus established just outside of the legionary fortress. Perhaps he might even learn a new magic trick or two from one of the itinerant conjurers who entertained crowds of drunken soldiers in the streets.

Scylla cleared his throat and went on. 'In the meantime, we must try to locate the Druids' base of operations. Cosconianus has been sending his scouts to search the marshes for any sign of the enemy. But there's nothing so far.'

Figulus clenched his brow. 'I've been in those marshes. They stretch out for miles and miles, and in places it's impossible to see more than twenty paces in front of you. Frankly, you could hide an army in there and we'd be none the wiser.'

'Quite so. Which is why it's vital that we uncover the traitor close to Trenagasus. Whoever tipped off the Druids about the weapons hoard must know where the warriors are hiding.'

Figulus scratched his jaw, a thought forming slowly. 'So the traitor – whoever he is – will lead us straight to the Dark Moon Druids?'

'Exactly.' Scylla eased back in his chair, his eyes burning brightly as he went on. 'Once we expose the traitor, we'll be able to learn the whereabouts of the Druids. Then we'll crush them once and for all.'

CHAPTER THIRTY-TWO

There was an air of excitement in the fort as the recruits toiled at their posts the following morning. News of the king's imminent visit had spread quickly through the ranks and each recruit landed blows at his training post with renewed vigour, desperate to make a good impression with the man they might be chosen to protect. Even Andocommius seemed to be concentrating all of his energies at his post, Figulus noted. Across from the thoroughfare a pair of auxiliaries were busy repairing the damage caused by the vicious storm that had raged the previous night. The lashing rain had washed away much of the heavy snowfall of the past few days, and now only a few scattered patches remained amid the large puddles and churned mud.

Figulus watched over the recruits with a lingering sense of unease. Placing the king's life in the hands of a partly trained native bodyguard struck him as a dangerous thing to do. Any sign of incompetence among his guards might persuade Trenagasus's enemies to make another attempt on his life. But Bellicanus was convinced that the recruits would prove their worth when they began their duties.

'All of my comrades have sworn a blood oath to protect the king,' he explained as he joined the optio and looked over the men training on the parade ground. 'They will do whatever it takes to keep Trenagasus from coming to harm, even if it means laying down their lives. They would not dare shame themselves by failing in their duty.'

'Even though some of your lot would rather see us banished from your kingdom?' Figulus asked, tipping his head at Andocommius.

Bellicanus glanced at the recruit and smiled faintly. 'It is understandable that Andocommius bears a grudge against Rome. He lost most of his family when your legion invaded our lands and attacked our hill forts. Many of his comrades died too.'

'Too bad,' Figulus responded flatly. 'That's the price you pay for following the Druids. Andocommius fought on the losing side. He should be kissing Fortuna's arse that he's still drawing breath.'

The Durotrigan noble shook his head. 'It is not that simple. Far from it. Andocommius did not side with the Dark Moon Druids. As a matter of fact, many of our warriors were compelled to fight against their will.'

'There's always a choice. No one put a blade to their necks and forced them to take up arms against the Emperor. They didn't have to fight against us.'

'Then I fear you don't understand the Dark Moon Druids,' Bellicanus replied coldly. 'All those of us who have defied their priests have paid a heavy price, Roman.'

Figulus stared at him. 'You really hate them, don't you? The Druids.'

'Only the Dark Moon sect. Most of our tribe are faithful to the wider cult. Our beliefs have been at the heart of our tribe since the dawn of time. But the Dark Moon sect are . . . different. They are intolerant. They insist that Cruach, our god of war, is angry that his lands have been desecrated by Rome. And that it is the sacred duty of every tribe in Britannia to spill the blood of the invader.'

'I thought that is what every Druid believes.'

'Not any longer,' Bellicanus responded quietly. 'Some of the other Druid sects are talking of making peace with Rome.'

'Bollocks! The Druids would never surrender.'

'I did not say surrender.' The Durotrigan frowned. 'One day, the Druids may sue for peace. Even their hatred of Rome has its limits. But the Dark Moon priests would never do such a thing. They are sworn to the absolute destruction of all those who oppose them . . . even their own people. Anyone who refuses to accept the Dark Moon cult is put to death. Men, women. Children. That is why we will lay down our lives to defend the king. Even men like Andocommius. Not because we have any great loyalty to Rome, but because the alternative is too terrible to contemplate. If our king dies, there is nothing to prevent the Dark Moon Druids ruling our lives.'

'Rome would never let it happen,' Figulus retorted. He thumped a fist into the palm of his hand. 'The legions would put a stop to the Druids before they took over.'

'I wish I shared your confidence. But the truth is, without Trenagasus there is no alliance with Rome. There is no obvious successor to the king, no blood relative.'

'What about the king's daughter?'

Bellicanus chuckled. 'Ancasta? Queen of the Durotriges? The council of elders would never agree to it. We are not like the Brigantes. There is no question of allowing a woman to rule us. No. If Trenagasus were to die, the Druids would exploit the uncertainty and take control again. Not even Rome could stop them then, I fear.'

'We'd never retreat from Durotrigan territory,' Figulus insisted. 'Not after so many lives have been sacrificed to win the new province.'

Bellicanus laughed and shook his head slowly. 'You Romans! Always so confident of victory, even when the gods do not favour you. But you cannot know what the future holds. As long as Calumus continues to inspire his followers, nothing is certain.'

'Calumus?'

Bellicanus nodded. 'You've surely heard of him? The one they call the Blood Priest.'

Figulus nodded. 'I've heard the name before,' he said, remembering his earlier conversation with Scylla soon after they had arrested Quenatacus. 'Isn't he the leader of those bastards in the Dark Moon sect?'

'That's the one. His followers are violent fanatics, too extreme even for the other Druid sects. It's said that Calumus was captured by the Romans and tortured. His face was burned and horribly scarred before he escaped. That's why he burns alive any soldiers he captures. To avenge his suffering. Some think he is a raving madman. Others believe he is the true voice of Cruach.'

'What do you think?'

Bellicanus shrugged. 'It does not matter what I think. But if Calumus is leading the Dark Moon Druids, then Rome has much to fear.'

Figulus was about to reply when he heard a loud rumbling groan from across the fort. He turned away from Bellicanus and saw the rough hewn timber gate swinging open. Several horsemen trotted into the fort. Trenagasus rode at the front on a neatly groomed white mount. He trotted over to the parade ground, flanked by his auxiliary bodyguard and followed by his inner circle of advisers, all of them resplendent in their brightly coloured trousers and extravagant gold brooches and torcs. The king pulled on his reins and eased his mount to a halt beside the parade ground. As he dismounted, Scylla emerged from the headquarters block and hurried over to greet him.

'Your Majesty. An honour to see you, as always. I trust you're well?'

'Quite fine, my dear fellow!' Trenagasus replied. 'Despite the best efforts of the thunder god last night!'

Scylla frowned at the deep puddles gleaming across the thoroughfare. 'Quite a downpour, I agree.'

'Ah, well. Can't let the weather dampen our spirits! I understand work is about to begin on my new royal home?'

'That's correct, Your Majesty. The plans have been approved by the governor's office and the engineers will begin construction at once.'

'Excellent news. It's about time I had a royal home worthy of the name. That mere villa Cogidubnus is building himself will pale into comparison with my palace!'

The envoy smiled and turned towards Centurion Tuditanus, the Batavian officer who had been placed in charge of the king's temporary bodyguard. 'I trust there have been no problems?'

Tuditanus stiffened. 'None, sir. Although a few of the locals have been moaning about the damage to their homes caused by that storm last night.'

Trenagasus sniffed indignantly. 'Honestly, a few damaged roofs and animal pens and my subjects complain bitterly. An unfortunate trait of our people, I'm afraid. Perhaps one of your engineers might take a look at the damage, Scylla.'

The envoy fixed his smile on the king. 'Of course, Your Majesty.'

The rest of the nobles and tribal elders climbed down from their mounts and stood round the king, Ancasta among them. Her eyes quickly settled on Figulus.

231

'My lady,' Figulus said. 'A pleasure.'

Ancasta nodded a greeting. 'Optio.'

There was a slight iciness to her tone that took Figulus by surprise. Before he could respond she turned away and Trenagasus clapped his hands.

'Now then, Optio. Perhaps you would be so kind as to introduce me to my new royal bodyguard?'

'Yes, Your Majesty,' Figulus replied quickly, shrugging off all thought of Ancasta. 'Please, follow me.'

Bellicanus joined Figulus as the Gaul guided the king around the edge of the parade ground, his large retinue following a few steps behind. Figulus steered the king away from some of the poorer recruits, instead pointing out the qualities of the warrior caste. At first Trenagasus seemed enthusiastic enough about his bodyguards, stopping occasionally to ask about a particular aspect of their training and feigning interest in the optio's answers. But after a while he fell into conversation with Bellicanus about some administrative matters or other, and Figulus found himself pacing a few steps behind the pair, alongside Ancasta. She stayed silent for a while. Then at last she turned to Figulus and cleared her throat.

'I'm sorry for being short with you, Optio,' she said at last, in a quiet voice so that Trenagasus would not overhear.

'Is it something I've said, my lady?' Figulus asked.

'Of course not. I'm grateful for everything that you've done for my father. You saved him from an assassin's knife, after all. Father is forever in your debt . . . and so am I.'

'Then what is it, my lady?'

Ancasta closed her eyes and looked away. When she spoke at last, there was a bitterness to her voice. 'I feel afraid, Optio. I have done ever since I returned here with my father. He has enemies on all sides. It's obvious that the people hate him and the Druids want to see him dead. Even though my concern is for Father, I also fear for myself.'

'You are well protected. But it must be hard, seeing your father threatened like that.'

'It is no different to your Emperor, I imagine. From what I hear there are some in Rome who would love to see Claudius cut down.'

She sighed. 'Forgive me. All this talk of death and conspiracy is quite depressing. I presume you will be leaving us soon, Optio, now that Father's new royal bodyguard is almost ready?'

'I suppose so, my lady. It'll be back to Calleva for me and the lads. At least until the snow clears and the next campaign season begins.'

Ancasta regarded him with her alluring gaze. 'It will be a shame to see you leave. Father greatly appreciates everything you have done for him. We both do.' She smiled softly. 'That reminds me. I found this. I believe it belongs to you.'

She reached a hand down into her pouch, pulled out a small silver medallion depicting the image of Fortuna and pressed it into his palm.

'My lucky charm!' Figulus exclaimed. 'I've been looking for this all over the place. Where'd you find it?'

'In the royal hall. One of our slaves found it. You must have dropped it when you were guarding Father.'

Figulus studied the medallion. It had suffered a fair amount of damage in the two years he'd carried it through the mud and marshes of Britannia and it was scratched and scuffed. He closed his palm around the charm and nodded at Ancasta.

'Thank you, my lady.'

She smiled at Figulus again as he tucked away his lucky charm. Ahead of them Trenagasus had reached the end of the parade ground. He turned and nodded appreciatively at the men in training.

'Very impressive,' he declared to Scylla as he stroked his neatly trimmed beard. 'I can see that your soldiers have taught them well.'

'Very kind of you to say so, Your Majesty.'

'They can begin their duties at once, I presume?'

Before the envoy could reply there was a commotion at the main gate. Figulus turned to get a better look and saw a cavalry scout galloping inside the fort and reining in before he slid from his saddle and sprinted off in the direction of the headquarters building. Shortly afterwards Cosconianus came striding across the parade ground, fiddling with the straps on his crested helmet. The prefect talked briskly with the duty centurion marching at his side before the latter hurried off in the direction of the barracks. Scylla and Figulus advanced towards the prefect to see what was going on, out of earshot of the Durotrigans.

'What is it?' the envoy demanded. 'What's going on?'

'The enemy have emerged from the swamp in force,' Cosconianus announced excitedly. 'According to the scouts, those painted bastards have attacked another supply convoy, six miles south of here, not far from the old hill fort.'

'How many, sir?' Figulus asked.

'The scouts say no more than a hundred. No horses or chariots. If we leave now we can cut them off before they disappear back into the marshes.'

'They might already have retreated,' Scylla said.

Cosconianus considered then shook his head. 'We can still catch them. They'll be loaded down with the spoils from the convoy and moving slower than my men. There's no time to lose.'

'In that case, take the optio and his men with you. They've finished their training duties here anyway.'

Cosconianus nodded briskly. 'They can join Centurion Ambustus in the First Century. His unit is under-strength. He could use the extra swords.'

'What about the king?' Figulus asked. 'Who's going to guard him?'

Scylla waved a hand in the direction of the parade ground. 'I'm sure Bellicanus and his men are up to the task. Trenagasus seems pleased enough with them, at least. The auxiliaries who've been guarding the king can return to the garrison at once.' He looked back to Cosconianus and added in a firm tone of voice, 'There's just one more thing.'

'What's that?'

'Capture some of the enemy alive if you can. It may be our best hope of finding the Druids' lair and destroying their vicious little cult.'

Cosconianus nodded. 'Of course.' The prefect switched his gaze to Figulus. 'Report to the barracks, Optio. We'll form up and move out at once!'

CHAPTER THIRTY-THREE

The sun was disappearing behind a thick bank of cloud as the Batavian auxiliaries marched out of the fort's eastern gate a short while later. Figulus and his legionaries took position at the front rank of the First Century while Prefect Cosconianus rode a few paces ahead. The remaining three centuries marched to the rear. Cosconianus was taking no chances and had left behind only a handful of men in the depleted Fifth and Sixth Centuries to guard the fort. A short while after the cohort had departed, Bellicanus and his bodyguards were issued with short swords and oval shields from the fort's stores and escorted Trenagasus back to the royal enclosure in Lindinis.

The Roman column followed a rough track south past the sprawling native settlement, a vast enclosure built on low ground and encircled by an outer ditch with an inner turf rampart, topped by a palisade. The occasional patch of snow still gleamed amid the slush and the sodden ground squelched underfoot as the soldiers marched at a steady pace. Figulus glanced to the west and saw the fringe of the marshes lying several miles away, bordered by a series of low broken hills and stunted trees. He automatically tensed at the thought of the Druid warband that was lurking somewhere beyond the mist. If Bellicanus was right, and the Dark Moon Druids refused to surrender, then there was only one outcome: a fight to the death, until the last of their priests had been killed and every last sacred grove razed to the ground.

After five miles they arrived at the edge of a vale between two forested hills. This was perfect ambush territory, Figulus realised. Cosconianus threw up a hand and ordered the cohort to halt. The men stood, wearied from the exertion of the forced march, their breath wreathing the column in puffs of air. A moment later there was movement on the side of the hill and Figulus saw one of the scouts who had remained to observe the enemy scrambling down the slope. The prefect dismounted and advanced to meet him and there was a brief exchange before Cosconianus followed the man back towards the crest.

'Think this is a good idea?' Figulus asked Rullus in a low voice as the column waited for the prefect to return.

'What's that, sir?'

'Leaving Lindinis so thinly defended.'

Rullus considered. 'It's only for a few hours. Anyway, I've had enough of the Durotrigans taking the piss. This is a good chance to catch them weighed down with loot, and in my book that's an opportunity going begging.'

His confidence helped to put Figulus's mind at ease, but he couldn't avoid a nagging concern at the back of his mind. 'I just hope the king's safe. That Andocommius is a bit off, don't you think?'

Rullus made a face. 'Do me a favour, sir. He's just like every other warrior in this godsforsaken land. Thinks his shit smells better than ours. Other than that, he's a useful man to have at your side.' He shook his head. 'That said, they're bloody stubborn bastards, the locals. And I thought the Batavians were arrogant.'

'I don't understand.' Helva tilted his head as he frowned. 'Life wasn't any better for this lot before we showed up. How can they look down on us, when they don't even have roads or baths, sir?'

'Roads and baths aren't everything, legionary,' Figulus responded. 'The warriors of these tribes cling to the past, when the Celts used to rule Gaul and Hispania. They can't accept that things have changed and they hate the idea of being ruled by Rome. They think we're the barbaric ones.'

They fell silent, adding to the growing tension in the air. A moment later Figulus caught sight of Cosconianus running back down the hill, followed by the rest of the cavalry scouts. The prefect summoned his officers to the front.

'The enemy's still there,' he reported breathlessly. 'Looting the convoy, by the looks of it. We've got them right where we want them, gentlemen. At long last this is a chance to teach the enemy a hard lesson.'

Figulus sucked in a breath before he voiced his concern. 'Why haven't the Durotrigans already left, sir? It's not like them to hang around after an ambush. They usually piss off as fast as they can.'

'What does it matter?' Cosconianus snapped. 'We've got a chance to stop them getting away with our supplies. We'll cut them to pieces and take a few of the bastards prisoner.' His eyes lit up with excitement. 'A neat victory over the enemy will be a fine way to impress General Plautius.'

Figulus saw it then. Cosconianus was less interested in saving the supplies than advancing his own career. It might smooth the way for a transfer to a more pleasant posting elsewhere in the empire. He gritted his teeth in frustration at the prefect's glory-seeking.

'We'll sweep over the hill and cut them off from the marsh,' Cosconianus decided, thinking rapidly. 'They won't see us coming until it's too late. When they do, they won't get very far. They'll have to fight us, or drop their loot and try to flee. Either way, they'll be cut off from the marshes. Questions?' Cosconianus looked at each officer in turn then nodded. 'Good. Prepare to advance!'

The officers saluted and returned to their centuries. They issued their orders in low voices and told the men to prepare for action. An excited murmur went up from the ranks at the prospect of finally engaging the enemy that had tormented them for so long, before their mood was cut short by angry hisses and swift blows from their officers to enforce silence. Prefect Cosconianus took one last glance over his command and then quietly gave the order to advance, and for the instruction to be passed on down the column. The cohort wheeled as the prefect led them off the track and at an angle up the slope towards the crest of the hill. Figulus felt the wet grass brushing at his calves as he gently flexed the grip on his sword handle before tightening his fingers. His ears filled with the soft rumble of boots, laboured breathing, the swish of the grass and the irregular patter of loose equipment.

As they neared the crest of the hill, Figulus caught sight of the Durotrigans' old hill fort less than a mile south of the vale. The vast multi-tiered mound of earthworks rose up from the plain, dark and foreboding. Figulus could see the wide plateau where the enemy's defensive enclosure had once stood. From end to end he reckoned that the fort measured half a mile, and even in its abandoned state the scale of the ramparts was impressive.

A short distance ahead, Cosconianus reached the crest of the hill and swept his sword towards the enemy.

'At the trot!'

Figulus and the other men in the leading ranks increased their pace and the motion rippled back down the column as the cohort flowed over the top of the hill and down towards the enemy picking over the remains of the convoy at the foot of the slope beyond. Ahead of them Figulus saw several heavy Roman transport carts in the middle of the track. The oxen harnessed to the carts were abandoned at once as their captors snatched up their weapons and turned to face the danger pounding towards them. The convoy's decurion and the rest of the escort lay sprawled on the ground at the side of the track, while Durotrigan warriors stood over the bodies, busy stripping them of armour and weaponry and anything else that might be of value.

One of the woad-painted warriors near the front of the convoy turned as he heard the heavy pounding of boots and frantically took out a horn and puffed his cheeks as he sounded the alarm. The sudden repeated blast broke the spell and the raiders immediately ceased their looting and readied their weapons. For a brief instant it looked to Figulus that they might stand their ground and fight. Then a large warrior bellowed an order and the enemy began retreating down the track in the direction of the hill fort, abandoning the transport carts. A few of the native warriors took to taunting the Romans as they fell back, shaking their fists and making lewd gestures.

Cosconianus snatched a breath and called over his shoulder, 'Keep up the pace, boys! Don't let 'em get away!'

The warriors continued to taunt the Romans, hurling colourful abuse and gesticulating wildly as they fell back. Figulus did not understand why the Durotrigans had been so quick to abandon their spoils. An uneasy feeling twisted like a knife in his guts as he moved forwards with his comrades at the front of the First Century, pursuing the enemy as they retreated at a steady pace. At last the warriors reached the outer defences of the ruined hill fort. As the Romans closed in they turned and fled, scrambling up the steep ramparts as fast as they could. As they reached the top tier of the earthworks, some of the Durotrigans briefly stopped and turned towards the Romans, shouting defiantly.

Cosconianus halted his column, a triumphant glint in his steely eyes as he sensed victory. 'Now we've got them!' he announced, his voice trembling with anticipation. 'We'll trap them in the hill fort. Tuditanus, take two centuries and cut round to the far side.'

Centurion Tuditanus nodded and gave the order to his men. The rearmost centuries turned away from the rest of the cohort and struck out obliquely towards the other side of the hill fort to try to prevent the enemy from escaping. Meanwhile, Cosconianus led his men up the track that zigzagged towards the main gateway. The auxiliaries were breathing hard as they passed over the outer ditch at the highest rampart and advanced through the collapsed timber ruins of the gatehouse. The surrounding palisade had been shattered by Roman siege weaponry during the Second Legion's assault on the hill fort months earlier. Now only the broken stumps remained, like rotting teeth.

As he stepped inside the hill fort, Figulus caught sight of the enemy. They had halted fifty paces or so across the small plateau contained within the topmost rampart and had turned to face their pursuers, bellowing insults as they beat their swords against the trims of their shields. Figulus felt a surge of delight as he guessed that the Durotrigans had not yet realised that Centurion Tuditanus and his men were racing round the rear of the fort to trap them. He began to think that Cosconianus's plan was going to work after all.

'Form line!' the prefect roared as he held his sword out to his side.

The men of the First Century hurried into two ranks and closed up. The following unit took their station to the left of the prefect while Figulus and his comrades recovered their breath and fixed their attention on the enemy. Despite the din the natives were making they made no attempt to attack.

'What the hell are they waiting for?' Helva blurted out, his javelin half raised.

Rullus shoved his shoulder into the young man. 'Lower your point before you do someone a fucking injury!'

Helva swallowed nervously and forced himself to ground the butt of the javelin.

'That's better,' Rullus said quietly. 'You're a bloody legionary. We set the example. What do you think these auxiliary bastards will think if they see you running around like a headless chicken? Stand your ground, straighten your back!'

During the exchange, Figulus had been casting an eye around the interior of the ruined fort. Smashed clay pots and torn shreds of clothing were scattered across the muddied ground. His attention was drawn to the skeletal remains of dozens of timber-framed houses standing amid the chest-high walls of stone – all that remained of the settlement atop the hill fort. For a moment Figulus thought his eyes were deceiving him. Then he stopped and looked again, and the blood instantly chilled in his veins. He turned to look up at the mounted prefect.

'Sir, we need to leave!'

'What the hell are you talking about, you fool?' Cosconianus snapped.

Figulus pointed towards the ruins. 'I saw movement over there! It's a trap!'

Cosconianus tugged on his reins and frowned. 'What? I don't understand—'

As he spoke, the terrifying war cries of the natives swelled in volume and an echo seemed to spill around the interior of the fort. The prefect froze, and the colour instantly drained from his face as hundreds of native warriors leapt out from their concealed positions behind the ruined buildings at either end of the plateau and charged towards the flanks of the Roman line. The raiders they had followed roared with triumph and surged forwards.

'It's a fucking trick!' Rullus snarled.

An icy dread clamped around Figulus's neck as he realised the cohort was surrounded, and he felt a surge of anger at the hotheaded prefect for leading the men into such a crude but effective ambush. At the same time Cosconianus shook off his stupor and cupped a hand to his mouth.

'Ready javelins!'

The first wave of Britons stormed towards the Batavians in a heaving throng, bellowing their terrifying war cries and spurred on by their Druid commanders. Many of the native warriors were brandishing captured Roman swords and oval shields and some wore chainmail armour and helmets. Dread coursed through Figulus as he quickly calculated that the enemy would easily outnumber the auxiliaries.

'Release javelins!' Cosconianus ordered at the top of his voice.

In the next instant the first line of men hurled their javelins at the charging Durotrigans. The Batavians' throws were panicked and ragged compared to the better trained men of the legionary cohorts, but the enemy was too close to miss and many of the javelins struck the front rank of Britons. Agonised cries pierced the cold air as the heavy iron heads slammed into the enemy ranks, impaling their victims. Dozens of warriors stumbled to the ground, spear shafts protruding from their bodies. Their screams were drowned out by the roars of those behind as they leapt over their stricken companions and charged at the soldiers. They were now less than twenty paces from the auxiliaries. The Batavians unleashed another shower of javelins, striking down more of the enemy at close range. Figulus hefted up his legionary shield as he took his place in the front line and faced the enemy.

'Hold the line!' Cosconianus yelled shrilly as the men on the flanks recoiled in fear. The Britons crashed against the Batavians pell-mell and there was a frenetic exchange of blows as the first warriors were cut down. But the sheer weight of the Durotrigan charge was pressing against the Batavians and even as Figulus held his place in the line he could see that some of the auxiliaries were being forced back by the enemy. Gaps began to appear in the shield wall as the second rank of Batavians hesitated to step forwards and replace their fallen comrades. Figulus barked at the nearest auxiliaries to hold their ground. Every instinct in his body implored him to run, but he knew that to turn his back on the enemy would lead to certain death.

A large shadow loomed in front of him as a powerfully built warrior clamped a hand around the rim of his legionary shield and wrenched it to the side. Figulus saw a flash of steel as the warrior drove his weapon towards his throat. Dropping onto his left knee the optio threw up his shield and the Briton's sword landed with a jarring

241

clatter against the boss. The Durotrigan snarled, cursing. Figulus drove his weapon between the warrior's legs and sank the blade deep into the man's groin. He gasped in agony and released Figulus's shield. Blood gushed out of the man's gaping wound as Figulus tore his blade free before punching out with his shield, slamming the boss into the warrior's face with a dull crunch. The Briton crashed into the seething mass of warriors behind him.

Abruptly the sun broke through the clouds and the light reflected off the melee of sword points and polished helmets fiercely contesting the plateau. Figulus glanced round and realised it wouldn't be long until the hard-pressed Batavians would be overrun. He saw another Durotrigan charging towards him, an older warrior with spiked greying hair and a wiry physique. He drove his thrusting spear towards Figulus. The optio yanked up his shield and there was a splintering crack as the tip punched through. The warrior tried wrenching his weapon back, yanking Figulus's shield towards him. The optio pulled at the handle, grunting with the effort and surprised at the warrior's strength. For an agonising moment both shield and spear were locked in place as the two men strained. Then Figulus roared and pulled with all his might, ripping his shield away from the Briton with such force that the spear tip tore free. Then he thrust his sword at the warrior before the latter could recover his posture, stabbing him in the guts with the tip of his blade. The warrior hissed sharply and fell away as Figulus wrenched his weapon free and struck again at another man.

A pained cry sounded above the grating rasps and brittle clatters of the battle and Figulus turned to see Cosconianus sinking to his knees further along the Batavian line as a burly native warrior cut him down with a savage blow to the shoulder. As soon as he had fallen away, a shout went up from a man close by.

'The prefect's down! Cosconianus has fallen!'

Panic instantly spread through the Batavian ranks. With their commander dead, any lingering sense of discipline and order in the cohort collapsed. The line wavered for a moment, and then the Britons pushed again and some in the front rank of soldiers turned and fled for the ramparts in a desperate attempt to escape the killing frenzy. Figulus rose up and glanced over the heads of the enemy before him, straining to see any sign of Centurion Tuditanus and his men, their only hope of salvation now. But there was no movement on the far side of the fort. He dropped into a balanced crouch and thrust at the nearest warrior. More and more auxiliaries turned their backs on the enemy. The gaps in the line were no longer being filled with replacements, and Figulus knew they could not hope to hold out much longer in the face of such overwhelming odds.

'Sir, we have to make a run for it!' Rullus shouted as the Durotrigans surged forwards, cutting down the fleeing Batavians.

Figulus hesitated. The thought of retreat disgusted him, but he knew there was no choice. If they stayed and fought, his men would surely suffer the same grisly fate as the auxiliaries. He turned back to Rullus and pointed to a dip in the ground a short distance away.

'Over there! Legionaries, on me!'

Figulus spun around and cut down an onrushing Briton with a vicious thrust to the neck. The man fell away as the optio turned to his comrades and filled his lungs. 'With me!'

Figulus turned and broke into a trot, leading his men towards the dip. He kept glancing over his shoulder to make sure that his comrades were close by. All around him native warriors were hunting down the defenceless auxiliaries without mercy, hacking at their bodies even after they had stopped drawing breath. Some of the Batavians scrambled over the ruined ramparts and down the slope, but they were easy prey for the Britons, who hurled spears at the fleeing figures, striking them down. Figulus glimpsed one auxiliary frantically throw down his shield and sword and hold out his hands, begging for mercy. A thickset Durotrigan clamped a hand on the man's shoulder and thrust him to the ground. The man cried out in terror as a cluster of warriors set upon him. Figulus averted his gaze, willing himself to run faster and cursing his heavy armour and shield for slowing him down.

As they neared the gully one of the legionaries called out. Figulus glanced back and caught sight of several warriors taking up the chase. He faced forwards and quickened his stride.

'Keep moving!' he bellowed. 'Don't stop!'

Figulus was snatching at his breath and he could feel his lungs burning with the effort. As he reached the edge of the palisade he heard a sharp cry of pain further back. He looked over his shoulder and saw Helva tripping over the leg of a fallen auxiliary and crashing to the ground, his sword falling from his grip.

'Shit!' Helva cried, hissing sharply between his teeth as he clutched his right leg. 'My ankle!'

Rullus immediately stopped and dropped to a knee to help the legionary to his feet. At the same time several of the mounted Druids galloped forwards and swarmed over the two men, encircling them and brandishing their curved blades. Figulus stopped in his tracks and turned to charge at the Druids, but the pursuing warriors were already streaming across the plateau towards the palisade, blocking his path to his comrades. Figulus saw that there was no way he could fight his way past the heaving throng of Durotrigans and save Rullus and Helva.

There was nothing he could do now except escort his few remaining legionaries to safety. He forced himself to turn away and lead his men over the side of the palisade, climbing over the shattered wooden stumps and dropping down into a narrow ditch worn into the side of the defences. A foul smell of human waste filled the air and Figulus fought a powerful urge to vomit. The ground underfoot was slick with mud and a swamp-like pool of sewage festered near the bottom of the gully, slowing the pace of the Romans' escape as they struggled to gain a footing in the slippery ordure. Below them lay the outer defences and beyond that, no more than half a mile away, Figulus could see the edge of the marshes. He felt a slight flicker of hope in his heart.

'To the marshes!' he ordered. 'We'll lose 'em in there.'

Just then a shout went up from the top of the gully as the pursuing warriors swept into view and caught sight of the Romans trudging through the filth. With an excited roar they began tearing down the side of the gully, intent on closing the gap on the fleeing soldiers. Figulus felt some sixth sense flare up at the base of his skull and he spun around just in time to see a scrawny warrior lunging at him, his lips drawn back in a savage snarl to reveal a set of yellow teeth. Figulus swiftly parried his opponent's blow with a metallic ring, then stepped outside the man and drove the point of his weapon towards his exposed flank. The blade punched through his ribs, piercing muscle and flesh, and the warrior gasped as the air exploded out of his lungs. Figulus spun away from the man as he sank to his knees in the filth. Around him the other Britons were swiftly cut down as the legionaries parried and thrust in the sort of gritty close-quarters fighting at which the Romans excelled. With the last of the pursuing Britons cut down, Figulus ordered his men to abandon their heavy shields. They rushed down the side of the ramparts as fast as their legs would take them. As they moved further away from the melee above them, Figulus felt a burning fury at leaving his comrades behind. He briefly wondered what had become of them, then pushed the dark thought aside.

As they neared the base of the outer rampart Figulus saw more figures away to his left; in the distance warriors seethed around a small knot of Romans fighting to the last around a standard held high over their heads. So that was what had become of Centurion Tuditanus and his detachment. Attacked long before they had been able to reach the far side of the fort. Figulus could spare them no further thought as the Britons pursuing the legionaries continued to give chase, streaming down the gully and hurling curses. But the warriors quickly found themselves bogged down in the mud and filth of the gully and Figulus and his comrades soon increased the gap between them. With a final chorus of jeers the warriors gave up their pursuit and turned back to rejoin the slaughter up in the fort.

Figulus and his men ran a little further across the open ground towards the dank fringe of the marshes. They reached the belt of stunted trees at the edge. A narrow track twisted between the dense gorse and expanses of stagnant water, leading north towards the river. His mind was filled with grief as he picked his way through the marshes. Any attempt to rescue Helva and Rullus would have been in vain, he knew. He'd had no choice but to flee the battle. All he could do was save what was left of his detachment and warn their comrades at the fort of the imminent danger to the settlement.

Lindinis. The terrible realisation struck Figulus that with the auxiliary cohort wiped out, the Druids and their well-armed troops might descend upon the settlement at any moment. With the size of their force they could quickly seize control of the Durotrigan capital and put Trenagasus to the sword. Without the unpopular king to keep his subjects in check, the Durotriges would surely rise up against Rome. If more tribes followed their example then a widespread rebellion would be impossible to put down, Figulus realised as he hurried along the track. The legions would be forced into a humiliating retreat. Every inch of territory the men of the Second Legion had fought and died for would be lost. His body cried out for rest but Figulus fought his tiredness and forced himself to keep pushing on through the rank marshes. He was determined to reach the fort and raise the alarm before it was too late.

CHAPTER THIRTY-FOUR

Darkness was beginning to creep across the land as the four Roman soldiers reached a small hummock of clear ground half a mile from the fort. For the past few hours Figulus and his men had been following a path through the edge of the marsh that they had stumbled upon. At times the track had disappeared beneath pools of brackish water and they had been forced to find their own way through the quagmire. Their slow progress was a source of immense frustration to the optio, but he knew it was too risky to venture out into the open ground beyond the marshes in case they ran into the enemy.

Figulus had briefly considered abandoning the attempt to return to the fort and making for the safety of the garrisons of Durnovaria or Vindocladia. Both were a day's march away, assuming that he and his comrades could evade the roaming patrols of rebels. But the other garrisons were too small to intervene decisively at Lindinis, and in the end he decided that he had no choice but to return to the fort as soon as possible and warn the envoy of the threat to Lindinis and Trenagasus.

After several hours of hard marching the men reached the edge of a gently meandering river. They continued east along the bank, concealed from sight by the dense forest running parallel to the river. Twice they narrowly avoided being spotted by roaming native horsemen, until at last they approached a clearing dotted with stunted trees cut down by Roman foraging parties and Figulus knew that they were drawing near to the fort. A sudden wave of relief washed over him. It was tempered by a sense of shame at retreating from the enemy, even though it had been the rational thing to do.

'What do you think happened to the others, sir?' Vatia asked softly as the soldiers paused to rest on the dry ground.

Figulus shrugged wearily. 'Killed on the spot, if they're lucky.'

'And if they're less fortunate?'

Figulus did not reply. During the long, uncomfortable journey through the marshes he had tried to avoid all thought of his comrades' fate. In all likelihood they were dead, cut down the moment the enemy had them surrounded, just as the rest of the column had been slaughtered.

'Get moving,' he ordered. 'We've got to make the fort before sundown and warn 'em about the Druids.'

'It might be a bit late for that, sir,' Vatia said quietly.

'What do you mean?' Figulus asked, frowning.

Vatia pursed his lips as he pointed to the south. Figulus followed his line of sight. No more than half a mile away stood the native settlement. In the fading light Figulus noticed several columns of smoke drifting up from the roundhouses, choking the darkening sky. For a moment he thought the smoke might be coming from the hearth fires that burned within each of the native huts. But there was far too much smoke for that. His eyes were drawn to a faint orange glow reflecting off several sections of the palisade atop the rampart. Fires were raging inside Lindinis. Several of them. Figulus felt a cold tingle of dread. He was too late.

Lindinis had already fallen.

Figulus broke across the open ground and raced towards the fort's main gate. His guts tightened into an anxious knot as he marched towards the narrow ramp leading over the outer ditch. He stopped and cupped a hand to his mouth as he shouted towards the watchtower. 'Romans approaching!'

There was a moment's silence and then a nervy sentry peered down from the tall wooden watchtower overlooking the gate. 'Password?'

'Castor! Now open the fucking gate!'

The sentry disappeared from view and shouted down to the duty officer. A few moments later Figulus heard a deep groan from the other side of the gate as the locking bar slid out of its bracket. Then the gate swung inwards and Figulus led his three remaining legionaries up the ramp and into the fort.

A chaotic scene greeted them inside. Exhausted soldiers were slumped around the approaches to the gate, their armour and faces spattered with mud and dried blood. Survivors of the ambush, Figulus realised. And not many of them. Some of their comrades who had remained at the fort passed from man to man, giving each survivor a sip of water from his canteen. Orderlies hurried over from the direction of the infirmary, inspecting the wounded. Those with the most severe injuries were placed on stretchers and carried away to be treated. A loose throng of anxious-looking merchants from Lindinis sat on the parade ground, surrounded by the limited possessions they had snatched up before fleeing to the fort.

Figulus swung his gaze ahead and saw the imperial envoy hurrying over from the direction of the headquarters building. He was flanked by Ancasta and Centurion Vespillo, the senior surviving officer. Scylla looked pale and fearful.

'Optio! Thank the gods! I was beginning to think you weren't going to return.' The relief in his voice was genuine.

'It'll take more than a few Druids to get rid of me,' Figulus grunted.

Scylla ran his eyes over the other exhausted legionaries. 'Where are the rest of your men?'

Figulus felt his throat tighten. 'Didn't make it. What happened here?'

'What does it look like?' Scylla threw up his hands in despair. 'It's a complete disaster. The Druids swept into Lindinis and took control of the settlement. Our plans are in ruins.'

'The king?'

Scylla grimaced. 'Trenagasus was in the royal compound when the Druids showed up.' He gestured to the king's daughter at his side. 'Only Ancasta managed to escape.'

Figulus looked to her. Tears welled in Ancasta's eyes as she spoke. 'Everything happened so quickly. I was inspecting the market while Father met with his wise council. Then the Druids crashed in. It was chaos. People running and screaming.'

'How did you get out, my lady?'

'Andocommius escorted me to safety,' she replied, her voice shaking as she nodded towards a large figure squatting by the gate. 'We were the last ones out. There was no way we could get to

Father. The Druids had the hall surrounded.' She bit her lip and looked away. 'I knew this would happen, Optio. The Druids have been trying to destroy my father from the moment we returned. Now they have got their wish. My father is as good as dead. If they haven't killed him already.'

Figulus turned his gaze on the duty centurion. 'Didn't you try to stop them, sir?'

The bluntness of his question took Vespillo by surprise, but this was no time for decorum or respecting rank. The centurion managed to compose his features and shook his head. 'There was too many of the bastards. There was nothing I could do.'

'How many men do we have left in the fort, sir?' asked Figulus.

'Including the stragglers who managed to escape the ambush, a little over a hundred men.'

'Not enough to retake the settlement, then.'

'Not even enough to defend the fort.'

'No.'

Scylla's eyes widened with panic. 'Do you think the Druids might try to take the fort?'

Figulus narrowed his eyes and formed a quick appraisal of the situation. 'More likely than not, I'd say. Now the Druids have seized Lindinis, we're the obvious target. They'll want our heads as trophies to impress the rest of the tribe. To show that we can be beaten. Nothing inspires the enemy like a few piked Roman heads.'

If the garrison had been anywhere near full strength, thought Figulus, they might have stood a chance of holding out until the reinforcements arrived. But Cosconianus's rush of blood to the head had cost them dearly. With most of the auxiliary cohort killed or captured, the Druids had been free to stroll into the native settlement and remove Trenagasus from his throne. And they could just as easily overrun the few defenders left inside the fort. Such a reversal of fortune here in Durotrigan territory would be bound to inspire rebellion amongst some of the other tribes of the new province. Just at a time when the Roman forces were thinly spread, in order to free troops up for General Plautius's army. The situation was critical indeed, yet Figulus was powerless to do anything to prevent it.

Just then there was a shout of alarm from one of the sentries on the gatehouse. Vespillo rushed over with Figulus and Scylla hurrying close behind. The three men entered the timber-framed gatehouse and climbed the ladder leading up to the boarded platform running above the main gate.

'What did you see?' the duty centurion demanded of the sentry.

'Men approaching, sir!' the auxiliary cried, his voice quavering as he pointed to the south.

Figulus leaned on the wooden rail and peered out at the gloomy expanse of land beyond the outer ditch. In the murky light he spied a handful of riders bunched together slowly approaching the fort from the direction of the settlement, their long, dark robes flapping in the sharp breeze, their faces hidden beneath their hoods as they headed across the patches of snow and mud. The shadowed figures reined in their mounts a short distance before the fort's outer ditch. Then one of the riders advanced ahead of his companions. As he drew near, one of the auxiliaries armed with a bow prepared to shoot an arrow at the man. Scylla thrust out a hand and glared at the soldier.

'No! Let's hear what he has to say.'

The archer reluctantly lowered his bow. The rider halted while the other horsemen remained further back in a tight circle, gripping their reins and ready to reach for their weapons at the slightest provocation from the Romans. Then the rider pulled back his hood and lifted his gaze to the gate. Figulus felt a cold chill of fear as he caught sight of the black crescent moon tattoo on the man's forehead.

'Romans!' the Druid called out. 'I send you greetings from Calumus, High Priest of the Dark Moon lodge.'

Anxious whispers and gasps sounded up and down the wall as the Batavians regarded the Druid with a mixture of curiosity and fear. Many of the auxiliaries had grown up listening to stories of the Druids' mystical powers and cruelties, but few had ever seen one of the priests in the flesh. This was as close as most of them would ever get. Vespillo called the auxiliaries to silence and waited for the Druid to continue.

'Our leader has a message for you.'

'Why doesn't he come and tell us himself?' Vespillo growled under his breath.

'Maybe he's scared to show his face,' Scylla suggested hopefully.

Figulus looked doubtful. 'Somehow I don't think this lot shit their breeches easily.'

The Druid messenger continued, 'For too long the Durotrigans have suffered under your rule. Today, Romans, your wrongful occupation of our lands is over. We have reclaimed Lindinis from that wretched dog Trenagasus. Tomorrow a great audience will gather to watch Calumus sacrifice the treacherous Roman puppet. Trenagasus will be skinned alive, and his hide will be offered to Cruach, the god of war, to decorate his great hall. You need not share his fate. Surrender your fort, leave Durotrigan territory and Calumus promises safe conduct as far as Calleva.'

'Does he think we were born yesterday?' Figulus snarled. 'This fucking lot will cut us down as soon as we step outside of the fort.'

'Silence!' Scylla hissed before the Druid went on.

'Refuse our demands, and tomorrow we will seize the fort as easily as we crushed your comrades earlier today. Any survivors will be tortured and put to death. And now, Calumus wishes you to witness something.'

The messenger turned and gestured to the other riders. The horsemen parted and a trio of figures staggered forwards dressed in tattered red military tunics. Their hands were bound behind their backs and their necks were tethered with rope. A rider walked his beast forwards from his companions, dragging the three men along on a leash. Figulus froze in horror as he recognised the faces of his comrades. Helva and Rullus stumbled along next to a thickly bearded Batavian. The three soldiers struggled to stay upright on the sodden ground. Gasps of shock went up among the auxiliaries as the rider drew near.

'Shit! They've got Ambustus!' one of the Batavians cried.

Figulus looked on helplessly as the horseman slid down from his beast. Nausea tickled the back of the optio's throat as the Druid messenger gestured towards the prisoners.

'These men were captured by our warriors today,' he announced. 'Tomorrow, all those soldiers taken alive will be executed with the dog Trenagasus, and our people will see that the armies of Rome can be defeated. No longer will our tribe cower in fear at the sight of your standards. Calumus gives you until dawn to surrender. After that you will share the fate of this man.'

The messenger signalled to the horseman. The latter grabbed Ambustus and untethered the rope from his neck. Then he kicked the auxiliary centurion in the back and forced him to his knees. Ambustus stared up in despair at his comrades as the horseman pulled out a cleaver from under his cloak. In a blur of motion the horseman swung the cleaver up and then hacked deep into the centurion's neck. Ambustus spasmed and the horseman struck again and this time decapitated the Batavian with a single blow. Cries of anguish went up along the palisade as the centurion's head rolled to the ground and his body slumped to the side, blood disgorging from the neatly severed stump. Then the horseman turned away and climbed back on his mount. The Druid messenger shouted an order to his fellow riders. Then he jabbed his heels into his beast's flank and the Druids trotted back towards the settlement with the remaining prisoners stumbling alongside. Figulus watched the sinister robed figures fade into the encroaching darkness.

Then they were gone.

CHAPTER THIRTY-FIVE

'Fetch the centurion's body!' Vespillo ordered before he climbed back down the gatehouse ladder.

Figulus and Scylla were quiet as they emerged onto the main thoroughfare. Three auxiliaries tentatively removed the locking bar and opened the main gate just wide enough to permit a man to slip through. One of the men cautiously made his way through the gap and returned a few moments later carrying Ambustus's severed head. The other two followed close behind, dragging the centurion's body. Out the corner of his eye Figulus noticed Ancasta watching with a shocked expression as she stood by the gate.

Meanwhile Vespillo ordered those auxiliaries fit enough to wield a sword to make for their positions along the palisade in case of an enemy attack. Others were sent to the stores to fetch bundles of javelins and quivers of arrows to stack at the foot of the rampart, ready for use. Figulus instructed Vatia and the other two legionaries to take up their places on the palisade among the Batavians. The soldiers went about their tasks in a grim mood.

As they made their preparations, Scylla weighed up the Druids' ultimatum.

'It's obvious we can't agree to their terms,' he said at last.

'No,' Figulus replied softly.

'Even if surrender was an option, we can't trust this Druid priest to honour his word and grant us safe passage.'

'Honour?' Figulus laughed cynically. 'I don't think the Druids know the meaning of the word.'

'Then it's clear what we must do. We wait for the reinforcements from the Second Legion to reach us. Once that happens we can drive the enemy out of Lindinis. Two cohorts of legionaries ought to be sufficient for the task. The Druids' rebellion will be short-lived. And then we shall avenge those we have lost.'

'And if the enemy attack us first?'

Scylla glanced round to make sure no one was listening. 'It might be for the best if you and I take the spare horses in the stables and meet the relief column on the road from Calleva. The auxiliaries can fend for themselves until the column reaches the fort.' He saw the look of disgust on Figulus's face and frowned. 'I'm the official representative of Emperor Claudius in Britannia, Optio. Not some piddling Batavian ranker. I can't afford to be captured by the Druids. Think of the embarrassment it would cause back in Rome.'

Figulus could not help sneering. It was obvious that the envoy was more afraid of being captured by the Druids than any political consequences back in Rome. He thrust aside his anger and pointed in the direction of the native settlement.

'What about the king? You heard Calumus's messenger. They're going to sacrifice Trenagasus tomorrow.' He pursed his lips then added quietly, 'And my comrades, too.'

'What can we do, Optio? Our hands are tied.'

'We could try and negotiate their release.'

'Out of the question. We're dealing with fanatics. There's no negotiating with such scum. Besides, they're not interested. They only care about driving every last Roman from Britannia.' Scylla cursed bitterly. 'Our defeat here will have serious implications for our future on this island. Once the other client kings learn that we have failed to keep Trenagasus from harm, they might be tempted to reconsider their treaties with us.'

'Why would they do that?'

'The likes of Cogidubnus are already coming under severe pressure from their people for entering into alliances with Rome. There are those who would have preferred that their tribes continued to fight us instead of making peace.'

'That's putting it lightly.'

'As you may know, the client kings are only able to stay in power thanks to imperial backing. Without our support, they wouldn't be able to reign over their people. If that happens, the tribal alliances we've fought so hard to forge will collapse.'

Figulus gave a wry smile. 'So we'll do what we always do and send the legions in. Nothing like a bit of muscle to make the natives think twice, in my experience.'

Scylla shook his head. 'We cannot rely on the legions to prop up the client kings. Not given the current situation. Many of our garrisons are under-strength, and our regular legions are busy stamping out resistance to the south and pushing back the Silures and Ordovices. If Cogidubnus decides to break his treaty with Rome, in truth there is little we can do about it. Worse still, our main supply base is in his territory. Should Noviomagus fall into enemy hands then the province is as good as lost.'

'Then it's down to us,' Figulus replied fiercely. 'We have to do something.'

'Such as, Optio? The Druids are in no mood to negotiate terms. There's little hope of saving Trenagasus, and if he is killed then his tribe will be sure to go over to the Druids. Even if there are no wider consequences, it will still require our legions to conquer these lands all over again and appoint a procurator to administer the people.'

'Annex the kingdom? The Durotrigans will never stand for that. They're too proud. Even those who support us would rather die than be governed by a procurator.'

'We'd have no other choice.'

Figulus listened with a heavy heart. The envoy's suggestion would spell disaster for the natives and for Rome. Annexing the kingdom would inspire every settlement and village to rebel against the Romans. Garrisons would be overrun, forts attacked and pro-Roman sympathisers driven from the province. The legions would become bogged down in a lengthy conflict to reclaim the land and any hope of establishing a bond of trust between the Durotrigans and Rome would be lost forever. Figulus frantically searched his mind, trying to think of some way of rescuing the situation. In the end there was only one way to bring a lasting peace to the Durotriges, he decided; one last chance to rescue the situation before it was too late.

'We have to rescue Trenagasus.'

'Pfft!' Scylla scoffed. 'And how do you propose to do that?'

'I'll enter the settlement and find out where they're holding the king,' Figulus explained. 'Then I'll rescue him, and the rest of the hostages too, including my men.'

The envoy looked at Figulus with a shocked expression. 'You can't be serious.'

'What else can we do? I look like one of the natives. I speak their tongue well enough. Paint some woad on me, find me a native cloak and I could easily pass for a local warrior. There's hundreds of 'em in the settlement so I wouldn't stand out from the crowd.'

Scylla narrowed his eyes and stroked his chin as he regarded Figulus. 'You do have a striking Celtic appearance. But for the sake of argument let's say you succeed in finding Trenagasus. What will you do then?'

'I'll try to smuggle him out with the others and get them back here to the fort. When the reinforcements arrive, they'll be free to assault the rebels and take back the settlement.'

'Even then, what guarantee have we that we can hold out long enough for your comrades from the Second to save us?'

'None,' Figulus replied curtly. 'But it's that or sit here, let the king die, and wait for the enemy to overrun us. Unless you have a better idea?'

The envoy thought for a moment. 'No, I don't. It's your funeral. But there's one obvious problem with your plan.'

'What's that?'

'How do you intend to get in and out of Lindinis? You can change your appearance all you want, but I imagine the gates will be heavily guarded, and the rebels aren't going to let you stroll through simply because you look like a Durotrigan.'

'There must be some other way in. Ancasta might know.'

He called her over and she approached, Andocommius staying close to her side. She listened intently to Figulus as he explained his plan.

'*Na*,' she replied after he'd finished speaking. 'The only way in and out is through the main gate.'

'There must be another way,' Figulus said desperately. 'We have to try, before it's too late.'

'I know a way, Roman,' Andocommius said.

257

'How?' Figulus asked, his pulse quickening.

'The palisade. A section collapsed during the storm last night. The king sent me to examine the damage early this morning. There's a gap large enough for a man to pass through.'

Scylla listened and stroked his chin thoughtfully. He narrowed his eyes at the bodyguard. 'You're absolutely sure of this?'

'I am certain,' he replied. 'I saw it with my own eyes.'

'That's it, then,' Figulus decided. 'That's how I'll get in.'

'Presuming the Druids ignore the damage caused to the palisade, of course,' Scylla countered. 'It's entirely possible the rebels have stumbled upon this breach in their defences and taken measures to seal it up.'

Andocommius laughed and shook his head. 'The damaged section is near the midden. Druids are many things, but they don't like filth. They wouldn't go near the midden without good reason.'

Scylla fell silent for a few moments as he considered Figulus's plan. Finally he sighed. 'Very well. Frankly I can't decide whether this plan of yours is bold or completely reckless. But given the critical situation we find ourselves in, I have no choice but to agree to it – on one condition.'

'What's that?'

'Take Andocommius with you, if he's agreeable.'

The native warrior was still a moment and then nodded his assent.

'The mission is far too risky for one man to undertake,' Scylla continued. 'Besides, you'll need him to guide you to the damaged section of the palisade.'

Figulus doubted that one extra pair of hands would make much difference if they ran into trouble inside the settlement, but he nodded anyway. 'Fine. We'll leave as soon as it's dark. There's less chance of us running into an enemy patrol then.'

'What about your appearance? How do you intend to pass off as a native?'

'I can paint him to look like a rebel warrior,' Ancasta offered. 'I've done it before. But I'll need supplies for the dye. And some slaked lime for the hair.'

Scylla nodded. 'You should find what you need in the infirmary. The fort's surgeon keeps a healthy stock of native plants for treating various ailments. As for your cloak, speak to the merchants. The natives traded their cloaks for wine. One of them will have something you can use.'

'I should go too,' Ancasta said. 'He's my father, after all.'

Scylla shook his head sharply. 'Absolutely not. It's too risky, my lady. It's much safer for you to remain here in the fort, where our soldiers can protect you.'

'For how long?' Ancasta retorted, a fiery look in her eyes. 'Until the Druids attack again tomorrow and overrun us?'

'I understand your frustration,' Scylla replied in a calm tone. 'But Figulus and Andocommius will be in great danger if you do go. There are too many people in the settlement that might recognise your face, and the chances of Figulus succeeding are slim enough as it is. No, you must remain here. The matter isn't up for debate.'

Ancasta stared for a moment at Scylla. Then she nodded. 'Very well. I understand.'

'Good.' Scylla straightened his back and clapped. 'Now, I suggest you get to work disguising the optio. There's no time to lose if we're to stand any chance of rescuing the king.'

CHAPTER THIRTY-SIX

In the dead of night the gate on the eastern side of the fort creaked open and two wild-haired figures slipped out into the darkness. The sky was overcast and the pair moved silently across the snow-patched ground. Half a mile to the south Figulus could see the native settlement, the palisade illuminated by the faint light of several small fires burning within.

Ancasta had done a fine job of making him look like a native warrior. First she'd mixed a woad dye out of crushed roots and plants boiled over a fire. Then she had instructed him to remove his military tunic and strip down to his loincloth, and by the light of the fire she'd applied the dye to the Gaul's skin, tracing intricate blue patterns across his chest, arms and neck. Once the dye had dried Ancasta then washed his hair with slaked lime, pulling the hair back towards the nape of his neck and spiking the ends. A thick brown cloak borrowed from one of the merchants completed the look. Even Andocommius had grudgingly declared himself impressed with the finished disguise.

Now the two men followed the course of the river east, eyes darting left and right as they looked for any sign of roaming enemy lookouts. A bank of silvery cloud smothered the moon and there was little danger of being seen in the pitch black. Both men carried legionary swords. Most of the native warriors at the hill fort ambush had been equipped with the shorter Roman swords and Figulus was certain that they would not stand out among the rebels carrying their legionary weapons. In addition Figulus carried his lucky charm, tucked into the folds of his loincloth. Although his comrades often made fun of his superstitions, Figulus refused to go on a mission without his charm. He knew he'd need all the luck Fortuna would grant him to succeed in his task.

At length they veered away from the river and headed south, passing a few abandoned farmsteads as they approached Lindinis. The brief opening in the cloud suddenly bathed the landscape in silvery moonlight and Andocommius dropped to a crouch and scanned the land ahead, his distinctive torc gleaming around his neck. In the distance Figulus could just about see the main gate.

'Which way now?' he whispered.

Andocommius pointed to the eastern side of the settlement. 'Follow me.'

The two men trotted parallel to the settlement, staying as close as they dared to the outer ditch, ears and eyes pricked for the slightest sign of enemy movement. Twice Andocommius thought he heard a voice. Both times he stopped and they lay flat on the ground, not moving a muscle. Once they were sure that it was nothing sinister they moved forwards again across the frozen ground.

At length they reached the far end of the settlement. The clouds finally began to break up and fully reveal the moon, casting its pale light across the land. A foul odour of rotting meat and animal manure drifted under Figulus's nostrils and he realised they must be close to the midden. Andocommius abruptly slowed his pace and edged forwards. Figulus crept alongside him, trying to ignore the powerful stench coming from the heaps of rubbish and waste that had been dumped in the ditch. After fifty paces Andocommius dropped to the ground and crept forwards on his belly until he was just short of the outer ditch. Then he turned and beckoned to Figulus. The optio crawled alongside Andocommius.

'Up there, Roman.'

Figulus lifted his gaze to the top of the turf rampart. In the pale moonlight he could see the tall wooden palisade encircling the rampart, each stake twice as tall as a man. The section directly above Figulus showed obvious signs of damage caused by the recent storm where the soil at the base of the palisade had given way, sliding into the ditch and causing some of the stakes to fall down, leaving a narrow gap, just wide enough to permit a man to slip through. For once he was grateful for the miserable British weather.

261

Both men remained still for a short while, listening for any sign of life from the other side of the palisade. There was nothing except the distant din from the far side of the settlement as the rebel warriors celebrated their victory. Satisfied that the immediate approach was clear, they began crawling towards the palisade. Andocommius suddenly stopped in his tracks.

'What is it?' Figulus whispered.

'Listen.'

Figulus pricked his ears. At first he couldn't hear anything. Then he caught a distinct sound in the distance: the dull scuffling of footsteps on the frosted ground. He glanced back in the direction they'd come from and saw a cloaked figure moving towards them.

'Shit,' Figulus hissed. 'Keep still.'

Both men lay flat on their fronts in the ditch. Figulus carefully watched the figure and slowly slid a hand down to his sword, ready to unsheathe the blade. Now the figure was less than ten paces away. Figulus knew he had to cut down the enemy before they could raise the alarm inside the settlement. He took a deep breath then sprang up from the ditch, wrenching his weapon free from its scabbard as he rushed forwards.

'Wait!' the figure cried shrilly.

Figulus froze. Relief and confusion swirled inside his head as Ancasta pulled back the hood from her cloak. 'My lady! What are you doing here?'

'I've come to help.' She frowned at his sword. 'Although it seems I'm in rather more danger of being killed by a friend than an enemy.'

Figulus lowered his weapon and glanced around, making sure she hadn't been followed. 'What in Hades do you think you're doing?'

'I couldn't stay behind. I can't bear the thought of sitting around at the fort while Father's held prisoner by the Druids. I want to help.'

'No chance. It's too dangerous. Think what the Druids will do to you if you get caught.'

'He's right,' Andocommius said. 'You shouldn't be here.'

'I can handle myself, if that's what you're worried about,' Ancasta said defiantly as she drew back her cloak to reveal the outline of a dagger hanging from her belt.

Figulus shook his head. 'I can't risk it, my lady. Go back to the fort.'

Ancasta stood her ground. 'Trenagasus isn't just the king. He's my father, and it's my duty to help rescue him. Besides, if you send me away now, I might get captured before I can make it back to the fort. You can let me come with you, or you can send me away and hope that I don't get taken alive by the enemy. Make up your mind.'

Figulus gritted his teeth. Ancasta was right. It was too risky to send her back to the fort, and he had no way of forcing her to leave. 'Fine. Come with us. But you'll do exactly as I say. Stay close to me at all times and don't do anything unless I say. And for gods' sakes keep your hood up in case anyone recognises you.'

A slight smile crept across Ancasta's lips. 'As you wish, Optio.'

He turned to Andocommius and motioned for him to keep moving. The Durotrigan nodded and crawled up the rampart until he reached the gap in the palisade. Figulus and Ancasta moved up behind him. As they reached the top, Figulus put his hand on Andocommius's shoulder.

'I'll go first.'

Easing himself through the narrow gap between the thick stakes, Figulus entered the settlement. A chaotic sprawl of animal pens and native roundhouses stretched out in front of him. Pools of orange light spilled out of the open doorways as the hearth fires burned brightly within the huts. In the distance he spied a pair of rebel warriors patrolling between the huts. Figulus waited until they had disappeared from sight. Ancasta joined him a few moments later, followed by Andocommius. They lingered in the shadows of the nearest hut for a short while, making sure they hadn't been seen. Then they moved at a steady pace through the winding lanes, taking care to watch out for the enemy.

'The prisoners are most likely to be in the royal enclosure,' Andocommius whispered.

It was eerily quiet this side of the settlement. Some of the huts had been ransacked, Figulus noted. Grain pits had been emptied, the inhabitants' meagre possessions tossed into the filthy street. Several corpses were sprawled in the darkened alleys running between the huts, their bodies stripped naked and horribly mutilated. Most of the natives remained in their huts, huddled around the warmth of their hearths, not daring to venture outside.

Several fires were blazing towards the middle of the settlement, not far from the royal enclosure. Figulus headed towards the glow of the flames. As they pushed deeper into the settlement he saw more evidence of the Druids' reign of terror. The foundations of the king's new palace had been torn down, the auxiliary engineers decapitated and their severed heads put on display on wooden stakes lining the street. The altar dedicated to the imperial cult lay smashed in pieces. Figulus pushed on, his nerves jangling with fear. If they were caught, the Dark Moon Druids would surely show them no mercy. They would be subjected to every imaginable torture, followed by a long and painful death.

A large throng of warriors and Druid supporters stood around the open market area a short distance from the royal enclosure. The merchant stalls and inns had been wrecked and the ground was strewn with shards from shattered clay amphoras and broken trinkets. In the middle of the market the fires continued to burn. By the largest a handful of natives had been lashed to a wagon. They screamed in terror as a pair of warriors approached. Some of the victims pleaded with their captors to spare them. Others shouted prayers to their gods as one of the warriors poured pitch over the wagon, dousing the natives in the sticky substance. Then the other guard stepped forwards and tossed the torch onto the wagon before quickly retreating. The crowd let out a throated roar as the fire quickly spread. The victims howled in agony and twitched hopelessly against the ropes binding them to the wagon in a desperate attempt to escape the flames. Their screams reached a new pitch of terror and agony as the flames engulfed their naked torsos, prompting another cheer of delight from the rowdy spectators.

Figulus looked away in disgust and growled. 'How can those bastards do that to their own people?'

'When the Dark Moon Druids take over a settlement, anyone who opposes them is given a choice,' Ancasta explained. 'Accept the high priest as their one true leader, or die. These people have refused.'

Figulus frowned deeply. 'But I thought the Druids were on their side?'

'It's not that simple. The Dark Moon Druids don't tolerate the other cults. They insist theirs is the only true one. Anyone who refuses to follow Calumus is considered an enemy.'

Figulus felt his stomach knot in disgust. This was far worse than anything he'd witnessed under the reign of Trenagasus. This was something much darker. Out the corner of his eye he noticed Andocommius staring at a series of makeshift crucifixes lining the rough thoroughfare leading towards the main gate. Figulus squinted in the gloom and felt a surge of nausea in his throat as he recognised the men of the royal bodyguard. Bellicanus and his men hung from the frames, the skin on their stomachs peeled back and their bowels emptied into glistening heaps at their feet. Andocommius clenched his fists and bit back on his grief and anger at the sight of his comrades.

Figulus turned away and gazed around the market. At the far end he spotted a sprawling cluster of grain sheds. Four warriors squatted on the ground just outside a large animal pen opposite the sheds. Their spears were rested against the gate as they shared a jar of wine looted from the market. Figulus pointed out the guards to his companions.

'That might be where they're keeping my father,' Ancasta whispered.

'If it is, we'll have to find a way past the guards,' Figulus said quietly.

Ancasta bit her lower lip. 'How, though? There's four of them and only three of us.'

Just then a shout went up. Figulus glanced back at the market as a line of prisoners was marched forwards by some of the rebels. Each victim had been stripped to their loincloth with their hands bound behind their back. More warriors flocked towards the market and cheered as the first native in line was dragged towards a pack of long-limbed hunting dogs. The dogs strained at their leashes, snarling viciously and baring their teeth. The native began trembling with terror as the dog handler bent low and pointed him out then released the beasts. At his command the dogs leapt forwards and pounced on the man, tearing at him. The victim sank to his knees, shrieking in agony as one dog mauled at his face. Drunken jeers went up from the crowd as the victim voided his bowels. The hunting dogs continued tearing at his limp body as the next man was shoved forwards.

With the warriors' backs turned Figulus spied an opportunity. He turned to Ancasta. 'Wait here.'

'Where are you going?'

'There's no time to explain. Wait here.'

She flashed a quizzical look at him as he paced quickly over to one of the fires burning by the edge of the market and seized a torch stoked in the flames. Another terrible scream pierced the air as the dogs set upon their next victim. Figulus moved around the fringe of the market, making sure that no one was watching him. But the warriors were transfixed by the gruesome spectacle unfolding in front of them and no one paid attention to Figulus as he made his way towards the grain huts. Taking one last look around, Figulus dropped to his knees and tossed the torch inside the small opening at the front of the hut. Then he spun round and hurried around the back of the storage huts and animal pens, screened from view of the warriors at the market. The flames were already spreading across the hut as Figulus emerged from the shadows close to the ruined gateway.

One of the guards at the animal pen spotted the rising flames and sounded the alarm to his companions. The men quickly abandoned their positions, sprinting in the direction of the royal hall to fetch water. At the same time more warriors raced over from the direction of the market and began quickly removing the grain from the nearby storage huts before the fire could spread. Amid the panic Figulus rejoined Andocommius and Ancasta. There was a deafening roar as the flames consumed the storage hut.

'Hurry!' he exclaimed breathlessly. 'Now's our chance!'

They slipped towards the pen, moving steadily and trying not to draw attention to themselves. Figulus stopped beside the pen and peered through a small gap in the surrounding willow weave wall. He glimpsed a huddle of figures sitting on the soiled straw floor, their wrists bound with rope. Most of the prisoners wore ragged military tunics. In the middle of the enclosed space Figulus spotted an older man slumped on the ground.

Trenagasus.

Figulus saw that the Durotrigan king was bleeding from a wound on the side of his head.

'The king!' Figulus whispered excitedly. 'He's there, I see him!'

There was a slight pause and then a gruff voice from the other side of the wall said, 'Sir? Is that you?'

Figulus felt his heart beating faster as he recognised the voice. 'Rullus. Are you all right?'

'We're alive. How'd you get in here?'

'Long story. We're coming to rescue you. Wait there.'

From inside the pen Rullus snorted. 'It's not as if we can bloody go anywhere else, is it?'

Figulus worked his way around to the gate. Then he pulled on the stout wooden bolt. But the bolt was stiff and he struggled to slide it free.

'Hurry!' Andocommius urged.

'Shit,' Figulus cursed, 'it's stuck. Give me a hand here.'

As he worked the bolt he heard a sudden dull slap at his side. Andocommius gasped and Figulus saw a look of shock on the face of the Durotrigan warrior. Then the optio lowered his eyes to the dagger tip protruding from his throat. Andocommius spasmed as the blade disappeared from behind with a wet squelch. Blood spewed from the wide gash in Andocommius's neck, splashing down his tattooed chest. The warrior looked despairingly at Figulus and gasped again before he slumped to the ground clutching his throat.

Figulus instantly spun around. Ancasta stood over the dying warrior, blood dripping from the tip of the Celtic dagger in her right hand as her lips parted in a thin, cruel smile. Figulus instinctively reached down for his sword, but he was too slow and before he could wrench it free Ancasta had the tip of her dagger pressed against his throat. He stood frozen to the spot.

'Keep your hand where it is, Optio,' Ancasta said icily. 'Don't give me a reason to cut you down. It'd be a shame to kill you now, before the Druids have had their fun with you.'

Figulus was still as she called out to the rebels. Already there were shouts coming from the royal hall as men turned in her direction. Even if he did manage to overpower Ancasta, there was no way he could fight his way past the other warriors. Figulus reluctantly lifted his hand away from his weapon.

'What the fuck do you think you're doing?'

Ancasta smiled. 'Come on, Optio. Surely even you can figure it out.'

The awful realisation suddenly hit Figulus. He glowered at Ancasta. 'You're the traitor.'

'I prefer to think of myself as a loyal Durotrigan. Unlike Father.'

'That's why you followed us here. So you could stop us from rescuing Trenagasus.'

'That wasn't my original plan. I was going to try and open one of the gates at the fort for the rebels, but they were constantly guarded. I couldn't get near them. But when you came up with your plan to rescue my father, I followed you to make sure you didn't succeed. Now you're finished. Calumus will be pleased when he finds out I've foiled a plot to rescue the king, and taken a Roman officer hostage into the bargain.' She smiled again.

Figulus glared bitterly at Ancasta. 'How could you do this? Betray your own father?'

The smile disappeared and an icy look formed in her eyes. 'That's where you are mistaken. I didn't betray anyone. It is my father who is the traitor. He has betrayed his people, his bloodline. He betrayed us the moment he struck a deal with your Emperor.'

'All this time you've been serving the Druids?'

'Not always, no. Believe it or not, I once supported my father's desire to forge a stronger bond with Rome, years before the invasion. But when the Dark Moon Druids exiled us, I saw with my own eyes how Rome treats its allies. How the people of Gaul had suffered under Rome. Most are little better than slaves in their own land, mired in poverty and scratching out a living while Roman landowners grow rich and fat. Except for those that throw in their lot with Rome.' Her eyes narrowed. 'Like you . . . I knew then that I had to stop our people from suffering the same fate. When Father announced that the Emperor was going to restore him to the throne, I made it my sworn duty to do everything in my power to stop him.'

A wave of anger exploded inside Figulus's chest. 'You'll never get away with this.'

'Oh, but I already have.'

At that moment footsteps approached the pen and several warriors hurried over brandishing their swords. One of them stepped forwards and spoke to Ancasta in Celtic.

'Drop the weapon.'

Ancasta shot a look at the warrior. 'I'm on your side, you fool.' She nodded at Figulus. 'This man is a Roman soldier. I just stopped him from helping the king to escape!'

'We'll see about that,' the man responded tonelessly. 'Now drop the blade or there'll be trouble.'

Ancasta hesitated. Then she tossed aside the dagger and glowered at the warrior. 'You'll be sorry when Calumus hears about how you've treated his most trusted spy.'

'Tell him yourself,' the warrior said.

Then he stood aside and a tall, robed figure with a heavily scarred face stepped out of the shadows.

CHAPTER THIRTY-SEVEN

Ancasta bowed before the priest.

'Calumus . . . my lord.'

The leader of the Dark Moon Druids raised a hand and signalled for the warriors to lower their weapons. His dark eyes rested on Figulus for a moment before settling on Ancasta. A loud hissing noise sounded from the storage huts as the small party of men dealing with the fire doused the rising flames.

'This is a surprise, my child,' Calumus rasped in a soft voice. 'I didn't expect to see you here. You're supposed to be waiting at the fort to help our attack tomorrow.'

Ancasta straightened her back. 'I had no choice but to abandon the plan, my lord. These men were plotting to help the prisoners escape.' She pointed to Andocommius's lifeless corpse. 'The dead man is one of Father's bodyguards. The other is a Roman soldier. Once I learned of their plan I followed them here and put a stop to it.'

Calumus turned his sinister gaze on Figulus. The optio felt a wave of revulsion as he took in the Druid leader's hideously disfigured face. Calumus had the tattoo of a crescent moon inked onto his forehead and, unlike the warriors he commanded, his hair was grown long. A smile trembled on his lips as he looked back to Ancasta.

'I can see you've done well, my child. Very well indeed. Once again you've proved your tireless devotion to our cause. Cruach will reward your efforts, I'm sure.'

He looked briefly towards the grain huts and worked his scarred features into a deep frown. By now the party of warriors had managed to put out the fire and trails of smoke were churning up from the charred hut into the night sky.

'It's a pity you didn't stop them before they torched our grain. We're going to need all the supplies we can get our hands on if we are to defeat the enemy, as Cruach has foretold.'

'Apologies, my lord. But I had to wait until their backs were turned. I had no idea the Roman was going to set fire to the huts. By the time I realised what he was doing, it was too late.'

'A small price to pay for foiling their plot, I suppose,' the Druid mused. 'How did you manage to get into the settlement? My men have strict orders not to admit anyone through the gate.'

'A section of the palisade was damaged during the storm yesterday. I would have warned you about it, but I had to make my way to the fort as soon as your warriors arrived.'

Calumus nodded. 'I see. We'll have to post a few guards there until it is repaired. Perhaps you can point out the breach to my men once we're done here.'

'Of course, my lord.'

'Did you at least get a good look at how many of the enemy are bottled up in the fort?'

'No more than a hundred or so. Some of them are injured. And they are badly shaken by the defeat they suffered at the hill fort. They barely have enough men to line the palisade.'

'Excellent. Then they will present no great threat when we attack the fort tomorrow.' There was a moment of silence as Calumus turned to Figulus and stared curiously at him. 'So this is a Roman. By Lud, he looks more Celtic than some of my own men.'

'He's a Gaul, my lord.'

Calumus arched an eyebrow in surprise. 'A fellow Celt? Does he have a name?'

'Horatius Figulus, Optio of the Second Legion,' Figulus responded in the native dialect with as much authority as he could summon.

Calumus paused a moment. 'So you're an optio? I didn't realise Rome was in the habit of promoting such young men. Or perhaps the occupation of our lands has taken a greater toll on your forces than I'd imagined.'

Figulus stared defiantly at the Druid leader. 'I'm just bloody good at cutting down Britons.'

A brief look of anger flashed behind Calumus's eyes and they widened dangerously for an instant. Then he smiled faintly. 'I presume you know who I am?'

Figulus nodded. 'You're the one they call the Blood Priest.'

'That's what my enemies call me, yes. But do you know why?'

'Because you're a sick, murdering bastard.'

Calumus shook his head. 'You're mistaken, Gaul. I kill only those who deserve to die.'

'What about these people?' Figulus replied, indicating the severed heads on display around the market. 'What have they done that justifies butchering them?'

'They have been corrupted, Gaul. They have forgotten the true way of our gods.' There was a sad timbre to the Druid's voice as he spoke. 'Rome has corrupted our land with its depraved culture and beliefs. Now the kingdom must be cleansed.'

'Sounds like an excuse to murder anyone who doesn't agree with your twisted ideas.'

'How is that any different to Rome?' Calumus replied with a sneer. 'Anyone who defies the Emperor is killed. Thousands of our brethren have been slaughtered by your legions. Many more have been condemned to slavery. You're no more than butchers.'

Figulus shook his head vehemently. 'No. We're soldiers. We do our killing on the field of battle. We don't murder for the pleasure of it.'

His response seemed to enrage Calumus. He stared at Figulus, his eyes boring holes through him as his facial muscles twitched with anger. 'No, Gaul. We are merely appeasing Cruach. Your legions angered our god when they invaded our lands. Your troops destroyed our sacred groves, banned our cults and forced us to worship foreign gods. Cruach has demanded the blood of Roman soldiers, and we will do whatever it takes to please him, and drive you back into the sea.'

'You can't win. Surely you can see that.'

'Can't we?' Calumus stepped closer and Figulus caught a whiff of the Druid's rank breath. His teeth were neatly filed, Figulus noticed. 'We proved today that we can defeat your soldiers. Our victory at the hill fort will inspire others. Thousands more will join our cause and swear a blood oath to Cruach, to crush the invader. We will never surrender. Never! We won't stop until the last drop of Roman blood has been spilled.'

There was a look of absolute hatred in his eyes. Calumus spoke with the fervour of a true fanatic, and Figulus could see how he'd inspired so many of the disillusioned natives to join his cause. There could be no reasoning with him. Calumus believed in the absolute victory of his cult over Rome, and nothing Figulus could say would persuade him otherwise. Such a man was capable of dragging the Durotrigans into a long and bitter war, inspiring the downtrodden natives with fiery rhetoric to take up arms against Rome. A campaign against Calumus and his followers could drag on for years.

'This tribe has already suffered enough,' Figulus responded angrily. 'All you're going to do is add to their torment.'

The Druid shrugged. 'Cruach demands that his followers make sacrifices. The king's skin is going to make a fine offering once it has been removed from his flesh and nailed to the doors of the royal hall. Cruach will be very pleased.' A wicked smile played out on his mutilated face. 'As for you and your fellow soldiers, I've got a special surprise planned.'

Figulus simmered with rage. He said nothing. The Druid's lips trembled in cruel anticipation.

'Tomorrow, before the king dies, there will be a big crowd to watch you and your soldiers burn,' Calumus went on. 'I'm going to have you die last. You will watch each of your comrades screaming like infants, knowing that you will suffer the same fate as them at the end. What do you think of that, Gaul? You can even decide who dies first.'

Figulus exploded with anger. He stepped towards the priest but the guards reacted first and grabbed him, pulling him away. 'You black-hearted bastard! You'll pay for this. I swear by Jupiter, best and greatest!'

Calumus moved closer to the optio. There was a look of pure evil in his eyes as he continued in a low, seething voice. 'Let us see how brave you are tomorrow, when we set fire to your comrades.'

CHAPTER THIRTY-EIGHT

The torments of the native prisoners continued through the night. Figulus sat in a corner of the stinking animal pen with his forearms resting on his knees, listening to the terrified screams of the victims, punctuated by the roars of drunken laughter from their rebel tormentors. Around him the other dozen prisoners sat in dejected silence, their faces etched with foreboding at the grim fate awaiting them the following day.

'We're really in the shit this time, sir,' Rullus muttered as he sat slumped against the wall.

Figulus glanced around the pen and swallowed hard. 'Looks like it.'

After his confrontation with Calumus the guards had shoved Figulus inside the pen, binding his wrists with rope. A leather collar was fastened around his neck, tethering him to the other prisoners and making it impossible for one man to stray far from the others. The straw floor was spattered with puddles of animal manure and a thick stench of piss and sweat hung in the air. Some of the prisoners stared at the ground. Others tried to make themselves comfortable in their squalid surroundings. Only Helva refused to give in to the morbid atmosphere. He squatted near the gate, peering through a gap in the willow weave, watching the enemy movements, as if waiting for an opportunity to escape. It was a forlorn hope, Figulus knew.

'What happened to the king?' he asked.

Trenagasus lay on his back in one corner of the pen. His tunic was ripped in places and spattered with blood and dirt, and a deep wound glistened on his scalp. His breathing was shallow and he was barely conscious.

'Him? He took a blow to the head when the Druids attacked the royal hall,' Rullus said. 'One of the bodyguards told us, when they were here earlier.' He paused. 'Before they got taken away.'

'The king doesn't know about Ancasta, then?'

'No.'

'Probably for the best.'

Rullus shrugged. 'Doesn't matter now, sir, does it? He's for the chop in a few hours. Along with the rest of us.'

Helva turned away from the wall and shook his head. 'This can't be it. There has to be some other way out, surely.'

'No chance, lad,' Rullus grunted. Figulus stiffened his jaw. As much as it pained him to admit it, Rullus was right. Any attempt at escaping the pen was doomed to fail. Apart from the ropes and the collar tying the prisoners together, Calumus had posted several of his men on guard duty outside the gate. Even if they could somehow slip past the guards, they were in the middle of a settlement teeming with Rome's sworn enemies. They wouldn't get very far before the rebels spotted them and raised the alarm.

'Maybe the reinforcements will get here?' Helva suggested hopefully. 'There's still time.'

'I wouldn't get your hopes up, lad,' Rullus responded. 'Even if the relief column does show up, the Druids will cut us to pieces before we can be rescued. Either way, we're fucked.'

'Rullus is right,' Figulus added ruefully. 'We can't rely on the relief column. They won't be able to save us.'

Helva looked distraught. 'So that's it, sir? We're done for?'

Figulus shrugged and looked away. A black wave of grim resignation engulfed him. He had failed the king, and his comrades. His efforts had been in vain. Now the prisoners would pay a terrible price, burned alive in front of hundreds of cheering natives. Figulus shivered at the thought. Over the past few hours he'd tried hard not to think about his impending execution but now he finally succumbed to the horrific mental images. He imagined the excruciating pain as the flames ate at his limbs, scorching his legs before engulfing his torso, the smoke filling his nostrils with the acrid stench of his own burning flesh . . .

He suddenly felt very tired. Every limb ached and he longed for rest, in spite of the terrible dread consuming his mind. Finally he rested his head against the wall. He gazed up at the twinkling stars and closed his eyes.

At last the screams abated and a warm glow tinged the sky as the first streaks of sunlight crept over the horizon. Figulus watched the sun rise for the last time, his stomach muscles tightening with dread as the moment of his execution drew near. From outside the pen he heard several loud grunts and shouts as the Druids roused their men from their slumbers and ordered them to prepare for the attack on the fort. As dawn came the air was filled with the aroma of roasting pork, wafting through the air into the animal pen, churning Figulus's already nauseous stomach. Further away he could hear the general hubbub of a crowd gathering in the marketplace, the din punctuated by murmurs of excitement.

'Looks like they're building a fire,' Helva reported as he peered outside. 'They're putting up some wooden frames around it in a circle, sir.'

'Bastards,' Rullus muttered quietly. 'Won't be long now.'

Figulus nodded slowly.

Helva spun away from the wall, his expression fearful. 'This is it, then? We're really going to die?'

The optio lowered his head. 'I'm sorry, lad.'

Helva cursed bitterly under his breath and slumped against the wall. A dreadful tension hung over the prisoners. Some of the men buried their heads in their hands and mumbled prayers to their gods. Others were inconsolable, convulsing with fear and beating their fists against the soiled ground in despair. A few simply stared into the middle distance with blank expressions, already resigned to their deaths.

Figulus looked away, angry and frustrated at the hopelessness of their situation. All his efforts had been for nothing in the end. Now he would die. Put to death by his enemies, not even afforded the dignity of a proper Roman funeral. He closed his eyes and briefly wondered what would become of Lindinis after he'd died. The relief column would surely drive the rebels back from the settlement, but any Roman victory would be short-lived. Despite the optio's bold assertion to Calumus that Rome would triumph in the end, he knew that victory against the Dark Moon Druids was far from assured. The Druids might not be able to hold on to the settlement, but word of their defeat of the auxiliary cohort would soon spread across the region, encouraging more native warriors to join their ranks. Eventually they would have a large enough force to crush Rome's under-strength garrisons and outposts. Nothing would stand in their way then. Calleva, Noviomagus, Londinium . . . none would be safe. Figulus clenched his jaw. The nightmare of a Druid uprising in Britannia was unfolding before his eyes, and there was nothing he could do about it.

In the corner of the pen he noticed Helva staring disconsolately at the ground between his feet. Figulus turned to the legionary. 'Afraid, lad?' he asked softly.

Helva looked up and gulped. 'Terrified, sir.'

Rullus looked the young man hard in the eye. 'Just remember, you're a soldier of Rome. You're better than this lot. When the time comes, don't show these bastards you're afraid. Don't give 'em the satisfaction.' He pointed at the gate. 'When you go out there, you die like a fucking Roman.'

'Yes, sir.'

'You in there!' one of the guards shouted from outside. 'Shut your mouth, or I'll come in there and cut out your tongue.'

The guards laughed amongst themselves and the prisoners fell into morbid silence, not needing any translation of the guard's threat. Rullus looked warily at the gate then shook his head. 'Looks like I'll never make it to my retirement after all, sir.'

Figulus smiled faintly. 'I hear Syria's overrated anyway.'

Rullus opened his mouth to reply. Just then Figulus heard a sudden commotion outside the pen. There was a deafening crash from the other side of the settlement, interspersed with urgent shouts and the frantic pounding of footsteps hurrying away from the market. Figulus crept forward and peered through a narrow gap in the willow weave. Beyond a screen of native roundhouses he glimpsed a flurry of activity as scores of rebels grabbed their weapons and streamed towards the main gate, shouting at their companions to follow. The crowd around the market started to disperse as the locals hurried back inside their homes, eager to avoid getting caught up in any further conflict. Another loud crash sounded and the gate's stout wooden timbers shuddered on their hinges.

'The Romans are attacking!' a voice cried out.

'Bastards must have crept up on us during the night!' said one of the guards outside the pen. 'Come, lads! To the main gate.'

'What about the prisoners?' another man asked.

'Leave 'em to the Druids. A quick offering to Cruach will help us beat back those scum at the gate.'

The guards grabbed their spears and raced off down the rough thoroughfare leading towards the main gate as another loud crunch thundered across the settlement. In the distance Figulus could see a heaving throng of armed rebels amassing by the gate, roaring with excitement as they waited to repel the Roman soldiers on the far side. He spun away from the wall and faced his comrades. 'It's the relief column from Calleva, lads! Has to be.'

Helva thumped a fist against his thigh. 'Thank the gods, sir! We're saved!'

Figulus shook his head. 'The Druids might kill us before the reinforcements can break into the town. We can't wait for them.'

'What's to be done, sir?'

The optio jerked his thumb at the gate. 'The guards posted outside have left to join their mates. Now's our chance to escape. We'll cut our way out of here before the Druids show up. We can escape the same way I got in here, through the gap on the far side of the palisade.'

'Aren't you forgetting something?' Rullus raised his hands, indicating his bound wrists. 'How are we supposed to break out of these bloody things?'

Figulus said nothing. He reached down into the folds of his loincloth and rummaged around, to quizzical looks from the other prisoners. Then he found what he was looking for and pulled out the damaged silver medallion he'd carried with him from the fort. He held it up to the dim morning light. The medallion was chipped on one side, the worn narrow edge just sharp enough for the task.

'My lucky charm. Ancasta returned it to me yesterday. She found it in the royal hall. I must have dropped it there when we were on bodyguard duty.'

'You've been carrying it all this time?' Rullus asked in disbelief. 'That's got to chafe a bit.'

Figulus grinned. 'I never go anywhere without it. Looks like it'll come in useful after all, eh?'

Rullus stared at him. 'Just hurry up and give me your wrists, sir.'

Figulus handed over the lucky charm. Helva crept forwards and kept watch at the gate while Rullus quickly went to work on the optio's bindings. He concentrated hard, gripping the chipped medallion between his thumb and forefinger and working at the rope with the sharpened edge. The frayed strands soon began to part. As Rullus worked at the rope another thundering crash sounded from outside the settlement, followed by a throated roar from the rebels, and Figulus knew that it would not be long before the battering ram had smashed through the natives' crude defences. At last Rullus cut through the remaining strands and Figulus pulled his wrists free before tearing off the leather collar fastened around his neck.

'Now the king,' Figulus said. 'Quick.'

Rullus handed over the medallion. Figulus hurried over to Trenagasus, his heart beating rapidly. The king had regained consciousness and regarded Figulus with a dazed expression. His eyes were heavily lidded and his lips were parched.

'Optio . . . ?' he croaked, blinking at his surroundings. 'What's going on?'

'We're getting you out of here, Your Majesty.'

The king glanced at the other prisoners. 'Ancasta . . . safe?'

Figulus bit his tongue. There would be plenty of time later for the king to learn of his daughter's betrayal. 'She's not here. Now hold still.'

He took the charm and frantically sawed through the king's bindings. The rope seemed to take forever to cut through. Finally he managed to free Trenagasus. The king groaned and touched a hand to his reddened wrist as Figulus ripped the collar from his neck. Then he turned towards Rullus. But before he could get to work on the legionary's ropes Helva suddenly spun away from the gate, his eyes wide with fear.

'Enemy's approaching, sir!'

Figulus hurried over to the gate and looked through the gap. Two

279

burly-looking rebels were trotting purposefully across the market towards the animal pen. He turned and dropped to a knee beside Rullus.

'Give me your wrists. Hurry. We don't have much time.'

Rullus shook his head. 'No, sir.'

For a moment Figulus was too stunned to reply. He stared at his friend in disbelief. In the distance he could hear the footsteps of the two rebels approaching. 'Are you fucking mad? The enemy's going to be here any moment.'

'That's why you have to go, sir. It's too late for us. You have to get out of here while you still can. There's no time to free us, but you can still save the king.'

'Bollocks! I'm not leaving you behind.'

From the gate Helva cried, 'They're almost here, sir!'

Rullus glanced at the younger man then turned back to Figulus. 'What are you going to do instead, sir? Fight 'em off? There's hundreds of the enemy and a handful of us. We've got no chance. You have to escape now. It's our only chance of getting the king out of here before Calumus and his mates send him for the chop.'

'But—'

'Sir!' There was a firmness to the veteran's voice that took Figulus by surprise. Rullus looked him steadily in the eye. 'Listen to me. You must go. No one's going to miss an old bastard like me. But if the king dies, this lot win.'

For a moment Figulus was still, weighing up the situation. The thought of abandoning his comrades made him sick to the pit of his stomach, yet there was no time to free the other prisoners. If he stayed then it would mean certain death for all of them, including Trenagasus.

'I'll come back for you,' he said.

'I'll hold you to that, sir.' Rullus smiled grimly. 'Now get bloody moving.'

Figulus hurried over to the king and helped him to his feet. Trenagasus groaned weakly, moving with some difficulty as the optio escorted him past the puddles and filth towards the gate. He rested the king against the wall and then tried reaching over the gate to unfasten the bolt on the other side. The wooden peg was tantalisingly out of reach and Figulus had to push up on the balls of his feet to clasp it. As he strained to pull the stiff peg free from the receiver he heard a hoarse shout. Figulus looked up and saw the two rebels a short distance ahead. One of them had stopped in his tracks as he caught sight of the optio leaning over the gate. The other man roared manically and sprinted forwards. Gritting his teeth, Figulus wrenched the peg free with all his strength and the gate flung open, hurling him forwards.

He crashed to the ground a few paces in front of the onrushing rebel, but sprang to his feet as the Durotrigan thrust his spear at him. Figulus dodged to one side to avoid the leaf-shaped tip and then stepped forwards, slamming his shoulder into his opponent. The man let out an explosive grunt and stumbled back. Then Figulus floored the rebel with a vicious punch to the jaw, and there was a dull crunch as his eyes rolled into the back of his skull. The rebel fell away, releasing his grip on his spear. Figulus reached down and grabbed the spear as he turned to face the next rebel. The man had drawn his sword and charged towards the Gaul, snarling with savage intent. There was no time to act. Figulus pulled back his throwing arm and launched the spear at the onrushing rebel with all his strength. The spear arced through the air and thudded into the Durotrigan's midriff. The man cried out as he sank to his knees, the shaft protruding from his stomach. His cry had alerted his companions at the market and several shouts went up among the warriors and Druids who'd been preparing the sacrifice.

Figulus grabbed Trenagasus, throwing an arm around the king's waist to support him. As they hurried away from the pen he heard a deep, dull crack at the main gate and he glanced round to see the locking bar splitting in two. For a fleeting moment the gate threatened to open and a crack of light appeared between the timbers. With a roar the rebels rushed forwards, pushing against the gate with all their strength before the Romans could force their way inside. It remained shut and the two sides ground to a standstill as they pressed their respective weights against the thick timbers.

Figulus turned his attention to the voices coming from the market. He saw Calumus and Ancasta rushing forwards, accompanied by eight or so rebel warriors brandishing their swords. She pointed out the king to her comrades.

'They're escaping!' she yelled. 'STOP THEM!'

Figulus spun away and set off with the king in the opposite direction to the market, heading down one of the narrow alleyways that snaked between the roundhouses in an attempt to throw off their pursuers. He glanced around and tried to establish his bearings. Ahead of them, a short distance beyond the huts, stood the royal enclosure. Figulus knew from his time serving on the king's bodyguard that there was a side street on the other side of the enclosure that would take him to the far end of the settlement. From there they could try to sneak across to the breach in the defences and escape to the fort. It was a faint hope, but he had to try. He pushed on down the alley, the cries and shouts of the bitter struggle at the gate diminishing. Figulus glanced over his shoulder and saw that their pursuers had been lost from sight, and for a moment he dared to believe that they might have got away.

The two men struggled on, staying close to the middle of the alley to avoid tripping up on the piles of manure and rubbish dumped outside each home. Trenagasus slithered on a puddle and almost lost his footing, but Figulus grabbed him at the last moment and they hurried on. By now the king was gasping for breath and struggling to keep up the pace, and Figulus knew it would not be long before their enemies caught up. He could hear the sounds of their pursuers getting closer. Ahead the alley opened up onto the main thoroughfare next to the royal enclosure.

'Hurry, Your Majesty!' Figulus urged. 'We're almost there!'

The king winced between ragged breaths. The faint clatter of equipment behind them grew louder as the rebels drew near, shouting their murderous intent. Figulus looked back and saw that their pursuers were no more than fifteen paces behind. He faced forwards and stumbled on, his heart thumping so loudly inside his chest that he could barely hear the pounding footsteps of the chasing enemy. At last they reached the end of the alley and emerged onto the main thoroughfare in front of the royal enclosure. The timber gateway had been smashed apart and the severed heads of the Druids' victims lined the surrounding palisade. Several warriors were rushing out of the ruined gateway, carrying spears and swords. They were in a mad rush to join their companions at the gate and none of them noticed the optio and the king making their way towards the gloomy side street.

As they neared the street Trenagasus let out a sharp cry of pain as he slipped and fell headlong, landing with a dull grunt. Figulus stopped in his tracks and dropped down beside the groggy king to help him to his feet. A short distance behind them, the first of the rebels were sweeping out of the alley and drawing close.

'Your Majesty! Get up!' Figulus implored.

Trenagasus winced as the optio hauled him to his feet. At the same moment Ancasta rushed out of the alley and screamed furiously at the rebels to catch the prisoners before they slipped away. The rebels spilled out across the thoroughfare, cornering the optio, blocking his path down the side street. Figulus saw them closing in, their weapons drawn and ready to strike him down. He stopped in his tracks and felt his heart sink. He lowered his head, burning with anger and shame. They were surrounded. It was over. His escape bid had failed. He would die today after all.

The rebels parted and Calumus stepped forwards, grinning sadistically. Ancasta stood silently at his side. In the distance the sound of the struggle at the main gate grew increasingly frantic. Trenagasus shook his head and rested his piercing gaze on his daughter. His skin was pale and his expression hardened into one of bitter rage.

'You . . . ! Daughter, how could you betray your own flesh and blood . . . your king?'

Ancasta spat at his feet. 'You left me with no choice. You betrayed your birthright the moment you sided with Rome. Now you're going to die.' Her cold blue eyes rested on Figulus. 'Both of you.'

'Fuck you!' Figulus said defiantly.

Calumus turned to his followers. 'What are you waiting for? Take them to the market. We must make the sacrifice to Cruach at once.'

A few of the rebel warriors lowered their weapons and stepped forwards. One grabbed Trenagasus while two others clasped Figulus by the arms. As they started to drag them away, a sudden crash erupted from the main gate, immediately followed by a chorus of panicked shouts. Figulus and the rebels simultaneously looked towards the sounds. In the next instant the gate leapt back on its hinges and a long column of hundreds of Roman soldiers spilled through the shattered opening, surging into the ranks of the warriors massed in front of them. Those warriors further back from the gate turned and fled. The triumphant look on Ancasta's face crumbled as she caught sight of the legionaries, the golden eagle of the raised standard glinting in the morning light as they cut their way through the rebel warriors.

'The Romans!' one of the rebels cried. 'They've broken through!'

CHAPTER THIRTY-NINE

Figulus felt his heart surge with hope as the relief column swept inside the settlement. For a moment Calumus and his followers looked on in horror. A handful of Durotrigan warriors in the front rank hurled themselves at the legionaries in a futile bid to halt or at least delay their advance, hacking and slashing at their opponents for all they were worth. But the legionaries hefted their shields and presented a solid front to the rebels, stabbing at them as they rashly exposed their bodies to attack. As the front rank crumbled beneath the Roman onslaught, the rebels turned and ran. Some of the Britons darted down side streets and were pursued by the Romans. The bulk of the rebels retreated towards the royal enclosure. The leading centurion bellowed an order and his men released their javelins at the fleeing rebels. A wave of missiles crashed down over the Britons, impaling dozens of them no more than twenty paces from Figulus. One man let out a gurgled scream as a javelin punched through the back of his neck, the iron head protruding from his throat as blood spewed down his front.

Calumus looked on in a cold rage at the unfolding chaos. He turned to the retreating rebels and pointed with his spear tip at the advancing Romans. 'Stand and fight! Cruach commands you not to run from the Roman scum!'

As he spoke, another shower of javelins arced through the air, thudding into the backs of the retreating Britons. Pockets of the rebels obeyed their leader's rallying cry and turned to face the advancing Romans, raising their shields. But the momentum of the attack was with the legionaries and in the next instant they tore into the Britons with a savage flurry of stabs and thrusts. Those rebels closest to the

285

Romans disappeared beneath their blades as they were cut down where they stood. Soon the thoroughfare was littered with the dead and the dying, and blood ran freely through the streets, mixing with the mud and the ordure.

From the rear of the rebel troops Calumus stood his ground, imploring his men to stand firm. Figulus saw Ancasta tugging at the Druid leader, urging him to fall back. The optio glanced at the man at his side. The warrior stood dumbly watching the battle unfold as if under a spell. Figulus tensed his neck muscles and jerked his head forwards, smashing his forehead into the bridge of the Briton's nose. There was a crack as the bone shattered and the rebel grunted as he staggered backwards. Figulus followed up before the man could recover, stepping into his opponent and punching him hard in the guts. The rebel folded at the waist, gasping. The weapon fell from his grip. Figulus quickly snatched up the fallen sword before the man could dive for it. Then he sprang forwards and punched out at the Briton, sinking the short blade deep into his guts. The rebel fell away as Figulus tore the blade free and looked across, searching for the king.

His blood turned to ice as he caught sight of Trenagasus being dragged away by Calumus's men. The Druid leader and his followers were hurrying down the thoroughfare towards the far end of the settlement. Calumus shouted an order to a pair of burly warriors and they instantly set off in the direction of the market to fetch the other prisoners. The legionaries were busy attacking the main rebel force and had failed to notice the Druid leader slipping away. Figulus turned to give chase. A heavily tattooed warrior blocked his path, teeth bared into a menacing snarl. He stabbed out at Figulus. The optio deflected the blow then feinted with a quick thrust aimed at his opponent's throat. The massively built rebel parried the attack with his oval shield and lunged forwards again, this time driving his blade towards the optio's guts. Figulus sidestepped to the left, evading the blow and then driving the point of his sword under the Briton's armpit and into his chest. The warrior gasped. He grunted and reached out, clamping his hand over Figulus's face and trying to gouge the latter's eyes out. Figulus thrust the blade deeper, piercing the man's heart. The rebel's eyes bulged. Then his arms went slack, and he collapsed in a bloodied heap on the ground. Figulus wrenched his weapon free and looked around but there was no sign of Calumus or Ancasta. They had disappeared from sight, along with Trenagasus.

A shout went up behind Figulus and he looked over as the rebel forces scattered. Some of them fled towards the palisade, hoping to climb to escape from the town. Others threw aside their weapons and tried to surrender, but the Romans were in no mood to show mercy and they ruthlessly cut down their enemies even as they begged for their lives to be spared. Out the corner of his eye Figulus spied a glimmer of movement as a shadowed figure charged at him, sword arm drawn back. The optio saw the man's legionary helmet and armour and instantly threw up a hand to protect himself.

'Wait!' Figulus cried. 'I'm a Roman!'

The legionary hesitated but held his sword warily in place, thrown by the optio's perfect Latin. Around them dozens of limp native corpses were sprawled across the thoroughfare. In the distance Figulus could see pockets of legionaries hunting down the few surviving rebel Britons as they tried to escape the killing spree.

'Bollocks!' the legionary muttered.

Figulus kept his sword arm lowered and replied as steadily as he could. 'I'm Horatius Figulus, Optio of the Sixth Century, Fifth Cohort, Second Legion.'

Confusion flashed in the legionary's eyes. 'You're Ocella's junior?'

Before Figulus could reply, a tribune with a dark, swarthy complexion trotted forwards. The man had the plump but broad-shouldered physique of one who knew how to fight but also how to indulge in life's finer pleasures. Both his breastplate and expensive-looking cloak were spattered with fresh blood and mud. Figulus recognised him immediately. Tribune Vitellius.

'I recognise this man,' Vitellius announced. 'Even beneath all that damn woad.' He wrinkled his nose and curled up his lips in disgust. 'Good grief, Figulus. What in the name of the gods are you doing dressed like that? And what is that smell?'

Figulus stiffened to attention. He felt faintly ridiculous saluting the tribune in his loincloth, his hair spiked and his body covered in Celtic patterns. He shook his head. 'There's no time to explain, sir. Calumus is escaping. He's taken the king with him, and some of our lads too.'

Vitellius knitted his brow. 'Calumus?'

'Yes, sir,' Figulus responded breathlessly. 'The High Priest of the Dark Moon Druids. He's their leader.'

'I know who he is, Optio,' Vitellius snapped impatiently. 'We ran into one of the auxiliaries yesterday. He told us all about the Druids. Told us how the Batavians got ambushed at the hill fort too.' A wry smile formed on his lips. 'I must say, it's damn lucky we ran into the fellow. Looks like we got here just in the nick of time, eh?'

Figulus took a deep breath, fighting the tension building in his chest. 'Sir, we have to stop Calumus before he gets away. He's got the king. He's going to sacrifice him.'

The tribune snorted. 'He won't get very far. The Eighth Cohort's under orders to cover the gate and pick up any stragglers who might try and make a run for it.'

Figulus shook his head then pointed towards the far end of the settlement. 'There's a gap in the defences, sir. The rebels will have gone that way, I'm sure of it.'

Vitellius's smug expression crumpled. 'Right. Get after them. We'll take care of this mob.' He gestured to the grizzled centurion at his side. 'Centurion Mergus and his men will accompany you. Hurry, man!'

Figulus grabbed a shield from one of the fallen rebels. Then he turned and charged down the thoroughfare, determined to rescue Trenagasus from the Druids. Centurion Mergus and his men hurried alongside him, the legionaries' boots thudding against the ground as they kept pace. The struggle inside the settlement had descended into a series of running battles being fought in the streets as the legionaries broke off into sections and hunted down the pockets of fleeing British rebels, and the air was filled with the pained cries of the wounded punctuated by the wails of terrified women and children running for their lives.

Figulus ran on. Beyond the sprawl of animal pens he glimpsed the damaged section of the palisade. Several rebels were slipping through the gap and scrambling down the side of the turf rampart. The optio raced towards the palisade, the fury of battle coursing through his veins as he took out his rage on the nearest rebel. The man's face was frozen with fear at the sight of the huge, wild-haired Gaul bearing down on him. His expression turned to shock as Figulus slammed his blade into his stomach, punching through the Briton's guts and ripping through his organs and muscle. Figulus booted him away, freeing his weapon while around him the other legionaries made short work of the remaining rebel warriors.

With the enemy cut down, Figulus leapt over the shattered palisade and charged down the rampart ahead of the legionaries. Beyond the ditch he could see a party of sixty or so rebels retreating across the open ground to the west of the settlement, led by Calumus and Ancasta. His heart skipped a beat as he spotted a bedraggled line of prisoners being dragged along to the rear. Among them he picked out Helva and Rullus stumbling along barefoot. Their British captors shouted at the prisoners to keep up, using them to cover their escape. For a moment Figulus wondered where the rebels were going. Then he saw the stunted trees screening the marshes, and he suddenly understood. He turned to Centurion Mergus as the last of the Roman soldiers scrambled up the outer ditch in pursuit.

'They're making for the marsh, sir,' Figulus exclaimed. 'We've got to stop them before they get there, or they'll give us the slip.'

Centurion Mergus turned to his men. 'At the double, lads!' he yelled. 'The bastards have taken some of our lads with them. The first idiot who throws his javelin will find himself on a fucking charge.'

The century swept across the open ground, chasing after Calumus and his followers. The rebels were slowed by the line of prisoners but the legionaries were starting to flag. Figulus pushed on, gripped by the need to rescue his comrades, and the Durotrigan king.

As they approached the trees at the edge of the marshes, Figulus saw the thin white threads of mist clinging to the dense undergrowth of gorse and hawthorn. The stormy weather of two days ago had made the ground soft and the men were breathing heavily as they kept up their dogged pursuit of the enemy. Figulus was exhausted. He could feel the dull ache in his leg muscles, the tiredness deep in his bones as the stress of the past few days finally took its toll on his weary body. But he ran on alongside the centurion and his men. He thought of all the friends he'd lost in Britannia. He thought of Blaesus dying in the snow. He would not let his comrades die today.

Ahead of them the rebels reached the edge of a rough track running between the low hills, leading directly into the heart of the marsh. The Britons raced on towards the mist-shrouded marsh, sensing that they had made good their escape.

'One last effort, lads!' Centurion Mergus gasped.

The legionaries kicked on. The Romans were physically fitter than their native counterparts and they moved at a good pace in spite of the heavy armour and equipment weighing them down. But the rebels had a good head start and it was going to be a close thing, Figulus realised. If the enemy reached the haven of the marshes before the Romans could catch them, then all was lost. His comrades and Trenagasus would be lost to the dense mist, dragged away to be tortured and sacrificed. Any pursuit into the marshes would be hopeless. The patchwork of dark still waters and small copses was impossible to navigate without knowledge of the land, and there was always the chance of running into an enemy ambush lurking somewhere along the narrow gorse-choked tracks. Once the Druid and his followers entered the marshes with their prisoners, the latter would never be seen again.

'Hurry, sir!' Figulus urged Centurion Mergus. 'Bastards are getting away.'

Calumus and his men were too far ahead. Mergus grasped the situation and cursed between ragged breaths.

'We're not going to catch 'em,' he gasped.

Figulus sprinted ahead, running as fast as he could. His senses were heightened by the prospect of finally defeating the Druids. His throat was burning. His muscles ached. He tried to forget about the pain. This was it now, Figulus told himself. One last effort. One last chance.

A short distance ahead, Calumus glanced over his shoulder and saw the Romans breathing down his neck. Realising that the legionaries might yet catch his men before they disappeared into the marsh, the Druid leader shouted an order to his followers. They turned as one to face the soldiers bearing down on them, forming up in a crude line while Calumus and Ancasta spun away from the rebels and hurried along a narrow track leading into the marsh, accompanied by half a dozen of the Druid's bodyguard and the prisoners. The rebels dug their heels in and raised their weapons against the charging Romans, hoping to buy their leader enough time to escape.

The two sides met in a clatter of shields and blades. Although the rebels were outnumbered, they fought with astonishing ferocity, no longer caring for their own lives. The frigid morning air was filled with the sounds of the frantic struggle and the gasps of exhausted men. This was brutal hand-to-hand fighting. On either side of Figulus the legionaries were fighting intense personal duels against the enemy. The nearest rebel thrust out at Figulus with his sword, grazing the optio's cheek. Figulus felt a hot burning sensation as blood trickled down the side of his face and he cursed the fact that he wasn't wearing any armour. He feinted and stabbed the man high in the chest. Then Figulus yanked his weapon free and searched for his next target.

Beyond the melee he spied Ancasta and Calumus fleeing with the prisoners in tow. Trenagasus lagged several paces behind, struggling to remain upright as a pair of rebel warriors shoved him along. Figulus spun away from the melee and set off after the prisoners, the clang and clatter of sword clashes ringing in his ears as the furious struggle raged all around him. A warrior spotted him and tried to block his path but the optio knocked him down with his shield and ran on as fast as his tired legs could carry him.

Further along the track Calumus looked back and saw the two rebels struggling alongside Trenagasus. The Druid leader barked an order and the rebels promptly stopped dragging the king. One of them booted Trenagasus in the small of his back and sent him sprawling face down in the mud. In the same instant the second rebel raised his sword and shaped to plunge the blade into the nape of the king's neck.

The optio froze for the slightest moment, gripped by a terrible indecision. Already Calumus and Ancasta were disappearing into the marshes with his comrades and the other auxiliary prisoners. If he saved the king, his comrades would surely be lost to the mist. But he knew his duty and charged at the two rebels standing over the king, with a deafening bellow.

The rebels looked up, momentarily distracted. They were young, muscular warriors and they stared in confusion at the sight of the half-naked Gaul rushing at them. They turned fully towards Figulus. The taller Briton gripped a spear and his companion wielded a short sword. The spearman noted the optio's lack of armour and his eyes gleamed as he anticipated an easy kill. He lunged forwards and feinted. Figulus threw up his shield and the broad tip clattered against the metal boss, glancing off to the side. The man thrust again, and Figulus jerked to the side, narrowly avoiding the spear and then slamming his shield into the Briton's face, stunning his opponent. Figulus glimpsed the swordsman driving at him from an angle and he spun towards the man, desperately parrying the attack. Before the swordsman could recover, Figulus drove his sword low into his opponent's groin. The man sank to his knees, pawing at his wound and groaning.

Out the corner of his eye Figulus saw the spearman driving at him, howling wildly. The optio spun around before he had a chance to wrench his blade free from the swordsman and hefted up his shield just in time to deflect his opponent's blow. Figulus felt the violent impact shudder up the length of his arm. The Briton kicked out at Figulus and sent him stumbling backwards. Figulus regained his balance and caught sight of the spear tip aiming at his neck. He quickly dropped to his haunches and then thrust his shield horizontally into the spearman's stomach. The metal rim crunched as it slammed into the Briton's guts, winding the man. But rather than stunning the rebel warrior, the blow merely seemed to enrage him. He reached out and grasped the edge of the optio's shield and easily wrenched it free. Figulus froze for an instant as the warrior moved towards him. A cruel smile played out across the man's face as he made to plunge the spear tip down into the helpless Gaul.

Suddenly the spearman lurched and collapsed to the ground and Figulus saw Centurion Mergus standing behind the warrior. The other legionaries were cutting down the last of the rebel warriors stading in their way. The centurion wrenched his blade free from the dead man and Figulus nodded his thanks. A pair of legionaries rushed over to Trenagasus and helped the king to his feet. Figulus blinked the sweat out of his eyes and looked around him. The rebel party had been wiped out. None of the enemy had been taken prisoner, preferring to die rather than see their Druid leader captured.

He breathed a sigh of relief. The king had been saved.

Then Figulus glanced across to the point where the track merged with the marshes, hoping against hope that his comrades were still in sight. But there was nothing but the bank of white mist obscuring the track.

His heart sank.

Calumus and Ancasta were gone. And so were the prisoners.

The smoke was still rising from several ruined buildings as Figulus returned to the settlement. At the shattered main gates the optio handed over Trenagasus to a pair of orderlies, and they escorted the king back to the fort's infirmary to have the surgeons tend to the wound to his scalp. Then Figulus reported to Vitellius. The tribune stood in the main thoroughfare, surveying the devastated settlement. Dozens of legionaries were rounding up the captured rebels and marching them outside, to be imprisoned in one of the empty barracks blocks at the fort. Once Vitellius had given the order for his mounted cavalry scouts to cover the surrounding land and round up any rebels who might have slipped away, he turned to Optio Figulus. He listened attentively as the Gaul made his report.

'I suppose congratulations are in order,' Vitellius conceded as he gazed across the settlement. 'You've saved the Durotrigan capital, Optio. Or whatever's left of it.'

Figulus shifted uneasily. Any relief he felt at having rescued Trenagasus from the Dark Moon Druids was tempered by the terrible guilt at having abandoned his comrades.

Vitellius eyed him sympathetically. 'It's unfortunate that you couldn't retrieve the other prisoners, but a couple of lost legionaries and the odd Batavian is neither here nor there in the grand scheme of things.'

Figulus stared bitterly at the rising smoke. 'If you say so, sir.'

Vitellius studied the optio. 'You were close to your men, I presume?'

'They are like brothers to me, sir.'

The tribune nodded sagely. 'I've lost enough men in my time in the Second. But at the end of the day that's what all soldiers have to face up to, Optio. The prospect of death.'

'I'm not going to abandon my men, sir.'

A look of mild irritation flared on Vitellius's smooth face. 'Look here, man. I understand you're upset. But for gods' sakes you can't let grief cloud your judgement. Your friends are probably already dead. If not, we can be sure the Druids will kill them soon enough. The prisoners won't have any value as hostages. Calumus is smart enough to realise that.'

'We could try going after them, sir,' Figulus insisted.

Vitellius raised an eyebrow. 'Send my men into the marshes? Have you lost your mind, Optio? We'd be walking into a disaster.' He snorted then added, 'Besides, I hardly think we need to concern ourselves with Calumus and his band of crazed followers. We've dealt the Dark Moon Druids a crushing blow today. Lindinis has been retaken. The king's alive – just. The Druids' army has been defeated. Calumus won't pose much of a threat now, not after the heavy losses he's suffered.'

'Sir, I know Calumus. I've met the man. He won't stop fighting us. Not until the day he stops drawing breath. As long as he's at large, he's a threat. He might have lost today, but in time he'll raise another army of rebels willing to die for his cause. It could take months to hunt him down, years even. But if we strike now, we can end this once and for all.'

Vitellius seemed briefly taken aback by the optio's assessment. Then he straightened his back and feigned a smile. 'Even supposing this Calumus is as dangerous as you suggest, I see no reason why I should risk sending my men into that marsh on a wild goose chase.'

'We cannot afford to let Calumus remain at large, sir,' Figulus insisted.

Vitellius glared at Figulus. 'I've made up my mind, Optio. I simply cannot risk it.'

'Then let me go, sir.'

'Eh?' The tribune furrowed his brow. 'What the hell are you talking about?'

Figulus took a deep breath. 'Let me search the marshes, sir. I'll find my men.'

'Out of the question.' Vitellius shook his head determinedly. 'The chances of you lasting a day in those marshes are minimal. You'd be cut down long before you could locate your friends. No. You're to return to the fort and await further orders. Dismissed.'

Figulus considered arguing the point further, but rank got the better of him and he clamped his lips shut. He gave a rueful salute and trudged off towards the fort, a heavy weight clamping around his heart. His comrades were doomed. There was nothing he could do to save them. Nothing at all.

CHAPTER FORTY

Three days later

A throated roar went up from the crowd as the rebel prisoner stepped into the makeshift arena. He looked round nervously at the heaving throng of off-duty Roman soldiers, traders and Britons gathered on the earth embankments.

'This'll be over quickly, sir,' Vatia said. 'That skinny one doesn't stand a hope in Hades. Not against that big bloody bastard.'

Figulus glanced at his comrade then looked on as a pair of orderlies dragged away the lifeless corpse of the previous fighter. Blood disgorged from a deep wound across the slain Briton's chest, leaving a glistening wet trail on the damp grass. The gaunt prisoner briefly stopped in his tracks as he caught sight of the dead fighter, before one of the legionaries on arena duty shoved him forward. Several paces away stood his opponent. A towering Durotrigan, his bare torso covered in swirling tattoos and rippling with taut muscle. He gripped a short sword in his right hand and glared at the next challenger. The swordsman had already seen off three opponents in a series of brutal fights to the death, with the winner staying on. Now the crowd hushed in anticipation of the last bout of the day's games.

The grim public spectacle had been arranged by Trenagasus. As soon as the king had begun to recover from his injuries and was well enough to leave the infirmary, a team of engineers had begun hastily erecting the earth and timber arena in a low vale situated between the fort and Lindinis. The games were intended to provide some much-needed entertainment for the Roman garrison as well as the king's beleaguered subjects. They would also serve as a warning of the punishment awaiting all those who would dare to defy the Durotrigan king.

296

While they awaited further orders, Figulus and the surviving rankers in his detachment had decided to take in the action. Since noon the crowd had looked on as forty pairs of rebels had taken to the arena with a variety of weapons, in a crude imitation of the gladiator contests held back in Rome. Some fought with long Celtic swords. Others wielded tridents or broadaxes, and one bout even featured two Britons fighting bare-knuckled. A few of the prisoners had turned their weapons on themselves, preferring death over fighting their fellow rebels, but most had fought willingly enough since Trenagasus had declared that the champion would be spared death and instead be sold into slavery.

'What d'you reckon, sir?' Vatia asked. 'Who's your money on?'

Figulus rubbed his bristly jaw as he assessed the fighters. The swordsman was several inches taller and considerably bulkier than his opponent. But the effort of the previous fights had taken its toll on the huge Durotrigan and he looked tired, Figulus thought. His chest muscles were heaving up and down as he caught his breath.

'I reckon the challenger's got a chance.'

'That lanky streak of piss?' Vatia spluttered. 'Sorry, sir. But there's more chance of finding an honest man in the Senate than the skinny one winning.'

Figulus glanced at Vatia and smiled. The short, squat legionary had been born in the slums of the Aventine district in Rome, and the cocky young rogue was never short of an opinion.

'Fancy yourself as an expert, do you, lad?' Figulus grinned.

'If there's one thing I know, sir, it's gladiator fights. I used to be a ticket tout at the Statilius Taurus amphitheatre. I've seen all the great fighters down the years.' Vatia counted them off on his podgy fingers. 'Britomaris, Tetraites . . . even Pavo. And I reckon the swordsman's going to win this one by a mile.'

'As long as it's a good fight, I couldn't give a shit who wins,' muttered Pulcher, another of the surviving legionaries. 'Half of these scraps have been bloody useless. I've seen Greek schoolchildren fight better than this.'

Figulus turned back to the arena as the umpire for the occasion, a Centurion Minucius from the Eighth Cohort, introduced the two fighters. A hushed silence descended over the arena as one of the

297

legionaries stepped forward and thrust a spear into the challenger's right hand. The prisoner looked down at his weapon, wielding it awkwardly as he tested its weight. Opposite him the swordsman flexed his muscles, the point of his bloodstained short sword glinting under the pallid winter light.

'Fight's about to begin, sir,' Vatia said, rubbing his hands gleefully.

Figulus smiled uncertainly. Normally he would have been excited about the contest. He enjoyed a good gladiator bout as much as the next man, but for the past few days he'd been wracked with guilt over Helva and Rullus. In his darker moments Figulus tormented himself with images of his comrades in the enemy camp, grimly awaiting their fate. Or perhaps they were already dead, he thought. Their heads parted from their shoulders, or burned alive in one of the Druids' terrifying wicker effigies . . .

A sharp crack split the air as the umpire lashed his whip. The crowd erupted into a deafening roar as the fight began.

'Here we go!' Pulcher said, punching a fist in the air.

The swordsman wasted no time in charging at his opponent, eager to make a quick kill and claim his prize as champion of the games. The spearman quickly stepped back out of range, as the larger Briton thrust at him, and almost lost his footing on the blood-slicked ground. He caught himself and staggered backwards as the swordsman lunged, the latter narrowly missing with a quick thrust at the vitals. The Romans and traders in the crowd roared their encouragement. The Britons were more subdued, uneasy about witnessing the public killing of their fellow Durotrigans, and many of them looked on sullenly as the two rebels fought to the death.

Figulus glanced away from the contest and lowered his gaze to Trenagasus. The Durotrigan king sat close to the action, flanked by his sizeable entourage and the two sections of battle-hardened legionaries who'd been assigned to his temporary bodyguard. Trenagasus still looked weak, Figulus thought. His skin was pale as chalk and a large dressing covered the wound the king had taken to his scalp. Despite his injuries, Trenagasus sat rigidly upright, a smile trembling on his lips as he watched the contest unfold below.

Figulus looked back to the action as the muscular Briton caught his breath then charged at his opponent. The challenger's face was a picture of concentration as he sidestepped the blow and in a lightning blur spun around to the side of his dumbfounded opponent before drawing his weapon across the back of the swordsman's legs. The crowd let out a collective gasp as the spear tip slashed open the Briton's calf, spilling blood across the ground in a red spray. Then the spearman jabbed the butt of his weapon into the man's back and the swordsman crashed to the ground. In a flash the spearman moved towards his opponent and kicked the sword out of the man's reach. Then he hefted up his weapon in a two-handed grip as he prepared to plunge it down at the swordsman's throat. Pockets of the crowd rose to their feet, desperate to catch the moment of the kill.

'Get up, you idiot!' Vatia urged.

The challenger brought his weapon down towards his stricken opponent. But the swordsman quickly rolled to his right, narrowly avoiding the spear as it thudded into the ground. He scrambled to his feet as the challenger twisted at the waist and thrust at the larger Briton. This time the swordsman evaded the blow and then clasped a huge hand around the spear shaft, pulling it towards him and forcing the challenger to lean forward. At the same time the swordsman brought up his right knee and slammed it into the challenger's face. There was a sharp crack as the smaller Briton's nose shattered. He staggered backwards, groaning nasally as he released his grip on his weapon.

'Finish him!' Vatia implored at the top of his voice.

Grabbing the spear with both hands and swiftly reversing it, the swordsman lunged at his disorientated opponent. The challenger saw the danger too late. He howled in agony as the spear punched into his stomach. Then the swordsman gave the spear a twist, skewering the other man's vitals and drawing a huge cheer from the crowd. Blood spewed out of the wound as the swordsman ripped his weapon free. The challenger wavered on the spot for a moment before collapsing. Cheers rang out around the arena as the swordsman tossed aside his weapon, pumping his fists in the air in a defiant posture of victory.

'The swordsman wins!' Vatia turned to Figulus, grinning. 'What did I tell you, sir?'

Figulus said nothing. In the corner of his eye he spied Trenagasus signalling to the umpire. The latter barked an order at the legionaries forming a circle around the edge of the arena and the three soldiers nearest to the action promptly stepped forward and approached the victorious Briton. Two of the legionaries grabbed the man by his arms. The Briton glanced around in alarm. At the same time the third legionary drew his sword and the rebel immediately understood what was happening. He tried to wrestle free from the two soldiers but they had a solid grip and they forced the Briton to his knees.

'What's going on, sir?' Vatia asked. 'Thought the old fool had promised to spare the winner.'

'Looks like Trenagasus has changed his mind,' Figulus replied, frowning.

A surge of nausea rose in the back of the optio's throat as the soldiers prepared to carry out the execution. All around the arena the natives were muttering angrily at this unexpected denouement to the games while the soldiers and traders roared for the Durotrigan rebel to be put to death. The spectators looked towards the king as he rose unsteadily to his feet. Trenagasus paused as he regarded the rebel with a look of cold indifference. Then he turned to address his subjects.

'My people, hear me!' the king declared, struggling to make his frail voice heard. 'There can be no mercy shown to our enemies. None! Those who would dare to defy me . . . who would dare to betray their king and the tribe that gave them life have forfeited their right to draw breath. They must die like the traitorous dogs they are.' His voice trembled with rage and Figulus could see his bony hands shaking at his sides as he glanced defiantly around the arena before continuing. 'This I command, as your rightful king and ruler!'

Trenagasus gestured to the umpire before he slumped back down on to his seat. Minucius shouted an order to his men, and the legionary who'd drawn his weapon traced the point of his sword across the Briton's stomach.

'They're going to gut the bastard,' Pulcher muttered.

The Briton tensed his muscles. He lifted his gaze to the crowd and stared defiantly at his fellow tribesmen as he shouted to them.

'What's he saying, sir?' Vatia asked.

'He says he does not fear death,' Figulus translated queasily. 'He says the Dark Moon Druids will rise once again and cleanse the kingdom of the Romans invaders. All those who have betrayed the tribe's gods will suffer. Calumus, their high priest and the loyal servant of Cruach, has foretold it.' He listened for a moment then went on. 'Soon the land will run red with Roman blood, and the legions will be driven back into the sea.'

The Briton finished talking and clamped his eyes tightly shut. His muscles visibly convulsed as the legionary drew his sword arm back. Then the legionary slashed his blade across the Briton's stomach in a single clean blow, ripping open the man's guts. The Briton let out a hideous garbled scream as his bowels slopped out of the wound and slid down his front, spilling to the ground between his feet in a glistening red and grey heap. Some of the natives seated closer to the arena looked away in horror. Figulus forced himself to watch as the two legionaries holding the Briton by his arms released their grip and let the man flop to the ground. Then the third legionary thrust down with his bloodied sword, sinking the tip behind the man's neck just above the collarbone. The Briton jerked briefly as the sword cut through his spine. Then he went limp.

A tense silence descended over the arena. As soon as the execution had been carried out the king gestured to the Roman officer in charge of his personal bodyguard. Centurion Minucius turned to his men and barked at them.

'All right, lads. Fucking move yourselves! Clear a path through this fucking rabble.'

The legionaries snapped to attention and began escorting the king out of the arena, shoving aside the crowd with their shields and drawing several curses and angry glares from the sullen natives. Centurion Minucius marched a step ahead of Trenagasus, his sword arm gripping his sheathed weapon, ready to lash out at anyone who tried to step too close to the king. After Trenagasus had departed, the rest of the crowd slowly began to stream out of the temporary arena, trudging back towards the settlement to the south and grumbling discontentedly amongst themselves. As the last of the spectators quit the arena the orderlies began clearing up. Teams collected up the weapons that had been used for the games and loaded them on to a cart to return to the fort's stores, while others dragged away the dead rebels to be dumped in the local midden for the wild animals to feast on.

'How about a drink, then?' Vatia suggested, glancing around at the faces of his comrades. 'I've worked up a decent thirst after that, sir.'

Before he could reply, Figulus noticed a clerk hurrying over from the direction of the fort. The clerk glanced around the arena, quickly searching the faces in the crowd shuffling out of the various exits. He caught sight of Figulus and marched briskly over.

'Optio! There you are,' said the clerk as he caught his breath. 'Been looking all over for you.'

'What do you want?' Figulus demanded.

The clerk stiffened. 'Message from the tribune. He wants to see you at headquarters.'

Figulus frowned heavily. 'All right. Let's go.' He turned to Vatia. 'Looks like that drink will have to wait.'

CHAPTER FORTY-ONE

'At ease, Optio,' Vitellius ordered.

Figulus was standing in front of the desk in the tribune's private quarters in the headquarters building. An iron brazier was flickering in one corner, heating the room to a pleasingly warm temperature. Scylla sat to the right of Vitellius on a padded leather stool. The wan light from the oil lamps emphasised the deep lines in the imperial envoy's wizened face.

Figulus allowed himself to relax slightly. Vitellius looked up from the stack of scrolls on his desk and ran his eyes over the optio. 'I must say, it's good to see you looking somewhat more civilised for a change. Wouldn't want one of my men to go mistaking you for a native again, would we?'

'No, sir,' Figulus mumbled in reply.

'The king wishes to pass on his thanks,' Scylla began. 'If you hadn't succeeded in freeing Trenagasus, it's very likely that the Druids would have executed him long before we could have rescued him. There's some extensive damage to the settlement, of course, and the rebels have plundered the royal hall, looting anything of note. But all things considered, it could've been much worse. So, well done.'

'Just doing my duty,' Figulus replied gruffly.

'Let's get on with it, shall we?' Vitellius muttered as he reached for his wine goblet. 'I haven't got all night, gentlemen.'

Scylla shot a reproachful glance at the tribune. Figulus detected some undercurrent of hostility between the two men. No doubt Vitellius loathed having to defer to a mere servant from the imperial palace.

'The tribune and I have been discussing your plan,' Scylla explained to Figulus. 'And I – *we* – think it may have some merit.'

Figulus felt his heart skip a beat at the chance to rescue his imperilled comrades. He listened keenly as the envoy went on.

'At the moment Calumus poses no great threat to the kingdom. But in a few months the situation might well have changed. Indeed, we've already received reports of natives from the outlying settlements flocking to join his cause. No doubt they've been persuaded by that mystical claptrap the Druids peddle.' He added with a sneer, 'It seems that Calumus retains a loyal following among the Durotriges. Especially since he now has the support of the king's daughter. Indeed, some of the local nobility are openly wondering whether Trenagasus is up for the job. They're questioning how the king can protect his people, when he cannot even control his own daughter.'

'What's to be done, then?' Figulus asked.

'Clearly we cannot allow Calumus to roam free in the marshes. We must press home our advantage while we still can, and deliver a fatal blow to the Dark Moon Druids before they have a chance to regroup. But according to the tribune, a large-scale advance into the marshes is out of the question.'

Vitellius bristled at the envoy's scathing tone. 'I'm all for defeating the Druids. But no commanding officer in his right mind would send his forces blundering recklessly into the marshes without knowing where to find the enemy. We'd suffer the same fate as those bloody Batavians.'

'Quite, Tribune,' Scylla responded, smiling diplomatically. He turned back to Figulus. 'As you can see, Calumus presents us with something of a headache. He's hiding, but we don't know where. Leave him alone, and he will inevitably grow stronger. Pursue him, however, and our troops run the risk of getting cut down in an ambush.' He cleared his throat. 'However, there is a third way.'

'Oh? What's that?'

Scylla exchanged a quick glance with Vitellius before replying. 'We send in a small party to reconnoitre the marshes and find the Druids' secret lair. Once we know where the enemy is hiding, the cohorts can move in and crush the Druids once and for all, putting an end to our difficulties in this kingdom.'

Figulus tensed. He could guess what was coming next. 'You want me to go in and find the lair?'

'Correct.'

'What about the prisoners we took? Don't they know where to find the Druids?'

Scylla shook his head. 'Our interrogators have been working the rebels over since yesterday. So far all they've done is spit curses and pray to their gods.' He smiled wickedly. 'Those who still have their tongues, at least.'

'Only a matter of time,' Vitellius countered. 'Torture a man for long enough and he'll eventually tell you anything you need to learn.'

'Sadly, I don't think that applies to the Druids.' Scylla turned his gaze back to Figulus. 'You're our best hope of locating the lair, Optio. You did a commendable job infiltrating Lindinis to rescue the king, you look like one of the natives and you can speak their tongue. You're perfect for the task.'

'A fool's errand if you ask me,' Vitellius scoffed.

Scylla ignored the tribune. 'I won't lie to you, Optio. This is a perilous mission. Now that we've driven the rebels back from Lindinis, they'll assume we will be moving into the marshes to finish the job. Which means that they will regard any strangers they encounter as Roman spies. If you run into the rebel patrols, I'm afraid the best you can hope for is a quick death. But if you succeed in your task, the Emperor will not be ungrateful.'

'What about my comrades?' Figulus demanded, angry that the envoy and the tribune had seemingly forgotten about the Roman prisoners being held by Calumus.

'Dead, in all likelihood,' Vitellius muttered dismissively.

'I'm afraid the tribune is right,' Scylla added. 'But if you find the camp and the opportunity presents itself, you may attempt a rescue. But only if it does not compromise your mission. Understood?'

Figulus thought for a moment. 'Let me get this straight. You want Calumus dead, but you can't risk sending in the cohorts and you can't afford to lose a scouting column. But you can afford to risk losing a soldier. Namely, me.'

'That's a rather blunt way of putting it. But yes.'

'I'll do it,' Figulus said. 'But on one condition.'

Scylla smirked. 'You're hardly in a position to make demands, Optio.'

'Actually, I am.' Figulus replied steadily. 'If I say no, you've got no chance of finding Calumus before the winter is out. Without me, you're buggered.'

The imperial envoy kept smiling but his eyes were cold and grey. 'Very well. One request. Name it.'

'A transverse crest,' he said.

Scylla furrowed his brow. 'I beg your pardon?'

'I want to be promoted to centurion.'

A stunned silence filled the air. Scylla stared at him in silence for what felt like a long time. 'What about your centurion? What does he have to say?'

'My centurion applied for a transfer back to the Praetorian Guard,' Figulus said evenly.

'Ocella?' Vitellius stroked his chin. 'Ah, yes, I recall. Best thing for all concerned, really. Let the Praetorians have him.'

'I'd like his job, sir,' Figulus said. 'I want to be the new centurion of the Sixth Century.'

Vitellius frowned. 'This is the Second Legion, man! Not some bloody provincial bureaucracy. You earn your promotions the hard way. Optios don't just go around demanding to be promoted. And certainly not in return for volunteering for some virtually futile mission.'

Figulus stood his ground. 'I have earned my promotion, sir. I've been in action ever since we landed in Britannia and seen more than my fair share of battles. Killed more than a few of the enemy, too. I've fought as a ranker and I've led this detachment as an optio. Now I'm ready to lead the rest of the lads in my century.'

Scylla coughed and shifted uncomfortably. 'This is a highly unusual request, you understand. And it would have to be approved through the official channels. We can't have civilians treading on military toes.' He glanced at Vitellius before continuing. 'But it sounds a reasonable suggestion to me. I'm sure we can come to an arrangement.'

In the corner of his eye Figulus could see Vitellius shaking his head in disgust.

'I'll be going alone?'

'Absolutely not. It's far too dangerous a mission for one man. You'll take someone with you. That way at least one of you stands a fighting chance of making it back alive.'

Figulus thought then shook his head. 'None of my lads will be able to pass themselves off as a local. They can't speak the language for a start.'

'They won't need to,' Scylla countered. 'Your cover story will be that you're a trader travelling the kingdom and looking to sell your wares to the locals. Your comrade will pretend to be a mad half-witted servant in your charge. From what we understand, the Durotriges believe that the witless are under the influence of their gods, and bring good luck to all those who come into contact with them.'

'That'll work?' Figulus asked sceptically.

'Oh, it won't hold up if you run into the Druids, or their patrols. But it ought to suffice for chance encounters with the natives. After all, who'd dare harm a well-meaning trader and his touched servant?' Scylla narrowed his cold grey eyes. 'Are any of your men capable of playing the role of a half-wit, Optio?'

'I can think of one.'

'Good. You'll also need to be accompanied by a guide, of course. One of the locals will go with you. I have just the man. A former bodyguard to the Druids. He claims to know his way through the marshes. So he says, at least.'

Figulus clenched his brow. 'Can we trust him?'

'I should think so. He volunteered for the mission. Besides, we don't have much choice. None of the other guides are willing to enter the marshes, regardless of how much silver we offer them. It seems they're just as scared of the Druids as our own men.'

'Either that, or they're still loyal to the enemy,' Vitellius added.

Scylla shrugged.

'When we do leave?' Figulus asked.

'Well before dawn. There's less chance of you being seen by the enemy if you enter under cover of darkness. Any questions?'

Figulus shook his head.

'Then I suggest you get moving. There's plenty to attend to before you leave.'

Scylla rose from his stool, signalling that the meeting had come to an end. Figulus abruptly stood and saluted at the tribune. Then he turned and marched out of the headquarters building, and made his way towards his barracks block, excitement and dread swirling inside his chest. He was being sent deep into enemy territory on the whim of two powerful men, and the forlorn hope that he might stumble upon the enemy lair. The odds of him returning from the marshes were slim, Figulus knew. But it was a chance to rescue his comrades, and put a stop to Calumus once and for all. He would not fail his friends, Figulus vowed to himself. He would save them, or he would die trying.

CHAPTER FORTY-TWO

A few hours later Figulus emerged from the relative warmth of his quarters and made his way towards the fort's eastern gate. There had been no time to rest after his briefing with Scylla and Vitellius, and as he trudged down the darkened thoroughfare a heavy fog settled behind the optio's tired eyes. As soon as the briefing was over he'd sought out Vatia in the barracks block assigned to their detachment. Of the four men left under his command, Figulus felt that Vatia was best equipped to accompany him into the marshes. His fearless attitude and common sense would be useful when they were miles from the safety of the fort, and when it came to handling himself in a fight there were few men in the legions who could match the stocky legionary.

'Let me see if I've got this straight,' Vatia had said after Figulus had explained the mission. 'That snivelling good-for-nothing envoy, the same Greek bastard who got us into this mess in the first place, now wants us to go and find the Druids' lair in that stinking marsh?'

'In so many words, yes,' Figulus had responded.

Vatia shook his head in disbelief. 'What happens if we run into the Druids?'

'Let's just hope we don't.'

'That's it?' Vatia looked incredulous. 'That's the plan?'

'I didn't say it would be easy.'

Vatia threw back his head and laughed. 'That's putting it mildly, sir. It's a bloody suicide mission.'

Figulus had pursed his lips. 'If you're not up for it, then don't come.'

'And let you take all the glory? With the greatest respect, sir, fuck off.' He smiled grimly. 'Besides, Rullus still owes me a drink from our last game of dice, and I'm not going to let that bastard get off that easily.'

The two soldiers had shared an easy laugh then, but as they paced down the main thoroughfare past the barracks blocks, Figulus felt a growing sense of dread. They were heading into almost certain death. No wonder the envoy had been so quick to agree to his demand to be promoted, Figulus thought miserably. It was unlikely he'd ever return from this mission.

Scylla had made all the necessary arrangements. Three horses had been commandeered from the king's stables, since the tribune could not afford to spare any mounts from the depleted cavalry squadrons. And the native horses would look less conspicuous than the larger foreign breeds. In place of their military uniform both Figulus and Vatia wore simple tunics with grimy brown cloaks over the top, frayed at the edges and caked in mud. Vatia also wore a leather thong in his hair in the Greek style to make him appear less Roman. They both carried leather knapsacks filled with provisions to last for three days, and both had daggers fastened to leather belts tied around their waists, with their legionary swords wrapped up inside bundles. Figulus also carried a satchel weighed down with cheap imported trinkets, purchased from a Syrian merchant for an extortionate sum, to help with his cover story. Everything else he'd been forced to leave with Pulcher, including his helmet and chainmail armour.

Scylla stood by the entrance to the stables, the light from the flickering tallow lamp throwing his shadow across the wall. He pulled his cloak tight across his slender shoulders in an effort to keep himself warm. The days had turned mild but the temperature still dropped sharply at night and Figulus shivered beneath his cloak as he marched over to the imperial envoy. His eyes were drawn to a dark-haired figure squatting to one side of the building. Scylla beckoned him over.

'This is Petrax,' he explained. 'He's the guide I told you about.'

Figulus cocked his chin at the thickset Briton. He looked to be only a few years older than the optio and he had an unkempt beard and a large pinkish scar running down the side of his face. He grinned, revealing several gaps in his front teeth. Figulus wrinkled his nose as he caught a whiff of the man's foul-smelling breath.

310

'Do you speak Latin?'

'Some, Roman,' Petrax replied in Latin, but with a thick accent. 'Enough. His Majesty says we must all speak tongue of our allies now.'

Figulus detected a trace of bitterness in the Briton's voice. He nodded at the man. 'Reckon you know your way around the marshes, eh?'

'*Sa!*' Petrax said. 'I spent my childhood in marsh. Hunting deer.' He thumped his chest in obvious pride. 'I make good hunter, Roman. Once I hunt deer. Now we hunt Druids.'

'That's a long time ago,' Vatia mused.

'Don't worry, Roman. I not get us lost.'

'I should fucking hope not, friend,' Vatia replied. 'Because if we run into the Druids, I'll make sure they're the least of your worries.'

Petrax stared levelly at the legionary for a long moment. Then Scylla clapped his hands. 'It's time, gentlemen.'

The envoy stood back and watched as the three men mounted their horses. Figulus threw his leg awkwardly over his horse, cursing his breath as he struggled to seat himself properly. At his side Petrax gracefully climbed on to his mount and gripped the reins with the ease of someone who had learned to ride from a very young age. Once they were ready to depart Scylla raised his eyes to Figulus and nodded.

'Good luck, Optio. May Fortuna be with you.'

Vatia laughed meanly as the three men twitched their reins and moved at a slow trot past the stables towards the main gate. 'Fortuna, he says! That bitch hasn't done us any favours so far, sir. Something tells me she's not about to start now.'

'Must be the only woman in Britannia who hasn't fallen for your charms,' Figulus replied with a grin.

Vatia forced a smile as they approached the gate. Two guards stood in front of the solid oak timbers. An order was given by the duty centurion, and the locking bar made a grating noise as the guards slid it back into the receiver and heaved open the timbers. The gate swung inwards and Figulus guided his mount out of the fort alongside Vatia, tightly grasping the reins. Petrax jabbed his heels into his horse's flank and moved quickly across the frosted ground. A bank of grey mist hung over the unending tract of marshland to the west, faintly illuminated beneath the pallid glow of the crescent moon.

As Figulus headed towards the marshes he shivered with foreboding. Deprived of his armour and shield and the companionship of his fellow soldiers, he felt naked, and as the small party made its way towards the series of broken hills screening the marshes Figulus turned in the saddle and cast a final look back at the fort that had been his home for the past few months. The fort was softly illuminated beneath the star-pricked sky and the optio permitted himself the grim thought that this might be the last time he ever set eyes on it. Then he looked forward and headed towards the marshes.

As the sky gleamed with the thin light of pre-dawn they stopped to rest their mounts at the side of the track. Figulus and his companions had moved quietly across the barren expanse of land lying between the fort and the edge of the marshes, straining their ears as they listened for any sound of the enemy above the thud of their horses' hooves. After several miles they reached the stunted trees screening the fringe of the marsh. Petrax had reined in his mount and scrutinised the way ahead before proceeding down one of the tracks that led into the dark sprawl of bogs and thickets. Figulus could feel his nerves jangling as the two Romans led their horses down the rough track after Petrax. The marsh was eerily quiet except for the occasional distant call of a curlew bird or the rustle of dead leaves, and a wave of relief swept through the optio as the darkness began to dissolve into the early morning light and they found a small clearing to rest in.

'This fucking marsh,' Vatia grunted as he slumped against the trunk of a willow tree. 'Tell you what, sir. When we find Rullus and Helva, I'm going to give the pair of 'em a slap for making us come out here.'

Figulus grinned. 'Maybe we'll get our hands on some of the Druids' loot. That'd make it worth our while.'

'Wouldn't get your hopes up, sir. Not the way our luck's been going lately.' Vatia fell silent for a moment. 'Do you think they're still alive?'

Figulus pursed his lips. He'd been asking himself the same question ever since his comrades had been dragged away. The honest answer was that he simply did not know. Vitellius was right, he realised. Calumus had no reason to keep the soldiers alive. Helva and Rullus carried little value as prisoners, and the envoy had made it perfectly clear that Rome had no intention of negotiating with the Dark Moon Druids. The optio bristled with anger at the thought of his friends being executed, and he was surprised at his strength of feeling for his comrades. There was nothing he would not do to set Rullus and Helva free. They were as brothers to him. The three of them had fought alongside each other, and Figulus knew he would gladly give his own life to save theirs.

'I don't know,' he sighed. 'But as long as there's a chance, I have to try and find them.'

'What's the plan then, sir?'

'Petrax reckons there are a few small farms to the west of here.' Figulus nodded at the Durotrigan guide. He was squatting on the track by his horse several paces ahead of the Romans, scanning the track. 'Someone there might have seen or heard something about the rebels.'

He cast a wary glance at the track ahead. The mist hung low over the marsh, hemming the Romans in on all sides and making it impossible to see more than fifty paces. Dense corridors of gorse and hawthorn flanked the well-worn track and the air was thick with the filthy stench of rotting vegetation arising from the dull, brackish shallows. In places the track disappeared entirely beneath the thick undergrowth.

'Speaking of which.' Vatia lowered his voice and tipped his head at the Briton. 'What do you think about him?'

'You don't trust Petrax?'

'Him? You must be joking, sir. I trust him about as far as I can piss. And I don't piss very far. Who's to say he's not leading us into a trap? To take the pair of us hostage and hand us over to his old Druid muckers so they can burn us alive.'

Figulus considered for a moment. 'We haven't got much choice. But we'll watch him closely, eh?'

They climbed back on to their mounts and pushed on. Soon the mist began to lift, burning up as the winter sun struggled free from the clouds. Figulus lifted his gaze to the pale yellow disc and from its position in the sky he guessed that it was late morning. The men had travelled for miles and seen no sign of anyone else. It could take days, if not months, for them to locate the Druids' lair, Figulus thought to himself bleakly. And that was assuming they managed to avoid rebel patrols. By the time they found the enemy, it might be too late. Helva and Rullus might already be dead.

'How much further?' Figulus asked in the native dialect as he trotted alongside Petrax on one of the innumerable tracks criss-crossing the marshes. 'To the nearest farm?'

The burly Durotrigan narrowed his eyes at the track up ahead, calculating the distance. 'Two miles. Maybe less.'

Figulus nodded. 'Do you think the farmers will help us?'

'Depends, Roman. Some are still loyal to the Dark Moon Druids.'

'Even after everything they've done?' Figulus asked, recalling the horrors he'd seen at Lindinis.

'It's all they know,' Petrax responded quietly. 'It is all I knew, once.'

Figulus felt a chill tingle running down his spine. 'How'd you mean?'

Petrax hesitated to answer. He stared ahead at the thinning mist, a distant look in his sad eyes. Then at last he spoke. 'When I was a boy, a Druid agent arrived in our village,' he said. 'He chose the strongest of us and took us away to his village to the south of here. Not far from the Great Fortress. We trained for years. In the mornings we learned how to fight. In the afternoons, a priest taught us the craft. At the end of our training we swore a blood oath to protect and obey the Dark Moon Druids, and lay down our lives to save them.'

Petrax paused, glancing from side to side before continuing.

'One day we followed the priests to a village. It was the first time I had been back in many years. The Druids ordered us to round up all those who had refused to follow the Dark Moon cult. Men, women. Even children. The priest declared them traitors to their own tribe.' Petrax spoke in a flat tone of voice but Figulus could see the emotion swirling behind his eyes. 'My father, he was among them.'

Figulus shuddered. 'What happened?'

'The Druids put them all to death,' Petrax said coldly. 'They were lined up in front of their families, cut down and their flesh was fed to a pack of hunting dogs. Then their heads were taken and nailed to the sacred oak tree outside the village, as a warning to all those who would defy the will of Cruach and his loyal servants. Even now, I can still hear my father's screams as the Druids took the knife to him. My mother watched too. She died a few months later. Without my father, there was nothing for her to live for.'

'What did you do?' Figulus asked.

'I knew I had to escape the Druids. I fled and hid in a forest. I lived in the wild for years, like an animal. I only returned when Rome arrived and the Druids retreated into the marshes.' He balled his hand into a fist. Figulus could see his knuckles whitening with tension. 'They have brought misery to my people. To my family. Now I will make them pay for what they have done.'

'That's why you volunteered?'

'*Sa!*' He patted the dagger fastened to his waist. 'I live to kill Druids. I do not care for Rome or your Emperor. But Calumus and his priests have twisted the minds of our people. They have turned us against one another and brought our tribe misery. That is why I fight, even if we cannot win.'

'Calumus can't defy us forever,' Figulus insisted. 'We'll defeat him sooner or later. It's just a question of when.'

'That may be true, Roman. But even once you destroy Calumus, do you really think the Druids will disappear?'

'Of course not. But with the Dark Moon sect out of the way, the others will be quick to sue for peace.'

Petrax gave out a bitter laugh and shook his head sadly. 'That is where you are wrong. The Dark Moon cult will not die with Calumus. There are other tribes ripe to fall under the priests' influence, ready to serve Cruach. That is what makes the Druids so powerful. They alone can rise above the petty rivalries of our land and unite the tribes against Rome. You may destroy Calumus. But mark my words. Your troubles will not end until you have slain every last Druid in this land.'

CHAPTER FORTY-THREE

As the morning wore on, the sky darkened and they moved deeper into the marsh, sticking to the narrower tracks and avoiding the better-worn paths to lessen their chances of running into the enemy. Petrax became more anxious, constantly glancing left and right and stopping every so often to prick his ears and listen for movement nearby. On several occasions the Durotrigan seemed unsure of the direction they were heading, and the small party would stop for a brief rest and feed their horses while the Briton ran his eyes across the marsh and tried to establish his bearings. Their progress became frustratingly slow and Figulus began to fear that they would not arrive at the farm until nightfall. The prospect of spending the night trawling through the hostile marshes, miles from the safety of the fort, filled him with unease.

By midday the rain lightened to a steady grey drizzle and after another mile the track opened up. Petrax abruptly halted atop his mount, throwing up a hand and signalling to the two Romans to stop behind him. While Vatia scanned the track to their rear Figulus moved his horse quietly forward and drew up alongside Petrax. Without saying a word the Briton pointed further down the track, towards an isolated patch of land that barely rose out of the surrounding marsh. In the middle of the land stood a large Celtic roundhouse along with a few smaller huts and barns and a pair of animal pens. A scrawny-looking man piled slops into one of the pens for a handful of pigs to feed on. The other pen stood empty. Two children were playing in the dirt outside the hut.

'This is the place?' Figulus asked Petrax.

The Durotrigan nodded. '*Sa.*'

'Looks peaceful enough to me, sir,' Vatia mused softly as he trotted forward and ran his eyes across the farm. 'What's the plan?'

'Let's go and have a word with them.'

They left their mounts tied up a short distance away from the farm and approached on foot. One of the children caught sight of them and pointed as he cried a warning. At the same time Vatia slipped into his role as the mad fool, beating his fists against the sides of his head and grinning inanely. The legionary cut a ridiculous sight and Figulus had to bite back on his tongue to stop himself from chuckling.

The farmer turned away from the animal pen and narrowed his eyes suspiciously at the approaching men. He shouted at his children to stay by the hut before marching down the track towards Figulus and his companions. From the age of his two young boys Figulus guessed the farmer was in his middle years but he looked considerably older, with his hollow cheeks and sunken eyes and weathered face, the telltale signs of a hard life scratching a living from this pitiful land. Petrax stepped forward and exchanged a few pleasantries with the farmer before gesturing to the two Romans at his side. The farmer glanced warily at Figulus. Behind him, the two boys were squabbling over a crude straw toy. The smaller of the brothers clutched it close to his chest, ignoring the high-pitched pleas from his sibling to let him play with it.

'So you're a trader, eh?' the farmer growled at Figulus in the guttural native tongue.

The optio patted his knapsack and nodded quickly. 'That's right. We've travelled down from Corinium. We heard there's business to be done here. I'm Boduogenus, and this is my servant Tocitamus.'

Figulus waved at Vatia then reached for his satchel. He opened the flap and shoved it towards the farmer, showing him the assortment of jewellery and decorative trinkets he'd brought along with him.

The farmer grunted. He lifted his gaze to Figulus and narrowed his eyes to knife slits. 'We're not interested, trader. Take your business elsewhere. You too, small man.'

He directed the last words at Vatia. The Roman legionary stared back, blinking uncomprehendingly. A look of puzzlement flashed in the farmer's eyes. He took a step closer to Vatia and prodded a gnarled finger at the latter's chest.

'What's wrong? Can't you speak, friend?'

Figulus subtly nudged his comrade. Vatia understood and immediately began jumping up and down on the spot, waving his arms and gurning as he shouted his assumed name over and over. 'Tocitamus! Tocitamus! Tocitamus!'

A faintly amused smile crossed the farmer's lips. He looked to Figulus. 'Your servant is a fool.'

Figulus shrugged. 'His mother dropped him on his head as a child. Been a simpleton ever since.'

The farmer relaxed his face slightly, entertained by Vatia's antics. Now that the tense mood had lifted Figulus decided to try his luck.

'Perhaps you can tell us where to find some customers to barter with? We've heard there might be some bigger settlements around here?'

The man suddenly became defensive. He folded his arms across his chest and tightened his expression. 'Can't help you. We don't get many visitors round these parts.' He waved his arm in a broad arc at the surrounding marsh. 'As you can see.'

'But you must know something?' Figulus insisted.

The farmer opened his mouth to reply. Just then the smaller of the two boys let out a hysterical scream as his brother snatched the straw toy away from him. The child burst into tears, wailing at his sibling and pleading with him to give the toy back. The farmer shouted at his children to shut up then turned back to the optio, glaring at him with a darkened expression.

'I can't help you. Now get off my land.'

The man stepped back and tipped his head in the direction of the marsh. Figulus hesitated for a moment and glanced around the farm. With a heavy sigh he made to turn away and head back down the track, resigning himself to another long trawl through the marsh in search of the next farm.

At that moment the leather cover pulled across the small opening at the front of the hut swept back and a fat woman burst out wearing a long winter cloak. She hurried over to the children, shooting a reproachful glance at the older boy and cuffing him around the side of the head. Then she noticed the three men standing next to her husband and turned towards them. Figulus noticed that she was wearing a decorative silver torc. A pair of serpent's heads gleamed at either end of the torc. It seemed oddly familiar to Figulus and he pointed to it.

'That's an interesting piece. Do you mind me asking where you got it?'

The woman narrowed her eyes suspiciously at Figulus. 'What do you care?'

'I'm just interested in the competition around these parts, that's all,' Figulus responded innocently.

'None of your bloody business,' the woman replied, touching a hand to the torc.

Figulus took a step towards the woman, his gaze fixed on the torc. Then he remembered where he'd seen it before, and the blood instantly froze in his veins. Andocommius had worn the exact same torc. He had been wearing it when Ancasta had stabbed him through the throat. And now it was wrapped around the neck of the farmer's wife.

'That torc belongs to Andocommius!' Figulus growled as he abandoned his cover story.

The woman backed away, shaking her head. At the same time the husband thrust out a hand, blocking the optio's path and glaring at him. 'Right, I warned you once. Get off our fucking land.'

The farmer reached for the dagger on his belt but Figulus reacted first, bunching his right hand then hammering his fist into the Briton's guts. He folded at the waist, letting out an explosive grunt of pain before Figulus hooked him on the jaw and he crashed to the ground. His wife screamed hysterically and grabbed her two sons as she turned to hurry inside the hut, but by now Vatia and Petrax had surged forward and the thickset ex-bodyguard quickly moved to block the doorway. Vatia stood over the dazed farmer, his cloak pulled back to reveal the dagger fastened to his belt. Closer to the hut the fat woman had a protective arm wrapped around her children as she held them close. She glared at Figulus with hatred.

Figulus ignored the woman. He took a step closer to her husband as the man lay on the ground, clutching his pained ribs. 'That torc belonged to one of the king's royal bodyguard,' the optio snarled. 'I'd recognise it anywhere. There's only one like it. Now tell me where you got it. I won't ask a third time.'

The farmer struggled for breath as he clutched his pained guts. His eyes narrowed at Figulus accusingly. 'You're no trader.'

'Last chance!' Figulus roared. He tore his dagger free from its hilt and pointed the blade at the farmer. 'Tell me, or I'll cut your balls off, so help me.'

The farmer's eyes widened with terror as he saw the look of madness in the optio's eyes. 'It was a g-gift,' he bleated. His voice took on a pleading tone. 'P-please. I don't want any t-trouble. It was a gift. That's all.'

'Who the bloody hell do you think you are?' the woman hissed.

'Shut up!' Figulus thundered at her. He turned back to the farmer and tightened his grip around the dagger's ivory handle. 'Who gave you the torc?'

The farmer hesitated as he glanced anxiously at his wife. Then he looked back to Figulus and gulped. 'D-druids,' he said meekly. 'They came to us. Two days ago. They said their s-s-supplies were running low. One of their commanders offered us a d-deal. Meat and g-grain in exchange for the torc . . . and some other gifts.'

'Where are they now?' Figulus snapped, his chest swelling with anger.

The farmer blinked. 'Who?'

'The Druids. Where are they hiding?'

The Briton pursed his lips, his mind working furiously as he tried to think of a response. 'I–I don't know.'

'Bollocks! The rebels were right bloody here, two days ago. You know.'

'Please,' the farmer whined. 'I beg you. If they find out I told you, they'll kill my family.'

Figulus suddenly exploded with rage. He spun away from the farmer and reached out to his wife, clasping a hand around her wrist. She cursed the optio as he pulled her away from her screaming children and pinned his left arm across her chest, pressing the dagger tip to her soft, plump neck. The woman abruptly stopped struggling and instead hurled abuse at Figulus, calling him every imaginable name. From the doorway the two children burst into tears and wailed for their mother. The farmer got to his knees, begging the optio to let her go. Figulus stared down at the pitiful Briton.

'I'm giving you one last chance. Tell me where the rebels are hiding, or I swear to the gods I'll cut her throat and save the Druids the bother.'

The farmer pressed his lips shut and stared helplessly at his wife. Figulus could see the torment playing out on the man's face and pressed the blade tighter to the woman's neck, drawing a gasp of terror as the tip pricked her skin.

'Wait!' the farmer cried. 'Don't . . . please! I'll t-talk!'

'Tell me,' Figulus replied evenly, holding the blade in place.

There was a pause as the farmer took a deep breath. Then he looked Figulus steadily in the eye. 'They came from the n—north. From the direction of the s-sacred lake. That is all I kn-know. I swear!'

Figulus looked to Petrax. 'Do you know the place he means?'

The Briton thought for a moment then nodded uneasily. '*Sa*. The lake was a sacred place to the Druids. Long time ago. But they abandoned it many years ago. No one has lived on the islands since.'

Figulus grunted. 'Sounds like the rebels have moved back in.'

'Let me go, you bastard!' the farmer's wife yelled.

Figulus lowered his arms. The woman backed away from him and hurried over to her husband and children, weeping openly. The older of the two boys stared at Figulus and the optio could see a lifelong hatred for Rome forming behind his bright blue eyes. He turned away from the Britons and hurriedly explained the situation to Vatia. When he'd finished, the legionary cracked his knuckles and nodded at the family.

'We should kill 'em, sir.'

Figulus stared at his comrade. 'Kill them? What for?'

'To cover our tracks. Think about it, sir. That wretch will go blabbing to his Druid mates as soon as we've buggered off. Then we're well and truly fucked. Better to just slit their throats and be done with it. No one will notice that they've disappeared. Not for a while, at least.'

Figulus pursed his lips and contained his revulsion. As a soldier of Rome, he had cut down dozens of Britons in his time. But that was in the heat and chaos of battle. There was a world of difference between the instinctive act of slaying an enemy in war and butchering a family in cold blood. He swung his gaze back to the woman and her children. They were still huddled next to the roundhouse. The woman was soothing her tearful offspring while her husband stared blankly at the floor, rubbing his bruised jaw.

'Leave them,' Figulus commanded, sheathing his dagger.

'Sir?' Vatia looked aghast. 'But what if he spills his guts to the Druids? That'll put the enemy on alert.'

'He won't,' the Gaul replied stiffly. He waved a hand at the farmer. 'If he goes running to the Druids, it won't take them long to figure out that he told us where the enemy was hiding. They'll kill the man and his family for betraying them. He won't risk the lives of his wife and children. Trust me, he won't talk. He's got as much to lose as us.'

Vatia seemed unsure but the discipline of rank got the better of him and he nodded in agreement. 'What now, then?'

Figulus turned to Petrax. 'This sacred lake of yours. How far away is it?'

The Durotrigan thought quickly, scratching his thick beard. 'From here? No more than four or five miles.'

'If we leave now we can make it to the sacred lake before nightfall.'

'I hope you're right, sir,' said Vatia, glancing doubtfully at the surrounding marsh. 'Don't fancy wandering around here after dark.'

'We have to push on. It's our only chance to save our comrades. It's either that or we give up and head back to the fort, and leave our friends to die.'

Vatia stared at the optio. 'For a hairy-arsed Gaul, sir, you certainly have a way with words.'

CHAPTER FORTY-FOUR

'Say what you like about the Druids, but they know how to find a good hiding place,' Vatia muttered as he gazed towards the rebel camp.

Figulus grunted in agreement. They were lying on their fronts on a low hummock east of the sacred lake, concealed from view behind a tangle of gorse and long grass, with their mounts tied to stunted trees further down the track. A hundred paces away a long causeway stretched out from the wetlands across the dark, rank-smelling waters towards the largest of a series of small islands. The main island had been extended with a man-made system of log piles driven deep into the bed of the lake, reinforced with a thick layer of brushwood mixed with clay. A low palisade defended the settlement within. Separate causeways linked the island to three smaller islets set further back from the marsh. Two appeared to be sparsely inhabited. The rearmost islet was sealed off by a tall wicker screen with a substantial towered gate above the causeway. Beyond the screen Figulus could see a dense ring of trees, black as ink against the pale grey sky.

They had reached the enemy lair in the late afternoon. Shortly after leaving the farm a dense bank of leaden grey cloud had darkened the sky. Then it had started to rain, disturbing the dank waters and slicking the ground underfoot, slowing their pace. Eventually the men were forced to climb down from their mounts and continue on foot. For a few hours Figulus and his companions trudged on through the quagmire. Figulus's leg muscles burned with the strain and he sweated freely under the extra weight of his soaked winter cloak. By the time the three men arrived at the screen of low hills obscuring the lake, they were out of breath and Figulus could already foresee difficulties entailed by an attack on the enemy's ramp. Each bolt thrower would have to be broken down to its constituent parts then transported across in carts, slowing the advance of the cohorts to a near crawl.

'It's hidden away, all right,' Figulus conceded as he looked back to the islands. 'But it won't save 'em from the Second Legion. We smashed apart their hill forts, and we'll beat them here too.'

Vatia looked doubtful. 'Wish I could share your confidence, sir. But look at this bloody place. The only direct line of attack is along the main courseway. Our lads will be sitting ducks if they try that.'

As he cast his eye over the island defences, Figulus grudgingly acknowledged that Vatia was right. Calumus had chosen the perfect location to hold out against an attacking force. The lake formed a natural defensive barrier, with the only approach to the islands across the causeway leading to the main island. At the far end of the causeway stood a thick timber gate with a crude watchtower above and flanked by a pair of sturdy redoubts, from where rebel warriors could shower the advancing enemy with arrows and slingshot. The causeway itself was so narrow that the attackers would be forced to advance no more than four abreast. In the shallows either side of the causeway a party of natives was hard at work planting sharpened wooden stakes in the water bed, to impale any soldiers who tried to avoid the projectiles raining down on them. The island presented a formidable obstacle. Attacking it would present the men of the Second Legion with a vastly different problem to the hill forts they had assaulted the previous year.

He turned to Petrax. 'Looks like your friends have been busy.'

'Not my friends.' The Briton grunted. 'Druids my enemies.'

'Either way, I don't envy the poor bastards who'll lead the assault,' Vatia murmured. 'Going to be hot work getting across that causeway, sir.'

Figulus nodded slowly then turned his attention to the rearmost island. It seemed eerily quiet and dark compared to the others. The black limbs of several branches poked out of the rising mist on the island, dark and foreboding. He pointed it out to Petrax.

'Any idea what's going on there?'

The ex-bodyguard pursed his lips. 'It looks like one of the Druids' sacred lairs,' he replied, his voice tinged with anxiety. 'Only the Priests of the First Ring are permitted inside. No one else. Not even other Druids. It is where the high priest makes sacrifices to Cruach, the god of war.'

Figulus strained his eyes at the islet. 'Looks empty to me.'

'For now. But soon it is the feast of the full moon. That is when Cruach feasts on the burning flesh of his victims, so that he may smite his enemies and bring darkness to the world.'

Vatia shivered and pulled a face. 'Can't say I care much for this Cruach bastard.'

Petrax shot the legionary an icy stare then muttered a native insult under his breath. Vatia glared at the Briton. Figulus ignored them both as he scanned the main island. 'No sign of the prisoners,' he said softly.

'No, sir.'

'Only one thing for it,' Figulus decided.

'What's that?'

'We'll have to take a closer look. They must be keeping Rullus and the other prisoners somewhere inside. If we can get close enough, we might be able to figure out a way to rescue them.'

Vatia frowned at the optio. 'How, though? We'd never get past the main gate.'

Figulus clenched his jaws then turned to Petrax. 'Is there no other way in? Another causeway or a ford? Anything at all.'

The Durotrigan thought hard then shook his head. '*Na*. Only one way in and out.'

'Looks like there's only one thing for it, sir,' Vatia said. 'We'll have to swim across.'

Figulus grimaced at the prospect of swimming across the lake. But he knew he had to get on to the island if he was to stand any chance of saving his friends, and he could see no other way of getting across the water. He pointed out a dozen dark shell shapes resting on the bank some distance from the main gate and then turned to Vatia.

'See those boats? There must be a gap in the palisade next to the landing platform. We can use that to get inside the camp. We'll wait until it's dark to move. As long as we don't make too much noise, we should reach the landing without any trouble.'

'What happens once we get across the lake, sir?' Vatia asked.

'We try and find a way inside the camp and rescue Rullus and Helva.'

Vatia spat on the ground and grunted. 'Going to be hard to find the prisoners among that lot, sir. The place is bound to be crawling with rebels.'

'Then we'll have to make sure we're not seen,' Figulus countered stiffly. 'It's that, or we give up. And I'm not leaving our comrades behind.'

Vatia lowered his head and fell silent. Figulus knew he was taking a terrible risk in approaching the enemy camp. If he and Vatia were discovered they would share the fate of their comrades. The opening in front of the landing platform was likely to be guarded. And if by some miracle they managed to sneak inside the camp, then what? There had to be hundreds of rebels on that island, battle-hardened Durotrigan warriors determined to resist Rome and her armies. How could they expect to slip past the enemy and find the prisoners? It was a reckless mission, Figulus knew. But he was driven by a deep desire to save his comrades. He remembered the desperate looks on their faces as they had been dragged away into the marshes, and the awful fate awaiting them if he failed. He had made it this far in his attempt to rescue Helva and Rullus. He would not abandon them.

Petrax turned to Figulus. 'What about me?'

'You'll head back to the fort and report to Vitellius.'

The Briton balled his hands into tight fists and snorted through his flared nostrils. 'No! I come with you! Kill Druids.'

'Quiet!' Figulus hushed. He paused before continuing in the local dialect. 'We need someone to tell Vitellius where to find the rebel camp in case we don't make it back.'

'Why me?' Petrax demanded. He cocked his head at Vatia. 'Why not the short one?'

'You know the marshes better than us. He'd only get lost. It has to be you.'

A fiery glow flickered behind Petrax's eyes. He shook his head angrily. '*Na*. I made a blood oath to the gods. I avenge my father, kill as many Druids as possible. Not run away from them.'

'You're not running away. You're helping to defeat the Druids.'

Figulus placed a hand on the Briton's broad shoulders and stared levelly at him. 'Look, unless we get a message back to the tribune, Calumus and his rebels will be free to hide out here and grow stronger. Then it'll be too late to defeat them. If you really want to deal a blow to the Druids, you have to tell Vitellius.'

Petrax hesitated for a moment then nodded reluctantly. 'Very well, Roman. I go. But later, we kill Druids.'

'Later.' Figulus breathed a slight sigh of relief. 'Now listen carefully. Get back to the fort as fast as you can. Don't stop for anything. Understood?'

The native nodded. 'You're really going into the camp, Roman?'

'Yes. My brothers are in there.'

Petrax shook his head sadly. 'It is madness. The Druids will kill you the moment they see you setting foot on the island.'

Figulus reflected for a moment. 'But I have to try. I have to do that, at least . . .'

CHAPTER FORTY-FIVE

As the light of day began to fail Figulus and Vatia crawled forward from the track and rested briefly beside a dense growth of reeds and bulrushes at the water's edge. After Petrax had departed on his mount the two Romans had settled into their position and observed the enemy while they waited for darkness. Shortly before sundown the last of the warriors retreated inside the main island. Fires were lit inside the camp and a chorus of raucous noises and drunken laughter filled the air. Some sort of celebration was going on, Figulus decided. No doubt the Britons were starting the festivities early in anticipation of the coming of the feast of the full moon.

He waited in the biting cold alongside Vatia, listening to the enemy's celebrations. After a while the hubbub of drunken voices and singing fell quiet, and Figulus signalled to Vatia. The two soldiers edged forward, making their way around the edge of the lake until they reached a point in the narrow track directly opposite the landing platform. The marsh was quiet except for the occasional booming cry of a bittern or the splash of a water vole scurrying about the reeds. Figulus gazed out across the lake at the Druids' camp on the main island, no more than a hundred paces away. Several fires flickered within the palisade, basking the roundhouses in a warm orange glow. Once Figulus was satisfied that the landing platform was not guarded, he turned to Vatia and nodded.

'Let's go.'

The Romans stripped down to their tunics and rolled up their cloaks and dumped them by the reeds next to their knapsacks and daggers. They kept their swords in scabbards fastened around their waists, taking up their inflated waterskins as they approached the dark waters. A pungent stench of decaying matter drifted up, mixing with the foul odour of human waste, and Figulus wrinkled his nose in disgust as he realised that the natives must be using the surrounding lake to dump their rubbish. At that moment he would have rather faced a horde of angry barbarians than slide into the water. He wanted nothing more than to turn around and leave this place. But Figulus knew he could not abandon his friends.

'Fuck the gods . . .' Vatia hissed as he caught a whiff of the rancid waters. 'Even the sewers in the Aventine smell better than this.'

'Keep your voice down! Want to draw the attention of every Druid in the village?'

'Sorry, sir. Just prefer not to be up to my neck in shit,' Vatia added in a hushed voice. 'Seems to be happening to us a lot lately.'

Figulus sucked in a breath as he slid into the freezing waters. The cold seared his skin as he stroked forward from the reeds, kicking underwater and gripping on to his waterskin. Figulus propelled himself forward as quietly as possible, but his technique was clumsy and after a few erratic strokes he felt he was struggling to stay afloat. Vatia had a natural talent for swimming and he glided easily alongside Figulus. Lumps of detritus floated on the brownish waters all around them, bobbing on the surface and slithering along their arms and legs, and Figulus fought a strong urge to vomit as they swam. They moved at an agonisingly slow pace to avoid making a splash and it seemed to take ages to reach the island.

He quickly tired from the constant strain of kicking out and he could feel himself starting to sink below the surface. Drops of water splashed into his face and a terrible fear gripped the optio that he would lose his grip on his waterskin and sink into the fetid depths of the lake. He swallowed back the bile rising in his throat and struggled on, kicking out for all that he was worth. After a few more ragged strokes Figulus blinked water out of his eyes and saw that they had almost reached the edge of the landing platform. With a final push he struggled forward and grabbed hold of a wooden post and gasped for breath.

Figulus pulled himself up and rested on the embankment for a few moments, his leg muscles aching and his lungs burning from the effort of swimming across the lake. His hands and feet were numbed from the freezing waters and he shivered violently beneath his drenched tunic. His relief at crossing the lake quickly turned to concern that their splashing might have attracted the attention of a nearby guard. He squatted by the landing platform for several moments and listened for any sign of the enemy. Then he looked back to Vatia.

'Ready?' he asked softly.

'As I'll ever be, sir.'

Figulus nodded. 'Follow me.'

They left their waterskins at the landing platform and edged forward, moving slowly in case a sudden noise attracted the attention of any nearby sentry. Figulus could hear laughs and shouts coming from the middle of the camp. The Romans crept towards the outer palisade then slipped through the opening and moved in the shadows between the huts and the palisade. Figulus watched the ground, careful not to disturb any of the drinking horns and bowls scattered outside the huts. He paused by the hut nearest to the landing platform. From within he could hear the ecstatic groans of a couple in the throes of passion. He beckoned Vatia over and then stared out across the camp.

In front of them stood the usual sprawling assortment of native huts, dimly illuminated by fires burning in the open ground between the shelters. To the left stood a cleared space just inside the main gateway where the natives had been busy reinforcing the defences. Towards the middle of the camp a loose throng of warriors sat around a large fire, along with a few women and children. The warriors clutched their drinking horns as they cheered on a pair of rebels arm-wrestling over the stump of a felled tree. Most of the other warriors had passed out drunk in the streets or retired to their huts. Figulus carefully scanned the dense arrangement of huts and sheds, searching for his friends, but he couldn't see any obvious place where they might be held.

'Sir,' Vatia whispered as quietly as possible. 'Over there.'

Figulus chased his line of sight. The legionary was pointing towards the far end of the camp. To their right stood a handful of animal pens filled with sheep and pigs, along with a few larger enclosures containing horses. Most of the pens nearer to the palisade were empty, a sure sign that the rebels' supplies had gradually dwindled and that they could not afford to hold out for much longer. Beyond the crude enclosures Figulus spied a dozen Druids in front of a separate causeway leading to the rearmost islet. They squatted around a pair of small fires, chewing on chunks of meat. A thrill of terror flowed through the optio as he saw that the causeway behind them was lined with human skulls on posts. If the prisoners were being held in the camp that was as likely a place as any, Figulus decided. He motioned to Vatia for them to move closer to the Druids.

The two soldiers slipped around the back of the huts and crept towards the animal pens, their footsteps masked by the sounds of the couple inside the hut. The ground between the pens and the foot of the palisade was a waterlogged mass of churned mud from where the water level had risen, and offered the best chance of approaching the Druids' causeway without being spotted. The optio could feel his hands shaking as he edged forward and not just from the cold. Every step took him deeper into the rebel camp. He felt certain that they would be discovered at any moment.

They dropped to the ground beside the animal pens, hugging the freezing mud as they crept towards the far end of the camp. In the distance Figulus could see one of the peasants pitching feed into a nearby enclosure, and he prayed to Fortuna that the Durotrigan was not able to hear the Romans as the ground sucked and squelched beneath them. It seemed to take for ever to crawl past the animal pens but at last Figulus and Vatia emerged from the quagmire. Figulus noticed a hut situated just beyond the pens with a small cart next to it half-filled with sharpened wooden stakes for driving into the shallows. Moving as quickly as they dared, the soldiers approached the cart. The ground here was soft and slippery and Figulus had to watch his step to keep himself from falling over. At last they reached the cart and dropped to a crouch.

The optio glanced quickly around. No sign that they had been seen. Then he looked towards the causeway. Straining his eyes in the gloom, Figulus saw a pair of Druids squatting beside a small fire. Next to them stood a wooden cage. Two bedraggled figures were crouched inside. In the dim glow of the torches he could see that the prisoners had been stripped naked and their torsos were covered in filth. As the optio looked on a Durotrigan approached the cage carrying a bowl.

331

The prisoners eyed the bowl greedily and crawled towards the bars. One of the Druids promptly stood up and snatched the bowl from the rebel, tipping the slops on to the ground in front of the cage just out of arm's reach. One of the prisoners thrust out an arm between the bars, desperately reaching for the rotten food. The nearest Druid picked up a club and jabbed it at the prisoner, forcing him to snatch his arm back and shrink away from the bars, drawing a roar of laughter from the other guard.

At that moment Figulus caught a glimpse of the prisoner's grizzled features. His heart skipped a beat as he recognised the man.

'Rullus . . .'

Figulus felt his heart sink. There was no way he could get to his comrades. Not without being discovered by the Druids guarding the separate causeway. Even if he and Vatia could cut down the Druids and manage to free the prisoners, the rebels would surely discover them before they could make their escape. It was hopeless, he conceded. Utterly hopeless.

'Sir,' Vatia said after a few moments. 'There's nothing we can do here. We have to go back.'

Figulus clenched his jaws and nodded grudgingly. To attempt a rescue now would be madness and would only succeed in getting them both killed. He had come this far, but despite his best efforts he couldn't save his comrades. Helva and Rullus would die, and there was nothing Figulus could do about it.

With a great heaviness in his heart, he turned away from the cage and set off in the direction of the animal pens. As Figulus moved ahead he suddenly lost his footing and fell heavily against the cart. A deafening noise filled the air as the wooden stakes spilled across the bare ground. For a moment he stood rigid, frozen with horror as he looked to Vatia. Neither man dared to move. Towards the causeway one of the Druids rose to his feet and clasped his spear, shouting a challenge in their direction. Hearing no response, the Druid moved closer to the huts and called out again into the darkness.

'Shit!' Vatia hissed urgently. 'He's coming, sir!'

Panic seized hold of Figulus. It was clear that there was no time to hurry back to the landing platform. They were too far away and it was only a matter of moments before the Druid spotted them. Figulus frantically scanned the area immediately around them, searching for somewhere to hide. He saw only one place that might afford them a possibility of hope.

'Over there!'

Figulus pointed out an empty animal pen slightly removed from the other enclosures, abandoned to the waterlogged ground beside the foot of the palisade. Under the reflected glow of the moonlight the pen seemed horribly exposed but it was their only chance.

'Hurry!' he whispered. 'Before the bastard sees us!'

They ran towards the small pen, abandoning all pretence of silence now. They had only an instant before the Druid reached the huts. Figulus hurried across the glutinous mud and quickly reached the gate at the front of the pen. Then he grabbed the wooden bolt fixed to the front of the gate and pulled on it, frantically working the peg free from the receiver. With a faint grating noise the peg came free and Figulus pulled open the gate, ducking inside after Vatia. Then he reached down to the other side of the gate, scrambling to reach the bolt and slide it back into the receiver. Figulus couldn't quite reach the bolt. He silently cursed.

'Quick, sir!' Vatia hissed. 'He's almost on us!'

The sound of approaching footsteps spurred Figulus on. Gritting his teeth, the optio extended his arm down to the other side of the gate and fastened his hand around the peg. Then he shunted it back into the receiver, securing the gate before he squatted out of sight. A pungent odour hit Figulus as he realised that the ground was smeared with dried faecal matter and soiled straw. He wrinkled his nose as he lay on the ground for a moment, his heart pounding as he caught his breath.

Figulus turned to the legionary and whispered. 'Keep quiet, and whatever you do, don't fucking move. Got it?'

Vatia nodded and lay low on the straw. Then Figulus crawled forward. The pen was surrounded by a wicker wall with several small gaps in it and Figulus peered out nervously as he watched the Druid approach. The Druid glanced around the pens before he wandered over to some enclosures close by. He stopped to inspect a couple of the pens, passing by less than fifteen paces from Figulus and Vatia in their hide-out. The optio trapped his breath in his throat and carefully slid his right hand down to his sheathed sword, firmly clasping the handle. If the Druid stumbled upon them, they were done for. He resolved to cut down as many of the enemy as possible before he was killed. It was a pitiful way to die, but infinitely preferable to the hideous fate awaiting them if they were captured.

For a few moments the Druid lingered by the pens and Figulus felt sure they were about to be discovered. He stayed perfectly still, not daring to breathe. At last the Druid moved on, and Vatia breathed a light sigh of relief.

'Thank you, Jupiter, best and greatest.' the legionary panted under his breath. 'That was close.'

Figulus swallowed anxiously. 'Maybe. But we're not safe yet.'

Vatia flashed a quizzical expression, and the optio nodded in the direction of the landing platform. A young Durotrigan warrior had emerged from the hut where Figulus had heard the sounds of lovemaking, hastily throwing a cloak over his shoulders and clutching his war-spear as he came to see what all the fuss was about. The Druid caught sight of the man and marched over to the hut, shouting at him furiously. The Druid shoved the Briton in the direction of the landing platform, kicking him in the buttocks as he sent the man on his way. Then he marched back over to the causeway while the Durotrigan took up his position in front of the opening in the palisade, shaking his head and clasping his spear.

Any relief Figulus might have felt at evading the Druid instantly turned to despair. Now that the Durotrigan had resumed his sentry duties there was no way off the island.

They were trapped.

CHAPTER FORTY-SIX

Figulus lay low inside the animal pen, shivering under the wan glow of the moon and feeling more wretched than he'd ever done in his life. Beside him Vatia lay perfectly still. The two Romans had been stuck in the pen throughout the night, their damp tunics clinging to their frozen limbs. A black despair seized hold of Figulus and he cursed himself for volunteering for this mission. Not only were his comrades going to die, but now he was trapped in a stinking pen with Vatia, surrounded by hundreds of Rome's fiercest enemies. He consoled himself with the thought that at least he had managed to send word back to Vitellius of the whereabouts of the rebels' camp. He had not wholly failed in his mission, then. His death would not be in vain.

Neither of the soldiers dared to utter more than a few whispers, for fear of alerting a nearby guard and being cut down on the spot. So they passed the night largely in silence, giving Figulus plenty of time to appraise their grim situation. As long as they remained in their hide-out they were reasonably safe. The wicker wall meant that they were well concealed from view and they were sufficiently far from the bustling activity around the rest of the camp. There was always a chance that one of the natives might wander over and take a closer look at the pen, but the surrounding enclosures were devoid of life and there was no reason for anyone to approach. The greater risk lay in trying to leave the pen. Shortly after Figulus and Vatia had ducked into the pen a group of carousers had settled close by, and their drunken singing and drinking continued well into the night and still showed no signs of abating. Any attempt to escape the pen was doomed to end in failure. They would be spotted the moment they left the pen, cut down by the enemy before they could escape from the island.

But sooner or later one of the natives would eventually stumble upon their hiding place, Figulus knew. Their only hope was to remain inside the pen and pray that the cohorts arrived in time to defeat the enemy. But there was little prospect of a swift victory over the rebels, Figulus acknowledged bitterly as he recalled the formidable defences awaiting the legionaries. It would be a prolonged struggle to seize the rebels' island camp. An overwhelming weariness suddenly weighed down on the optio. There was nothing they could do now except wait.

'If only those bastards would stop singing and go to sleep, sir,' Vatia barely whispered. 'Then we might have a chance of getting out of this bloody pit.'

Figulus shook his head. 'We'd still have to get past the sentries. One of 'em would raise the alarm before we could cut them down. We'd be killed before we could reach the far side of the lake.'

'So that's it, then? We're stuck here?'

'What else can we do? We'll just have to wait.'

'What for, sir?'

'I don't know,' said Figulus. 'I don't know.'

Vatia fell silent for a long moment. 'Tell you what, sir. If we ever make it out of here alive, you'll owe me a bloody drink.'

Figulus smiled slightly. 'If we make it out of here, we'll both need a drink.'

The first glimmer of dawn arrived, and the carousers finally retired to their huts. The sound of their singing was swiftly replaced by several weary voices as the warriors roused from their slumber, and before long Figulus heard the repetitive brittle clash of weapons as the men trained some distance away from the pens. Later in the morning several loud splashes came from the direction of the lake. Figulus crawled over to the opposite side of the pen and peered out through a gap in the wicker wall. The section of the palisade around the waterlogged ground appeared to be shorter than the rest and the timbers sagged slightly from where they had sunk into the mud. Above the stakes he could just about see one of the smaller islets situated midway between the Druids' isle and the main island, linked to both by a pair of short causeways. At least a dozen rebels were wading through the murky waters, carrying large bundles of withies and wicker branches on their backs from the dense forest on the bank opposite the islet where a cluster of tree stumps marked the place they had entered the water. Figulus noted that the water barely came up to the Durotrigans' knees and he guessed that they must be using some sort of underwater passage that linked the islet to the forest for easy access.

The hours passed slowly. Every moment brought with it the fresh terror of discovery and Figulus found it impossible to rest. His body was numb with cold and exhaustion. Several times he heard the footsteps of peasants approaching and emptying slops into some of the other pens, swiftly followed by the grunting noises of the pigs as they ate. On each occasion Figulus gripped his sword handle, ready to fight. But no one came. The Durotrigans never ventured up to their hiding place.

In the early afternoon a shout went up from the main gate. Figulus crept across the pen and looked out in the direction of the gate just as a party of rebel scouts hurried through the opening. A cluster of warriors had rushed forward, accompanied by several Druids. Calumus stood among the throng with Ancasta at his side. Figulus pulsed with anger and he was gripped by a compulsive desire to rush out of the pen and cut them both down. He looked on as the scout made his report to Calumus, pointing frantically towards the marsh. The Druid barked an order at the warriors, and consternation quickly spread through the camp.

'What's going on, sir?' Vatia asked softly.

Figulus pricked his ears, straining to catch an exchange between two nearby warriors as they called to one another. He listened for several moments then looked back to his comrade, grinning wearily.

'Looks like Vitellius is on the way. One of the rebel patrols has spotted his column entering the marsh.'

'Bloody great,' Vatia replied with relief. 'We'll be out of here soon enough, then!'

'Don't get your hopes up just yet. The tribune has got to get the artillery train through that bloody marsh first. And once they get here, they've still got to advance across that causeway.'

'Shit,' Vatia cursed. He nodded at the main gate. 'How many of them do you think there are?'

Figulus made a rough estimate based on the numbers he'd seen around the fires and huts over the past several hours. 'Three hundred warriors or so, I reckon. Another thirty Druids, say. Plus the women and children. Enough to hold out for a few days.'

'At least, sir. We'd never last that long.' Vatia's shoulders slumped. 'Unless we can find a way out of here, we're bloody done for.'

Figulus made no comment. He peered out through the wicker wall, looking on as the rebels began their frantic preparations to defend against the imminent Roman assault. The optio heard a shout from close by to the pens as one of the rebels called on his comrades to fetch arrows and javelins from the weapon stores. Figulus stared in the direction of the main causeway, gripped by an acute sense of longing. He yearned to be alongside his comrades right now, marching towards the enemy and preparing for a brutal fight. Instead he was lying in a filthy animal pen in the middle of an island teeming with Rome's bitterest enemies, cold and hungry and tired. Figulus had never felt so helpless.

'Sir, look!' Vatia whispered.

Figulus snapped out of his dark thoughts. Vatia was nodding towards the Druids' isle. Figulus looked in the same direction and saw a huge man-made structure rising into view as it was hauled into position by several long ropes. A cold chill clamped around the optio's neck as the structure finally stood upright and towered over the palisade. They were looking at a crude effigy constructed of wicker and twisted withies. A number of cages had been built into the effigy's torso. Some had been filled with chickens and sheep and their bleating and squawking noises carried sharply across the frigid air. Another few cages stood empty, Figulus saw.

Vatia shuddered. 'Won't be long before they set fire to that thing, sir.'

'No,' Figulus replied quietly. 'No, it won't.'

He glanced anxiously back in the direction of the main gate. Everything now depended on Vitellius. Unless the cohorts arrived soon and fought their way through the enemy's defences, Rullus and

Helva would burn alive. And more than likely Figulus and Vatia would join them.

For the next few hours the frenetic pace of activity inside the camp continued. There was a heightened sense of anxiety among the natives from the snippets of conversation that Figulus overheard. Some of the rebels shouted enthusiastically at their companions, thrilled at the prospect of cutting down some of their sworn enemy. Others made prayers to their gods, begging for one last victory over the hated Roman invaders. As the afternoon wore on the rebels' preparations became more hurried and another party of scouts soon returned with a further report on the enemy's progress. From what Figulus could glean, Vitellius had almost advanced through the marsh and was approaching the rebel lair. Any excitement the optio felt at the news was instantly replaced by a feeling of dread at the prospect of the cohorts having to cross that heavily defended causeway.

In the late afternoon the braying note of a Celtic war horn sounded and a chorus of frantic shouts went up from the gate. At once the Durotrigan warriors, who were scattered across the camp, stopped whatever they were doing and hurried over to the palisade, pausing only to grab their weapons and shields. Figulus and Vatia looked on through gaps in the wicker wall as the warriors streamed over to the main gate and took up their positions on the defences, bellowing at one another in encouragement. From the other side of the camp they could hear panicked shouts as women and children hurried back inside their huts, desperate to avoid getting caught up in the imminent fight. One of the natives emerged from a hut close to the pens and called out to a warrior rushing past. Figulus listened as the warrior quickly explained the situation. Then he turned to Vatia, his heart beating fast.

'Vitellius has arrived!' he exclaimed. 'Let's hope he'll attack before it gets dark.'

'Won't the lads be tired after slogging through the marsh, sir?'

'Perhaps,' Figulus responded after a moment's consideration. 'But it's that, or give the enemy a chance to escape during the night.'

He returned to the gap in the wall and studied the main gate. By now hundreds of Durotrigan warriors had formed up along the front of the palisade. Some clutched their spears. Others were armed with bows or slingshot. A few hurled insults at the Romans across the lake as they worked themselves up into a war-like frenzy. Below them stood a handful of Druids dressed in their flowing black robes, gesticulating to the skies and invoking their gods to crush the invaders with guttural chants. A few wild-haired women stood among the men, shrieking at the Romans as they inspired their men to battle. Calumus and Ancasta stood amid the rebels, both imploring the rebels to resist the enemy waiting for them on the other side of the lake.

The faint, brass note of a trumpet sounded above the din. Figulus recognised the sound at once. It was a sound familiar to every legionary's ears.

'Vitellius is about to attack!' he said excitedly.

Vatia clenched a fist in triumph. 'Now we'll give these bastards a good kicking.'

In the next instant a series of distant cracks sounded as the ballistas unleashed their missiles and a shower of flaming iron bolts arced over the palisade and smashed into the rebel camp. He briefly wondered at how quickly Vitellius had been able to deploy his artillery. Figulus had seen Roman artillery at work many times before, but he'd never been on the receiving end of it and the experience was terrifying. Some of the bolts slammed into the rooftops of a cluster of native huts near the middle of the island, setting fire to the thatched reed roofs. Others struck down some of the natives as they fled for cover, piercing them through the chest and skull, and the agonised cries of the wounded penetrated the air.

The bolts were quickly followed by other thuds as the catapults added their weight to the barrage. Figulus craned his neck and gazed up as the heavy rounded stones launched in a steep angled trajectory over the lake. They seemed to hang in the sky for a cold moment before crashing down to the earth. Most of the stones fell short of the camp and Figulus heard loud splashes as the missiles plunged uselessly into the waters around the island. A few stones landed just inside the palisade and the rebels at the main gate had gone to ground, diving down from the defences and retreating to a line just beyond the range of the Roman artillery. Now they were safely out of range, the rebels jeered at the unseen enemy.

'That lot didn't do much good, sir. We hardly scratched the main gate,' Vatia observed.

Figulus shook his head. 'They're not trying to destroy the defences. They just want to drive the rebels back for long enough for the lads to cross the causeway.'

As he spoke a second wave of flaming bolts fired, this time with greater accuracy as the artillery commanders aimed their missiles deep into the rebel camp. Figulus watched a dozen roundhouses burst into flames as the bolts landed behind the defensive line, scattering the rebels in every direction. The flames quickly spread to the nearby huts and thick columns of black smoke eddied into the grey skies. Panic erupted among the natives as the flames took hold. One of the older warriors shouted out to the sentry posted at the front of the landing platform, frantically waving him over to help deal with the burning roundhouses. The sentry hesitated for a moment and shifted on the spot, torn between helping out and abandoning his duties. Then he hurried forward, racing past the pens towards the rising flames and leaving the opening in the palisade unguarded. Figulus turned to Vatia.

'Quick! Now's our chance.'

They clambered stiffly to their feet. Figulus hurried over to the gate and risked a glance over the top, making sure that the immediate area was clear. The rebels were hunched in a mass close to the middle of the camp, and those men not dealing with the fires were tending to their wounded companions or seeking cover from the catapult stones being hurled at them. Taking a deep breath, Figulus stood on the tips of his toes and reached down to the other side of the gate. His hands were trembling as he worked the peg free from the receiver. Figulus dropped back down before pulling the gate open slightly. Then he moved through the gate, with Vatia following close behind.

As they ducked outside a shout went up close by. Figulus glanced past his shoulder and saw a peasant rushing out from one of the stables carrying a leather bucket filled with water. The man drew up in surprise as he watched the two soldiers creeping away from the pen. Then he turned to his companions and frantically pointed out the fleeing Romans, screaming at the top of his voice. A trio of warriors swiftly turned away from the burning huts and charged across, gripping their long swords and oval shields. Figulus broke into a run alongside Vatia. There was nothing for it now but to rush towards the edge of the island and escape before the warriors could catch up with them.

He raced alongside Vatia, running as fast as his stiff leg muscles allowed. They struggled through the waterlogged ground beyond the pens, their pace slowing as the foul, swirling mud sucked at their boots. Figulus gritted his teeth and pushed on through the mud, straining with every sinew in his body to reach the landing platform. A triumphant shout sounded behind them and Figulus glanced at his back. He saw with some surprise that the pursuing Durotrigans had closed the gap on them.

Just then a warrior swept into view from behind one of the huts and ran towards the Romans, blocking their path. The man had flowing white hair and he gripped a hunting spear in his right hand. He bared his rotten teeth and let out a savage roar as he drove his spear tip down at an angle, piking Vatia in the hip before he could evade the blow. The legionary cried in pain as the tip tore into his flesh. Figulus roared madly and charged at the Briton before the man could work his spear free, slamming into him shoulder-first and knocking him to the ground. Then Figulus wrenched his sword from his scabbard and sprang forward, driving the point of the sword into the warrior's neck. The blade punched through his throat with a soft wet crunch.

Figulus tore his weapon free as the man lay writhing and gurgling horribly. He spun around and looked to Vatia. The legionary had dropped to a knee a few paces behind and was clamping a hand to his hip, trying to staunch his wound. The pursuing rebels were closing in behind as Figulus rushed over to his comrade and helped him to his feet. Vatia stood up and tried to take a step forward, but the pain was too great and he fell down again, cursing the gods through his gritted teeth. He tried to stand once more and managed half a step before he collapsed. Vatia looked at the optio with a flash of dread in his eyes.

'It's no good, sir. I'm not going to make it.'

'Come on!' Figulus shouted. 'Get on your feet!'

Vatia winced painfully and shook his head as he drew his sword. 'I can't, sir. You go. I'll hold off these bastards.'

Figulus stared at his comrade. 'No.'

'There's no time, sir. I'm done for. But you can still get away.' Vatia managed a grim smile. 'Guess you'll have to buy me that drink in the afterlife.'

Figulus hesitated briefly. But he knew he could do nothing more for his comrade. He gave Vatia a final nod then turned and ran on, hurrying through the opening in the palisade and sprinting down to the water's edge. As he drew close to the boats a defiant roar sounded and he glanced back to see the three warriors descending on Vatia. The legionary parried a thrust from the nearest Briton and narrowly ducked a blow aimed at his head from the second man. Then the third warrior lunged at Vatia, thrusting at his torso and the legionary let out an explosive grunt as the blade sank deep into his chest. He fought back, aiming a ragged blow at the Briton and parrying wildly as he tried to keep the warriors at bay for as long as possible. Then the second rebel feinted and drove his sword into the soldier's armpit, and Vatia let out a final defiant shout as the warriors finally closed around him, hacking and slashing at his bloodied torso.

Figulus sheathed his sword as he turned and rushed into the lake, kicking out for all that he was worth as he struck out across the dank waters. Above the sound of his splashing he could hear the furious shouts of the Durotrigans as they reached the water's edge. One of them hurled a javelin at Figulus and he caught a glimpse of the projectile as it struck the water a short distance to his right, breaking the surface with a splash. Figulus swam on, snatching at the air, his muscles screaming with pain, but no more missiles came. At last he reached the far edge of the shore and he pulled himself up, gasping for breath. Over at the landing platform the Britons stood shaking their fists at him in anger. Then the warriors turned and hurried back inside the camp, joining their companions as they took up their positions along the island's defences.

Figulus turned his gaze towards the Roman end of the causeway. The artillery fire had ceased its shooting and the first century of legionaries marched forward in tightly closed ranks on to the causeway. The Britons massed along the palisade immediately shot their arrows at the first ranks of soldiers, while the half-naked slingers unleashed a savage volley of shot at the advancing Romans. Figulus

343

looked on in horror as the first deadly wave of missiles smashed into the front ranks of the cohort. Agonised cries split the air as the barrage smashed bones and clattered off shields and helmets, while arrows plunged into the soldiers and struck down several men. The cohort's steady advance slowed to a crawl as the legionaries struggled to defend themselves from the furious shower of arrows and shot pouring down on them from the rebel defenders. Other men lost their footing on the causeway and fell into the water, some impaled on the sharpened stakes driven into the shallows. Already Figulus could see that the attack was faltering in the face of the heavily defended gateway.

Any relief he might have felt at escaping the island turned to despair as he watched the brutal struggle unfolding along the causeway. Then Figulus looked back to the smallest islet lying between the main island and the Druids' isle, and he realised that there was a chance to turn the tide of the battle.

He took a deep draw of breath and set off down the rough track that skirted around the edge of the lake. He had to reach Vitellius in time to prevent any further unnecessary loss of life amongst his comrades.

To stop the bloody butchery taking place on the causeway.

CHAPTER FORTY-SEVEN

Figulus raced towards the Roman column, forcing his way along the gorse-choked shore of the lake. A screen of ash and willow trees grew along the edge of the track and the branches snagged on the Gaul's tunic as he pushed on. He continuously glanced to his right, looking between the trees at the futile attempt to break into the enemy camp. Already the shallows either side of the causeway were littered with Roman bodies. He could see several legionaries sinking in the water, dragged down by their heavy armour and kit. Others were limping back towards the Roman end of the causeway. The remaining men of the century were crouching behind their shields to defend themselves against the vicious storm of arrows and shot raining down on them from the palisade.

As Figulus looked on, a war horn sounded its strident note and the Britons in the two redoubts hurled javelins at the front ranks of the century as they advanced into range. A handful of javelins punched into the century's vulnerable right flank, goring several men. At the same time the rebels massed on the palisade continued to loose arrows and shot at those ranks to the rear of the marching column. The centurion and his optio were struggling to maintain order amid the chaos and the entire century now appeared as little more than a tangled mess of abandoned scaling ladders, the dead and wounded, and pockets of legionaries trapped under the relentless shower of missiles being hurled down at them from the enemy defences. The Durotrigan rebels were more than holding their own and Figulus could see that the attack on the main gate was doomed to failure.

He broke through a gorse thicket on to a track and spotted a small patrol of mounted legionaries. One of the men on the patrol caught sight of the bedraggled Gaul and pointed him out. The others turned quickly towards Figulus. One of the men raised his sword and prepared to charge. The optio threw up his arms and waved desperately at them.

'Wait!' he exclaimed. 'I'm a Roman! Roman!'

The decurion reined in his mount and looked at Figulus in surprise. 'Optio! Shit, I almost didn't recognise you dressed like that.' He turned to his comrade and ordered the man to lower his weapon, then looked back to Figulus. 'What the fuck are you doing out here?'

The optio glanced down at his front. His tunic was smeared with mud and he looked nothing like a legionary. He took a breath to compose himself then addressed the decurion. 'There's no time to explain. I must report to Vitellius at once.'

'Tribune's busy.' The decurion nodded stiffly at the main island. 'In case you hadn't noticed we're in the middle of a fucking assault.'

'That's why I must speak with him,' Figulus insisted. 'We've got to act now if we're to save the cohorts.'

The decurion made no reply. He considered the mud-spattered wretch in front of him. Then he nodded slowly. 'All right, Optio. Come with me.'

Figulus mounted up on the decurion's horse and gripped hold of his saddle horns as the patrol wheeled around and trotted quickly back towards the Roman ranks assembled further back from the lake. Their standards fluttered in the dank afternoon breeze. The Ninth Cohort stood on a gently rolling slope next to the artillery train. There had been no time to construct a marching camp with Vitellius desperate to attack the rebels before they had a chance to escape under the cover of darkness. The remnants of the Batavian auxiliary cohort stood in support to one side of the Roman units, with a small contingent of archers standing among them. The Batavians looked on anxiously as the first century from the Eighth Cohort took a battering on the causeway.

As the patrol made their way towards the mass of troops Figulus turned his attention back towards the island. The Roman advance had ground to a halt. The shallows around them were stained dark red with blood and in places the soldiers could not move forward for the dead littering the causeway. The centurion was nowhere to be seen but his optio stood behind the rearmost ranks, barking at the men and driving them on with his wooden staff of office. But with the ranks in front of them forced to a standstill the causeway became a tight press of exposed bodies that the rebel defenders gleefully attacked with an unrelenting volley of arrows and slingshot, interspersed with javelins aimed at the exposed right flank.

At last the cornus sounded its shrill call and the legionaries fell back. Dozens of wounded limped along. Others lay on the ground, pawing at the arrow shafts protruding from their limbs. One of the retreating soldiers lost his footing amid the pools of bloodied mud and slipped off the causeway, crashing into the stakes amid the shallows. Others helped their wounded companions along and they slumped on the near bank of the lake with exhausted looks etched on to their bloodied faces. Orderlies rushed over to those wounded who were not able to walk and carried them away on stretchers. Along the palisade the Britons cheered wildly. At least thirty dead soldiers lay sprawled along the causeway, with perhaps the same number injured. The attack had failed miserably.

A stillness hung over the lake, broken only by the pained cries of the wounded and the fading cheers of the defenders. Then a call went up as the centurion ordered the next century of men from the Eighth Cohort to their feet. The shattered ranks of the first century stepped aside, making way for a second attack on the causeway. Moments later a sharp crack split the air as the arms of the bolt-throwers snapped violently forward and the Roman artillery barrage resumed its onslaught. The Britons knew what to expect and swiftly withdrew from their positions as the iron bolts whirred above the lifeless bodies slumped along the causeway and crashed into the palisade either side of the main gate, smashing apart a few of the timbers. One Briton stood brazenly on the palisade, pumping his fists in defiance at the Romans until a bolt skewered him through the guts and whipped him out of sight. Then the catapults' long arms slammed against their cross beams as they hurled their heavy stones, driving down like giant fists on the thatched roofs of the huts inside the camp. At the same time the next century stepped warily forward and hefted their shields as they waited for the signal to commence their advance down the bank towards the causeway.

A cold dread ran through Figulus as he dismounted and hurried past the sprawl of wounded men and sentries towards Vitellius. Perhaps the tribune had simply failed to grasp the severity of the situation confronting him. Or more likely, in his supreme arrogance Vitellius truly believed that victory was in his grasp. That he was on the cusp of defeating the rebels, and all it required was a renewed assault along the causeway. If so, then he was playing right into the enemy's hands. Calumus and his rebels held the advantage. They could hold out on the island for days, going to ground every time the Roman artillery fired and then cutting down the legionaries as soon as they made their approach along the causeway. If Vitellius continued to blindly pursue his strategy, the attack was in grave danger of turning into a bloodbath.

The catapults continued to crack and whir as Figulus approached Vitellius. The aristocratic tribune stood on the grassy slope overlooking the bank alongside his staff, his attention fully focused on the island as the artillery battered the rebel defences. Petrax stood to one side, his scarred arms folded across his chest as he looked on at the struggle. Vitellius threw up an arm and there was a final crack as the last of the catapults loosed its missile. A trumpet blared and the next century of men from the Eighth Cohort, led by Centurion Minucius, advanced cautiously down the causeway towards the main island. As soon as the artillery barrage ended, the Durotrigans broke forward and returned to their stations along the palisade, ready to pick off the approaching column with javelins and arrow and shot.

Vitellius heard Figulus approach and looked towards him. A brief look of surprise crossed his face as he regarded the filthy Gaul. 'Optio! Good gods, man. Where the hell have you been?'

Figulus pointed across at the island. 'In there, sir.'

'All this time?' Vitellius shook his head in disbelief then nodded at Petrax. 'It seems your friend was right, then. He mentioned something about you going off to try and free your friends.' He frowned. 'Where's the other one?'

'Vatia.' Figulus felt his throat constrict. 'Dead, sir.'

'I see. And the prisoners?'

'Still trapped inside, sir. I couldn't get near them.'

'Hardly a roaring success, then.' Vitellius straightened his back and

348

nodded at the causeway. 'Well, as you can see your comrades won't be trapped for much longer. Now we've got those rebels right where we want them, we'll break through soon enough.'

Figulus cleared his throat and stiffened. 'Sir, forgive me. But the main gate is impregnable.'

'We'll incur some losses, undoubtedly,' the tribune responded. 'But it can't be helped. Calumus has chosen to make his stand here, and we must attack. I'm not going to let him get away from us again.' There was a gleam in his eyes as he added, 'The rebels' leader will make a fine prize. I should think we'll all be in line for a reward from Claudius for finally lancing this particular boil.'

'Yes, sir.' Figulus swallowed and tried again. 'But I've seen the inside of the camp. There are hundreds of defenders bottled up in there. Fighting men. They're well armed and they know how to handle a sword. They could hold out on that island for days if we keep throwing men at 'em.'

'What would you have me do?' Vitellius snapped. 'In case it's escaped your attention, there's only one way in and out of these damn islands.'

'Sir, there is another way.' Figulus pointed to the small islet, off to the north of the main island. 'There's an underwater path between the marsh and that islet. If we can move a force of men across to the islet we can use that to launch an attack on the main island and flank the enemy. We might be able to distract them long enough for the rest of the lads to force their way in through the gate.'

'An underwater path, you say?' Vitellius asked doubtfully, cocking an eyebrow. 'How do you know about that?'

'I saw some of the natives going across it, sir. I know where to find it.' He saw the uncertain look in the tribune's eyes and went on. 'Unless we do something now, we're not going to take their camp. This is our only chance. It's that, or we keep throwing men at the gate until the cohorts are finished.'

Vitellius shifted his gaze to the causeway and stared silently in thought. Below the slope the men of the follow-up century were struggling to hold firm as bodies continued to pile up around them. Amid the melee Centurion Minucius shouted an order at his men, bellowing at them to keep their formation. He let out a throated cry

349

of pain as an arrow punched through his neck and knocked the centurion out of the column. Vitellius slapped a hand against his thigh, cursing under his breath as he turned back to Figulus.

'Very well, Optio. Take the Batavians. Centurion Vespillo is in need of an optio anyway. Take the archers with you.' He waved at Petrax. 'This brute can accompany you too.'

Petrax grinned at the prospect of cutting down the enemy while Vitellius turned to the auxiliaries and beckoned over their commanding officer. Vespillo approached and stiffened to attention.

'Sir?'

Vitellius gestured to the Gaul. 'Optio Figulus here claims there's another way across the lake. Some sort of hidden passage. Cross it if you can and relieve the pressure on the men at the main gate.'

Vespillo nodded gruffly then turned away and marched over to his men. The tribune looked back to Figulus.

'Find a shield and a helmet from somewhere. Don't want you getting killed. Not until you've shown the others the way across this so-called path of yours, anyway.'

'Yes, sir.'

'And, Optio?' Vitellius added as Figulus turned to leave.

'Sir?'

'You'd better hope that you're right about this. Because if you're wrong, I'll hold you fully to account for any disaster.'

Figulus nodded. Then he turned away from the tribune and hurried across the slope, grabbing a helmet and a shield from a barely conscious legionary lying amid his wounded comrades on the bank. Then he made his way over to the Batavian ranks, with Petrax at his side. Vespillo drew his sword and bellowed an order to the small auxiliary force to form up. A hundred and twenty men, Figulus estimated, including the archers, armed with second-rate armour and equipment.

Vespillo addressed his men. 'There's no time to explain, lads. Just stay quiet and move fast and follow the optio's lead. But I can promise you one thing. Once we're in position we'll teach those rebel bastards a lesson they won't forget in a hurry.'

The men grunted in approval. They had been cooped up in the fort at Lindinis for many months, living in fear of the Dark Moon

Druids, and now they had a chance to exact a brutal revenge over their enemy.

Vespillo shouted for his men to move out. They followed Figulus as he made his way down the slope alongside Petrax, past the lines of broken soldiers and stretcher bearers, towards the track that snaked around the edge of the surrounding marsh. The thin line of gnarled trees screened the Batavians' approach from the rebels lining the palisade and as Figulus hurried down the track he took one last look back at the causeway. The men of the Eighth Cohort were still pinned down under the hail of enemy missiles and he doubted they would be able to withstand another attempt on the gate. Everything now rested on Figulus's shoulders, and the existence of an underwater path somewhere along that lake.

CHAPTER FORTY-EIGHT

The battle continued to rage along the causeway as Figulus led Centurion Vespillo and his men down the track, retracing his steps along the edge of the marsh. They moved at the double-quick, and soon the sounds of the battle were barely audible above the soft thud of their boots and the faint chink of their equipment. Every so often Figulus glanced beyond the line of trees at his flank to check on the Eighth Cohort's progress. The men were still struggling under the stream of missiles pouring down on them, and towards the rearmost ranks he could see a handful of legionaries trying to bring a battering ram forward. Figulus hurried on ahead of the auxiliaries. He had the strange sensation that the gods had placed this final test in his path, that he wouldn't be worthy of the rank of centurion unless he saved his comrades from certain death. He made a silent prayer to Jupiter, best and greatest, and promised him a votive offering if he managed to survive this battle.

Figulus slowed and quickly scanned the track, searching for the precise spot where he'd seen the rebels make their crossing to the islet. The crossing had seemed clear enough from his vantage point inside the animal pen, but now as he picked his way through the dense tangle of trees and hawthorn it seemed much harder to find. After fifty paces the track disappeared entirely and Figulus began to worry that he might have led the Batavians astray. The awful feeling seized hold of him that he would fail to find the crossing point in time to rescue the cohort.

'There, sir!' he said with relief, pointing to a cluster of felled tree stumps a short distance from the dense sprawl of forest to the north.

Vespillo threw up his arm, calling the men behind him to halt.

The centurion moved forward and eyed the water suspiciously. 'You're sure this is it?'

Figulus nodded. 'I'll cross first, sir. Just to make sure. Once I've made it over and checked for the enemy, you can bring the men across.'

Moving quickly, he stepped towards the stagnant waters, picking his way through the slippery rocks and bulrushes running along the bank. The water seemed dark and impossibly deep and Figulus nervously felt his way into the water, feeling for the hidden passage. Once he'd established a foothold he began wading tentatively through the freezing waters towards the small islet. A pair of large ash trees dominated the far bank, marking the spot where Figulus had seen the rebels emerge from the lake the previous day. His progress was achingly slow as he tested each step in front of him, feeling for the soft mass of dead and fallen matter lurking beneath the surface, and he was terrified that the Britons on the main island would spot him before he made it over to the far bank. But their attention was fully focused on the main attacking force at the front gate and soon he was standing on the bank of the islet, dripping wet beneath his tunic.

Figulus crouched by the damp rocks and ran his eyes across the open ground in front of him. There was no sign of life on the islet and he guessed that the defenders had joined the rest by the main gate. He turned back to the lake and then beckoned for Centurion Vespillo and his men to cross. At once the Batavians plunged into the water and moved along the hidden causeway in single file, the contingent of archers followed by the hundred or so auxiliary soldiers. They followed the same line as Figulus, moving as quickly as the conditions and their heavy armour and weapons allowed. Petrax was the last to make the crossing. Once the auxiliaries began to assemble on the far bank, Vespillo signalled for his men to form up. Then the centurion gestured to the rebel camp and grinned.

'We've got 'em now, lads. As soon as we reach the main island.'

The men grunted in approval. There was no time for the sort of flowery, rousing speech that the senior officers in the Second Legion were so fond of, but the Batavians understood that they were about to play a vital role in determining the outcome of the battle. Figulus sensed their determination and desire to avenge themselves and the comrades they had lost at the hands of the Druids and their fanatical followers.

'Optio, I want you at my side,' Vespillo added, nodding at Figulus before turning back to his men. 'As soon as our archers have got their attention we'll hit 'em with everything we've got. Wait for my command, and don't stop until every one of those rebel scum is dead. Got it?'

The auxiliaries nodded grimly.

'Let's go.'

They advanced towards the causeway linking the two islands, keeping their noise to a minimum. The previous day Figulus had noticed a pair of sentries posted at either end of the causeway but there was no sign of them now. His heart was pounding with excitement as he led the Batavians across the short causeway and he experienced that familiar tightness in his guts and dryness in his mouth at the prospect of a fight. In a few moments they would reach the rebel camp. The key was to strike hard and fast, Figulus knew, cutting down as many of the enemy as possible. The element of surprise wouldn't last for long but they would have to distract the enemy for long enough to allow the men of the Eighth Cohort to break through the gate. Only then might they have a chance of turning the tide of battle in their favour.

They crossed the causeway at a brisk trot, the cries of battle getting louder as they swept through the outer palisade. By now the fires inside the camp had consumed several huts and swirling tendrils of black smoke darkened the sky. To his right Figulus could see a handful of peasant men and women struggling to contain the flames. The rest of the rebels were massed around the main gate, launching missiles at the Romans on the far side of the palisade and utterly unaware of the Batavians at their flank. One of the peasants turned away from the fire at the sound of men approaching and his face flashed with alarm at the sight of the auxiliary soldiers entering the camp. He turned to shout a warning to his comrades along the palisade. At the same time the auxiliary archers notched their arrows to their bowstrings and then Vespillo gave the order for them to shoot.

The archers loosed a volley of arrows at the rebels. The dark shafts of the arrows streaked through the sky, disappearing momentarily behind plumes of smoke before darting down into the thick horde of Durotrigans along the palisade. A few arrows thudded into the stout timbers but most found their targets and screams split the air as scores of Britons fell like leaves. Figulus saw one rebel staggering down from the palisade, letting out a guttural cry as he pawed at a feathered shaft jutting out of his eye. The Batavians shot again, loosing their arrows as fast as they could before the Durotrigans could find cover. Some of the Britons turned away from the gate and ran for cover behind the nearest huts. Voices screamed in agony as the arrow heads, occasionally clattering off the oval shields of the few rebels who'd managed to heft them up in time, mostly punched deep into flesh.

The steady shower of missiles had the intended effect, drawing Britons away from the palisade and leaving only a few determined souls who were too engrossed in the attack on the main causeway to realise the new threat at their flank. Panic spread through the native ranks as the archers kept loosing arrow after arrow in a vicious deluge. Most of the Britons lacked any armour and the missiles had a devastating impact, piercing exposed torsos and limbs. By now many of the rebels had been forced to abandon their positions, leaving the palisade undefended except for a handful of defiant warriors, drawing a lusty cheer from the Batavians.

Amid the chaos Figulus caught a glimpse of Calumus. The Druid stood in front of the gate, shielded from the arrows by his personal bodyguards. He was furiously pointing out the Batavians, raging at his troops to attack as more arrows thudded around their position. Most of the rebel warriors were scattered across the front of the camp and only a few managed to respond to their leader's desperate cry. Vespillo looked on, waiting until the archers had shot their final volley. Then he filled his lungs and drew his sword, bellowing at his men.

'Charge, lads! Fucking get 'em!'

The Batavians echoed their centurion's cry as they wrenched their swords free and broke forward, bearing down upon the enemy. Calumus roared at his men and those who had not sought cover now climbed down from the palisade and turned to confront the onrushing auxiliaries. Figulus gritted his teeth and charged forward, slowing his pace slightly to keep in line with the heavily armoured soldiers in the front rank. Petrax raced alongside him, gripping his sword. A long line of native warriors stretched out in front of Figulus, at least two hundred men. He made for the nearest enemy, no longer caring if he lived or died, only that he succeeded in helping his comrades breach the gate. The Batavians were outnumbered and Vespillo's men no longer held the element of surprise. But the men around Figulus showed no signs of fear, placing their faith in their superior training and equipment and their prayers to their gods.

The two sides met in a shimmering frenzy of sword points and spear thrusts, the dull thud of shields and the sharp clatter of clashing blades ringing out above the throated cries of the men. A huge warrior lunged at Figulus, thrusting his long sword at the optio's throat with astonishing speed and strength. Figulus instinctively threw up his shield and deflected the blow with a clatter. His opponent let out a snarl as he drew his arm back and kicked out at the bottom of the optio's shield in the same breath. The Gaul felt his grip weaken on the handle as his shield tipped forward, and he stumbled half a step towards the Durotrigan. The wicked glint of a blade caught the light as the rebel thrust at the optio's face. Figulus quickly evaded the blow and there was a sharp grating sound as the point of the Briton's sword thrust an inch or two to his right, the edge of the blade scraping against the rim of his shield. Figulus punched out with his shield, smashing the boss into the rebel warrior's side and winding his opponent. Then he thrust with his sword arm and struck the Durotrigan in the stomach with the point of his weapon, driving the blade home.

Figulus stepped away from the dying Briton and looked above his shield. The auxiliary charge had lost its impetus and all around him men were grunting with the strain of the fight. The Durotrigans shouted their war cries and insults while Vespillo yelled at his men to hold firm. The intensity of the struggle took even Figulus by surprise as both sides refused to give ground. At either side of the optio the Batavians tore into the rebels in a manic flicker of thrusts and stabs. The archers joined in with the struggle, slinging their bows and drawing their swords and tearing enthusiastically into the enemy. Although the closely fought nature of the battle favoured the auxiliaries, whose short swords were more suited to hand-to-hand fighting than the longer Celtic swords used by the Durotrigans, Figulus knew they could not hold out for much longer. The sheer weight of numbers would soon begin to tell. Unless the men of the Eighth Cohort broke through soon all would be lost.

'Keep it up, lads!' he roared in encouragement. 'Kill every one of the bastards!'

He quickly turned to face the next warrior who'd singled him out, a heavily scarred veteran with thin greying hair. There was a vicious gleam in the man's eyes as he saw that Figulus lacked the heavy armour of his comrades. The Briton thrust out at the optio's face but Figulus easily deflected the attack and the blow thudded against his shield. The warrior was quick for his age and thrust out again. Figulus evaded the blow then feinted, driving his weapon at his opponent's exposed lower half and striking him in the thigh. His opponent let out a curse at his wound. Then Figulus stepped forward and smashed the pommel of his sword into the man's weathered face. The Briton grunted before stumbling backwards, stunned by the savage blow. His arms fell by his side and then Figulus moved in for the kill, driving his weapon into the Durotrigan rebel's chest. There was a crunch as the sword tip punched through bone and cartilage. Blood sprayed out of the man's gaping wound as Figulus tore his weapon free and he felt warm droplets spatter his face.

How long the battle lasted, Figulus could not tell. He could feel his arm muscles beginning to ache from the strain of continually stabbing and blocking and parrying with his shield. Then he heard a thunderous crash from the direction of the gate. He looked beyond the writhing melee just in time to see the heavy timbers shudder on their rope hinges. His heart soared as he realised that the men of the Eighth Cohort had reached the gate and were smashing it open with their battering ram. A moment later the gate shook again and one of the thick timbers split apart, to a chorus of enthusiastic cheers from the far side. The few Durotrigans remaining on the palisade frantically hurled down shot after shot against the attacking force, but the momentum was irresistibly with the Romans now and a moment later the locking bar gave way with a loud crack and the gates crashed open.

'We've got 'em now!' Figulus thundered. 'The Eighth's here!'

The Batavians tore into the rebels with renewed vigour, sensing an imminent victory. Calumus and the other Druids stood amid the

357

rebel ranks, imploring the Durotrigans to stand firm in the face of the hated enemy. But the rebels were fatally trapped between the Batavians and the century of Roman soldiers sweeping through the open gate and were too thinly stretched to defend themselves on both fronts. The men of the Eighth Cohort set upon the nearest Britons, shields raised and blades thrusting left and right as they cut down scores of rebel warriors. Those few natives remaining on the palisade immediately dropped down to join the fight but they were no match for the skill and determination of the Romans. The Durotrigan ranks finally broke and the Romans pressed home their advantage, cutting down anyone who tried to surrender. Some of the warriors stood their ground but others turned and joined the women and children fleeing in the direction of the causeways leading to the separate islets.

Figulus ran his eyes across the camp, searching for Calumus. There was no sign of the Druid priest among the scattered rebel combatants. In the corner of his eye he spotted a pair of Druids breaking towards the rear of the camp. Figulus felt his throat tighten with dread as he realised they were heading directly for the prisoners. He spun around and looked for Petrax. The native was thrusting his weapon at a huge warrior standing firm in front of the gate. The optio looked away and turned towards the nearest auxiliaries.

'You two!' he rasped, thrusting an arm in the direction of the prisoners. 'With me!'

The Batavians nodded without question and broke into a jog, following Figulus as he hurried forward. Around him the battle had deteriorated into a killing frenzy as fear and panic spread through the native ranks. The remaining warriors had abandoned any sense of discipline and were fighting individually or in small pockets around the camp. Figulus passed the bodies of dozens of fallen warriors, their faces smashed in and their torsos covered in stab wounds. Across at the gate a few warriors, half-mad from the thrill of battle, tried to stem the wave of legionaries pouring into the camp. But they were hopelessly outnumbered and swiftly overrun. Victory was assured now. Calumus had gambled on being able to keep the Romans at bay for long enough to break their will, and he had lost. All that remained to be decided was how much more blood would have to be shed before the Durotrigans finally surrendered.

Figulus scuttled past the burning, blackened huts towards the far end of the island. Twenty paces ahead the Druids had reached the prisoners. One of them was reaching for the locking pin. Figulus quickened his stride and ran faster, surging ahead of the Batavians, who were straining under the weight of their kit. One of the Druids heard the pounding of footsteps and spun around just in time to see the huge Gaul bearing down on him.

'Come on, you black-robed bastard!' Figulus roared.

The Druid lunged at the optio with his thrusting spear, aiming the leaf-shaped point at his guts. Figulus parried the attack and stabbed out, but the Druid was deceptively nimble and sidestepped the blow before driving his spear low at his opponent's exposed flank. A hot pain exploded in Figulus's leg and he clenched his jaws in pain as the spear tip sank deep into his thigh. The Druid tore his weapon free then stepped out of range before Figulus could thrust at him. The Druid bared filed teeth at Figulus and thrust again, this time driving his spear at the optio's throat. Figulus dropped to his haunches before lunging forward and burying his sword deep into his enemy's stomach. Figulus jerked his weapon up, stabbing into the Druid's heart and drawing a pained gasp from the man. As he ripped his sword free the Druid fell away, clutching at his bowels. The other two auxiliaries made quick work of the Druid by the cage, cutting him down with a precise series of thrusts and stabs.

Figulus wiped his blade clean on the slain Druid's flowing robes then dropped down beside the front of the cage. A fetid smell of piss and shit violated his nostrils as he looked at the two figures squatting inside. Both Rullus and Helva were filthy and covered in painful-looking welts and bruises, but alive. Rullus inched towards the bars and blinked in shock at the sight of the Gaul.

'Sir?' Rullus said gruffly. 'By the gods, sir, it's you!'

The Gaul managed a half-smile. 'You didn't think I was going to let you two kick your heels in this cage when there's soldiering to be done, did you?'

Rullus grunted. 'Just get us out of here.' He nodded at the youthful-looking recruit next to him. 'Word to the wise, sir. Don't ever share a cage with this one. He never bloody shuts up.'

'That's rich, coming from the one who shits like an elephant. It smells worse in here than a piss-collector's armpits.'

Rullus grinned. 'Now you're starting to talk like a true ranker, lad.'

Figulus chuckled at his comrades then used his sword handle to hammer out the locking pin, springing open the door. Rullus and Helva crawled outside and stretched to their full height, rubbing their stiff and sore limbs. The two legionaries scooped up the weapons from the lifeless Druids and then one of the auxiliaries let out a cry. Figulus turned towards him and followed his pointing finger. Then he stopped cold. Calumus was slipping around the fringe of the animal pens, accompanied by Ancasta and his trio of personal bodyguards as they hurried away from the battle. They were heading towards the opening in the palisade, Figulus saw.

'Shit!' he cursed as he turned to his comrades. 'Calumus is going for the boats. We've got to stop him!'

The Romans rushed towards the huts, moving obliquely to intercept the rebels before they could escape. None of the other soldiers had noticed the fleeing priest, with the Romans too busy killing the last few pockets of resistance in front of the main gate. Calumus hurried along at a fast pace but Figulus and his comrades were gripped by a fiery determination to avenge their fallen brothers and they quickly closed the gap on the Druid. As Calumus moved past the blazing roundhouses some sixth sense made him glance over his shoulder. The Druid stopped in his tracks and turned to face the soldiers charging towards him, drawing his curved blade from beneath his flowing robes. At the same time the bodyguards gripped their long swords and closed ranks around Calumus, determined to protect their sworn leader from this new threat.

The two sides were evenly matched and the bodyguards immediately set upon the two auxiliaries. Rullus launched himself madly at the third bodyguard while Ancasta wielded her ornate dagger and slashed at Helva. Figulus made straight for Calumus. The Druid priest attacked first, swinging his sickle at the optio. Figulus jerked back, narrowly stepping out of range as the curved blade swept inches in front of his chest. Calumus curled his lips back into a sinister smile, his eyes burning brightly in the reflected glow of the flames.

'I'll eat your heart, Roman,' Calumus rasped.

Figulus gripped his sword handle tightly. 'We'll see about that.'

The Druid priest snarled and brought his weapon crashing down in a wide arc. Figulus read the move and dropped to a knee, hefting his shield above his head. Calumus was surprisingly strong and the blade clattered against the shield with a shuddering impact, numbing the optio's tired forearm, and for a moment he thought he might lose his grip. He shot to his feet and lunged forward, seeking out Calumus with the point of his sword and hoping to stab him before he could strike again. But the superior reach of the priest's weapon meant that Figulus couldn't get close enough to land a blow without exposing himself to attack.

Calumus effortlessly avoided the optio's thrust then dropped to a crouch and swept his sickle along the ground, trying to draw his opponent into lowering his shield. Figulus hopped backwards and lost his footing, landing on his backside. Then his opponent brought the sickle crashing down in a rapid arc towards the Gaul's face. Figulus reacted in a flash, rolling to the side and then rising to his feet in the same smooth motion. The sickle sank into the ground as Figulus regained his balance and drove his sword at the priest. Calumus sidestepped him again and then slashed crossways at the optio, nicking the latter's bicep and drawing a trickle of blood. Figulus swore under his breath and moved backwards again, staying out of range. In the corner of his eye he could see that the fight was going badly. The bodyguards had the measure of the auxiliaries and one of the Batavians lay slumped on the ground. The other was bleeding heavily from a gash on his leg. The three guards were now hacking wildly at Rullus and Helva while Ancasta hurried away towards the boats.

Figulus looked towards Calumus and dropped to a crouching stance as the Druid swung at him once more. This time Figulus stepped inside the blade then sprang up, punching up with his shield. Calumus gave a light grunt as the shield's metallic boss slammed into his jaw. Then Figulus lunged at the priest, stabbing him deep in the guts. Calumus gasped in agony and surprise. His pale, wrinkly fingers thrust out at Figulus's face, searching for his eyes. Figulus bunched his muscles and jerked upward, twisting the blade beneath the Druid's ribs. Calumus wavered on the spot for a moment, teeth clenched.

Then his arms went slack and he fell to the ground in a bloodied heap in front of Figulus.

'Calumus is dead!' the optio thundered at the bodyguards. 'It's over! Surrender!'

The bodyguards looked across and saw their leader writhing in a pool of blood. They hesitated at first, and for a moment Figulus feared they might fight on in revenge for the killing of the Druid. But then the first bodyguard stepped back from the fearless Gaul and threw his shield and sword to the ground. The next man followed. Across the camp the fighting drew to a sudden end as word spread that Calumus was dead and the remaining warriors lost any lingering heart to continue the fight. Figulus looked across at his friends and frowned.

'Ancasta?'

Helva nodded towards the palisade. Ancasta was still heading towards the boats, ducking between the pens. The optio made to run after her but a shout went up as a party of advancing legionaries moved towards her, bellowing at the king's daughter to surrender. Ancasta ignored them and ran on. Then from the shadows Petrax leapt forward and tackled her to the ground. Ancasta reached for her fallen weapon but Petrax kicked it away and shaped to kill her. Just then a shout punctuated the air as the commanding officer called for the Briton to spare the king's daughter. Petrax reluctantly lowered his sword arm and dragged Ancasta to her feet while around the camp the other soldiers rounded up the surviving Durotrigans. Figulus and the men around him slumped to the ground, drenched in mud and sweat, breathing erratically.

'It's over, sir,' Rullus gasped, smiling through the blood spattering his face. 'Thank the gods. It's really fucking over.'

CHAPTER FORTY-NINE

Two days later Figulus reported to the headquarters block at the fort outside Lindinis. After the end of the fighting on the island he had made his way back over to the marching camp with the other bloodied and weary soldiers. An orderly had taken one look at the deep gash in his thigh and ordered Figulus to the field hospital, where a pinch-faced surgeon had cleaned and sutured the wound. He'd spent the past two days nursing his injury and getting drunk with his friends in one of the modest taverns in Lindinis. Now the optio moved stiffly as he marched across the parade ground in the crisp morning light. The last of the snow had melted away and there was a mild warmth in the air. Soon the bitterly cold winter would be nothing more than a distant memory.

Work on the public buildings inside Lindinis had begun almost as soon as the rebels had surrendered. Teams of Roman engineers lay the foundations of a gleaming new temple dedicated to the Roman gods, while others toiled away at the king's lavish new palace. The works were designed to symbolise the new alliance between the Durotriges and Rome, with the costs paid for by a crippling tax imposed on the natives. At the same time the first land agents and slave dealers had arrived in the kingdom to profit from the unsuspecting Durotrigans. Figulus almost felt a pang of sympathy for the defeated Britons. Their once proud tribe had been humiliated on the field of battle and Trenagasus had been imposed on them as their ruler. Now they would be forced to fund the extravagant lifestyle of the king and his inner circle, while the rest of the natives remained mired in abject poverty. Figulus doubted the natives would warm to the foreign invaders anytime soon.

A few bloodstained carts and battered equipment remained outside the infirmary. Those who had been too badly injured had been carted back to the fort, while the Roman dead had been burned on a funeral pyre the morning after the battle. The dead rebels had been thrown into the lake or dumped in mass graves, while the survivors had been rounded up and escorted back to the fort under heavy guard. The women and children would be sold off to slave dealers at the earliest opportunity, while the rebels and Druids were housed in a special compound that had been constructed just outside the fort, watched over by a force of auxiliaries. Figulus shivered as he remembered the cold looks in the Druids' eyes, burning with hatred in defeat. Ancasta had not been among the prisoners. She'd been escorted immediately to the palace by several of the king's royal bodyguard as soon as they returned to Lindinis. Trenagasus had not yet decided her fate.

'Congratulations, Optio,' Scylla announced as Figulus entered the envoy's quarters. Scylla seemed to have shed the concerned expression of a few days ago and he spoke enthusiastically as he gestured for the optio to sit on one of the padded stools. Vitellius stood to one side.

'There is much to celebrate,' Scylla continued. 'Calumus is dead. The rebels have been defeated. The Druid threat to this kingdom is over. Trenagasus is now well established on the throne. It's worked out even better than I'd hoped, even if Trenagasus remains rather unpopular with his subjects.'

'That's putting it mildly,' Figulus responded.

The envoy dismissed his concerns with a wave. 'Can't be helped. Besides, now that the rebels have been wiped out no one will dare try to rise up against Trenagasus. Not for a while, at least. But it won't matter by then. The king's old and weak. He doesn't have long left.'

Figulus shrugged. 'So?'

'Isn't it obvious? The king has no heirs, and in a year or two he'll have served his purpose in Romanising his people. The more civilised ones, at least. Then we'll be free to formally annex the kingdom.'

Figulus stared at the envoy in surprise. 'But— I thought we wanted to avoid annexing the Durotriges?'

'Emperor Claudius has made it clear that we can't go on propping up these client kings for ever. It's a costly exercise and there's too much risk of someone assassinating the king and undoing all our good work. No. Sooner or later these unruly brutes must be brought into the empire proper. Far better to have them inside the tent pissing out, rather than outside the tent pissing in. Isn't that how the saying goes?'

'So Trenagasus was nothing more than a temporary measure? Then why go to the bother of installing him in the first place?'

'To smooth the transition. Without the king we'd have had to impose Roman rule directly on these savages, and that would likely have provoked outright rebellion. This way Trenagasus can gradually introduce the locals to our customs and culture. Then he'll have served his purpose and we can dispense with him.' Scylla sipped his wine. 'Then it's just a question of appointing an imperial procurator to run the kingdom.'

'What about me, sir? I'm to return to Calleva now?'

'Afraid not, Optio,' Vitellius replied. 'The new campaign season will begin in a few weeks. We'll be pushing west into hostile territory. From what our scouts have reported the Dumnonii are tough fighters and I'll need every good man I can get. Men like you, Optio.' He paused for a moment and relaxed his face into a smile. 'Or should I say . . . Centurion.'

'Sir?' Figulus asked, frowning.

Vitellius folded his hands behind his back. 'I received a report from Calleva this morning. Legate Celer will be arriving with the rest of the Second Legion in a few weeks, now that the resistance on Vectis has been wiped out. The Fifth Cohort will be coming with him. Minus the Sixth Century's centurion.'

Figulus's mind worked ahead of him. 'You mean—'

'Ocella's transfer back to the Praetorian Guard has been approved.' Vitellius tipped his head at Scylla. 'Thanks to some gentle persuasion from the envoy, I might add. Ocella is on his way back to Gesoriacum as we speak.'

For several moments Figulus was speechless. He'd worked towards this moment since he'd first joined the Second Legion. He had fought so hard and for so long that there were times when he thought it might never arrive. And now it had, and Figulus could hardly bring himself to believe it was happening. The silence lasted a moment longer. Then Scylla leaned forward and fixed a smile on him.

'Well?' he asked. 'What do you say? Are you ready to lead the Sixth Century, Centurion Figulus?'

HISTORICAL NOTE

The client kings of first-century Britain played a crucial role in the years after the Roman invasion. After a flurry of initial military successes, the legions soon found themselves bogged down in a prolonged and bloody conflict against a determined enemy. Confronted by unruly tribes, large swathes of unconquered terrain and vulnerable supply lines, the Roman army in AD 44 was dangerously overstretched. Direct military rule was both costly and burdensome (as recent conflicts have painfully reminded us). Instead, Rome sought alliances wherever practical with the tribes of the newest imperial province. Faced with the choice of waging a futile war against the invaders or seeking peace, many native rulers chose the latter.

Politically, the support of the client kings was vital. In return for ensuring the loyalty of their tribes, men like Cogidubnus enjoyed military support and lavish villas, as well as the material benefits of being part of the Empire. Some were even granted Roman citizenship. Gradually, they encouraged the growth of a pro-Roman native aristocracy that developed a taste for wine, togas and gladiator fights. But the relationship was not an equal one. The British kings were little more than puppet rulers, subservient to the Emperor. They risked the wrath of their own tribespeople by imposing crippling taxes and agreeing to give up their weapons and ways of life.

Few tribes were as bitterly opposed to Roman rule as the Durotriges. One can easily imagine their defiance continuing even after their armies had been routed and their hill forts destroyed. We do not know whether the Durotriges ever had a puppet ruler imposed upon them. But those kings who gambled on cooperating with Rome would eventually pay a heavy price. By the end of the first century the tribal confederations of Britain had all but disappeared, their legacies turned to dust and replaced by a vast imperial administration. But the support of the client kings would have given Rome vital breathing space in a province riddled with conflict. Without the support of men like Trenagasus, Rome might never have been able to fully tame the warrior tribes of Britain.

THE ORGANISATION OF
THE ROMAN ARMY IN
BRITANNIA, AD 44

L ike every other Roman legion, the fighting men of the Second Legion were among the finest soldiers in the ancient world. They were highly skilled, well equipped, disciplined and subjected to a gruelling training regime best described as 'bloodless battle'. But they were also expected to be able to construct forts and marching camps, build roads and bridges, as well as fulfil a rich variety of peacetime duties in the provinces they conquered. Often spending years at a time on the treacherous frontiers of the empire, the legionary was a soldier, engineer and local administrator combined into one.

One of the reasons for the legions' success on the field of battle was their efficient structure. Each legion had roughly five and a half thousand men. At the bottom of the structure was the century: the basic Roman military unit of eighty legionaries. Six centuries formed a cohort, with ten cohorts making up the legion; the first cohort was double-size. Commanding this impressive mobile army was the legate – an aristocratic man who was inevitably on the rise in the political circles of Rome. He was served by a staff of six tribunes and a military tribune, all from privileged backgrounds. Below these men were the centurions: the backbone of the legion, gritty officers who each commanded a century. Below each centurion was his deputy – the optio.